THE ENDLESS SONG

Also by Joshua Phillip Johnson

Tales of the Forever Sea
THE FOREVER SEA
THE ENDLESS SONG

THE ENDLESS SONG

Joshua Phillip Johnson

DAW BOOKS
New York

For Agnes and Rachel, my favorites.

A child said, What is the grass? *fetching it to me*
  with full hands;
How could I answer the child? I do not know what
  it is any more than he.

I guess it must be the flag of my disposition, out of
  hopeful green stuff woven.

—WALT WHITMAN, "SONG OF MYSELF"

The storyteller sits in Twist-that-was-Arcadia and listens to a scream cut the early morning air.

"Sing," he whispers to the darkness, to the chains heavy against his papery skin.

He is silent and still as questions are asked around the city, as disbelief turns to shock, as decisions are made. The shifting of power from one set of shoulders to another long ago lost any interest for him.

A woman has died, her body become an empty relic. Another will take her mantle and dream her dreams. A race without beginning and marked by endings. A race that, if run, can only be lost.

He packs the book carefully, giving the last half-filled page a final look before stowing it in his bag.

While Twist reckons with the change, the storyteller prepares himself for the end of the tale, the flowering of history into present. He lets the memories rise from where he has buried them, hidden from the slow forgetting that takes more and more of him every day.

Until now, he has told a story that is not his own. No more.

"Sing," he whispers, for himself now. "Sing, memory."

A home on the edge of the Sea. A family broken and broken again. A secret held across generations, hidden behind an archway of stone.

All of it returns to the storyteller, but the battles and the struggles and the myths and the magic mean so little to him now. He sifts through it all, an old man letting dirt and detritus fall through his loose, cupped hands to find the few grains mixed in.

A young boy, shoulders hunched against the night and all its terrors, creeping along a hallway, looking for shelter.

That same young boy, head full of stories and eyes pulled to the horizon, dreaming of adventure, of glory, of finding and taking his place in the world.

And later, much later, a voice full of new-dawn hope, saying, "I'll see you after."

This, the storyteller dwells on, letting the words weigh on him, as if they might hold down the loose tatters he has become after all this time. He fills in the timbre and melody of that voice, piecing it together slowly. Rediscovering every fragment and facet, relishing the pain as he cuts himself on the jagged edges of remembering.

Here is his gift, the memory becoming as fresh and clear as ever it was, painful and pure.

And here, too, is his penance, riding close behind, payment for a bargain made long ago, yes, but in some way, payment for all of this. For the world this world has become.

Once, he sought the peace Kindred found in all of it, but such peace was smoke in his hands. Gone with the barest breath of hope.

When Praise comes to get him, the storyteller has resurrected teeth and lips and face and eyes and hair—pulled them back and given them life again in his memory.

A new First walks with Praise now, a tall man, young and wide-eyed. He might live into old age. He might not.

Praise says nothing of the change. Death is a close friend here, always nearby. To be surprised by it is weakness, stupidity.

"Did you sleep all right?" Praise asks, a nervous question. Last time, he did not ask, and perhaps it is this change, so slight and unimportant, that helps the storyteller decide.

Penance, he has come to learn, is not something paid alone.

"Of course," the storyteller lies. They'll know the truth soon enough, and have forgotten it soon enough, too. No need for complications.

"Are you hungry?" the new First asks, his voice like an echo of one the storyteller has heard before, and though it takes him a moment—a long, long moment—he finds its source.

"Tae. Twyllyn Tae. Does that name mean something to you?" he asks this new First, whose wide eyes grow even wider at the sound of his voice. "A father? Grandfather, maybe?"

The First swallows and casts an anxious look to Praise before responding.

"My grandmother's grandfather."

Had the storyteller air in his lungs to sigh, he might have. He could have shaken his head and looked about, noting the passage of time like a river running ever on or a plant growing ever up. Shock and vague sadness might have curled his lips and darkened his countenance.

So long. It had been *so long*.

Instead, he nods and says, "A good man. A wonderful sailor."

I'll see you after.

Now that he has resurrected that voice, the storyteller cannot stop the memories from rising in him, specters of a past embodied in his every movement, his every word. What is he if not a plant grown in that old graveyard soil, fed by those long-ago waters, reaching for the light of a sun pulling ever farther away?

The First has spoken to him again, and Praise, too.

"What was that?" he asks, pushing the memories down, knowing they will return. He needs to resume the story now.

"Are you hungry for anything?" this descendant of Twyllyn Tae asks again.

"No, thank you," the storyteller says.

Praise unlocks the chains and leads the three of them back out of the house, back through the overgrown streets of Twist, back to the fires and the dais and the listeners, all of them hungry and waiting.

"We have all had a challenging morning," the First says, speaking with growing confidence to those assembled. "What better to soothe our hurt than the completion of a promised tale?"

He gestures to the storyteller, who mounts the dais and lets his eyes rove the audience, ringed again around their fires. One by one he finds their eyes, noting those who look away in shame and those who stare back, angry and proud.

At the back, angriest and proudest of all, is Praise, and when the storyteller finds this man's eyes, he does not look away.

Yes, he will be the one. A fitting payment for a tale well told.

"Did the fires consume the whole Sea?" someone shouts.

"Did Kindred make it to the Sea floor?" another asks.

"What happened to the pirates and to Arcadia?"

"Did she find the Marchess?"

They have chewed these questions all night, working and wondering at them. They expected a story, neat and tidy and complete. An escape.

The storyteller accepts an offered cup of water from one of Praise's men, and after letting the water touch his lips, he steps forward. A raised hand quiets the questions.

"My tale thus far has asked many questions, some still on your minds, I see. Today, you shall have answers," he says, letting his eyes drift to the youngest among the group, children with no idea of his mistreatment, no sense of what the leaders of Twist have done and will do again to hold on to even the smallest protections.

In the faces of these children he finds again that wry, clever joy, the suspense and wonder found only on the precipice of a story soon to be sung.

I'll see you after.

"I have told you already of Kindred Greyreach, first among the hearth-fire keepers of Arcadia, who, through trickery and manipulation, took her ship and its crew out past safe grasses and into the Roughs, where monsters from the deep and pirates of the surface dwelled. I have told of her grandmother, the Marchess, who was said to disappear from her ship into the Sea, stepping down into the black below. I have told of Kindred finding the Once-City, home to those pirates. I have told of the mysteries there, and the banal realities, too. A struggle for water, a struggle for power, and Kindred at its center.

"When last I spoke, Kindred had escaped the crumbling Once-City and set fire to the flattened grasses of the Sea around Arcadia, creating a temporary barrier between the pirates and the island itself. In a boat made of grass, Kindred, now a captain, along with Ragged Sarah and Seraph, sailed below the Sea, down toward whatever waited below."

The listeners had shifted forward, most without realizing it, their eyes on the storyteller, their breaths slowing and evening out against the rhythms of his telling. Soon they would all breathe together, a chorus of silent voices, held completely in his power.

But not yet.

I'll see you after.

He is caught for a moment in the memory of what comes next, the threads of past, present, and future knotting together in him.

"First," the storyteller says, holding up a finger and grinning down at the kids, who watch him with greatest interest, unguarded and honest, "let me tell of another. Hold on to the burning Arcadian Sea for a moment, and to Kindred's joyous dive beneath, and instead see a boy. Young, like some here. Dreaming of adventure, of heroism, of great deeds done by his own hands. Dreaming, too, of a family that was and might be again. If Kindred's name should be known by all, sung in every language, revered and loved, then let this boy's name be a forgotten curse. Let it dribble from the corner of your mouth in dreaming, lost again upon waking. A bare memory, already disappearing."

The storyteller pauses, not to draw out the tension nor to stoke the fires he sees in every eye watching him.

He pauses because this is the moment the forgetting will commence. When he utters that single syllable, the name he carries with him always, the slow wash of oblivion will begin to slacken mouths and glass over keen eyes. All will slowly be lost save for the barest memory of him, a hollow remembering for a hollow man.

And when he speaks, a being out in that darkness beyond Twist will turn its vast attention toward him. It will cock its head, listening as he spills out this story, and then it will approach, skimming and sliding through the endless night, unhurried.

It has done this before. It will do this again.

The storyteller pauses in the last moments before the end.

"As we begin our story, this boy is sitting with his family on what will be one of his last good days. One of his last happy moments. His name is Flitch o' the Borders. A boy, nothing more, searching for his story."

CHAPTER ONE

———◆◆◆———

"She set the Sea on fire!"

"On purpose?"

"That's what they're saying."

"*Who* is saying that?"

"Everyone! Just look at the smoke!"

"I heard only five or six birds were able to make it through the smoke to deliver reports. Only five or six!"

"Father said the King's casters have been working all day and night to keep the flames back from our grasses."

"Aren't Mainland grasses protected by magic?"

"*All* flattened grasses are protected by magic, you child."

"Don't call me child."

"Then don't ask silly questions like a child would, *child*."

"Both of you shut up! This person—Kindred . . . Greylights or Greyscare or something—released the flames from a *hearthfire*. The basic spells in place to keep the grasses flat and free of fire were no match for it."

"But if the King's casters have been working to protect our grasses, then it's okay, right? It's going to be okay?"

"Why would someone do something so stupid? All those lives and livelihoods just so she can . . . what?"

"That's the best part! She's getting chased by pirates sailing the *Once-City*—"

"Wait, that's real?"

"No way, that's a kids' story."

"Then I'm surprised you don't believe it, child!"

"I said don't call me that, Aster!"

"Wait, how were they *sailing* the Once-City? I thought it was a city."

"It was a floating city! Just one big ship."

"That sounds impossible. This can't be true."

"What would you know about *true*, child?"

"Would you two *knock it off* and let me finish?"

"Yeah, be quiet—you, too, Zim—I want to hear this."

"So, Kindred is getting chased by this whole floating city full of pirates, and there's Arcadia ahead of her, teeming with people who don't like her either, and so she sets fire to the whole Sea and *dives down below.* She's the daughter or granddaughter of some famous captain who jumped off her ship in pursuit of whatever was below, so this woman, Kindred, had to follow, I guess."

A silence—the first of the morning since the siblings had sat down to breakfast—followed. The four of them sat or stood around the enormous oval table, the gleam of the polished wood reflecting their faces where it wasn't covered in heaping plates and bowls of food. Charred green snout and red-rye spread and sliced root salad; gleaming slices of apples, bowls of raspberries and blusterberries, and clutches of moonfruit; glasses of every juice a body could crave and cups already half-drunk nearby; filleted starve-ant cooked three ways; broiled landhawk seasoned with sage, with callinae, with silver salt; breads of all different kinds, shapes, and colors, in slices or yanked away in thick hunks.

It was a feast.

It was breakfast in the Borders Baron's house.

Idyll, oldest of the four siblings—a group often called the Borders Brats among other barony nobility and in the King's court—sat upright and still, speaking only occasionally, and listening much more. They were tall and narrow, with serious eyes and long black hair. A small smile hovered perpetually on their face, and they wore faded robes in the colors of the Borders barony: black and gold.

Next to Idyll sat Aster, second oldest, standing to reach one long arm across the table to refill her plate. She wore the loose-fitting garments of a caster, already having been out training that morning before her other siblings had cracked their eyes on the new day. She was in her final year of study at the King's academy, and her arms showed the shifting muscles of serious practice, her fingers and hands the scarred-over burns of many mistakes at the casting fire. Aster's wolfish smile grew wider as she tormented her younger sibling Zim, appending "child" to nearly every sentence meant for him.

Zim, barely touching the food carefully arranged on his plate, sat upright like Idyll, but whereas Idyll's lines were those of someone who had carelessly mastered gracefulness, Zim struggled for it. He wore the high-necked, stiff clothing—jacket and pants—of the bookkeeping office where he worked, though he had not yet found comfort in them. Even as he snapped back at Aster, only a year his senior, Zim fiddled with the scratchy collar of the jacket and shifted uncomfortably against the belt and boots. He'd recently begun to grow in a beard, and it, like all of his attempts to be old before he was old, was only slightly successful.

Last, youngest, and loudest, was Flitch, baby of the Borders Brats, only sixteen. He had the same dark eyes, the same light brown skin, the same long nose as his siblings—a gift from their mother—but while the rest of them wore the clothes of their station—even Idyll who had not yet selected a formal role in the barony, wore the family colors—Flitch wore the plain clothes of youth. They were nice enough to gesture at his status, of course, but several years old and perfectly mended whenever possible instead of replaced, as was the expectation among the nobility.

And this was the secret etched in the lines of the old wood and stone of the Borders family home, in the tangled wilds of the woods growing on their lands, in the hollow sockets on the shelves of their libraries, in the faded colors of Idyll's clothes and the small, careful stitching of Flitch's—the secret, known to all and carried like a weight around each of the Borders Brats' necks, was that their family *had been* great.

Borders had once been strongest among the baronies, most favored by the kings and queens of old, its children accepted into and at the head of the best schools, the most secretive and elite groups. Borders ships once dominated the Mainland ports and grasses, its sails myriad among the crown's own fleets. The Borders Baron once sat at the place of honor on the royal council.

Once, Borders was mighty.

Once, Borders was grand.

Once.

Now, hunched and lurking behind every smile and in the shadow of every joyful word uttered by these siblings was the heavy truth that they were the last hope of a fading, failing dynasty.

"So, *that's* where all this smoke on the horizon is coming from," Flitch said, turning from the massive windows of the dining room, which faced east toward Arcadia and showed a hazy, fuzzy sky, the Sea chaotic in the heavy winds of the morning.

While the others sat at the breakfast table, Flitch had spent the morning peering through the longsight, scouring the eastern horizon for any sign of a ship emerging from that haze of smoke. A vessel bringing news. Or survivors.

Despite the few crow-callers who had managed successfully to get their birds back after sending them into the haze, no real information about the state of the Sea or Arcadia was known, at least not that Flitch had heard. The smoke was too thick, they said. The fires too aggressive and their spread too fast.

"I wonder if it has anything to do with the increase in mid-Sea creatures coming to the surface," Idyll said, propping their chin up with the long fingers of one hand, sharp elbow pressing into the wood of the table. "Two wyrms almost came ashore last span, and apparently more of the King's ships have been repurposed to deal with the beasts from below."

"But that all started before the news of the fire, right?" Flitch tried to remember exactly when the strange tidings about the Sea began, whispers from their barony's sailors, fear and uncertainty in the eyes of captains known to be brash, confident, and capable.

"Maybe we'll find out what's really going on at the King's meeting this afternoon," Aster said. It had been her bit of news that sparked the conversation that morning. She'd been practicing her casting forms out on the north deck of the estate and had overheard their father, the Borders Baron, talking with one of his sibilants. "*All* the barons are invited, along with their advisors and staff, after all."

That stopped the rest of them for a moment. How long had it been since their father had been invited to the castle for anything beyond the occasional pleasantry and individual meeting? This King gathered sobriquets like a child gathering leaves at the turning of the seasons: the Warring King, the Loveless King, the King in Shadow, the Unruled King, Faineant the Luckless, Faineant the Widower, the Unaging King—but his most recent felt truest among the siblings at the table: the Fickle King.

King Faineant's love and favor shifted quicker than the wind, but neither ever seemed to touch on their father, oldest and most forgotten of the four barons who controlled the areas surrounding the Mainland capital.

"Maybe he's finally going to give Father a real seat at the table?" Zim said, though even he didn't seem to believe it.

"More likely he's going to take additional vessels from our fleet," Idyll said, tipping their head to the side as they mimicked King Faineant's voice. *"For the good of the kingdom."*

"What are we if not servants to our greater cause?" Aster said, adding her own impression. Even Zim laughed at that.

Flitch couldn't stop smiling as he turned back to the window and squinted once more through the longsight, He felt restless and excited, like a child again, back when all of his siblings were always around and the substance of their lives had been only this: talking and laughing and joking and snarking at one another. Creating their own mischief and games on days that felt rich with possibility and purpose, their imaginations racing one another, making mainsails out of trees and stretches of sea out of grassy fields, monsters out of shadows and heroes out of themselves.

It had been like a play where Flitch had always known his lines, always understood and cherished his part and the purpose it gave him. He'd known who he was with his siblings around and had loved them for it.

But now Aster and Zim were away daily for their duties, her to school and training, him to the bookkeeping offices near the capital, both more and more often sleeping away in their apartments in the capital, going spans without returning home. And Idyll, too, spent greater portions of their time in the royal library, researching and writing their stories, preparing themself to become the next leader of the Borders barony.

They were all leaving Flitch behind, and he couldn't run fast enough to catch them or the ghost of what they had once been together.

But today felt different. The time had come and gone that should have seen Aster leaving for her classes, and both Idyll and Zim should already have been preparing for their journey into the capital for the day.

Instead, some quiet magic held them all there, each sibling falling again into the old patterns of speech, their old roles as peacemaker or instigator, oldest or youngest. For a moment, everything felt right again, and Flitch thrummed with joy.

"You're sure no one has returned from Arcadia yet?" he asked. Through the longsight's grimy glass, he watched one of the King's vessels, *Glory's Bellow*, cutting across the harbor, casting fires ablaze, royal casters ready to send errant beasts from the deep back to the darkness.

Flitch adjusted the dials on the longsight to bring the masts of the ship into focus, smiling a little at the flare of runes inscribed there, the handiwork of Borders carvers. Without their hold on mast-building, Borders would have crumbled away to nothing long ago. Other baronies had robust and growing trade spread around many different goods, while Borders was left behind, still keeping its miser's hold on the secret work of mast-building, but with little else to pad its fortunes.

Zim's work responsibilities had him attempting to address this problem, but to hear him describe it, it was a little like starting a footrace a day late and with stone shoes.

Flitch pushed all of that aside and instead let his mind roil with the possibilities and potential of a day like this. If fate truly existed, it had finally, *finally* turned its golden eyes toward Borders. All the siblings were still in the house, and mysterious news swept like a wildfire along the lines of their imaginations.

"We'd have heard if someone made it back," Aster said. "Although every barony—us included—have ships out there trying, and I heard Father saying *someone* should have returned by now."

Flitch continued to scan the stretch of Sea that had served as the siblings' source of inspiration and imagination as children, the Borders estate having been built many generations before, on the cliffs at the edge of the Mainland, close enough to spit into the Sea from the edge of their backyard.

"I don't see any ships out there," Flitch said, one eye squeezed shut as he continued looking. "It's just the King's vessels patrolling for deep-Sea threats. I heard one of Father's sailors say that some of the creatures seemed to be targeting some boats over others. Some are saying it seems to have something to do with the size of the hearthfires or the amount of captains' bones they're carrying. Oh! It looks like one of the ships just found— Wait! There's something out further!"

"What is it?"

"A ship? Is it a ship?"

"It might be," Flitch said, leaning forward until the edge of the longsight met the glass of the window with a soft *clink*. "The smoke is so thick; it's hard to tell."

"Well, look harder!"

"That doesn't even make sense, Aster. How could he—"

"*You* don't even make sense!"

"Enough, you two."

"Yes!" shouted Flitch, sending his voice up through the susurrus of his siblings like a bright flower emerging from the green mess of the Sea. "It's a ship! Coming from the east!"

"What are their colors?"

"Whose ship is it? One of ours?"

"The King's?"

The other three siblings launched a volley of questions at Flitch, and as he squinted to see, they abandoned their places at the table to jostle around, each squinting out at the harbor and the smoke-veiled Sea beyond. The ship was a speck in the haze to the bare eye, and soon they were fighting over the longsight, a chaos of limbs and laughter.

"Give it back!"

"I have the best eyesight, though!"

"I'm the oldest!"

"Hey, Flitch! Give it!"

"Ouch, Aster! Not my ribs!"

"Hey, no tickling!"

They were a jostling mess, closer than they had been in years, and when Aster finally took control of the longsight, cackling in victory, the Borders Brats stayed entangled as she narrated what she saw.

"It's a three-master, huge hull! That has to be one of the widest ships I've ever seen. Two generations old, maybe, returning but badly damaged— either that or it's being sailed by someone with Zim's ability at the helm."

"Hey!"

"Shhh!"

"The ship's listing hard to port, burns along the hull, sails are . . ."

Flitch flicked through the lists he kept in his mind of ships and captains, crews and casters, fleets and armadas, colors and sigils. He might have been too young to truly begin pursuing his path in the world, but he had it there in his heart. A captain of his own ship, searching the wide Sea for adventure and riches, fame and glory, sailing always under the proud banner of the Borders barony. Like his siblings, and in his own way, he would return the dignity and power of the Borders name.

"Deep blue?" he asked, finishing Aster's sentence for her.

"Yes!"

"That's *Prairie Bounty*, sailed by Captain Halfstorm, Paths barony," Flitch said, speaking in a rapid clip.

"Flitchy!" Aster said, grinning at him and slinging an arm around his neck. "Look at you! Little soon-to-be captain!"

Flitch grinned and felt tears touch at the corners of his eyes, as much in response to that old nickname as the compliment itself. Idyll, still holding Zim in a headlock, smiled at Flitch and nodded. Although they were the oldest and Flitch the youngest, Idyll had always been Flitch's closest companion in the family. Their rooms were next to one another on the third floor, and some of Flitch's earliest and happiest memories were of sneaking down the cold, dark hallway during storms to crawl into Idyll's bed. Idyll would whisper made-up stories in the darkness to distract Flitch from the too-bright flash of the lightning and the bone-deep press of the thunder.

While Aster was loud and energetic, Zim rule-bound and stiff, Idyll had always offered a calm steadiness for Flitch. They were a well of peace, the Sea calmed, a sky banked with endless, fluffy clouds.

When Idyll had grown old enough to gain charge of their own vessel— a gift still offered by the Borders Baron to his children despite his waning fortunes—they would take Flitch out with them, the two siblings whooping and joyous at the prow, wind in their faces, smiles stretched to breaking. Aster often joined them, and even Zim sometimes, too, though the two of them grew increasingly interested in their own studies and pursuits, leaving Idyll and Flitch to sail off around the harbor with the small crew that piloted and worked the vessel itself.

In all things, Idyll was there to show Flitch the right path.

Idyll helped Flitch with his lessons; Idyll showed him the shape of knots and told him their uses; Idyll pointed out the cooks in the estate who would smile at clumsily pilfered snacks and the ones who would use the wooden spoon.

Idyll showed Flitch the secret language of the world, and in return, Flitch gave to them a fierce and loyal love.

A quiet had settled over the siblings, all of them still tangled together. Aster continued to peer through the longsight, but she roved the harbor with it now, lazy as she peered among the grasses. Zim finally succeeded in removing his head from Idyll's hold, and he stood with a glare before returning to the table for a forkful of food.

Flitch could feel the beginnings of them pulling back, the possibility and magic of the morning seeping away. He could already hear the slow indrawn breath, the casual glance around, followed by one of them saying, "I suppose I should . . ."

No, came a voice from deep inside Flitch. *Not another morning of them all leaving me behind.*

"The council meeting isn't until this afternoon, right?" he said, giving his voice an edge of mischief.

"Right," Zim said, leaning down to pick up the work bag he'd set next to his chair at the start of breakfast. "I'll be in the office until then, but—"

"And if that ship is from the Paths barony," Flitch continued, fixing Zim with a smile before looking at his other siblings, "then it should be returning to their docks, right?"

"That's usually how it works, Flitchy," Aster said, peering back curiously at him.

"What are you thinking, Flitch?" Idyll asked, studying him.

"That ship will have news of the Arcadian fire, maybe even information about the pirates and the Once-City," Flitch said, looking around at them. "It's too bad it's not one of ours. Then we wouldn't have to wait until the council meeting at the castle this afternoon to find out whatever they know."

"Nothing for it," Aster said, shaking her head and looking out at the harbor. "Paths are just as protective of their private docks as we are. Without a signed agreement from the Paths Baron, no one rests a vessel there."

"Gwyn Gaunt doesn't sign *anything*," Zim said, frowning around at them. "My office has been attempting to broker a deal with Paths over a stretch of land that could provide excellent chances for timber production. It's almost unused right now, and the waterways alone might be our chance to finally leverage some of our remaining political power. The lead negotiators on the project have—"

"Yes, yes, you're very important and so is your incredibly boring work," Aster cut in. "We understand. Get on with it."

Zim offered a huff and glare in response before continuing.

"The project might have gone through formal negotiations and been signed by now, but the famous Paths Baron, Gwyn Gaunt, refuses to attend meetings! She always sends a councillor or staff person, someone who asks odd questions and makes promises to deliver the information back to the baron."

"Even still," Flitch said, doggedly holding on to the day's hope—his siblings together again, one more adventure—"maybe we could sneak onto the dock. We could pretend to be on official barony business. It's a busy dock, and in the time it takes them to figure out we don't have the documents to rest our ship there, Captain Halfstorm would have returned, and no one would bother with us anymore in all the excitement."

It was weak, and Flitch knew it, nothing more than a child's hope. But he didn't have anything else. Any moment, Zim would leave for the office, and Aster would say something about needing to practice some of her forms at the school facilities, and Idyll would put their hand on Flitch's shoulder as they stood to go.

Zim shook his head at the thought of breaking so many inter-barony agreements, but he was always going to be an impossible sell on such a plan. Even when they were kids, Zim was the last to join in their imaginary play if he caught even a whiff of potential danger or rule-breaking.

For their part, Idyll offered only a soft *hmm* and let their eyes drift once more to the window, the expression on their face unreadable even to Flitch.

Most surprising was Aster, who had always been first to take a leap of uncertainty, to climb a tree or eat a strange bug or jump from a ledge that seemed just a little too high. Brave or reckless, wild or dangerous, free or mad—whatever a person could say about Aster, none would ever accuse her of caution.

But here, she was frowning at Flitch, the look on her face conveying her uncertainty in clear-enough terms that her low "It's a bit risky for us, isn't it, Flitchy?" seemed unnecessary.

Looking around at the faces of his siblings, Flitch felt the golden glow of the day fade into grey dullness. They would leave again, and he would stay. Maybe he would sail his ship over to the Paths dock anyway. Just him. Let them go off to their jobs and activities, the lives they led outside of the family. He would—

"I know someone," Idyll said, their voice quiet and slightly strained. When they spoke, they kept their gaze on the window and the Sea beyond. "From Paths. He'll be there. I could get us on that dock."

After a surprised pause from the other siblings, Aster said, "That certainly changes things." The clouds of uncertainty had cleared from her face, and she looked around now with the bright brashness Flitch thought of as her natural state. "Who is this person you know?"

"No one," Idyll said, the casual tone of their voice brittle and breaking.

"No one?" Aster said, smile sharpening into a wicked instrument. "I hope he's more than no one—it's going to take a higher-up in the Paths hierarchy to get us a spot on that dock. This can't be some nobody Gwyn Gaunt has working in the library with you, Idyll."

Idyll turned finally from the window and fixed Aster with a look that said, quite clearly, how easily and happily they would kill her if she didn't relent.

"He's an advisor to Gwyn, and I know he was overseeing operations on the dock this morning. I've worked with him at the library, and we are on good terms. I believe he will allow us to rest our vessel at their dock for a short while."

Even the music and fluidity of Idyll's speech had vanished, and though hope blossomed in his chest at the renewed prospect of their fate-touched morning, Flitch watched his eldest sibling with suspicion. Who was this advisor? Flitch had never heard Idyll speak of the other librarians or librarians-in-training beyond a simple remark here or there—an annoying cataloguer who wouldn't stop talking or an ambitious noble's child hounding the head librarians for favors.

A strange and unpleasant thought slid into Flitch's mind, a bare shred of raincloud portending a storm. He'd known that his siblings had their work and responsibilities, and he'd known that, in spending their days and many of their nights away for those responsibilities, they would meet other people and find their own ways in the world.

But here was the first moment that Flitch understood that all of them, that Idyll—his favorite, his closest sibling, maybe his closest friend—was living a life outside of the Borders home that didn't include Flitch at all. A life of friends and enemies, goals and successes and setbacks and all the rest, all the things that, once upon a time, Idyll had shared with him.

It wasn't jealousy or anger that gripped Flitch.

It was a cold shiver of sadness as he imagined a thousand different lives, all full, that Idyll was living without him.

It was loneliness, singing its empty song in his chest, even as his siblings continued their play.

"You're on *good terms*?" Aster asked, a mischievous smile quirking one cheek. "You and this gentleman are on *good terms*?"

"I'm going to throw you into the Sea," Idyll said, voice flat and eyes dangerous.

"I don't know about this," Zim said. "Won't it take too long to get a crew and vessel ready?" He held his bag in one hand, caught in the space between a decision he should make and a decision he wanted to make. The winds had changed on this conversation, and he knew it.

"We won't take one of the big boats," Flitch said, gaining momentum. "We can take a catboat! I still have the one I was using yesterday rigged up and ready to go!"

"I haven't been in a catboat since . . ." Aster began, her eyes going soft, one finger tracing the edge of her broad jawline as she tried to remember. Flitch was already thinking of the memory she sought, had been thinking of it most of the previous day as he moved around the harbor in the small vessel, the hearthfire burning steadily around his basic builds.

It had been almost eight years before, Flitch still young enough that he spent the whole of the voyage tied to the single mast so he wouldn't fall overboard. The four of them, plus their father, had crowded onto one of the catboats and cut across the harbor at speeds that felt impossible to young Flitch, their bow sending up sprays of seedpods and prairie fluff in the thick afternoon light. They sailed without destination or purpose, slowing to investigate interesting flowers and plants or to cast out for bugs whenever they felt like it.

Is this windflower, Father? Idyll asked in Flitch's remembering, their face—much younger then—tipped toward the tall stem boasting its purple, spiked flowers.

It is, the Borders Baron had said, smiling broadly for perhaps the first time since the baron had passed. *We're lucky to see them; they don't often make it to the surface of the Sea. Come on, everyone—Flitch, you hold on to me. Let's pick a few.*

It burned and shone like only memory could, brighter for the forgetting, every sharp word and moment of unhappiness lost in the glow of what remained: a happy day. A good day. Flitch's mother had passed away only a year or two before, and many of the family's days since had been long, hard ones, feeling and feeling again the loss.

But that day had been a happy one, bright and hopeful and quiet and loving, like a single perfect flower opening defiantly in a dreary field of green.

It was a day Flitch thought of as he sailed his tiny vessel around the harbor, sometimes with a crewmate or two, sometimes alone.

"I don't know," Zim said, still unmoving, indecision gripping him. "I really should work this morning."

"Don't you want to see the ship when it comes in?" Flitch asked, trying and failing to keep the pitch of desperation from his voice. "Don't you want to hear the stories from the sailors themselves instead of whatever filtered, shortened version we're going to hear at the council meeting? Don't you want to see Captain Halfstorm when she steps off the deck?"

"Haven't there been increased appearances from deep-Sea creatures in our grasses recently? Won't it be dangerous?" Zim's eyes had gone wide.

"That's what all the patrolling vessels out there are for!" Flitch said, excitement thrumming through him. This was going to happen. "And we'll stay close to the shore. Even if one came up on our short trip, it wouldn't be anywhere close to us. Come on! Let's have an adventure like we used to! All of us, together for another journey! The Borders Brats sail again!"

"Seems dangerous," Zim said, just as Aster raised the longsight like a sword and said, "Yes!"

With an arch look at Zim, she continued.

"I'm in. And I hope something *does* come up while we're out there. What's the point of being the best caster on the Mainland if I can't send some monstrosities from the deep back to the Seafloor?" Aster's cocky smile flared and then faltered. "Except there's no way Father will let us go."

Zim nodded and gestured with one hand, as if to say, *See? A doomed idea.*

"Father won't know," Idyll said, standing up. Their long black hair had gotten tousled in the scrum, and they retied it into a tail once more, the motions practiced and smooth. "He was in his study when I came down for breakfast, and he said he was going to spend the morning *downstairs.*"

Silence blossomed into the conversation as it did anytime anyone spoke of what lay below the Borders estate, the space beyond the archway that none of them had ever seen. The promise and curse of their family, a secret they had all pieced fragments of together from overheard conversations of the baron's and scraps of paper barely glimpsed in his study over the years.

It was not something they were supposed to speak of, and so, of course, they had spent many lazy afternoons of their childhoods speaking of and speculating about nothing else. The baron had never taken any of the children below, not since their mother's death, so it remained an open secret between them in those early days.

"I'm not sure—" Zim began, but Aster dropped the longsight and wrapped an arm around his neck, pulling him into his second headlock of the morning.

"Zim and I are *both* in," she said, eyes alight with mischief. "Idyll?"

Idyll's grin matched Flitch's own, and soon enough the Borders Brats, reunited for a day away from work and school and whatever singular lives they had all begun to lead, were racing each other down to the docks, aglow with all the morning might bring.

CHAPTER TWO

———◄◆►———

"*The Laughing Queen*?" Aster leaned precariously over the bow to inspect Flitch's paintjob. "I thought we named this *Thundering Rainfall* or something like that."

"*You* named it *Thundering Rainfall*, and I changed it," Flitch said from where he sat behind the wheel, piloting their small vessel along the coastline of the harbor, which, when looked at on a map, resembled a flattened half-moon scoop out of the Mainland's eastern coast, with Borders positioned at one far end of the harbor and Paths in the center. Farther along were merchant and public-use docks.

With so many places to land a ship, Falcate Harbor was one of the Mainland's busiest, and Flitch had spent many days on the shore or in *The Laughing Queen* just watching boats come in and out, whispering their names and their captains' names to himself, imagining their voyages and adventures.

Falcate Harbor had recently grown quieter, though, its grasses hosting fewer and fewer merchant vessels and harvesting crews, and not just because of the Arcadian fire, the smoke from which still hung to the east like a grey curtain.

"Isn't it bad luck to change the name of a ship?" Aster asked, pulling her body back over the gunwale. "Aren't you sailors supposed to believe in that kind of thing?"

"*Thundering Rainfall*," Idyll cut in before Flitch had a chance, "was this vessel's fourth name, if I remember correctly. I named it *Oakheart* back before Zim and Flitch were even born, and then Zim renamed it *Ghost*, and then I renamed it *Windflower*, and then you named it *Thundering Rainfall*, Aster."

Idyll smiled around at them, perfectly at ease on the cramped deck, seated and leaning with their head back against the single mast.

"If there was luck to be had with this vessel," they said, "we squandered it long ago."

"Do we have to go so fast?" Zim asked. Among them all, he was the least comfortable aboard a ship, regardless of whether it was a single-mast, beamy vessel like *The Laughing Queen*, where the cabin was little more than a storage space for casting tackle and a bedroll, or one of the larger, fully-rigged vessels—*The Lament*, with its forty-person crew, or *Starlight*, the longest, fastest vessel of any fleet in the Mainland, with its strange tiered sails and doubled hearthfire. No matter the ship, no matter the voyage, Zim had never found his sea legs, which was why he, alone among them, had tied himself to the mast, the coils of his leash piling at his feet.

"I'll slow us down," Flitch said, gesturing for Idyll to take the wheel while he moved to the small hearthfire and rearranged the simple build to give them stability in lieu of speed.

"It's nice being out here again," Aster said, trailing one hand overboard into the passing grasses, the slight *shush* and *hiss* adding to the swell of similar sounds made by the wide prow. "We spend so little time on actual boats at the academy."

"We spend *no time* on boats at the bookkeeping offices," Zim said, his knuckles four bright points on each hand as he grasped the gunwale. "We walk between buildings, or ride horses if it's too far. It's nice. No one ever fell a thousand miles to their death when they slipped on the road."

"Don't be so dramatic," Idyll said, rolling their eyes as they angled their face up into the sun, smiling at the warmth. "It can't be more than a few miles to the bottom of the Seafloor."

"You can't know that," Zim said, sinking down to sit on the deck opposite Idyll. "No one knows that, and so I choose to believe it's thousands of miles."

"I hope for Kindred's sake it's less than that," Flitch said, letting out a laugh. He felt expansive, as though his own forever had been locked inside his chest, but this moment—his siblings pleasantly arguing in those old rhythms and melodies, the sun turning the green of the Sea into something holy, the gently rocking deck of a boat beneath his feet—it was the key that fit snugly between his ribs.

He laughed again, this time deep from that opening place inside himself, a joyful noise for a joyful moment.

Off portside, the coast of the Mainland, still technically Borders territory, rushed by, tangled plants and clusters of unchecked weeds swarming the rocky soil, untouched by a gardener's careful hand in many years.

"I didn't realize Faineant had assigned so many vessels to defense," Aster said, peering out into the harbor, where, instead of the usual fare of harvesting and merchant vessels moving among the grasses, groups of two or three royal ships sailed in a carefully orchestrated patrol, the casting fires on their decks lit and visible even from where the Borders Brats watched on the deck of *The Laughing Queen*.

"The creatures have been appearing at greater rates every day," Flitch said, and then to Zim, "but only further out, and even the ones who've managed to get close to the coast take a long time to reach it."

"It's going to be fine, Zim," Idyll said, leaning over to put a hand on Zim's arm. "The people on those ships know what they're doing."

Aster made a small noise of protest, and Idyll held up a hand.

"Yes, yes—we all know they're nothing compared to the Mainland's finest caster, Aster o' the Borders, the Stormcloud Magus reborn, first of her name and feared across the land. We got it; everyone understands."

Aster, who had opened her mouth to offer the same sentiment, now closed it for a moment before saying, "It's good to know my fame has begun to spread." Her bright smile pulled deep dimples into her cheeks, and she made a show of patting one pocket. "And don't worry. I always travel with a few casting plants—just in case you all need saving."

Idyll gave her a long-suffering look and said nothing.

"Do we have time to cast out for some food? I'm hungry." After basking in the glow of her burnished reputation, Aster opened the tiny door to the cabin space below and began rooting around for a pole.

"We were just eating breakfast," Zim said. "How can you be hungry?"

"I'm always hungry." Aster's voice became muffled as she stuck her head and torso below. "Where's the casting equipment, Flitch? There's nothing but an old axe down here."

"I broke a pole a few days ago and haven't replaced it yet," Flitch said, laughing at Aster's cry of dismay. "We'll be there soon, anyway."

They talked of small things as they cut across the harbor, their conversation accompanied by the music of the sail catching and snapping in the wind, by the crack and rustle of the hearthfire.

Aster told tales of her time at the school, the eccentric teachers who molded the minds and abilities of the Mainland's most elite casters. Zim countered these stories with descriptions of the bookkeeping offices and their new renovations, offering loving details of their new pen racks and windowsills.

Even Idyll spoke some of the cataloguing project the librarians at the Rose were undertaking, and though they feigned boredom as they told of the private theoretical wars being waged between librarians over where and how and in what manner to organize the library's knowledge, Flitch could see the glimmer of real pleasure in Idyll's eyes.

"And what about you, Flitch?" Zim asked. "Have you decided what you want to do with your life? Father visited us at the bookkeeper's last span and spoke of a dearth of Border-friendly merchants willing to sail westward along the Mainland coast. Could be a promising career."

"Flitch isn't going to be a merchant in Father's fleet," Aster said, scoffing at the thought. "Merchants need to have business knowledge, an ability to make hard decisions, and the intelligence to know where the market is moving and why. Did you see how long it took him to decide what to eat for breakfast this morning?"

Aster's smile had turned wicked, but even her jabs could not puncture the happiness in Flitch, and he smiled back as he wrenched the wheel hard a-starboard, causing Aster, the only one still standing, to stumble and nearly fall.

"Oops," he said, still smiling. "I slipped."

Aster glared at him but dropped down to sit on the deck and relented with her teasing.

"What *are* you going to do, Flitch?" Zim asked, insistent. "The day is coming soon when you'll need to decide."

Idyll turned their attentions from the sun to Flitch, waiting for his answer with a smile. They knew already. Of course they knew. How many times had he confided his secret hopes to them? How many nights had he held up his dreams, only a little bashful, for Idyll's consideration and approval?

"I'm going to be a sailor and a mapmaker," Flitch said, letting his eyes rise to the Sea off to the east, to the smoke hanging there. He imagined for a moment he could see beyond it, to Arcadia, to the Roughs, to the barely mapped stretches of Sea and to the never-mapped stretches beyond that.

He saw himself, older, perhaps hardened by his time on the open Sea, a crew whose loyalty he'd earned moving in perfect concert around his deck, bringing their vessel back into port, the riches in the hull nothing when set next to the stories of adventure and heroism they had in their memories, and buried in all that richness, waiting among the triumph he would find out on the Sea, would be the glory Borders had slowly been losing over the past generations.

Flitch understood on some level that such dreams were childish. They were the longings of a little boy yet to grow up, and he knew his siblings would say just that if he were to utter his truest hopes.

So, he settled for *sailor* and *mapmaker*. The best kind of truths, laced with the liar's omission.

Only Idyll knew the heart of Flitch's dreams. Only Idyll could be trusted with something so precious to him, something so wonderful, so shameful, so hopeful.

And as they did with everything, Idyll handled Flitch's true aspirations with care and generosity.

That melancholy swept through him again, a wet slick of it gliding across his happiness, and Flitch thought once more of Idyll's life at the library, of this person they knew who could get them in to the Paths dock.

"Mapmaking is a fine profession!" Zim said, offering Flitch a lopsided grin. "So much unexplored coastline and stretches of Sea. You'll be a wonderful addition to Father's fleet."

"Maps are just doodles on paper," Aster said, winking at Flitch. "But I bet you'll doodle just as well as the rest of them."

Idyll only nodded at him, their small smile giving nothing away.

"Look!" Flitch pointed out into the harbor, glad for the distraction. *"Prairie Bounty* cleared the line of the King's patrol. We should meet them just as they reach the dock."

Aster had been right in her description: it *was* listing hard to portside and *did* have burns along the hull, but it was so much worse than that. One mast jutted off at an odd angle, and its sails hung in tattered strips. The burns along the hull had eaten away stretches of the wood, exposing the cabin to the Sea.

"Time to deliver on that promise, Idyll," Aster muttered, pulling their attentions away from *Prairie Bounty* to the Paths port, which was laid out like every other port in the huge harbor, each individual dock radiating out from the central patch of land like fingers on a hand, longest in the center and smallest on the sides.

On an average day, there might have been anywhere between fifteen and twenty-five ships docked there, some large and some small, crews and dockhands congesting the wooden walkways and filling the morning air with their bickering and dickering, their speculations and storying. The music of their lives.

Instead, Flitch counted three ships in total at rest there: the harvesting ship *Cloudless*, captained by Mehra Leon, and two vessels from Gwyn Gaunt's personal fleet, *Something Wicked* and *The Wild-Run*, both crewed and captained by whomever Gwyn Gaunt needed from day to day. Sometimes, Flitch had heard, Gwyn herself served as captain.

With so few vessels at rest there, Flitch's initial plan to sneak *The Laughing Queen* in amongst the chaos and bustle of the dock was revealed as pure fantasy. Despite the creeping melancholy he still felt at the thought of Idyll's life away from the Borders house, he saw now that that life was all that might get them a place on one of the short docks.

"Whoa there, sailors! Whoa!" came the rough voice of a dockworker, a man with sun-leathered skin and hard eyes. His beard, braided into three thin tails, caught the wind and bounced against his broad chest. Against one hip he wore a sword, and on one shoulder the sigil of Paths gleamed, giving his words and actions the shine of command.

Flitch banked the hearthfire, cutting the vessel's speed in jerky, juddering lurches. Zim let loose a shout and toppled over to the deck; he'd been squatting to get a better look over the gunwale, and he landed in a pile near the single, sturdy mast at the center of *The Laughing Queen*'s deck.

Aster, too, lost her balance and had to flail for a handhold to avoid Zim's fate. Idyll, still sitting, held on to their verticality with a grimace and hands splayed to the deck on either side of their crossed legs.

"Hold on," Flitch said, smiling around furtively.

"Thanks for the warning, Flitchy," Aster said, standing upright again but with a firmer hold on the gunwale now.

"These are private docks, young sailors," the man said, his feet planted at the edge of the dock where Flitch had planned to stop the ship. "Do you have the permissions to rest here?"

Flitch opened his mouth to respond and then shut it again, looking to Idyll, who rose unsteadily to their feet—the ship still hiccupping to a slow stop.

"We do not," Idyll said as they gave the man a soft smile, almost apologetic. "We're from the Borders barony with an urgent message for Ravel. If you tell him Idyll o' the Borders is looking for him, he should know what it's about."

"Ravel?" the man said, frowning.

Ravel. Flitch chewed on that name, imagining an array of men who might wear it—tall and muscular Ravels, short and lithe Ravels, smiling and sauntering, laughing as they shelved books with Idyll, the two of them sharing small jokes and secrets.

Flitch's melancholy twisted now with bitter jealousy, and he watched the dockworker wander off into the growing crowd of people clotting the ends of the docks, all of them watching the approach of *Prairie Bounty*.

"*Ravel,*" Aster said, infecting the word with all the euphemism and insinuation she could manage. Her eyes were wide as they found Idyll's, and that mischievous smile slicked back across her face. "Does he make you feel all tangled up inside?"

"That promise to throw you into the Sea still stands," Idyll said, keeping their eyes forward.

Aster gave a low, dark chuckle but said nothing else.

"I actually think it's wonderful that you've met someone," Zim said, giving Aster a disapproving look. "I can't wait to meet him."

"Thanks, Zim," Idyll said, their stoic expression cracking to reveal the utter suffering beneath.

"How long have you two been pursuing your love?" Zim asked, and it was enough to send Aster into fits of laughter. Even Flitch cracked a smile, the frantic, fragile joy of the moment enough to push his odd feelings about Idyll's secret life back into a dark corner of his mind.

Zim, who had probably read such a description of relationships in a book, looked around, confused.

"Maybe I'll throw myself into the Sea instead," Idyll muttered.

"If you'd just introduced him to us in the normal way, you might have avoided all of this," Flitch said, feeling a brittle smile on his face as he tried and failed to keep a petulant note out of his voice.

"I was going to tell you about him," Idyll said, their voice low and cutting under Aster's continued peals of laughter. "I just wasn't ready yet."

Any response Flitch might have given was interrupted by the return of the dockworker and a man who could only be Ravel.

He was tall and muscly, with hair cut close and an open, serious countenance—a man at work, busy but in control. Wide, roving eyes moved around the dock, noting various workers at their tasks and flicking constantly to *Prairie Bounty*, still some distance out but closing.

Ravel wore librarian's robes, the thick green fabric catching and filling in the wind, adorned only by a single rose woven into each shoulder, like floral epaulettes. Idyll rarely wore their librarian robes at home, claiming they were itchy and uncomfortable, but Ravel looked completely comfortable in the well-worn robes.

"The official envoy from Borders, is it?" Ravel said as he neared them, his gaze moving over the four siblings and lingering on Idyll for a long moment. Did the sober, sedulous demeanor flicker with something else then? Flitch squinted and searched Ravel's open face, but he couldn't tell.

"Official envoy . . ." Idyll said, misunderstanding giving their words a lilt.

"I didn't expect you until later this morning at the earliest," Ravel said, nodding and looking down at a densely covered roll of paper he pulled from a pocket. "No matter. You're welcome to rest your vessel here now."

Flitch began the work of pushing *The Laughing Queen* up to the dock, his thoughts returning to Idyll's secrecy and rewarding him with a sharp spur of pain from the hearthfire. He hissed and brought the whole of his attention on the clumsy task, singing his toneless song and urging the ship closer and closer to the wood of the dock until a soft *thunk* gave him leave to stop.

In the nonsense language of the hearthfire, Flitch sang words that were supposed to mean *stop*, or *rest*, or *surrender*. It all sounded the same to his untrained ear, but the books he'd read on keeping the hearthfire were clear on these simpler tasks. While the hearthfire on a larger vessel would forever remain out of his grasp and outside his interest, the flames of a small catboat like this one were easy enough to muddle through.

With a final, hitching judder, *The Laughing Queen* dropped down into the Sea and onto the chains of the cradle below, finally at rest.

"Edgar, will you please see to final preparations for Kathleen's arrival?" Ravel dismissed the dockworker with a nod, his eyes still flicking all around but always returning to Idyll.

"Kathleen?" Idyll asked.

"Kathleen Pentala Halfstorm," Flitch said, his memory firing almost immediately. He could see with clear-skied clarity the page in the most up-to-date copy of *Mainland Captains and Their Vessels* that featured Captain Kathleen Halfstorm, her small, sharp nose and angry, suspicious eyes. It was one of a few books Flitch carried with him everywhere at home, returning to it almost daily.

In the absence of his siblings, and with his father constantly at work keeping the Borders barony from falling further into obscurity, Flitch populated his daily life and imagination with captains old and new, with the shapes of their ships and the bits of biographical information lining their pages. Those nights when none of the siblings returned, more and more common now that each of them had their own lodgings nearer their work, Flitch would lie awake in his bed and whisper aloud the names of captains and their exploits, seeing in the play of moonlight on his ceiling the forms of famous crews and casters, adventurers and mapmakers, discovering labyrinthine hedges surrounding an unknown island or fending off waves of Antilles roaches as they rose through the prairie grasses.

In all of his fantasies, Flitch saw himself among the crew, perhaps their captain, perhaps a deckhand or quartermaster, part of the ship's tiny community, his imagined heroic deeds always so impossible and dramatic that they brought sharp tears of embarrassment to his eyes, the shame sugary, and caused him to clutch up the blankets to conceal the bright smile on his face.

"That's right," Ravel said, nodding at Flitch. "Not many people know Captain Halfstorm's full name."

"Our Flitchy knows all manner of useless information," Aster said, climbing from the ship onto the deck, ignoring Ravel's outstretched hand until she had gained her footing. "I'm Aster, Idyll's sister and personal hero. It's wonderful to meet you."

"Hello," Ravel said, smiling before casting his eyes out to the approaching *Prairie Bounty*.

"You were expecting us today?" Idyll asked, taking Ravel's extended hand and stepping off the ship. "Did we have a meeting I didn't know about?"

Ravel chuckled, his cheeks dimpling deeply, and Flitch found himself liking this man despite himself.

"That was a lie, Idyll," Ravel said, not unkindly. "Strictly speaking, I'm not supposed to allow anyone access to our docks right now, which I suspect you all already knew."

He gave them each a shrewd look.

"Hello, I'm Zim." Lacking either the social graces or awareness to navigate the situation, Zim awkwardly stepped off the boat and shook Ravel's hand, offering him a friendly smile.

"One of my brothers," Idyll said, nodding at Zim before gesturing to Flitch, who was the last off the boat. "And here's the other one."

"Hi," Flitch said, nodding at Ravel.

"It's wonderful to meet you all, though it's not how I expected to first meet your family, Idyll," Ravel said, looking back to Idyll. "And now that I've given you a spot for your boat and access to our dock, maybe you can tell me why a party of Borders nobility has arrived here without any warning and just before our vessel is returning from a dangerous mission through the smoke and fire?"

Opening his mouth, Flitch suddenly realized how their bright, brash idea—*his* idea, really—would sound to someone else, just as the games they'd played as children had never translated to anything rational or understandable when the siblings had explained them to their father. He felt suddenly foolish hearing the words in his head the moment before he spoke them, aware of how childish it all sounded. How reckless. How purposeless.

"We wanted to hear the news before anyone else, and since all of the siblings were home for the first time in so long, we decided to go together. Our docks are so close to this one, and we thought it would be fun," Flitch said.

There it was. The logic of every one of their childhood endeavors. The reason Aster climbed that tree when she was nine and why Idyll had run barefoot across those coals when they were twelve; the logic behind Zim dressing up as a great landhawk and screaming across their lawn one night.

We thought it would be fun, they had all said to their father and the various carers that had watched the Borders Brats after the death of their mother. *We thought it would be fun*, the siblings had said, as explanation and justification for every bit of adventuring and ill-considered daredevilry they had accomplished.

The other siblings had set aside that childish impulse the minute they stepped out of the Borders house with eyes toward their futures, leaving Flitch to care for it alone. Perhaps that's what gave the morning such a shine for him; for just a little while, they were all in their old roles again, and for just a little while, they were all moved and pushed by that same pure, honest, childlike impulse.

Why?

Because we thought it would be fun.

Now, though, Flitch watched discomfort crease his siblings' faces as that old phrase fell from his lips, and he saw them all as distant beings, older and gone away, his present nothing but a wrinkle in their past, his fire only a memory of warmth in their long ago.

He felt like a child, and he waited for his reprimand.

It never came.

When Flitch finally brought his eyes back up to Ravel's, he did not find the embarrassed, unintentionally condescending look he saw in the faces of his siblings.

"I don't have any siblings," Ravel said, his suddenly wistful voice at odds with the loud chaos of the docks and his previously earnest tone.

"We just got carried away by—" Idyll said, intending to say more but cut off by Ravel.

"I never did anything like that," he said, gaze sweeping around at them all, and when he smiled this time, it was youthful somehow, as though the man in charge had been only a mask, one that easily slipped and fell away. "You told me that your siblings liked to play games and go on adventures when you were younger, Idyll."

He let out a small laugh, the joy lighting his features.

"I didn't think I'd be so lucky to get to be in one of them."

A ruckus along one of the longer docks broke the moment and pulled Ravel's attention away, his gaze flicking back over his shoulder and the mask of his responsibility sliding back on seamlessly.

"You can stay," he said, distracted now. The group awaiting *Prairie Bounty*'s arrival had begun to disagree about something, by the looks of their faces and the sounds of their voices, and Ravel was already moving in that direction, turning his body away. "But don't get in the way."

He went then, striding off, his sheet of paper in one hand, moving among sailors many years his elder with calm and ease.

After a moment of silence in which Idyll's eyes followed Ravel across the docks and the other siblings exchanged looks with one another, Aster said in a low voice, "Close one."

"Too close," Zim said, looking ill and uncomfortable.

"Come on," Flitch said. "I don't want to miss it."

As *Prairie Bounty* neared, Flitch could make out a voice shouting commands—Captain Halfstorm, probably. That she and her crew were able to pilot the vessel in anything approximating a straight line was a miracle, but as Flitch and his siblings edged through the crowd to get a good view, they could see as the *Prairie Bounty*, still smoking from fires recently put out, looking like a ghost ship from nightmares, creaked and groaned forward, rocking dangerously.

"She's going to hit the dock," Aster said, rising up on her tiptoes.

"No, she isn't," Flitch said, rooted to the spot, watching with fascination as crew members rushed around the deck like extensions of the captain herself, the perfect execution of her desires. The hearthfire keeper, barely visible from this distance, was a flurry of song and activity as she moved around the fire, managing and manipulating her build to accommodate the fast-failing vessel.

Slowly, precariously, impossibly, the *Prairie Bounty* lurched to a stop along the largest of the decks, at which point the Paths workers waiting for their moment leapt into action, sliding several gangplanks out to the ship and racing along them with buckets of water and medicker supplies. Among them, Ravel moved with a calm efficiency, a mirror of Captain Halfstorm, ordering and maneuvering his people just as she ordered and maneuvered hers.

"Come on," Idyll said, pulling Flitch along the dock and onto the wide, flat patch of land from which the various roads to different parts of the Paths estate wound.

The Borders Brats moved among the other sailors and workers, who had halted their tasks to watch the *Prairie Bounty* come in.

"Down!" shouted a voice a moment before the damaged vessel sank down into the Sea, catching on the cradle of huge metal chains strung beneath it. Unlike the other ships at port, which sat snug and upright in their cradles, the *Prairie Bounty* leaned at a drunken angle away from the dock as it settled onto the chains, and it took some creative work from the dockworkers to get the captain and her keeper off the ship, the last two to disembark.

A happy cry went up from those waiting as Captain Halfstorm put boots onto the dock, and Flitch didn't realize he was cheering too until he found his siblings watching him in surprise.

"Let's get closer," he said before plunging into the crowd, edging around and between clumps of people, feeling himself like a full sail bellied out by the wind of this moment, this morning, this perfect confluence of events that found all of his siblings at home once more.

He made it to the front of the crowd, eliciting only a few mutters of disapproval, just as Captain Halfstorm had finished looking over her crew for major injuries, which were now all being treated by Paths medickers.

She was having a close, quiet conversation with Ravel, though even Flitch could tell she was anxious to move toward solid land. If Captain Halfstorm was going to say something before disappearing into the Paths estate and taking her stories with her, it was going to happen now.

Flitch cast a quick glance backward, to find his siblings waiting with open curiosity. A rill of joy ran through him.

Here we are, he thought, letting the possibility and magic of the moment fill him like a wind bellying out the sails of a ship pushing hard for home.

Captain Halfstorm broke away from Ravel with a nod and a quick smile, one hand gripping and leaving his shoulder. She was recognizable from the picture in Flitch's book, but whereas the lines on the page left her looking brusque and angry, her presence there on the dock was jovial and lively, her eyes wide and dancing with joy. Short and lean, with an arrhythmic step thanks to the smooth wooden leg attached below her right knee, Captain Halfstorm walked down the dock, her smoke-shadowed face breaking to show the smile she couldn't hold in.

"The *Prairie Bounty* returns!" she shouted, voice ragged and hoarse, climbing up on a few boxes to address the crowd cheering and waiting for her news. A roar of celebration erupted from everyone, and this time, Flitch wasn't the only Borders Brat cheering. Aster and Idyll hooted and whooped along with the rest, and even Zim let out a cheerful shout.

Here we are.

"Ten vessels left for Arcadia nearly a span ago," Captain Halfstorm said, her voice rasping out and capturing the listeners. It was a marvel how she spoke with such command and strength even after what had almost certainly been a harrowing voyage, even with a voice that sounded strained and at its end. "Four from the King's fleet, three from the Rivers barony, two from the Borders barony, and only one from Paths. And we are the first to return!"

Another cheer went up, and Flitch grinned around at his siblings, a happy loser in a game he didn't even know he was playing. Idyll laughed and pulled him close, slinging an arm around his shoulders and leaving it there.

"The others were pushed north and south by the racing flames, too slow or too cowardly to find the breaks in the fire. But my crew, my casters, my keeper—together we braved the fire and cut closer than any of them to the ruins of Arcadia!"

This time the cries were a mingled confusion, barony pride mixed with the sudden shock of despair.

"Ruins?" Flitch whispered, thinking of the beautiful buildings of Arcadia from his memory, the wonderful trips they'd taken there as a family to walk the streets and marvel at the sights and sounds, the smell of food and feel of the old buildings as he ran his hands along their facades.

Captain Halfstorm held up her hand for quiet.

"The fires swept inland some distance, and much of Arcadia was damaged or completely destroyed. We couldn't make it to the island itself, but we ran close enough to see signs of life well inland, where I made out casters and water workers fighting the oncoming flames. I don't know what Arcadia will be after this, but some still live there. Perhaps many."

She paused for a moment, and a quiet muttering could be heard, whispered prayers cushioned by the skin of hands rubbing together and the pull of fabric as hardened sailors shook their heads in disbelief.

Though Arcadia and the Mainland regularly jockeyed for economic and naval supremacy, neither ultimately hoped for the other's demise. They were too linked, businesses and governmental entities tied together through clandestine and public means alike. The best sailmakers were still in Arcadia, but the Borders barony were the only ones to make masts, and while the wood for hulls was grown and cut on land owned by the Rivers barony, it was smoothed and shaped into ships by Arcadian hands in Arcadian shipyards. The Mainland and Arcadia had both grown and prospered thanks to their relationships.

The fall of one was a blow to the other.

"But I bring news beyond Arcadia." Captain Halfstorm gestured at her ship. "You will see the damage to my vessel and the injuries among my valiant crew. Some of these were sustained by our proximity to the flames even now devouring the seas around Arcadia and pushing through the magical reinforcements no longer maintained by Arcadian casters. We were caught in the fires several times, but we always broke free to find avenues and lanes of grasses as yet unburned."

Flitch imagined it all, Captain Halfstorm, her commands rending the air and tearing her throat, her crew dumping water stores to put out the flames, casters working their magics to manipulate the ravenous fire started by that crazed keeper, Kindred Grey-something.

In his mind, it was all drama and daring, impossible moments and acts of heroism, gold and shining. Worthy of books and songs, of memory.

"But our damage was not caused by rampant hearthfire flames alone," Captain Halfstorm continued, her voice more and more ragged with each uttered word. "On the northwestern side of Arcadia, with the entire crew fighting desperately to hold off the flames reaching for our ship, we came upon a strange and unnatural sight: a pirate armada fleeing the flames, their vessels even worse off than ours."

She paused a moment, hacking out a rasping, wet cough. Flitch flinched at the sound of it. She wouldn't speak for much longer; that was clear. He pressed closer and felt his siblings just behind him doing the same.

"Pirates in Arcadian grasses?" shouted one of the dockworkers in disbelief.

"No," Captain Halfstorm said, shaking her head and taking a gulp of water from a skin. Some got in her mouth, but most spilled down her chin and onto her clothes. "Not anymore. When we came upon them, they were nearing Mainland grasses and closing in on *The Arcana.*"

Flitch cut a look to his siblings, eyes widening. *The Arcana* was a huge ship, the biggest in the King's fleet if the stories were true, and held the Mainland's best casters, who worked day and night to maintain the magics keeping the grasses flat and sailable around the Mainland. It was the heart of Mainland control over the Forever Sea.

"We," continued Captain Halfstorm, "along with the other vessels from the Mainland, subdued the pirate armada, and they are being led back to the Mainland by the King's ships."

The fantasies in Flitch's head exploded at this. Pirates! A whole *armada* of pirates!

He looked back at *Prairie Bounty*, assessing the damage to the ship with new eyes and seeing—really seeing—the lashes of angry magic, the flashes of power and bursts of burning energy hurled by pirates to carve channels in the wood like a manic pirate language, burned black and written in rage.

The battle would have been a furious one, Mainland ships of diverse origin and flying the colors of different baronies coming together to corral and subdue the pirate armada.

Had the pirates emerged out of the smoke and flames suddenly, appearing like deep-Sea creatures bursting forth from below? Certainly they had, and Captain Halfstorm, followed by the Borders barony ships and captains, had been first to notice, raising the alarm and bringing the ships into alignment. Pressed in by voracious flames on all sides, quickly losing sailable grasses in which to maneuver, the Mainland ships had mounted a fierce defense, taking only what lives they needed to and offering mercy to pirates who would never have offered the same back.

"Victory!" The jubilant cry came from someone behind Flitch, jarring him from his reveries, and soon it was taken up by others who surged forward, clapping captain and crew on the shoulders, examining the scarred and battered hull of *Prairie Bounty* more closely, amazed and joyous.

On their faces and in their conversations was the same fantasy that gripped Flitch, its fire built on the bones of Captain Halfstorm's words.

While her crew, those healthy enough to require no urgent attention from the medickers, fell to dockside tasks or into conversations with friends, Captain Halfstorm eschewed the eager congratulations of the crowd and set off for the wide, well-worn path that stitched itself up the cliffside and terminated at the Paths mansion, home to Gwyn Gaunt.

"We should go," Zim said, putting a hand on Flitch's arm.

"Okay," Flitch said, watching Captain Halfstorm go, Ravel walking next to her, the two of them speaking quickly, quietly.

Something in the captain's face, perhaps the slanting line of her mouth as she listened to Ravel or the distant reach of her eyes as she looked up toward the cliffside and the Paths house hidden above—*something* there in her face spoke of trouble, of uncertainty, of a danger at odds with the cheery celebration happening around her on the dock.

Had she lost crew? Had any of the Mainland ships? Or was she simply thinking of the ramifications of a wounded, battered Arcadia?

Flitch followed his siblings back to their tiny, undamaged vessel, wondering what troubled thoughts Captain Kathleen Halfstorm would deliver to the Paths Baron, Gwyn Gaunt.

⬛◆⬛

The Sea's soft whisper sounded against the hull, and Flitch let himself be lulled by it and the conversation of his siblings, which ranged from reactions to Captain Halfstorm's story to Aster's continued inquisition into the nature of Idyll's relationship with Ravel.

Waves of bluestem and sage grass swam in the same wind that scoured Flitch's face and snapped at the sail to remind him how inexpertly he'd positioned it.

"He's off again toward the horizons in his mind," Aster said, leaning close to Flitch and jostling him a little with one elbow. When he brought his gaze and mind back to his siblings, he found they were all looking at him, smiling in that familiar way.

The horizons in his mind.

It was a phrase oft uttered by their father to describe Flitch's tendency to sail off on an imagined adventure all while the rest of them were busy living in the real world. When he was younger, Idyll would sometimes sail with him, the two of them whispering back and forth, pointing at imagined beasts and uttering soft, awed breaths at the far-flung lands of the Forever Sea.

"You're just like your mother," the Borders Baron would tell Flitch, smiling sadly and pulling his son close. It was another legacy Flitch carried: the last of the Borders Brats to grow up, youngest of a failing, fading barony, and the son who lived in dreams and fantasies, just like his late mother, the last to hold and bear this part of her, as though he were the last flower planted by her imagination, reaching still for the sun.

"Come on back to us, Flitch," Idyll said, their voice gentle, smiling. With their back against the mast, legs splayed before them and hands folded against their stomach, skin and clothes aglow with the sun's favor, Idyll looked the perfect Sea-born lordling, effortlessly royal and perfectly at ease. How easy it was to imagine them ascending to take over the barony after their father stepped down.

How easy it was to imagine them leading an ascendant Borders barony, Idyll at the helm and Zim, Aster, and Flitch there beside, each filling their roles.

Zim said something, but Flitch was not yet returned from those horizons, not yet untroubled by those distant winds.

A smile creased his face as he imagined sailing back into port, hull filled to bursting with rare plants and treasures rarer still from unmapped lands—bones from a deserted island and books traded by sailors on a curious, many-masted vessel; the skin of a Sea-skimmer and the whispered secrets of a wretched sunbaby carried like a burden inside Flitch's mind. Perhaps he would follow Kindred below at some point before rising again, bringing back to Borders and to Idyll a new world of wealth and knowledge, mystery and wonder.

"Flitch?" It was Zim again, jostling his elbow and wrenching Flitch from his daydream.

"Sorry, what?" Flitch said, looking around.

"Still the same Flitchy," Aster said, laughing and looking out across the harbor. There were still no signs of the King's ships and their pirate captives, only smoke blotting out all but the barest hints of a horizon or Sea beyond. "Remember when Father used to sneak up on him when he was sailing off to the horizons in his mind?"

Idyll burst out laughing, and so too did Flitch, floating on the great joy of laughing at himself. Zim was the only one not enjoying the memory, which was nothing new.

"Shouldn't we—" Zim began, but Idyll cut him off.

"He'd tiptoe up behind him, a big grin on his face, and even though he could barely hold in his laughter, Flitch would never stir, never realize that he was in danger."

"Poor Flitchy would stare out a window or at a wall." Aster picked up the thread, tears of joy glistening in her eyes, her wide, constant smile a beacon. "He'd be gone, and even Father's chuffing laughter—remember how he would laugh?—it wouldn't be enough to warn Flitch, and then *wham!* Father would leap forward and lift Flitch in the air, tickling him and shouting about his long-lost son, who—"

"Who disappeared on the horizons in his mind," Flitch finished, the memory sculpting his present, pushing him to sit up straighter, to look with clearer eyes, to move forward with his sails bellied out by winds from the past.

For the rest of his siblings, this reminiscing offered a chance to inhabit again those people they were back then, the phrases they'd uttered and the roles they'd fulfilled but had long since left behind.

For Flitch, whose feet were still on the bridge he hoped was leading him away from that person and that role, it was simply nice to have some company again.

"Flitch!" When he spoke this time, Zim did not utter Flitch's name quietly, sidling into conversation in that way he sometimes did, through the side door or slipping in quietly nearby. He shouted, and Flitch was surprised to see wide eyes and flaring nostrils. Fear blooming into real terror.

"We're getting too far from the coastline," Zim said, his annoyance at having been ignored for so long belying a real fear below.

Even as he'd journeyed far and famously in his mind, Flitch had let their actual craft on this actual Sea drift away from the safety of the coast. Their hull now cut through deeper grasses, out where the big ships would normally have been sailing, harvesters crewed by thirty or forty sailors or merchant vessels with their huge outriggers and holds stuffed with goods from the west.

"Don't worry, sweet child," Aster said, sliding across the deck to sling an arm around Zim's shoulders despite his protests. "I'll protect you from the big bad creatures of the deep."

Zim's cries of dismay and anger were cut short by Idyll leaning suddenly forward, one hand braced against the gunwale as they gestured out to the east, where the curtain of smoke swished and churned, as though players in a drama were making themselves ready to enter.

"Look there," Idyll said, their finger marking vague shapes, the barest hint of sail and mast, hull and prow lurking.

"It's just like Captain Halfstorm told it," Flitch said, spellbound by the sight.

Slowly, and trailing tendrils of grey behind them, the pirate vessels broke through the bank of smoke, their line monitored by vessels from the King's fleet as well as a ship each from the Rivers and Borders fleets.

"Is that one of ours?" Aster asked, squinting at the parade of vessels.

"It's *Apogee*," Flitch said. "Twyllyn Tae's ship. Crew size around thirty, including six casters, but bunk space for thirty-eight."

"I didn't know Father had sent Twyllyn out," Idyll said, frowning. "When did he decide that?"

Flitch shrugged, though he knew when. It had been in the late morning four days earlier. Idyll had slept away at their lodgings in the capital for a few days—Aster too. Zim had returned the night previous but left before dawn had colored the sky.

"I really think we should be closer to the coast," Zim said.

Idyll would have been away with Ravel while Flitch sat at home, the only one around to watch their father send Twyllyn Tae off with one of their vessels, not knowing what the journey was about, its goal or purpose, no one around with whom to speculate or discuss the tidbit of information.

The chaotic rush of the waves against *The Laughing Queen*'s hull and the distant shouting of sailors on their vessels, the ubiquitous glow of the sunlight and the wind's symphony against sail and mast—all of it was suddenly too much for Flitch, and he wanted to be back home, ship safely docked, the quiet of his room covering him like a blanket.

"Something's happening over there," Aster said, pushing herself up to stand, grabbing for the longsight. "Do you see that?"

The stately procession of the captive pirate vessels continued through the harbor, ten or twelve ships in all, each of them looking as though they had sailed through a fiery nightmare—sails ripped or burned away, hulls torn and charred.

The ruckus came from the patrolling vessels, those sailing under the King's colors and monitoring the harbor for creatures from below.

Two of them, both sleek two-masters that were not in any of Flitch's books—recent additions to King Faineant's fleet, apparently—were cutting hard toward *The Laughing Queen*, the two casters standing next to their fires at the bow shouting and waving at them.

"What are they saying?" Idyll asked, concerned. Encounters with the King's people never went well for anyone from Borders.

"I can't tell," Flitch said. "The wind is too loud." The Sea was thrashing and dancing with it, sending up sprays of seedpods and prairie fluff.

But that wasn't right. The wind wasn't any louder than it had been, and though it gusted and blew, it wasn't actually loud enough to obscure the shouts of the sailors. The churn of the Sea was, though—the plants roiling and whipping around, sending up a great wave of noise to accompany the plant material.

"I think they're saying 'Get back' or 'Go back' or something like that," Aster said, peering through the longsight.

It was Zim's terrified look that finally lit the empty room of Flitch's mind and made him realize what was happening, what fundamental thing he had missed.

We're getting too far from the coastline, Zim had said.

The casters on the King's vessels were wrenching pure power from their fires, hands aglow in violent reds and blues, the colors vibrant and wrong in the soft light of the day.

"Oh, no," Flitch uttered, lurching forward to the hearthfire, but it was too late. The pirates, it turned out, were not the only players waiting to enter.

The creature erupted from the Sea in a colossal spray of green, a corona of ripped plants surrounding its thick, misshapen head as it screamed upward, shoulders and arms and wings and a body that tapered away into a tattered, clattering mess of bones stained red and braided together with still-growing vines. Skin a dusty goldenrod, long faded and somehow awful to behold, and eyes rolling madly in too-large sockets that never closed, never blinked—the creature formed a great crescent in the sky, touching the sun and sending the crew of *The Laughing Queen* into shadow for a long moment.

At its peak the creature screamed again, a cry too melodic and beautiful to come from something so monstrous and wrong. Its wings flapped feebly at the air, straining and stretching, catching the sun's light and flaring with it, the veins and long, thin bones threaded through the thin skin of its wings thrown into sharp relief. For one mad moment, Flitch felt certain those curls of blood and shafts of bone formed the shapes of a long-lost language, one he could understand, could read and hear and speak, if only given time enough. There in that branch of veins, and there, too, in that long slip of bone, he saw a strange sense.

Zim's high, terrified shout fractured the stillness of the moment, setting the world in motion once again.

Flitch lunged for the wheel.

Idyll threw themself down to the deck.

Aster loosed a defiant scream and plunged a hand into the hearthfire.

The beast fell.

Flitch preferred *The Laughing Queen* to the larger, many-crewed vessels for many reasons, one of which was how nimble it was. A huge two- or three-masted ship took forever to execute a command. It came down from the captain, who managed the wheel while a hearthfire keeper manipulated the flames, but even then, a maneuver required crew pulling at the sails to better cut through or run along with the wind.

But a tiny catboat like this one, with a hearthfire basin not much larger than a soup bowl and a wheel small enough to be managed with a single hand—a ship like this could *move* when it needed to. It didn't have the top speed of those larger vessels, and it would be useless in a fight, but for quick movements, little bursts of speed here or there, it was perfect.

A harbor-hopper, some of the sailors in his father's fleet called it, smiling and laughing at the sight of Flitch sailing it around Falcate Harbor.

Flitch slammed against the wheel, turning the craft away from the descent of the creature in a sharp, quick swerve that sent Aster to her knees and hurled Zim against the gunwale, and for a terrifying moment, Zim looked in danger of toppling over the side. He was saved by the rope he'd again tied around his waist, like an umbilical cord pulling him back to the belly of the ship and the mast at its center. With a strangled cry, he teetered there at the edge before wrenching himself back, bright-knuckled fist over fist, until he was fully on the deck again, splayed out and scrabbling to rise.

A great explosion of sound and force rocked the ship as the beast slammed back into the Sea, one wing ripping through the grasses where *The Laughing Queen* had been only a moment before.

Flitch sang into the noise as he wrenched the wheel harder, fighting the wind and force of the Sea, demanding speed of the hearthfire in his broken, shambolic understanding of the language, sibilants and plosives, fricatives and trills, consonants and vowels leaping from his tongue and teeth in a tangled mess, most of them overheard from keepers in his father's fleet and practiced over and over again in the quiet of his room.

The hearthfire flared, and Flitch leaned forward into the new velocity that would take them away from the monster thrashing and rising again in the grasses behind them.

But there was no new velocity.

Instead, *The Laughing Queen* hitched and lurched.

And slowed.

"Aster!" Flitch screamed as he looked around the wheel to see his sister standing, lips moving with the rhythm and melody of song, one hand trailing into the fire where casting plants fell from her open palm.

On a normal ship, hearthfires and casting fires were kept separate. Both used the power of the fire but for different purposes—while a hearthfire burned bones to keep a vessel afloat and offer increased stability and steering for the captain, a casting fire used the magic of burning bones and combined it with the latent power waiting inside prairie plants, releasing the magics for a caster to shape and use.

It was possible for a single fire to serve both purposes, but it would mean neither was as efficient or powerful as it might be. A vessel could not race on the fiery puissance of the hearthfire while it also burned plants for a caster, and a caster would find herself dealing with shreds and tatters of magic while pulling her plants' power from a hearthfire still giving a ship lift and momentum.

The Laughing Queen slowed despite the wind gliding gustily along its sail.

And Aster, self-proclaimed Stormcloud Magus reborn, first in her class and most promising student of the Mainland casting academies, wrenched a diaphanous slip of magic, grey-gold and flickering weakly, from the fire. With a dedicated fire, it might have been a shining lance or a terrible bolt of energy, something to rival the lightning of a summer storm. But with such a small fire, and one pulled in two directions, Aster's great assault amounted to a wisp of light that, from the wrong angle, disappeared altogether in the sun's glow.

Her own shout of dismay and anger rivaled Flitch's, and though *The Laughing Queen* lurched with the sudden drop in speed, and though the fire offered her the barest shreds of power, Aster made the most of it.

Her song changed mid-syllable, the cry of confusion setting her off on a range of notes that jangled against one another, discordant and angry. The skein of silky power slipping through the air in front of her tore apart, shreds of it leaping the distance between Aster and the Sea creature and slicing deep into its face and neck, scoring great burning lines along the plane of its skin and popping with sickening ease one of the delicate spheres of its eyes.

The creature sang in anger and pain, its cry eerily beautiful, and the huge bulk of its body thrashed in the grasses, a chaos of skin and muscle. The end of it, where a tail and back legs and hips should have been, was nothing more than an unfinished mess of bone and flesh, stained red but dry, with vines growing through it all—growing from *inside* the creature, roots deep in its body, and for a moment Flitch imagined its great heart, cavernous and thundering, threaded through with roots like veins, splitting and splitting endlessly until they were too small, impossible to distinguish from tissue.

Flailing and shrieking, the creature lashed out with its tattered backside and hit one of the approaching patrol vessels, slamming into the hull with a thick *crunch*, timbers buckling and shattering.

Flitch caught a quick glimpse of the ship listing hard, like a dog favoring one mangled leg after a fight, unable to make a straight line of its path forward but still pushing to return to the fray. Aboard the vessel, casting fires burned bright and high, and the King's casters shaped violence from plant and flame, bone and air, their magics rising from the broken, battered shell of their ship in crackling arcs that, unlike Aster's spellwork, slammed into the monster, carving channels into its flesh and lighting small, brief fires there.

It should have been enough to draw the monster's attention away from *The Laughing Queen*. The second of the King's vessels, unbroken and almost glowing with the energy of its casters, unleashed an arsenal against the creature, lances and lashes of power, meteors and gouts of destructive magics, purples and blues and reds burning from broadside to beast.

The assault was more concentrated magical power than Flitch had ever seen in the whole of his life, and though he still hauled hard on the wheel and sang his low, urgent song to the hearthfire for speed, he couldn't help but stare in awe at the corona of light and color that flared around the creature as it sustained an impossible amount of damage.

It should have been enough to pull it away from *The Laughing Queen*. What was such a tiny vessel in comparison to huge ships with hurtful, bright magics?

But amidst the cries of casters and creature, a lone voice rose above the chaos.

"Let Flitch sail the ship, Aster!"

It was Idyll, rising from the deck where they had been retrieving the axe from below, the chipped blade catching the thick sunlight and sharpening it. They knew enough about sailing and hearthfires to see why *The Laughing Queen* was moving so slowly despite the full sail and level grasses.

Their voice should not have cut through the madness of the moment, but it did, their fear and anger bright in the sudden pause of other shouts and screams, and though the beast from below burned and bled from attacks hurled by those other vessels, it turned whiplike to fix its remaining eye on Idyll and *The Laughing Queen*, still creeping sluggishly away and back toward the Borders port and the safety of land.

Wings unfurled and a surge of muscle preceded an explosion of movement from the creature, its impossible bulk rising higher in the Sea as it surged toward *The Laughing Queen*.

Aster flung herself back from the flames, ending her casting, and Flitch felt the return of the hearthfire's full power deep in his stomach a moment before the ship leapt forward, no longer hindered by serving two masters.

"Go, go!" Idyll shouted, keeping their feet despite the rush of acceleration, one hand braced against the gunwale and the other holding aloft the axe, so insignificant next to the mountain of flesh and bone and anger following them.

Zim huddled against the mast, his face pressed into the wood, teeth bared against the terror of the moment and the creature's song. Aster leaned in close, wrapping her arms around him, making of her body a shelter, whispering whatever safety she could.

Flitch sang in his broken, ragged way, watching the fire flare and rage and demanding more from it. He imagined the sounds of his song carrying their own meaning, imagined them to be a real language that the flames understood, impressing urgency and terror into every nonsense syllable.

Closer and closer the beast came. Its song soared in pitch and volume, so loud that Flitch could no longer hear his own, so loud that he could not hear whatever defiance Idyll spit back at their pursuer.

The beast's song peaked just before it lunged, and though Flitch understood what was happening and slammed his weight on the wheel to pull them out of reach, it was not enough; arms of dusty goldenrod, mottled now with burns and scored with bleeding wounds, reached out, clawed hands closing on Idyll, who cut off three of the creature's fingers before burying the head of the axe too deeply in its arm to recover, the blade biting into bone and refusing to release its hold.

When the creature screamed in pain and recoiled, the only remaining weapon on board *The Laughing Queen* went with it.

Thick lines of magic, burning white-hot and singing as they whipped forward, scored the beast's head and neck, an attempt by the King's vessels to draw the beast back, or perhaps to send it down below, or maybe even to kill it.

But the creature would not be deterred, its one, rolling eye still returning to Idyll, who stood weaponless and undefended, no longer defiant, no longer bold.

When he had first heard the story of Kindred burning the Sea and disappearing below, Flitch had been unable to imagine anything that could cause a person to do something so selfish and so stupid. How many would be killed or hurt by her choice? How quickly would the gears of society grind down to inaction because of her?

Yet now, as horrifying fingers reached for his eldest sibling, his best friend, Flitch thought he understood why a person would do something so grand, so stupid, so selfish.

He launched himself toward the fire, his song changing rhythm and melody, pitch and timbre, and when he grabbed the two longest, largest bones in the pile, the fire offered him the barest flicker of hot displeasure, the flares of pain along his fingers and knuckles promising pain later, if there was to be a later.

Song still on his lips and hands awash in flames the color of a sunrise, Flitch rushed forward, shoving Idyll aside with one shoulder before plunging the bones as deep into the creature's thick arm as he could manage, feeling the makeshift skewers shatter and break below the skin's surface even as the flames flared and spread.

With a dissonant roar of anguish, the creature slapped Flitch back, sending him sprawling nearly into the hearthfire, but the damage was done, and it turned away from *The Laughing Queen* and into the coordinated attacks of the King's vessels, which occupied it until it was forced to retreat below.

Dizzy and in pain, Flitch accepted Idyll's hand up, and together—Idyll at the helm and Flitch keeping the now-diminished remains of the fire as best he could—they sailed *The Laughing Queen*, the harbor-hopper, back into port.

CHAPTER THREE

Kindred Greyreach, captain of *The Lost*, sang jubilation in a language made for flames.

The cabin of her woven vessel flickered and danced with light from the hearthfire, gilded tongues and rufescent fingers of flame rising and falling and rising again. As she had done for years, Kindred guided the vessel around her, making tiny changes to the structure of bone and plant in the fire's heart to offer speed or lift.

Only, now she followed no orders but her own, and she sailed her ship down, articulating the curling whorl of a cyclone with her grass vessel, careening lower and lower. Long gone were the delights of sunlight and surface; even the smoke and heat of the prairie fire she had set were things of the past, unable to keep up with *The Lost*'s descent into mystery and darkness.

Finally, Kindred would see what lay below.

Finally, she would know what bones moved beneath the skin of the world.

"Sarah," she said, breaking off her song and looking up from the fire to where Sarah sat across from her, idly braiding a few strands of stray grass. She was ill at ease aboard *The Lost*, which had no caller's nest, no rigging to manage, no cargo to stow or fasten down.

"It's time?" Sarah asked, her sudden smile limned by the wild, shifting colors of the hearthfire.

"I think we're low enough," Kindred said, feeling her own smile matching Sarah's.

At first, they had descended while the grasses of the near-surface had sung against *The Lost*'s hull, and Kindred had been leery of opening the doors in case their ship took on any additional unwanted crew. Seraph had bobbed his head in agreement at this decision before launching into a list of the various mid-Sea creatures he had personally seen, which of course didn't include those he had only heard of from trusted sources, a different list again from those he'd read about.

"Stop," Sarah had said, holding up a hand. "Just stop talking. We're not going to open the doors right now, so stop."

Seraph opened his mouth to respond, but Sarah put her hand back up, palm flat.

"I'm in charge after Kindred, and that's a direct command from your superior."

Seraph's mouth had hung open at that, and when he'd turned to Kindred for confirmation, she'd been so focused on the fire and their initial descent that she'd only been able to say, "Sarah has more experience."

Seraph's initial displeasure faded once he realized the plaits of grass that composed the walls of the vessel had gaps in them large enough to serve as viewing windows, and he was once again a delighted man, up on his tiptoes to peer out the slanting cut of the gap in the grass to what lay beyond.

His low mumbles of delight, *ooh*s and *oh dear*s and *what could it be*s, were the melody of the cabin long after they'd dropped low enough for the plants of the Sea to have pulled back into their stems.

Now, though, Kindred could feel the emptiness of the space around their ship without looking; she could sense it in the ease of the fire, the quick response to her build, the sense of power and immediacy in every slight shift or change in her song.

Plants spread as they reached for the sun; every child knew that. Grass or flower, tree or shrub—it didn't matter. As they grew, they spread, like hands opening, arms uncrossing, mouths falling open to draw in the sweet breath, the brilliant everything of the sky.

And so it followed that the open hands of the Sea's surface would clutch into hard, closed fists below, a single stalk or trunk in the darkness supporting miles and miles of hopeful green above.

What would they look like? Thin, spindly, impossible lengths? Stout towers with failed, shriveled shoots fuzzing their edges, unable to rise with their siblings to the surface? Would their movement above have echoes below?

As Sarah undid the bindings holding one door closed, Kindred worked at the other, a part of her mind always listening to the fire's quiet melody, monitoring it for signs of unevenness or displeasure.

But it burned steadily now, and suddenly Kindred could hardly wait for the openness of the Sea. The cabin had become a shell that she needed to crack.

Her door opened with a whisper.

And beyond?

Arches. Endless arches glowing in the darkness. The great stalks of bluestem and thrice-root, sage grass and coneflower, prairie smoke and Rachel's joy—all of them were the same this far down: colossal beams, hundreds of lengths wide, big enough for a three-masted barque to fit comfortably inside them. They rose from darkness below in elegant, arc-ing glory, crossing one another to form a gallery of arches, doorways, portals—each one an invitation to wonder and marvel.

And the plants, all of them, *shone.*

Light seeped from green stalks: blue, like a cloudless sky, green, like the Sea itself caught full in a shot of sunlight.

The empty spaces between the stalks remained a rich, thick black— made richer still by the brilliant lines of the Sea cutting through.

"I'm here," Kindred whispered, loud enough for the others to hear. She didn't care. Gone was that timid woman from *The Errant*, afraid to ex-press her hopes and thoughts of the deep. She had found her people, her crew, and they would understand.

The air of the cabin had grown stale and still as they'd dropped farther below, the scents of each of their bodies intermingling into something unpleasant. But now, with the doors open, a cool wind cut through the vessel, a breeze that smelled of other worlds, dark and rich and strange and wonderful.

Stars of pink light, small and soft, scuttled along the stalks of the Sea. Their movement was erratic, leaping up or dropping down the lines of the plants in bursts before going totally still again.

"Are those bugs?" Kindred asked, still staring out her door, one hand pushed deep into the grass braids of the hull to steady herself.

"They move like bugs," Sarah said, her voice dreamy and distant.

"I thought so, too," Seraph said, surprising Kindred by speaking right next to her. "But look closer. Right *there.*"

Seraph extended an arm outside of the cabin, one finger quivering as he pointed to a slanting beam closest to them.

Kindred squinted and leaned forward, feeling as though she were again in that cell below the Once-City, going through a test that was meant to separate those who could live in and with the Sea from those who couldn't.

There she was, once more leaning out into the Sea, losing herself in it.

The mote of pink light lurched upward suddenly, scaling the strand of bluestem in a moment and resolving into a shape at once strange and familiar to Kindred.

"Is that . . ." Kindred began, her body stilling and going cold.

"Yes," Seraph said, letting his hand drop. "The lantern bearers."

It was a man, or might have been once, clinging to the side of the stalk with one hand, while he held the shattered, floating remains of a lantern in his other, the fragments orbiting slowly around the light at its center, a light that shifted from light pink to deep red and back again in a shuddering slide eerily like breathing.

Even as *The Lost* cut through empty air and moved down and away from him, the lantern bearer turned his head, and Kindred caught a brief glimpse of the leering grin cut slantwise across his face and the way his legs and feet extended far, far below him, as though he'd been stretched well past breaking but had not broken.

"I thought they were just in the Once-City," Sarah said, and Kindred felt her close behind, one of Sarah's hands coming to rest on Kindred's shoulder. "When I was a kid, I thought the lantern bearers were ghosts that haunted the Forest. I used to imagine that the trees were their homes."

But they weren't trees, had never been trees. Just as the lantern bearers above were only variations on the theme of people, the trees were nothing more than a shape the Sea had chosen to take as it expanded its hold on the Once-City.

Kindred thought of her final moments in the Once-City, of Little Wing encountering her lantern bearer and whatever peace it offered.

"The Once-City had more of the Sea in it than many people realized," Seraph said. "The Forest, yes. But much of the strangeness on the lower levels, of course, could not be explained as anything other than more gifts from the Sea. Or perhaps not gifts but pokes and prods. I always felt the Sea was reaching out, not for any purpose other than to encourage us to reach back."

Kindred turned to Seraph, surprised. It was a remarkably lucid and abstract statement from him.

He stayed lost in his thoughts for a moment before snapping back and nodding down at Kindred's hand, which still had her own gift from the Sea—the plants that grew from her skin, golden grasses swaying in their own phantom breeze.

"And, of course," he said, "there are those lucky enough to host some of the Sea themselves! Kindred, speaking of that—I was hoping I could take a few small clippings at some point, just to—"

"No," Kindred said, shaking her head and feeling the tense pull of those golden shoots curling in on themselves. "Absolutely not."

⊸◆⊷

With the doors open, it wasn't long until they saw what lived below.

"What do you think we're going to find down here?" Sarah asked, having returned to Kindred's side at the hearthfire.

"I don't know," Kindred said, raising her eyes to meet Sarah's. "People? Magic? The source of the Greys? I have no idea."

What a wonder to not know, to discover what had been below her boots for so long.

"Do you think we'll find *her*?" Sarah asked, her voice careful and low, eyes on Kindred. She didn't have to clarify. The Marchess's letter still rested in Kindred's pocket; her promise of what lay below still hung like a fog in Kindred's mind, permeating every thought, every question, every certainty.

"I don't know," Kindred said. And then, after a moment, "Yes."

"Good. Me too." Sarah's smile was lit by the flickering light of the hearthfire, and she leaned in close enough for her shoulder to brush Kindred's.

The Marchess moved through the dark hallways of Kindred's memory, stepping closer and closer as her ship dropped lower and lower. Would she laugh when Kindred found her? Bellowing out her joy the way she had always done? Would she shout in triumph? *I knew you would come*, she might say, raising her arms high in the strange light of the Sea, as giant as the plants themselves and as mighty.

Kindred imagined her already at work solving the problem of the Greys, moving among the sickened stalks with that look of intense focus, mouth drawn into a severe line, eyes wide and penetrating.

Finally, she would say, smiling as Kindred and the others emerged from the darkness. *I heard your song and felt you coming. Now come help me with this and tell me stories of sunlight and sky.*

"Captain," Seraph said from where he sat in one of the doorways, his legs hanging out of the ship, one hand hanging on to the wall, the other clutched on the low lip of the floor as it rose to the bottom of the doorway. "We are not alone."

Beyond him, framed by the door and lit by the Sea itself, were eyes.

A creature bigger than anything Kindred had ever seen floated along beside them, pacing their descent, maintaining a safe distance. It was bigger than the wyrm that had almost taken down *The Errant*, and stranger, too—a being that expanded and contracted as it moved, as if it breathed with the whole of itself, shrinking down to the size of *The Lost* before expanding to fill the increasingly huge space between stalks of the Sea.

Myriad eyes opened and closed along its spherical body, too many to count and scattered without any clear pattern. Its skin was a translucent, oily film that showed its insides—a loose collection of bones floating in some substance, disconnected from one another and seemingly without purpose or structure.

As it expanded and filled the space between stalks, lightning jagged and flickered inside it, dark blue and silvery white, leaping from one bone to another to another, filling the calm of the Sea with a brief light show.

The creature emitted a low hum as it moved, gliding through the negative space of the Sea along with *The Lost*.

"We don't have any defenses," Sarah said, holding up a pair of knives to illustrate the point.

"It isn't attacking," Seraph said, leaning away from the knives. "It's just *interested* in us."

Sarah didn't look convinced.

But Seraph had a point. The creature swam or floated or flew beside them, always at a safe distance, its massive eyes opening to stare at them for a moment before closing and reappearing elsewhere on its body. It was as if they were fish surfacing and then diving under again in a pool of water.

Breath whispered through Kindred's lungs as she watched, paralyzed not by fear but awe. Above, this being would have been a threat, would have been neatly slotted into a mindset of violence and competition. Could it be harvested? Was it attacking a ship? Destroying a crop or eating high-value plants?

Could it be used?

"It's okay," Kindred said, to herself as much as Sarah. "It'll be okay."

Keeping her eyes on the creature, she stepped back to the fire and whispered a song, letting her hands drift among the flames and smooth the lines of her build, drawing out a braid of grass here or an angle of bone there.

She built for calm and quiet, not wanting to disturb the creature. She mimicked its soft float with her song and breath, and *The Lost* responded with lift and lightness.

What would the keepers from Arcadia think of this? Or the few teachers Kindred had encountered in the schools who had scoffed at her approach to the fire?

Build according to the texts! they had shouted at her, over and over. *Clean lines! And sing the songs in the book! No more of these improvisations.*

Kindred lifted the remaining plant fibers and scraps of bones into a loose collection, plants frayed into a tattered cloak holding and hiding shards of half-burnt bone, the whole mass of it floating in the flames.

A shock ran through Kindred as she realized how little remained of their fuel. There was no closet there from which to draw out more bones, and they had long since left behind the parts of the Sea where such plants could be harvested. Down so low, the plants were thick, wide beams, and Kindred knew of no knife or power that could sever such things.

They were almost out of fuel, and if they didn't find land soon, their slow descent through the Sea would grow sharp.

Kindred cast a wary eye to her two crew members, both of them staring out at the creature in wonder. Both had followed her down there, both given up their lives and all the lives they might have had on the surface for this.

She let her song slow, imagining her vowels and consonants weighed down suddenly, a melody muddled by frozen lips on a chilly night, tongue thick in her mouth and sluggish as it shaped the words. The fire, in response, grew thick and slow, the flames moving and reaching up like bubbles rising slowly through honey. A gentle gold radiated out through the hearthfire, a color that made Kindred think of sunlight warming her cheek on a long afternoon.

The hull of *The Lost* shivered, the long grass braids shifting against one another and whispering dangers into the cabin's confines.

"Kindred?" Sarah asked, turning from the door and dropping down to kneel beside her. "What's going on?"

The bones and braids against her hands felt suddenly miserly to Kindred, no longer the bounty with which they had descended but a paltry, picayune build, stringy and weak.

"It's okay," Kindred said, biting back the truth. It would be okay. She would make it okay. "I just need to focus on the fire. You can keep watching it."

Sarah gave her a glance that lasted just a moment too long before nodding and moving back to the doorway.

The melody in the flames had grown slow and heavy, but the fire itself was airy and empty inside, the build burned down to a spider web's width in some places, bare fibers holding bone and bud together. It would not last long.

Kindred sang a calming, easy song, giving the flame what confidence she could and hoping it was enough. They needed land, and soon.

"It's leaving," Sarah said, her back to Kindred. "It's just— Oh. Oh, my."

Kindred looked up in time to see the creature floating away from *The Lost*, bending its path off into the darkness and *through* a series of plant stalks, each one thick enough to devour the creature as it passed through. One by one it moved through them as if they were nothing before emerging on the other side, floating and undamaged, its see-through skin shining with the light of the plants for a moment before becoming transparent again.

"How is it doing that?" Sarah said, awe running like a cool wind through her voice, and Kindred felt her own thrill—at the wonder and mystery of that creature, yes, but a sister-sense to Sarah's own joy. As they had descended and left behind the known world of the surface, doubt had sprouted somewhere deep inside Kindred: would Sarah regret her decision to come? Would the wonders of whatever lay below be for Kindred alone, empty of anything meaningful to Sarah, who would grow more and more discontented with such a foolish dream?

Those and a hundred other questions had clicked together like stones in Kindred's stomach as they dropped farther and farther down, and as Sarah stalked the lengths of the vessel with nothing to do.

But there she was, smiling, baffled, laughing with utter, joyous, complete disbelief.

"I have a few theories," Seraph said, "and top of the list is ghosts."

Sarah had already turned, perhaps to tell him to be quiet again, but she stopped at that for a moment before letting out another laugh.

The fire, strange as it was now, burned steadily if sluggishly, and Kindred could do no more for it at the moment, so she stood and joined her crew at the door, wrapping one arm around Sarah's waist and kissing her on the cheek, lips pressing against the slight dip of a scar there.

"Ghosts, Captain," Sarah said, flushing at Kindred's closeness but not pulling away. "How soon until we miss the known dangers of wyrms and pirates?"

"Never," Kindred said, ignoring Seraph's continued theorizing and seeing only Ragged Sarah, the myriad colors of her hair—fading now—glowing in the light of the hearthfire and the Sea, her smile wide and wicked and wonderful.

Kindred met that smile with her own, pressing her lips to Sarah's, once briefly and then again more slowly, savoring the nearness of her.

Seraph had stopped talking by the time Kindred and Ragged Sarah emerged from the shelter of their intimacy, and he stood aloof from them, staring out at the interplay of light and dark in the Sea.

Kindred disentangled herself from Sarah's arms, not without some regret, and turned back to the open door.

"What were you saying, Seraph?" she asked, but he waved a hand and shook his head.

"It wasn't anything, really," he said, smiling without any anger or sarcasm.

It seemed he wouldn't say anything else, that the three of them would hold on to that thick, heavy silence, still warmed by the mystery of what they had seen.

But Seraph spoke again.

"My name isn't really Seraph, you know," he said, not looking at either of them. Like his thoughts, Seraph's gaze usually flicked and leapt all over, meeting the eyes and then tracing along the ceiling or someone else nearby before returning to the eyes or skipping along the floor.

But he stared out into the Sea now, anchored to it.

"Seraph Three-Twist," he said, smiling a little at the words. "When you become a councillor in the Once-City, you take on a new name. Some people just take a new first or last name, while others change the whole thing. I, being the silly person I was when I became a councillor—the silly person I still am, I suppose—I left behind my old name entirely. I became Seraph Three-Twist. *Three-Twist* to show how proud I was of my ritual performance."

"What ritual?" Kindred asked.

He pulled at his robe, showing the flesh just below his neck, the ring of bruised, painful skin there, punctuated by scabbed sores.

"Hanged Council," he said, finally meeting their eyes, a ghastly smile on his face. "The name isn't just a metaphor, although much has been written in our own small histories about its figurative resonance."

He took a breath, as if needing a moment to realign his thoughts and trim away the tangents.

"They hang you with a length of catch vine. One twist around the neck is enough, but I wanted to show everyone who thought I was a weakling. Foolish, of course, but I was so young when I was made a councillor—there were so few others who had any skill whatsoever with the fires."

Seraph held up three fingers.

"Three twists, I asked for. Three times around my neck they wrapped the catch vine, and its suckers latched on to my skin, and the nettles pierced my neck in hundreds of places, stealing bits of me."

He shuddered.

"I've never felt pain like that, and even when the airflow was disrupted, it was the pain in my neck that almost took me."

Kindred looked closer and saw the three distinct twists of the vine around Seraph's neck, their lines etched in puckered and purpled flesh.

Questions bubbled through Kindred's mind: *Why hasn't it healed? Why do they make councillors do that? How many twists did the others do? How old was he when he was hanged?*

But she settled on the most important one, "What was your name before?"

Finally, he turned back and met her gaze, his dirty, curling beard framing a sad smile.

"I can't remember. It's one of the things the vine took. Isn't that funny?

I was born and given a name, and for a little while it was mine, and now it's gone and I'm Seraph Three-Twist, member of a council that doesn't exist anymore in a city that sank."

Sarah turned to him, and for a moment Kindred feared she would use the lash of her tongue again. She could be so kind, but so sharp, too.

"It's hard to leave a life behind," she said. "Or be left behind by one. You don't have to be Seraph Three-Twist anymore, not with us."

He nodded and was silent for a moment.

"When I was a little boy, before my parents were lost on one of the eastward voyages, I remember seeing a stand of prairie awn growing just within longsight of the Once-City. I spent every day up in the branches then, of course, in part to get away from the kids who would pick on me during our school time, but also because I couldn't get enough of the Sea and all its mysteries."

As he talked, some of the old excitement returned to Seraph, firing behind his eyes and flickering in the quick gestures of his hands.

"Everyone ignores prairie awn, of course," he said.

"That's because it's a weed," Sarah said, though not unkindly.

"Exactly," Seraph said, putting a hand on her shoulder, smile contorting his thin mustache and crusty beard. "It's a *weed*, big and spiky. It grows these long, rigid hairs—*awns*, they're called. The wind pulls at the awns until they and the attached seedpods get wrenched from the parent plant when it's time to propagate, and what started as a thin, skeletal plant gets even more thin and skeletal. No good for casting or cooking, and very minimal medicinal benefits."

"Tastes like shit, too."

Seraph nodded at Sarah, a giggle bubbling up from his stomach and crinkling his eyes closed.

"It does!" He shook his head for a moment, and when he opened his eyes, he looked at his crewmate, Sarah, and then at Kindred, his captain. "I used to watch the wind catch and carry those seedpods miles away, off to the horizon in every direction, and I would dream it was me, growing too big and strange and ugly for the place that had raised me. I wished it would pick me up and lift me away so I could grow somewhere else. I knew I wasn't like the other kids, and even though I served on the council, I knew I wasn't like the people there, either.

"I'm not Seraph Three-Twist," he said with a shake of his head. "Not anymore, and maybe not ever. I'd like to be Awn now, leaving behind my parent plant and carried away on a strange wind of my own." He reached out a hand to the hull of *The Lost*.

The wind that moved beneath the waves sounded gently against the side of the vessel, and through the open door, plants bigger and older than anything above swayed almost imperceptibly.

"I'm glad to have you aboard, Awn," Kindred said, reaching out and taking his hand in her own. His palm was sweaty against her own, and she could feel a slight tremble in his fingers. Kindred had seen Awn excited to the point of babbling and fearful enough of mortal danger to go silent, but this was the first time she had ever seen him terrified into truth-telling.

"Thank you," Awn said, the words quiet.

After a moment of silence, Kindred turned to Sarah, who was looking away from Awn and out the door on the other side of the cabin.

"Sarah?" Kindred asked, frowning. They might have started out badly in the Once-City, but Sarah could at least acknowledge Awn's attempt to become part of their small crew.

"Look," Sarah said, gesturing out the door, and for a moment, Kindred thought she was pointing at more of the lantern bearers, their lights a swarm of orangish points.

"Is that . . ." she began, but didn't finish.

Beside her, Awn let out a sigh of such longing that it sent pricks of gooseflesh running along Kindred's arms.

It wasn't the light of lantern bearers racing along the stalks of the Sea.

And it wasn't the uncanny shine of the Sea itself.

It was a fire. A fire on the ground, flickering against a field of huge, sharp rocks.

Sarah turned, her eyes wild, her smile fierce.

"Land sighted, Captain," she said, before turning to Awn. "Welcome to the crew, Awn. Let's go see what new soil you're going to sprout from."

CHAPTER FOUR

L and ho.

How often had Sarah slung those words down from her crow's nest? So many voyages brought to an end with just a few syllables, the banality of port and the smallness of Arcadian concerns rushing back with a simple call.

"Land ho, Captain," Sarah said again, and Kindred was able to see for the first time how Sarah smiled as she said it, how she shaped those simple syllables with a grin, her eyes half-closed. It was easy enough to imagine her in the crow's nest, seeing the world as her birds did, the play and rush of the Sea stretching out before her, the sliver of port growing on the horizon.

Would she miss it? Would the dark and deep hold enough to anchor Sarah where birds did not fly and the Sea became towering plinths arcing through movements slow enough to trick time and the eye?

Could Kindred be enough for her below the Sea?

Land ho, and it was noun and verb both now. Thing and doing. Land rose beneath them, but so too did they land, a bird brought carefully, if not gracefully, down.

No longer did it mark the end of a journey.

This was the beginning.

And it couldn't come soon enough.

"Prepare for landing," Kindred muttered, weaving her hands into the flames, which had begun to stutter and spasm as bits of the structure burned away to nothing, leaving the fire momentarily gasping for more fuel before it focused on one of the remaining bits. Fragments and fibers rubbed away to nothing against Kindred's hands as she reached inside, the diaphanous structure losing its last semblance of form.

"Hold on," Kindred shouted a moment before the fire flared and collapsed in the basin.

The Lost lurched downward, yawing in a slow, sickening spiral, like a ship without a captain at its helm. Awn cried out and fell to the floor, grabbing at the braids of the hull.

Sarah, too, dropped low, though she scuttled across the floor until she was near Kindred.

"What is it?"

"We're out of bones and plants," Kindred said, looking around for anything she might use. She had never taken the captain's exams or gone through the rituals, and so even her own bones were of no use there.

Kindred suddenly remembered the grass Sarah had been idly braiding before and reached a hand into one of Sarah's pockets, finding the small plait. It was not much, and it would do almost nothing on its own, but she didn't have anything else. "The hearthfire doesn't have anything to burn."

"Are we going to crash?" Sarah asked the question with surprising calm.

"Maybe," Kindred said, and her mind flashed to that brief glimpse of the Seafloor even as Sarah named the danger there.

"On those rocks?"

"It'll be okay," Kindred said, envisioning their rate of descent and the little control she still had over the flame. She could set them down. It wouldn't be pretty, but she could do it. "I . . ."

Even as she opened her mouth to reassure Sarah, even as she thrust the small braid of grass into the fire and raked a hand across the coals in search of anything else with which she might build a scant structure, a small thought pushed itself into her mind, cold and hard and suspecting.

What if Sarah reached the Seafloor and found only regret blooming inside her? And what if—when that regret flowered into melancholy, into bitterness, into anguish—what if she asked to leave and their boat, the only way they might return, lay wrecked on the Seafloor? What if she couldn't go back?

Kindred could land *The Lost* among those rocks, and surely they would survive, but the ship almost certainly would not. Could she do something so selfish? Could she burn the only bridge that Sarah might cross to return to her old life?

"Hold on," Kindred said again, this time with steel in her voice. She stretched the strand of braided grass in the fire, making of it a waving tower, weak and tenuous, buried in the paltry coals and shifting gently among the flames, which began to devour it immediately, their color shifting from a lazy, slow-burning gold to a fierce, hot red, angry and hungry.

The Lost lurched again, this time forward, slinging through the darkness with a rush of speed, and Kindred pitched her song at the flames in quick bursts, tipping the ship on its side so she could see the Seafloor below, the rows of rocks racing by.

"What are you doing?" Sarah shouted, her teeth bared against the sickening pitch of the vessel. "Just set us down!"

"Not . . . yet . . ." Kindred said through her own gritted teeth. She wouldn't do that to Sarah. She couldn't.

Ahead—a tiny patch and growing larger—was a stretch of smoother floor, ground littered with plants that had germinated and grown but found themselves too far from sunlight to reach very far.

Her voice tore with the strain of her song, and she could feel her throat burning with her effort.

Fly, Kindred sang in her ragged voice to the fire. *Fly!*

And they did, darkness and huge boles of Forever Sea grasses rushing by, *The Lost* sinking lower and lower with each moment. Kindred squinted to see past the red, red fire and out the door, trying desperately to track their progress and imagine their descent, to hear the fire and sing her song, to ignore, as best she could, the despairing voice inside that wondered what would happen if Sarah couldn't leave. What would happen if she were trapped with Kindred forever and wanted nothing more than to go back.

"Land!" Kindred cried, the word a cough of pain, and then *The Lost*'s hull was touching down, filling the cabin with a sonorous scraping as the ship cut into rock and earth and soil and plants and whatever else rested below the foundations of the Sea.

The ship came to a rest finally, sitting at a slight angle, and for a moment no one inside moved or spoke. A wind sighed through the open doors through which the Sea floor glimmered and glowed in the queer, beautiful light emanating from the plants themselves. Motes of pink-orange light moved along those perfect lines of the plants rising through the vast, empty dark, and beyond, too far away to see properly, huge shapes glided or leapt or walked or swam or flew, their every movement an invitation to know and see more.

Kindred turned back to the hearthfire, which had contracted into a small, angry thing, flames writhing and rippling with displeasure.

"Enough, enough, enough," Kindred sang, the words of her ending song familiar and worn, her voice reduced to a bare whisper.

"Rest." The word sighed from her lungs and throat, the last bit of air she had there, and for a moment, Kindred felt weightless at the bottom of the Sea, her lungs empty of air, her limbs still, heart hanging in the rest between beats.

In that moment, she felt the growth of the plants in her body, each one a gift from the Healing Glade and from the Sea itself. The golden shoots along her hand extended and waved in a wind all their own, and Kindred felt new growths moving along her body, not yet broken through the skin but soon, perhaps.

Between breaths and between heartbeats, Kindred became the Sea.

Her bones the bones of the world.

Her skin the thick, dense soil down there in the dark.

Her limbs and new-growth plants the dancing chaos of the prairie.

Her blood carried the same magic as the Sea itself, life's poetry singing along her veins like bright hope and deep despair and a forever that might hold joy itself.

All that magic was there, endless and wild and good. It was no hearthfire waiting to be guided and directed. It had no need of her or anyone else, but it was there, flowing through her, as though she were a tiny, tender stem, flowers still just green dreams, reaching out from the stalk holding up the world.

Kindred became vast.

Kindred became tiny.

She sucked in a long, rattling gasp, lungs on fire, throat torn and voice frayed. Sarah was there to catch her as she tipped to the side, exhausted and suddenly overcome.

"Kindred? *Kindred?* Back up, Se—Awn. Give her some space." Sarah lowered Kindred to the floor of the cabin and put a hand on either side of her face.

"I'm okay," Kindred said.

She retched once, pulling away from Sarah and throwing up only a trickle of water.

Sarah cursed and began frantically sifting through her robes.

"I left all of my healing supplies above," she said, before cursing at her empty hands.

"I'm okay," Kindred whispered again, sitting up.

"You don't look okay," Sarah said, leaning close and peering into Kindred's eyes one at a time, the medicker in her taking over as she moved efficiently to check Kindred's temperature and pulse.

"My throat hurts a little, but that's it," Kindred said, taking Sarah's hands in her own and kissing them. "Just too much strain."

As Sarah reached for Kindred's neck, sliding her smooth hands across the skin there, Awn smiled and said, "No matter! Whatever you did worked—look!"

He reached one trembling hand through an open door before returning with a fistful of dirt, grey-gold and glittering in the Sea's light.

Kindred reached for it, already imagining the feel of it, the cool of it as she sank her hands and feet into earth untouched and unseen by everyone above, maybe by everyone ever.

"Wait," Sarah said, holding Kindred down, concern edging into her voice. "Are these new growths, Kindred?"

Kindred lifted a hand to her neck, where Sarah's fingers guided her to the soft, supple skin at the base of her throat, right above the top of her sternum.

But instead of the slight, soft divot she expected, a small, hard *something* emerged from the skin there, which cracked and puckered around it, like dry, drought-stricken earth releasing a single shoot to reach above, some species persistent and rugged enough to survive where nothing else could.

"What is it?" she asked, meeting Sarah's eyes.

"I don't know." Sarah grabbed and held up Kindred's other hand, from which grew the stand of golden grass that had taken root during her time in the Once-City. Closed now, wrapped up in tiny, gilded curls, the grass would expand and wave about in a wind of its own from time to time. "It's not grass like this, and it looks like it damaged your skin as it came through. Does it hurt?"

"No," Kindred said, touching and pressing at her neck. Though hard as stone, there were folds in whatever grew there, lines and cracks in it that shifted under Kindred's touch.

"It's new," Sarah said, frowning, and then, "I don't like it."

"It is odd," Awn said, the dirt still clutched in his hand as he leaned back into the cabin to peer at Kindred's throat. "Though similar to the intrusions we saw in the Once-City."

"Intrusions?" Kindred asked, still playing with the growth on her neck. Now that the initial shock of it had worn away, she found she didn't mind it as much.

"Oh, you know," Awn said, gesturing haphazardly enough to sprinkle the cabin with bits of Seafloor dirt here and there. "The bits of plant growing from your skin and throat, the ones on Sarah's leg after her fall when you arrived at the Once-City, those striking blue flowers on our old friend, Barque—you remember him?"

"I remember him," Sarah said, words quiet and violence in her eyes.

"There were others, of course," Awn said, oblivious, still gesturing around as if those people were there and he would give them a benediction and blessing from the Seafloor. "Mostly those who were healed by the glade, like you two, but a few others experienced them as well. People who worked down in the Gone Ways or up in Breach. Ebb-La-Kem had an intrusion!"

He burst out laughing for a moment before continuing.

"He was so embarrassed about it—a little vine that grew along the side of one of his feet. He made everyone on the council swear that we wouldn't tell anyone." He smiled at each of them. "I guess I broke my promise."

"I just thought it was remnants from the Healing Glade," Sarah said, shaking her head. "Some byproduct of whatever magic healed people there. I didn't know intrusions happened outside of that."

Awn nodded, his attention already drifting back to the open doorways and the wonders that waited beyond.

It was where all of their attentions should be, and Kindred sucked in a breath as she sat up, nodding at Sarah as if to say *I'm okay; it's going to be fine.* Her throat still hurt, but everything else was in working order, and there was no way a ragged voice would keep her from seeing what lay below for one more moment.

"No ramp or anchor, I guess," Kindred said, rising and taking a step forward. She smiled at her crew before taking Sarah's hand and saying, "Let's see what mysteries are waiting for us."

Kindred stepped from her vessel and into wonder.

Once, as a child, Kindred's parents had taken her to the old-growth forests of the Mainland, an area called the World's Body because of how the trees looked like bones that might once have held the flesh and muscle of a whole world.

Kindred had spent the day walking hand in hand with her parents, Father on her left, Mother on her right, her eyes traveling up and down the massive trees that rose too high to ever capture with her sight. First awe and then terror and then wonder and then fear and then shock and then dread and then *joy* seized her mind and heart. This was a place too big for her, each tree too huge to ever fully see, to ever hold completely in her mind, and it made her feel at once small and enormous.

"I am we," Kindred said, whispering the same words her mother had whispered on that day long past, her face upturned, eyes half-closed, a smile so serene it broke open something in that young Kindred.

"Incredible," Sarah said, standing beside Kindred and looking out and up at the endless corridors and half-finished archways moving off into forever in every direction.

On Kindred's other side, Awn wept quietly. He had taken off his footwear and buried his feet deep in the soil of this place. Kindred followed suit, tossing her well-used boots back into the empty shell of their vessel and sucking in a breath at the joyous feeling of her toes buried in cool, soft dirt, her aching heels held and massaged by the granules.

The plants of the Sea there were like towers built by some perfect hand before time began. Where they broke from the soil, their illumination was most intense—a light that neared a white so bright, it was hard to look at. They were spaced unevenly and randomly but all far enough apart that the distances between them felt like vast, empty, vaulted arcades that might have held swaying priests or raging armies or burgeoning communities but held, instead, the song of a low wind and the promise of more.

Through those barren spaces, lines carved in strange hands cut and swirled across the grey-gold dirt. Some were tiny streams branching and running across the ground, sensitive to slopes slighter than any Kindred could see.

Most, though, were not streams but simply lines in the dirt, as though a great being had traced a finger through the thick, soft ground, leaving curlicues and arcing lines across the huge empty fields, idly drawing nonsense while waiting for the world to move on. It was reminiscent of Mainland farmers raking the tilled land, tracing even lines across it to make their planting easier, but these lines were neither straight nor part of any larger scheme. They cut through and around one another, leaving gentle mounds.

Like scars left on the skin, telling a story for any who might pay attention.

The lantern bearers were fireflies flitting through the still always-night of the Seafloor, somehow part of the peace even with their frantic movements and uncanny forms.

For a moment, for several, the crew of *The Lost* stood in and with the Sea, breathing its breath, feet sunk in its grave soil, eyes wide and full.

I'm here, Grandmother, Kindred thought, imagining the Marchess walking alone through one of those great fields, a tiny figure between the world's plinths, smiling. *Welcome, Kindred*, she would say. *Welcome home.*

"Why didn't you set us down back by the rocks?" Sarah asked. "Did you see something back there? Some danger?"

The truth felt so fragile, so sharp in her mouth that Kindred found she couldn't say it.

"It just seemed like a safer place to set down out here," she said finally, slanting truth-ward as best she could.

"Playing a little loose with our fuel, though, wasn't it?" Sarah asked even as she grinned at the danger, though she frowned in thought a moment later before looking around. "Speaking of fuel, where is it?"

"Where is what?" Kindred asked, following Sarah's eyes and seeing nothing but more black, more Sea, more everything.

"The fire. The one we saw among the rocks as we neared— *There!*" Sarah's hand leapt out in the darkness, a single finger pointing at what Kindred at first thought to be a lantern bearer shuttling close to the ground, but no. It was not a pale pink mote but a group of flickering, burning flames, orange as any torch found above.

And they were getting closer.

Sarah slid a hand into Kindred's.

"I don't like being in the open like this, just waiting for whoever or *whatever* is coming our way."

Where else could they go? Kindred looked around, seeing nothing but spaces to be out in the open. There was nowhere to hide there, nowhere to shelter from the Sea itself.

"Don't worry," Kindred said, squeezing Sarah's hand and staring ahead at the nearing lights. "We came here to see what lay below. So, let's see it."

"Yes," Awn said, stepping forward, his eyes still wet. "Let's see it."

Sarah shook her head and blew out a breath, but she stopped the hand that had been straying to where her knives waited against one hip.

"I still don't like it," she muttered. Her hand in Kindred's was slick with sweat.

Kindred wiggled her toes in the dirt and waited.

A strange assemblage resolved, picked out in the gentle, low light of the Sea and the flickering of the torches attached to it. Patched and partial, built of castaway shards and shreds, bits and scraps, a long, thin, low ship approached, skimming across the ground, barely kissing the dirt save for a keel sunk deep and leaving a trailing line behind.

Tiny, barely bigger than the little catboats Arcadian sailors used for short sails around the island, and as it grew closer, Kindred could see four people crammed aboard.

No sail cut the air above, and no mast rose from the single deck.

Instead, ropes made of intricately braided grass, some fastened to the boat itself and some trailing down from the deck, disappeared into the dirt in front of the vessel, pulled taut and connected to something below that left no trace of itself. No noise, no ground disturbed by its passing, but the evidence of it was clear in the forward rush of the ship.

"What an odd vessel," Awn said, taking a step forward and raising his hand in greeting. He turned back to them with a grin. "It seems to be sailing in the dirt itself. I've never heard of such a thing!"

The woman holding what Kindred had started to think of as reins, standing proud at the bow, let out a sharp whistle and jerked back hard on the braided grass, the various lines extending into the ground going suddenly slack. Two of the crew farther back jabbed long poles into the dirt, quickly stopping the vessel.

For a long moment, no one in either group spoke or moved.

The woman who had dropped the reins turned abruptly to the others and held a whispered, frantic conference, jabbing a finger back at Kindred and the others from time to time.

"At least they're not attacking us," Kindred said, turning to Sarah with a half-smile.

"Yet," Sarah said, her eyes trained on the group of strangers.

And they *were* strange, all dressed in raggedy clothing that looked to be neatly stitched together from several sources, silks attached to rough fiber-cloth attached to wool or cotton, faded scraps of green and red and brown and black all pieced together like some curious fabric puzzle.

Two of the four—the leader with the reins and a tall, fat man who had helped bring the vessel to a stop—had brown skin and wore their hair in long tails trailing along their backs. The leader, and clearly she was the leader, spoke most and did so with one of those tails held in her hand, jabbing forward the dark hair to emphasize her points.

The third was a short person, face scrunched in thought, thin and rigid and unmoving, pale skin looking waxy in the blue-green light of the Sea. They stood a little apart from the others, their eyes fixed on Kindred and her crew, mouth set in a grumpy slant.

The fourth was a child, perhaps seven or eight years old. She peered at Kindred, Sarah, and Awn with unabashed curiosity, aloof from the furious discussion. As the leader stabbed her braided hair forward again to accompany a hiss of words, this young child raised one hand and waved at the crew of *The Lost*.

Kindred waved back.

"Just shields," Sarah muttered, shaking her head.

"What?" Kindred asked, her eyes still on the child, who had ducked behind the man and was peering around him at her.

"They only have shields," Sarah said, gesturing to the strangers, who all, Kindred saw now, carried a shield strapped across their back. Even the child carried one, the plane of its face battered and cracked.

"They must have seen some combat," Awn said, frowning, and Kindred felt a sinking disappointment in her gut.

They had come below to leave such things behind, to slip the grip of such ugly things as fighting and striving and warring. Had she been naive to think such things wouldn't have been there, too? Had it been a child's hope?

They hadn't even met these people yet and already the world above returned, had perhaps never really left.

It was supposed to be different below. Better. Simpler.

The leader broke off, nodding at something the other long-haired crew member had said before starting across the distance between the two parties, her long-legged, jaunty walk almost a jig. As she stepped around the braids of grass buried in the dirt, the leader pulled a few scraps of food from her pocket and dropped them on the ground.

In an instant they were gone, the scraps pulled under with the barest flash of something red—a hand or paw or tentacle or snout or beak or *something* almost too fast to see, there for a blink and then gone, the star-speckled dirt barely disturbed and already settled.

"What luck touches the Lost Monarch's Traveling Court," the woman said, holding her arms out wide and smiling big enough to reveal a mouth half-filled with teeth. "We, our lost majesty's fiercest, most courageous finders, expected only another wreck fallen from above, and yet—miracle of miracles! Hope of hopes! We find living beings among the wreckage!"

It seemed a stretch to call *The Lost* "wreckage," especially given the effort Kindred had expended in securing them a safe landing, one that would preserve the vessel's integrity.

The leader stopped before Kindred and the others, arms still wide for a moment before realizing, perhaps, that no embrace was forthcoming.

"Hello," Kindred said, feeling her way with careful steps into her captain's role. Until now, that had meant only keeping the fire and making a few obvious and easy decisions with her two friends-turned-crew. Now it meant speaking for her crew in the face of whoever and whatever this was.

"I'm Kindred, captain of *The Lost*." She gestured to the vessel behind her, so small and insignificant in the mighty green-ribbed halls of the Sea floor. "This is Ragged Sarah, my second-in-command. And this is Awn, my . . ."

What was Awn? A deckhand? A loremaster? A caster? A second hearthfire keeper? They hadn't sailed for long enough to establish roles, and even if they had, *The Lost* was not a vessel that required much. Fire to move, sails to catch the occasional wind. It was a ship for the liminal spaces between true journeys.

"I'm not much of anything, really," Awn said, stepping forward and, to everyone's surprise, wrapping this woman in a hug. "I'm just happy to be here."

The leader of the other crew grinned and returned the embrace.

"We are all not much of anything," she said, keeping a hand on Awn's shoulder as the two of them parted. "It is in that not-muchness that we find what has been lost."

She turned to Kindred.

"Welcome to the Lost Monarch's land, Kindred, captain of *The Lost*, and to you, Ragged Sarah, second-in-command, and to you as well, Awn-who-is-not-much. You may call me Jest, though my true name is much longer," she said, pulling one of her braided tails across her chest and bowing deeply.

"And here," she continued, righting herself and motioning for the others to join her, "are the other members of the Monarch's Traveling Court."

The three other crew members jumped from the ship, the child with a triumphant peal of laughter as she leapt and walked over. The thin, unsmiling person introduced themself first.

"I'm Fourth-Folly," they said, nodding to each of them, face grim, eyes hard. "You cannot have any of my things."

An awkward pause followed, and when neither Jest nor Fourth-Folly gave any indication that this was meant to be humorous, Kindred said, "Okay." Sarah and Awn quickly added their agreement, and only then did Fourth-Folly nod and step back.

"This is Wylf," Jest said, pulling forward the man, tall and fat and solemn, who held Kindred's gaze for a long, intense moment before moving on to do the same with Sarah and then Awn. The whole time he was gazing at them, his lips were moving in quick, silent speech, words too fast to make out. "He speaks and sings very little—he traded most of his words during his time in Forever. His voice, if used too much, would bring about the end of his world."

Jest said this as though it were nothing, an observation about the soil quality or a statement about rain on the way.

"How fascinating," Awn said, taking a tiny step forward toward Wylf, just as Sarah muttered in Kindred's ear, "That can't be true."

"And I'm Madrigal," the final crew member—the child—said, jumping into the middle of the loose group and lifting her hands in the air. Like all of them, she was grubby, her clothes a rough assembly of scraps, her face smudged, hands rimed in dirt.

But like all of them, she seemed beyond it, as though her true self floated outside and above and beyond her circumstances, not constrained by ill-fitting clothing or defined by the life she led, clean despite the dirt on her and joyous despite the shambling wreckage around her.

It was intoxicating.

"Madrigal," Jest said, smiling down at the girl with obvious fondness, "is still looking for her myth. Soon, though, she'll have found it."

Madrigal smiled and stepped close to Kindred, moving with calm and ease despite having just met her.

"I like your robes," she said, taking some of the fabric of Kindred's clothing in her hands as if it were precious. "They're so beautiful."

They were robes that had once been black but had been browned by the sun. Various stains covered the fabric, which had gone thin and oily with time.

"Thank you," Kindred said, looking to Sarah with raised eyebrows, but Sarah had on that mischievous smile, the one Kindred loved so much, the one that said Kindred was on her own there.

"I don't have any others. I would give it to you if I did," Kindred said.

Madrigal was so close and seemed completely comfortable. What if Kindred had a knife? A cudgel? What if she meant these people ill?

"Leave her be for a moment, Madrigal," Jest said, though with a kindness that only someone acting as a parent could muster. Madrigal smiled up at Kindred once more before scampering back.

"Well, Kindred Captain," Jest said, the others standing around her and watching Kindred expectantly, "please tell us what has brought you from the fabled lands above to the Monarch's forgotten lands."

CHAPTER FIVE

"I'm never sailing again." Zim's declaration accompanied his flailing leap onto the dock once Flitch dropped *The Laughing Queen* onto the chains of the cradle below. Around them, the Borders docks, usually busy at this time of day, were quiet, most sailors either out on merchant or harvesting voyages or remaining on land until the ways to Arcadia were once again opened.

Zim's footsteps receded as he ran up the dock and hurled himself onto the safe certainty of land.

"I don't normally agree with Zim," Aster said, her voice sedate, motions calm and slow as she climbed off the ship and onto the deck. "But I also may take a short break from sailing."

She offered a small, brief smile before trotting down the wooden planks of the dock and dropping to the ground next to Zim, crossing her legs and folding her hands in her lap.

"Not completely the Stormcloud Magus reborn, apparently," Idyll said, stretching their back and watching Aster and Zim sitting quietly together. It was the first time Flitch had seen them sharing the same space without fighting or picking at one another, without their constant sniping and snarking.

"I don't know," Flitch said, hoping the shaking in his legs was not obvious as he moved on to the dock after checking once more to make sure the hearthfire was well and truly doused. "Did you see her attack? It was incredible even with the reduction in power."

"She's plenty talented; everyone knows that's true." Idyll put an arm around Flitch's shoulder as they walked, leaning on him and giving him someone to lean on in return. "I've heard people from the other baronies and even the minor nobilities talk about Aster's accomplishments at the school. She may be arrogant, but there's real fire there, too."

They looked along the line of the dock to the other two siblings, face still showing some of the fear they'd all experienced on their return voyage.

"No, it's not Aster's abilities that will be her challenge. It's her kindness. Down deep, underneath all the bravado and arrogance and jokes about Zim or me or our family is simple, honest kindness, and that's something none of those famed figures from myth had. All those stories I used to tell you, they all featured people who could do impossible, unbelievable things, but the more I read, and the more I talk with the librarians who have been around for longer than seems possible, the more I understand that those great captains and casters were, deep down, selfish and cruel in small, quiet ways, even as their deeds were sung to the skies and shone brighter than the sun."

Idyll gave his shoulder a squeeze.

"And Aster might be a selfish, cocky terror sometimes, but deep down— way, way, *way* down," Idyll said, grinning, "she's kind. Just like you. Just like Zim and me. It's how Father raised us. How Mother did, too. It's why Aster will never be the Stormcloud Magus reborn. She'll be something different. Something better."

Flitch could say nothing, only nod at what Idyll had offered. The vision of the beast from the deeps still swam in his mind, and the sound of its melodic cry still sang in his ears, and Flitch could not comprehend anything so true right then.

"Are you talking about me?" Aster shouted as Flitch and Idyll neared. "Admiring my incredible spellwork, perhaps? I could've destroyed that thing if Flitch hadn't been using the hearthfire to fuel our cowardly retreat."

"Way, *way* down," Idyll said, turning to Flitch, their voice low and smile mischievous.

"We should hurry back," Zim said, standing and brushing himself off. "The meeting at the King's court will start soon, and I want to bathe before we go."

The scrubby ground just beyond the docks, crushed into dirt and unyielding weeds by too many boots and too many barrels, reminded Flitch of the games they used to play down there, racing and running at the edge of things, the sounds of sailors and shipwork their constant companions.

For a moment, no one made a move to begin the walk back, each of them looking around and lost in thought, and Flitch wondered if they too were seeing the ghosts of the kids they once were around them, digging in the dirt for lost treasure or swinging tree-branch swords at warmongering pirates.

"We almost died out there," Zim said, and as the others nodded, Flitch understood that none of them were looking back as he was.

"It was a bad idea," Aster said after a moment. "Even if I *was* amazing."

"Flitch and I were the ones who actually saved us," Idyll said, frowning at Aster, but the bit of humor in their voice dissipated as they said, "But we probably shouldn't have gone in the first place. Why take the risk when we'll just hear the same news at the King's meeting?"

Flitch gave a bare nod, the adrenaline of their escape evaporating and leaving him tired and empty.

"At least we survived," Aster said, punching Flitch lightly in the shoulder, misreading his glum expression for lingering terror. "And no one has to know we were there."

"By no one, you mean *Father*," Zim said, picking at the skin on one finger.

"Exactly." Aster smiled around at them all, her confidence returning. "It can be our little secret. The final voyage of the Borders Brats."

The final voyage, Flitch thought as he followed the others up the winding path that would lead them home.

The Borders Baron was already astride his horse—gone, of course, were the days of a carriage—when the siblings came out the large front doors some time later, the carved, weatherworn wood protesting as Aster emerged, followed closely by Idyll, Flitch, and Zim.

The baron had been in conversation with one of his sibilants, a bald woman, the light skin of her head and neck covered in thin, twisting tattoos, standing up on tiptoe to offer the baron her information. She dropped back, startled, as the siblings came out of the house and raced across the rough lawn toward their father.

Flitch had always loved the sibilants, the whisper workers of the Borders barony. Espionage and clandestine maneuverings were a simple fact of life among the nobility and the crown, but every barony had their own approach. The King, who was technically a baron of the capital city, Halcyon, called his people whispermen. The Rivers barony had their spies.

Only the Paths Baron, Gwyn Gaunt, did not play the information game, at least not in the secretive way the other barons did. She was aloof and distant, often absent from court, her seat filled by one of her servants.

"I'd thought to attend the meeting alone; I was certain you all would have found your own activities for the day," the baron said as his children neared. His eyes searched their faces, mouth tensing from a smile into a pensive line behind the thick cover of his beard, gone grey before the hair atop his head. "Did something happen? Is something wrong?"

He was a powerfully built man, shoulders like mountains and legs like tree trunks. Some of Flitch's favorite memories were of afternoons passed riding atop those mountainous shoulders out in the fields and forests of the Borders lands, his siblings dashing and racing around, his father's rich laughter like sunlight turned melodic, bright and warm and good. *Flitchy*, the Borders Baron had called his youngest son, the pet name Flitch's siblings would take responsibility of when their father began to fade like his estate, widowed and weakening, lost and losing.

"Nothing! We're just excited about the meeting!" Aster said, gesturing to one of the servants nearby to fetch them their horses.

"We still can, can't we?" Flitch asked. He'd spent the time since they'd returned in his room, paging aimlessly through his books and poking his model ships around on the floor without much interest.

The baron looked them over, one dark eyebrow rising. His cheeks puffed out beneath the thick tangle of his beard as he *hmmm*'d—a sure sign that his answer was *yes*.

Idyll made it solid.

"Father," they said, speaking in their careful, slow way, "it would be a very good opportunity for us to appear at court and take part in offering whatever aid our barony can to the King."

The baron's unsure hum burbled over into a low laugh, and he nodded. Flitch could see the same magic that had pulled his siblings back together that morning, that had begun to stitch and mend the fraying bonds between them, was working, too, on their father. It had been many spans since the Borders Baron had smiled, and perhaps years since he had laughed.

Always working to prop up the failing reputation of his family, constantly striving to protect the interests of the people under his protection and command, the Borders Baron had worn a harried, frantic look for a long time, eyes constantly flicking about in thought during conversations, showing up late or not at all to most meals, spending most nights working in his offices.

"Come on, then," he said, looking around at them. "Borders will ride in strength today."

The five of them, accompanied by a few servants and guards, set out shortly thereafter, and Flitch let out a whoop of excitement as they did. The wind cut along through them as they rode, and it felt like change.

Borders was the thin band of skin stretched along the Mainland's eastern edge, and it took almost no time to ride out of it and into Halcyon, the capital of the Mainland and ancestral seat of the Larks. The hallway leading into the throne room of the Fickle King, Faineant Lark, was lined with statues of his ancestors, beginning with Dred Lark, first baron of Halcyon, and ending on an empty pedestal with *Faineant* chiseled into its name-plate. To see the King, one first walked his bloodline.

The streets of Halcyon were busy as Flitch rode in the Borders train into the city, carts and riders and walkers parting for the servant at the head of the party, the lance with the Borders regalia decorating it enough to gain swift passage through the throngs. Flitch couldn't help but wonder, though, if some of those people might have been less than willing to move if they'd looked more closely at exactly *which* nobles they were giving way to.

The newly built homes of the outer edges caught the morning sun, their clean angles and light colors turning them into bright, broken teeth, ugly and perfect.

Zim had a fondness for the new homes. Flitch rode beside him and watched his brother's eyes scan across the neat, boxy lines of them, vivid paints garish. Zim offered one of his rare smiles and turned to Flitch, huffing in a quick breath, the morning's terrors either forgotten or buried deep.

"One of our Third Pens purchased this row," he said, gesturing to the houses they were passing. "Our team helped ferry through the sale."

It was as close to bragging as Zim would get—*our team*, implying his own presence on it. Only a year into his bookkeeping practice, so close to the bottom of the ranks in the Borders bookkeeping office that he wasn't even a junior something-or-other. His title, he'd proudly told them after spending his first set of days working at the offices and sleeping in the apartments above at night, was "Callow Pen."

"And how many steps between you and the lead bookkeeper?" Flitch had asked him.

"She's called the First Pen," Zim had responded, snorting with laughter at Flitch's ignorance. "And I'm seventeen positions from hers."

The baron had nodded over his meal, the food long gone cold, since he'd arrived late. It was something all of his children learned about their father as they grew up: the baron did things the way they should be done, appropriately, with hard work, dedication, and a hope for some luck.

Borders had been in dire need of some luck for more than a generation.

"I didn't know we were in the housing business now," Flitch said as he nudged his horse to the right and onto the wide, well-worn road that would lead the party to the Fickle King's castle.

Zim grew serious, falling back to his natural state, and said, voice barely audible over the swelling sounds of the city and the dry clop of their horses' hooves, "We're all doing what we can to bring Borders back."

Flitch nodded, his own smile fading too.

Bring Borders back.

He set his gaze ahead, looking between the rising and falling forms of Idyll and Aster where the tall towers of the castle spiked above the architecture of Halcyon, the old city surrounding it like a protective barrier.

These new buildings might set his brother's heart speeding and provide some margin of profit for the people in Zim's office, but Flitch couldn't see the shine of them. They all looked the same, iterations on a theme. Big or small, stretched in a row or surrounded by grasses and trees, the buildings looked to all have been carved from the same hand, assembled using the same pieces. The streets between them were thin, miserly things, shadowed and harboring the possibility of violence, if even half the stories of the new city could be believed.

The old city, though, was a wonder.

Swirls of stone and elaborate facades of long-weathered wood grew up from either side of the narrow, paved street. Churches and sanctums, wind-wheels and drying houses, the homes of minor nobility and lodgings for visiting dignitaries, historic inns and dark, exclusive taverns—all crowding for space in the bounded confines of the old city, surrounded as it was by the expansive growth of the new city.

"There we are!" Zim shouted, gesturing toward a squat building, the front a latticework of dark wood, with a small hanging above the double doors reading Borders Bookkeepers. The baron looked over to where his son was pointing before giving him a broad, honest smile. The siblings all mirrored it until their father turned back around, and then they offered sarcastic swoons of amazement and overblown shows of astonishment.

Zim, as was his wont, offered a more direct gesture to let them know how appreciated their joking was. But even that was softened. Among siblings, what was teasing if not a slantwise whisper of love?

"Did you all have a nice morning at home?" the baron asked, his deep voice sounding underneath the bright-strike of horse hooves on road. "I'm sorry I wasn't around. Business below."

How long since they had sat on the floor or bed or chairs of their bedrooms, crowding into Aster's messy space or Zim's carefully cleaned one—how long since their whispered speculations about their family's secret?

After she died, Flitch thought, falling back into those dark, strange memories of his mother's death, the news shocking and impossible to a boy so young, only a few days away from his sixth birthday and incapable of imagining a world without his mother in it.

Whatever secret was in the basement of the house, whatever great treasure or great curse the Borders family carried, had played some part in the death of Flitch's mother, and though the baron never spoke of it in detail, his one rule—more of a promise, until then—became absolute: no child is allowed in the basement until the baron has died and a new Baron takes his place.

Childhood and adolescence passed this way for Flitch: his father absent working at or struggling with or puzzling out whatever secret, whatever weight he carried below, and the Borders siblings doing their own puzzling about the basement between games of pretend pirates or hide-and-seek.

As Halcyon passed by them on either side, a revelry of joyful cries and bitter shouts and every emotion in between, the Borders kids rode close to one another, laughing and joking, a short distance behind their father and his guard. Despite the events of the morning, or perhaps because of them, it was turning out to be one of the best days Flitch could remember.

"We didn't do much," Idyll said in response to their father's question, cutting a sharp glance at the other siblings as they spoke. "Went down to the docks to look at the smoke and fog."

"Quite a mess that woman made," the baron said, his eyes scanning the street around them before turning, a smile pulling deep down inside his beard. "I shouldn't say before we arrive at court, but I have some early information from Arcadia."

Flitch and the others led their horses closer, until the four of them swarmed their father.

"The King's vessels, along with a few from the other baronies, including Borders, found and captured—truly *captured!*—the survivors of a pirate armada! It's unclear what happened beyond the story I'm sure you've already heard about this keeper, Kindred Greyreach, who set fire to the seas over, as far as I know, a water dispute. But all that matters little in the face of this!"

He broke out now in a great, wide grin, eyes alight with expectant excitement.

"Real pirates, captured by our very own ships, and brought here to the Mainland! What do you say to such news?"

Flitch drew in a breath and held it, trying and failing to keep his eyes from sliding to those of his siblings, who all looked equally stricken.

The pause stretched to the point of discomfort, and just as Flitch opened his mouth to speak, hoping something plausible and believable would come out, he was beaten to it.

"I am shocked and amazed by this news, Father," Zim said, eyes wide as he looked to the baron, his voice a steady monotone that offered neither shock nor amazement.

"How are you so bad at this?" Aster asked, staring at him. "*You're shocked and amazed?* Honestly, Zim!"

"What was I supposed to say?" Zim's voice climbed an outraged octave.

"It was fine, Zim," Idyll began, but Aster spoke over them.

"Oh, I don't know, Skimmer," she said, using the sobriquet she'd come up with for Zim when they were young, the name referring to his tendency to move around the house in a constant state of restlessness. "Maybe you could have *shown* some shock and amazement? You're like an actor seeing his lines for the first time!"

"It wasn't that bad, Aster," Flitch said, joining the fray.

"It was, too!"

"You didn't say anything either!"

"We were all surprised, okay? Just leave it."

"We really should have talked about this before leaving."

"A plan! We needed a plan. I would've been okay with a plan."

"Isn't *don't get caught* the sort of default plan we're supposed to have all the time?"

"Only if you're a criminal!"

"Hey!"

"Hey yourself!"

The baron raised one hand, his eyes looking between his children, unperturbed by this whirlwind of words. If anything, he looked almost pleased by it, and Flitch found he felt the same. This poking, prodding, biting, joking, consoling mess that the four of them always fell into was like a song he knew deeply, profoundly, essentially. It was a melody he longed for during long, silent afternoons.

It mattered little what they spoke of or joked about or fought over, only that they were all there, all present, all speaking, using up every bit of air in their lungs with one another.

The four of them quieted as their father's hand stayed up. It was how he would get their attention as children, though he'd had fewer opportunities to use it of late.

"Clearly, my news was not so new," he said, his smile dimming.

Who would tell him? Could they get away with only telling him a bit? Cutting chunks off the truth and presenting it as something whole? Flitch doubted it.

"Who told you?" the baron said, continuing. "One of my sibilants? It was Halle, wasn't it? They're so good at gathering information and keeping it from those outside the barony, but that soft spot they have for you will be their doom."

"It wasn't Halle," Flitch said, leaping for the explanation their father had offered them. "But yes, we did hear from someone already."

The Borders Baron narrowed his eyes at the four of them before staring hard at Flitch. He guided his horse, a roan stallion who could be vicious to anyone attempting to ride him save the baron, under whose hand he was a tranquil, attentive companion.

"Not giving up your source?" The baron's eyes rolled skyward in the expression of resigned parents the world over. "I suppose I should be proud of that. It's an odd time when my children are more careful with information than my well-paid spies."

After a pause that filled with the sounds of their horses and the ruckus of the capitol, the baron's frown fell away and he let out a huge, full laugh.

"Oh, fine—you're not giving anything away. And you were going to find out about all of this regardless, so I shouldn't be upset. I suppose you've heard ten different tales by now about Kindred Greyreach setting fire to the Sea and diving below?"

Flitch smiled as he pictured it all, flames glinting and shifting across the spectrum as they devoured the old, dried grasses, leaping up like a young puppy to climb the hulls of the ships. Some of the black-hearted pirates leapt from the deck, choosing the green dive over the flames, but most stayed aboard, spreading sand ineffectually and screaming for the sailor at the helm to angle away. Some made it—those who would soon be captured by Mainland ships in stunning acts of heroism—but most perished in the flames.

The play in Flitch's mind was like something out of the old stories—a single sailor, with only her wits and power to hand, outsmarting the evil pirates chasing her. Although, in one of those stories, she would have been saved by a flock of kindly silver-winged shrikes, who would fight off the remaining pirates before stealing the hero away to her home or a mansion in the clouds or the other side of forever.

Astride his horse, he shivered with a discomfort bordering on disgust as he thought instead of her willing, knowing dive below.

"Apparently, they were nearing *The Arcana* and its defenses!" Aster leaned forward in her saddle, eyes bright with excitement. "I bet some of my teachers were on the King's boats that are bringing them in."

As one of the advanced casting students in her school, Aster was allowed to train with the King's finest casters, mages of such power and ability that a ship lucky enough to sail with one of them didn't need to include any other casters. That Aster trained with such casters as Trilyn West or Maxwell Myriad or any of the others was a great honor—or so it seemed, based on her need to bring it up in nearly every conversation she had.

"No doubt they'll be needing your help soon, too," Idyll said, one side of their mouth curving almost imperceptibly. "Underling caster, Aster o' the Borders, King Faineant's last great hope!"

Flitch and Zim laughed at that, although not too loud; Aster most easily gave the laughing prods and least easily received them.

"I'm not an underling anymore, Idyll!" she said, voice rising slightly. "I'm of the fourth ring now!"

Aster gestured to her right ear ,where the new ring gleamed with the others. It was made of a black material Flitch had never seen or heard of before, and when Aster had last visited home for any time—several spans before—she had been strangely cagey about the rings, obviously proud of her accomplishments but tight-lipped about what exactly they were made of or symbolized. She was progressing, one ring away from attaining the title of master—that's all she could say. Her visit then had been a single night before disappearing back down the road, heading back to her live-in school.

Zim and his First Pen and Callow Pen and all the levels between.

Aster and her secretive rings and exclusive education.

Even Idyll in their work at the royal library, the Rose, had begun to move up among the ranks of the librarians, gaining enough experience to gain access to more and more guarded archives and collections, the keys they carried on the keyring at their belt multiplying with each new, irregular visit home.

All of his siblings were climbing their own steps, walking further and further into their own territory and leaving Flitch further and further behind. It was as if each of their chosen roles had offered them a new way of being, complete with new clothing and language, and all of it served to make Flitch's siblings more unrecognizable.

Closer to the castle, the worn, warm press of shops began to fall away, and only a few buildings remained, spread out and surrounded by small green seas, their lawns cultivated and curated to resemble the Forever Sea itself. Tiny stands of bluestem and clutches of many-colored echinacea bending gracefully in the low, ever-present wind; spreads of lousewort, giant stalk, and faerie gold bobbing and ebbing in luxurious, dreamlike flows.

Aster pointed out the buildings of her school off in the distance, visible through the tangle of trees and grasses, and a short while after that, Flitch caught Idyll staring off at the single tall tower of the Rose, the red stones of its peak distinct even from a distance.

When the path below finally turned onto the castle's avenue and the guards at the head of it nodded them past, Flitch breathed a sigh of relief. Whatever awaited them inside was outside these new lives his siblings lived. They were not that fractured, wayward family anymore when they walked through those huge, jeweled front doors.

The castle of King Faineant, the Fickle King, was a mountain of stone, its outer walls and the points of its spires sloping inward. Made of all thick, dark stone, it had been the seat of power in the Mainland for longer than memory.

Around its front door, a swarm of courtiers and minor nobility waited, speaking together in tight circles, casting suspicious looks around at one another, no doubt juggling the various reputations present in hopes of gaining some advantage should any of their number be admitted. Those same calculating eyes widened and then narrowed again at the approach of the Borders retinue, almost certainly smaller and less grand than any of the other baronies that had already showed up.

The Borders siblings followed their father in dismounting their horses, which were promptly taken by some of the King's numerous guards.

"Leeches," Aster whispered, her glance flicking all around at the waiting nobility.

"Worse," Idyll said, their normally kind face taking on a look of withering disdain. "At least leeches have a purpose."

"Here we go," Flitch said, stepping close to his siblings, arm to arm with Idyll and Aster, with Zim on the other side of Idyll. One of the guards had beckoned them forward. Flitch's heart beat hard in his chest. Here they all were, together.

"Your job is to listen *only*," the Borders Baron said to his children, giving each of them a careful, steady glance. "It is an honor to be invited in by the King, and we will respect that honor. Remember the rules. Remember all I have told you."

He paused for a moment before speaking again, and this time, his voice was very low. Flitch knew what he was going to say before he said it. They all did, of course.

"Do not speak to anyone of what lies below Borders."

The siblings nodded together and followed their father inside.

The doors groaned closed behind them.

※ ◆ ※

King Faineant sat on his throne, eating peaches and watching his dogs fight. His seat, raised above the rest of the court by four steps—each meant to symbolize one of the baronies—was cut from a single piece of milky-white stone, at odds with the dark rock constituting the rest of the throne room and castle. Thin, slitted windows sliced high into the ceiling let in some light and emphasized the sheer size of the room.

It was a huge cavern, cold every time Flitch had been in it no matter how great a fire burned in the pit at the center, no matter what season it was or how many layers he was wearing. The ceiling was a half-seen vault above, and the walls receded away into darkness as soon as a person walked through the doors. Even the columns of stone—rough-cut and cracked—bent at a smooth angle up and away.

"Disgusting," Idyll said, their voice low, eyes narrowed as they looked on the massive cage erected in the center of the room, just below the white throne, where a pack of dogs, snarling and barking and yelping, attacked one another for the entertainment of the petty nobility standing nearby.

"Quiet, Idyll," the Borders Baron said, drawing in a short breath and taking in the room.

"But dogs, Father?" Idyll whispered. Since entering court, Idyll had withdrawn into themselves, growing watchful and quiet, on their guard against whatever insults or degradations another trip to court might offer the Borders barony.

"It is Faineant's court and he will do as he does," the baron said. "Now hush."

Faineant had grown markedly older since the last time Flitch saw him, his squashed nose and pocked cheeks having grown redder, populated by more burst blood vessels. Folds of skin overhung his sharp, bright eyes, and his hair had receded almost entirely from the top of his head, leaving only a few ghostly wisps behind, long and white and airy, floating up through the circle of his thin crown.

When Flitch had last been at court—more than eight years past by this point—the Fickle King had worn a crown thick with gold and gems, heavy and ornamented. Perhaps his neck had grown tired of holding such a thing up in the meantime.

The juice of his meal slicked Faineant's lips and cheeks, catching the firelight in bright streaks.

"Up, Tyrus!" he shouted at one of the dogs in the large cage. "Up, beast!"

One of the dogs, maybe Tyrus, rose above the scrum for a moment, teeth bared in a bloody snarl, and Flitch, like Idyll, like every member of the Borders delegation, looked away.

King Faineant likes hard, cruel things, Flitch's father had told him at a young age, the same as he had the other kids. Being one of the barons, even one often on the margins of the King's favor, meant that Flitch's father had had to learn the subtle and not-so-subtle intricacies of King Faineant's ways of being in the world. And it meant that his children had to learn these things too. Many nights had been spent with their father reciting an ever-growing list of rules for his children to follow while at court.

Do not laugh if the King is not laughing.

Do not find enjoyment in something the King does not enjoy.

When you enter a room at court, step first to your left and bow.

Do not speak unless the King asks you a direct question.

Do not speak to the King's whispermen, especially Nab, the one with long red hair.

If you must speak, speak only in sentences totaling an odd number of words.

Do not eat any food.

Do not drink anything.

Keep one hand hidden at all times.

The baron would say all of this in the firm but pleasant tone reserved for silly-but-important rules they must follow, often adding items to the list based on whatever new activity had captured the King's attention. Some of them gained a clear purpose over time; others remained silly, and Flitch and his siblings followed them only out of duty to their father.

But then the baron's eyes would grow serious, his voice dark and almost threatening as he repeated the one item that never changed, that the Borders children had learned from their first days. By the age of three or four, they would recite it along with their father as he spoke.

Do not speak to anyone of what lies below Borders.

As if any of them could with any certainty, Flitch had always thought, but still, he heard the refrain in his head even now, a dictate writ so deep down that he would never be rid of it.

The petty nobility surrounding the cage did not interest any of the Borders delegation, but those seated outside the press at raised tables around the dog cage did.

At one table a rowdy group sat, many of them already building a small collection of empty cups before them. The Rivers Baron, Cantria Shade, sat among her people, drinking and laughing along with them. Most loved of the nobility, her barony most favored and most profitable among the four, Cantria had little to darken her countenance. Her stringy blond hair framed a laughing, joyous face, sharp nose, and watery eyes. She was a large, powerful woman known for her prowess in the wrestling ring and her political ambitions. Even Flitch, who was often ignorant of the goings-on at court, had heard the news that Cantria's only child, a girl named Tacet, had agreed to marry King Faineant's second-youngest daughter in a ceremony that was promised to last eight days and nights.

Rivers was ascendant, they said, and every laugh and joyful slug of drink at their table was evidence of it.

Nearby was the Paths table, and when Flitch saw only a single person seated at it, his heart thumped hard against his ribs. Could it be Gwyn Gaunt, the Paths Baron, strangest and most absent of the major nobles? Flitch had only ever glimpsed her a bare handful of times in his life, and her absence in every other courtly situation had only fed the stories that flourished around Gwyn Gaunt.

She's immortal, people said.

Her feet have walked the rain-soaked lands on the other side of forever, people said.

She was born of the union between the sun and the moon, people said.

With a single word, she can bring anyone under her power for nine days and nights, people said.

As a child, she was swallowed by a wyrm and lived out her adolescence in its belly, emerging only when she had reached adulthood, people said.

The stories were myriad, each more magical, more impossible than the last, and Flitch had once collected them just as he collected facts and ephemera about the Mainland fleet now.

Gwyn Gaunt was a story told by everyone but herself.

So, Flitch was disappointed when it was not Gwyn Gaunt's small figure resolving out of the low light but instead Ravel, his broad shoulders and open, unassuming face becoming clearer and clearer as the Borders party moved toward their own table.

If he looked uncomfortable being the only person at his table, the lone representative of Paths, Ravel did not show it. His eyes moved slowly and methodically around the room, taking note of everything and everyone, and his hands remained folded in front of him on the table. The food and drink that had been laid out for him remained untouched.

When the Borders party moved into Ravel's field of vision, his gaze swept over each person in turn before settling on Idyll. His guarded, careful expression opened slightly, and his attentive expression softened with the hint of a smile.

"Absent again," the Borders Baron said, glancing toward the Paths table and huffing out a breath. "The Sea afire, pirates on our shores for the first time in living memory, an unprecedented call for an all-barony meeting, and that woman sends a lackey in her stead. Unbelievable."

"But a very well-muscled lackey," Aster said, nodding seriously at their father. "Obviously not one of Gwyn's best or brightest."

"Aster," Idyll said, their voice a low warning.

"Don't be quick to assume, Aster," the baron said, his eyes returning to Ravel, who had resumed his watch of the room. "Little from Paths is what it seems, I've found."

The great throne room was filled with pockets of nobles and merchants, emissaries from distant lands and major captains from the King's fleet, all speaking in quiet voices or watching the ongoing carnage of the dog fight. And though they moved about the room, some in tight clutches and others in wide, loose groups, none came close to the Paths table. Ravel sat alone in the busy room, seeming more at ease than anyone else, the King included.

He had traded in his scroll of dockwork scribblings for a bandolier strung across his chest, the slender handles of throwing knives shining against the worn brown of the leather.

"What are you talking about?" Zim asked, stepping around their father and joining the whispered conversation. "Did you see who's here, Idyll?"

"Yes," Idyll said, glancing away.

"Do you know that boy, Idyll?" the baron asked, eyebrows rising into thick, black arcs.

"Oh, they *know* that boy," Aster muttered, low enough that only Idyll and Flitch heard.

"*Aster*," Idyll hissed.

"What's going on here?" The baron was looking around, confused.

"It's—" Flitch began.

"*Well*—" Aster began.

"Nothing!" Idyll said, speaking over their siblings in a raised whisper. "I know him from my work at the library; that's all. His name is Ravel."

The baron nodded and gave an absent *hmmm*, though he said nothing else, and it wasn't until he turned away to continue his walk toward the Borders table that Flitch saw the quirk of a smile contorting the landscape of his beard.

Aster laughed quietly as she dodged a jab from Idyll, who left off but did not brighten with the contagious excitement moving among the other siblings. Even as Ravel disappeared behind a group of passing merchants, their clothes fine, their fingers gilded with rings and bracelets, Idyll maintained a look of detached impassivity.

Perhaps because they were oldest or perhaps because of what had happened with their mother, Idyll had always been the most reserved and pensive of the Borders kids, a figure somewhere between an older, protective sibling and a young, protective parent when their father couldn't be around. They were given to slow, quiet pauses and careful, thoughtful words. Here, in a moment of great possibility and uncertainty, Flitch would have been surprised if Idyll had been anything else but cautious.

Still, the day felt like a wave carrying Flitch forward, the disaster of the morning be damned. It was all momentum and purpose now. Finally something was happening. Finally they were all back together. Finally.

"Keep moving, children," the Borders Baron said, not looking at his kids as he spoke. He'd made his face into the mask of calm, gentle humor he wore when dealing with anyone outside of the family. It was the mask of a man in control, at ease in whatever situation he was in, competent and comfortable.

As a young boy, Flitch had been confused by this side of his father, so different from how he acted among his family: cold when he was normally warm, formal and distant when he was normally casual and close. But

Flitch soon learned the value of putting up such defenses at court, where the Fickle King's moods swung chaotic and cruel, and the petty nobility searched for any crack in which they could plant their noxious ambitions.

The Rivers table was raucous and chaotic; the Paths table was silent and watchful.

The final table was empty, a small, burnished sign at its center reading Borders. It was toward this that the baron made his way, followed by his still-whispering children. Idyll, as was their right and privilege, took their seat at the baron's right side, while the seat to his left remained empty in honor of his wife.

The others sat down in the remaining seats while Tally and the other guards took up their places standing just behind, silent and unmoving.

From his seat, Flitch could easily see the whole of the court, every noble resplendent in bright, rich colors of their minor house, the various climbers moving in excited, agitated leaps from conversation to conversation, always on the lookout for a better group to join, a slightly higher-quality collection of aristocratic graspers to hang from.

Faineant raised his chalice, a cup cut from the same milky-white stone as his throne, to acknowledge the Borders Baron, and the whole party was forced to rise and give deep bows in the King's direction before reseating themselves. Faineant's smile was still slick and wet, the juice from the peach glistening on his lips and chin, shiny on his fingers.

"What a shit," Aster said quietly through teeth clenched into a smile as she settled back into her seat beside Flitch. "He waited to notice us until we'd already sat, and *then* he gives his pompous wave with that idiotic cup."

"Hush," the baron said, giving her a disapproving look before sliding his court face smoothly back into place.

Flitch laughed, and Zim grinned, and even a few of their guards who stood close enough to hear let the thin, grim lines of their mouths quirk into brief shows of pleasure.

Only Idyll didn't smile or laugh. They had begun to fidget anxiously with the end of their ponytail, threading the thick black strands through their fingers in quick flicks, eyes locked on some point away from their table.

"What's wrong?" Flitch said, keeping his voice low enough so that just Idyll would hear.

"What?" Idyll asked, clearly distracted. "It's nothing." Their eyes, lighter brown than the rest of the Borders siblings, flicked to Flitch for a moment before leaving again, and Flitch followed Idyll's gaze to where it landed on the Paths table and its solitary occupant.

When he looked back, Idyll was chewing a handful of fried spicy wild-rye, their eyes still locked on the Paths table.

"*Idyll,*" Flitch hissed, reaching out to grab hold of Idyll's wrist as they made to grab another scoop from the bowl. The table was littered with various foods and drinks, each nicely labeled and held in pristine, shining dishware of silver and gold.

"What?" Idyll asked, looking at him for a moment before the fog in their eyes cleared and they glanced down, horrified, at their hand, buried halfway into the spicy snack.

"*Do not eat any food,*" Idyll uttered, their voice coming out slightly choked as they recited one of their family's court rules. Everyone else was so busy staring around and getting settled that only Flitch had noticed.

"It was only a little bit," Flitch said, shrugging as Idyll frantically wiped off their hand and took a pull from the flask of water they'd brought. In their rare court appearances, each of the siblings had always brought their own water. "And it's just one of Father's precautions. I'm sure it's okay."

Who could Ravel be to Idyll to make them into this anxious, forgetful person? This was not the calm, steady sibling Flitch knew.

"Right," Idyll said, nodding once before huffing out a shaky breath.

"I wonder what the Paths Baron is doing instead of attending," Flitch said, trying to stoke again the fire of their collective excitement, but Idyll only shrugged and offered a noncommittal *hmmm* as their response.

The dog fight had reached its gruesome conclusion, and Flitch spent the time it took Faineant's servants to clear it all away happily speculating with his siblings about what the King might say, what reports there would be from any of the captains present, and whether any of the stories about Gwyn Gaunt were actually true. The baron was absorbed in deep conversation with the same sibilant from before, the bald woman leaning down to whisper quietly in his ear.

"Friends! Children of the Crown! Your King speaks!" One of the King's servants, a smiling, bearded man dressed in impeccable robes, stood on the stairs leading up to the throne and brought the assembled parties into order. The conversations in the room died away as the last bits of drink were slugged down, the last bits of gossip exchanged. An expectant quiet took hold of the big room, a quiet that seemed amplified by the soaring ceiling and distant walls.

King Faineant Lark did not rise from his throne to address his subjects, but his voice rang out, practiced as he was at filling the emptiness of the court with his words.

"Welcome." The King raised his cup again, this time in a wide sweep to include everyone present. "Loyal subjects one and all. We are beset by ill tidings. The grasses of our Sea have grown unruly, more and more stretches of green going grey as the sickness continues its spread. Creatures from the deeps continue to rise in unprecedented numbers, posing risks to our ships and trade, and even posing threats to some of our most cherished nobility."

He paused, his rheumy eyes sliding across the room and pausing on the Borders table before he continued to speak. Flitch could almost feel his father's frown of confusion.

"And now, Arcadia, weak creature that she was, has fallen, her grasses burned, much of her fleet lost, her people fled or cowering in their island-bound homes."

He stopped to loose a thick, hacking cough, his eyes open and fixed on his subjects even as spittle and phlegm flew from his mouth in a wide, wet spray. Servants appeared almost immediately with cloths to clean up.

Faineant continued, unabashed, as though nothing had happened.

"Arcadia's fall has long been on the horizon, obvious to any with eyes and foretold by my own counselors." His heavy-lidded eyes shifted for a moment to his right, where a man with long, red hair stood in the shadow of the throne. Nab, chief of the King's whispermen, a ghoul that had haunted Flitch's nightmares as a boy, the stories of Nab's cruelty widespread and detailed.

Nab was almost a shadow himself—short, thin, dressed always in black, eyes set deep in the hollows of his face. Only his hair, bright red, long, and curled in tight, messy ringlets, gave him any life. It fell in luscious waves around his oily, sallow face, out of place and odd, like a stand of perfect, beautiful flowers growing in a dead, dry field.

Nab smiled in the darkness beside the King's throne and nodded once.

"Stranger stories have reached this court, stories I have allowed to slip beyond our royal walls and among the people. It is said the Once-City entered Arcadian grasses shortly before the burn began, the city entire racing for Arcadia, pirate citizens released onto ships and sailing beside it. The fire consumed the Once-City, perhaps. Or perhaps it was sunk before the fire could do its hot work. Regardless, the fabled pirate city is no more, and her citizens, those who escaped the ravages of the flames and the omnipresent dangers of the Sea, are on their way here. Now."

Whispers gave way to murmurs, which gave way to cries of distress and shouts of terror. Pirates on their way to the Mainland. They were ever only an Arcadian problem, Arcadia's grasses bordering the storied Roughs on which pirates were said to sail their own rough vessels.

But Flitch did not share in the fear running wild throughout the room. Armed with his knowledge of the truth, the figures from these stories were nothing but wind and a little rain against the firm stone of this castle, of the Mainland's might, of the baronies brought together into the same room, of the Borders Brats, joined again.

King Faineant watched the panic in his court with a knowing smirk. He drew the back of one hand across his face, catching and smearing some of the juice and spittle still lingering there.

"Worry not, loyal subjects," he said, reaching out with an empty hand, palm down, as if to smother their fear. "Your King has the situation well in hand. Already my fleet has surrounded and escorted the mendicant pirates to our harbors. They were detected by Mainland vessels as they neared *The Arcana* and met before they could do any damage. The pirates come here under our control, under our power, and according to our plans."

A hearty cheer went up from the assembled crowd at that, though Flitch understood the truth of the King's words. While some present heard Faineant's *our* as a word meaning *all of ours*, what it truly meant was the royal *our*. The King as a body containing his own spirit and those of his predecessors. This was his *our*, his *we*, singular and solo, multiple and myriad, all at once.

"Pirates on Mainland shores!" Aster whispered, leaning across the table to the other siblings. She was grinning, caught up in the excitement, and Flitch nodded to her, his own smile just as wide.

"Worrisome," the King said, looking pained for a moment, as if the worries of the world collected together on his brow, a burden he was willing to bear, but a hard, difficult one nonetheless. "Dangerous times, with the stench of change in the air. The Greys. Monsters from the deeps that even now my casters are fighting off on our shores. Pirates. Fire. But the Mainland is strong, our roots run deep, and we will remain a link between past and future, our hands reaching back and forward. Together, we will flourish. *Together.*"

The Fickle King spoke this last through the first salvo of another coughing fit, this one long and severe enough to press eyelids together and tuck his chin toward his chest. Again, servants appeared to clean up the spittle and phlegm and bits of his meal that sprayed out.

When he finally stopped, he took a long drink from his milky-white cup and bit into the flesh of a fresh peach, unconcerned with those watching and waiting for him.

"I have commanded the leaders of the baronies to join us today," he said finally, gesturing to the three raised tables, "so that the Mainland can provide a strong, united response to this moment. Rivers, you guardians of our waterways. Paths, you walkers of the land. And Borders, you shields at the edge, a light atop that unknown dark."

The King favored each table with a smile as he noted them, though every member of the Borders table stiffened at his description of them as a light atop the dark. His meaning was clear.

Faineant had long lusted after the secret of the Borders barony. He knew enough to know that he didn't know everything, and King Faineant was a jealous man, given to suspicion and envy.

The first Borders Baron, Flitch's great-great-grandfather, had been a sociable man at first, but after the construction of his home on the cliffs overlooking the Forever Sea, he had grown strangely quiet and aloof, eschewing society, cloistering himself in his estate, playing host to odd visitors from around the wide world. One of the little secrets that Flitch had been told was that his great-great- great-grandfather had died down in whatever lay below, having forgotten the beauty of the morning sky and the gift of the wind on his face.

His children, and their children, and their children, and all the way down to Flitch—all of them had grown up carrying the secret of their home, their family's secret—the key to their fortunes and the rot worked through their foundations.

King Faineant knew that Borders had a secret, and he lusted after it— that was known. But he did not have the power to simply walk into the estate of another barony and demand the knowledge he hungered for. Even the King did not have such authority.

And so he poked. He joked. He prodded and wheedled and sent his whispermen around to ask questions.

And Borders stayed strong.

Faineant let his words settle, waiting for any reaction before continuing, a hint of disappointment on his face.

"Although my casters were able to stop the fires before they destroyed our grasses—and *your* livelihoods—we are still in the grips of challenge," he said. "Arcadia, weak though she may have been, was a hungry creature, and she bought many of our goods, hired many of our workers. Needy though she was, Arcadia offered much in pay for us to satisfy those needs."

As those in the room nodded solemnly at this and murmured their ascent, Idyll scowled down at the table and whispered, "Must he call everything a *she*?"

"Quiet, Idyll," the baron said, though his look was a sympathetic one.

"An entire economy left in tatters, homes left empty, and grasses burned away to a blackened corpse far below the Sea level." Faineant shook his head before brightening suddenly, his old head snapping up, birdlike, until he was peering out into the near-darkness to where Ravel sat alone at his table. "One of our own Paths vessels was lucky enough to sail close enough to see Arcadia's shores, and we are lucky, tremendously so, to have a Paths emissary here to report on what they have found. The baron, it seems, was too busy to favor her King with an appearance."

Faineant's voice dripped sarcasm as he gestured to the Paths table.

Ravel stood, the motion fluid and unhurried, his eyes taking in the whole of the assembly. He removed a small sheet of paper from one pocket, a prepared statement, maybe. Flitch was vaguely aware that he was leaning forward in anticipation, the muscles along his arms tense as he squeezed his folded hands together.

"Here we go," he whispered to no one in particular.

The tension in the room built until it seemed the walls themselves might crack with the waiting, and then Ravel spoke.

"Arcadia and its grasses have burned," he said without any inflection, reading the words on the paper in a voice that spoke of boredom. He waited for a long moment before sitting back down. While everyone in the room still waited in stunned silence, Ravel nodded at the King to indicate that he was finished.

King Faineant leaned over to one side of his throne and spoke quietly to Nab, who nodded, first with a frown and then with a slick, wide grin. When the King was finished, the whisperman bowed and slunk back into the shadows, disappearing through a door at the back of the throne room.

"Thank you to Paths for this enlightening report from the front lines. And perhaps the baron's messenger might remind his lady that a King's summons is best not ignored," King Faineant said, peevish and hard.

"He's too afraid of Gwyn to do anything but talk," Aster whispered, leaning across the table and grinning.

"I'd be afraid of her too," Flitch said. "If a tenth of the stories are true—"

"Silence in this throne room!" Faineant spoke with a whipcrack severity, the reserves of calm, passive control gone as his eyes flew wide, the bright blue of them a shock after his heavy-lidded laze.

Every bit of Flitch went cold and still, the air in his lungs barely stirring, his mouth suddenly dry. He looked up from Aster's face, still frozen in a smile, and saw King Faineant staring directly at the Borders table, directly at *him*. Flitch gave a shaky nod, hearing his father's voice echoing in his head: *Do not speak unless the King asks you a direct question.*

How could he have been so foolish? So confident? So unthinking? The high of the day burned up in his veins, leaving him feeling sluggish and weak, every flicker of excitement gone now in the face of a King enraged.

Flitch's father stood, his chair making a harsh grating sound as he pushed it back.

"My King, I offer our deepest apologies. My children are simply overjoyed, as am I, to find ourselves in your capable hands in this difficult time. Our horror at the pirates' approach has turned to comforted delight with the knowledge that Your Majesty's vessels, under the King's guidance, have the situation well in hand."

The baron sat back down as his head guard, Tally, pushed his chair back in for him.

Faineant's eyelids had drooped in pleasure again as the baron spoke, his ugly snarl softening to a smug smile.

"Our friends from Borders are forgiven, of course. Who could blame such young, innocent children for their inexperience at court? Let the young be young while they can, eh?"

King Faineant laughed, long and rattling and punctuated by snarls of snot-laden coughs, and the court laughed with him. Even the Borders table, brunt of the criticism as they were, laughed, because they all remembered the rules now.

But the barbs caught deep in Flitch. He was the youngest of them but had long since left behind the mantle of childhood. Buried just below the surface of the King's honeyed words were the condescensions: Borders was not often invited to court, its children less so. Perhaps if the baron were stronger, more able, more profitable, more needed, his children would not lack this experience.

Flitch laughed along with the rest of the court at himself and his family, and somewhere deep down in his belly, a small fire grew bigger.

Idyll laughed too, though their eyes had grown cold and hard, and they stared their hatred at the King. Under the table, they reached out and held one of Flitch's hands, the squeeze of their long, thin fingers a comfort.

"I am sure," the King said, putting out a shaking hand to quiet the laughter, "the young nobles of the Borders house are still experiencing some shock after their near-disaster on the Sea this morning. It is a dangerous time to sail in so unguarded a way, Lord Baron. While the King's vessels are happy to protect all, I suggest you dig more deeply into your boundless wisdom before allowing your children to sail unprotected in such dangerous times."

The Borders Baron stilled as the King spoke, the only movement coming from the flare of his nostrils as he pulled in deep, steadying breaths. Without looking to his children, who were all staring hard at the table in front of them, the baron rose once again.

"My deepest apologies, Your Majesty, and my deepest thanks, too, for your never-ending protection and guidance."

He bowed his head before sitting down. And still he did not look at his children.

"It is right that we are speaking of Borders," the King continued, his smirk growing a little. "Ancestral protectors of the line between land and grass, *sentinels of the Sea.*"

Each of the baronies had begun with clearly divided responsibilities and places to manage: Rivers in charge of the waterways in and out of the Mainland, Paths in charge of roads and transportation on land, Halcyon in charge of the city itself, and Borders in charge of the land-Sea border. But the clear delineation between the baronies had evaporated over time as Rivers bought land for the lumber and Paths acquired its own sizable sailing fleet and Borders, according to Zim, moved into housing.

Those old roles were like clothes that no longer fit but had yet to be thrown out or given away, each carrying the memory of the person that had once worn them.

"These difficult times are sure to strain us all," Faineant continued. "We will, each one of us, need to add our strength to the whole. Because, loyal subjects of the crown, the situation is more dire than you know."

At that moment, Nab returned, appearing beside the King's throne with a thick book held in his hands.

"We have been looking through old texts of late, seeking wisdom from the past to guide us through to the future. And we have found prophecies troublesome indeed." Faineant gestured and Nab stepped forward, opening the book and holding it open for the King. "I read to you now from the collected writings of Laire, explorer of death and dismay, greatest of our prophets."

Faineant bent to the book and began reading.

> *When the Sea blooms red with heated flame,*
> *And fell sails clot the horizon's line,*
> *Then rise, defenders of land and sky,*
> *For come those Few, Supplicant children returning,*
> *Let crown lead, heed kingly advice, else land with Sea will burn.*

Nab stepped back and closed the thick book with a sharp *snap* while King Faineant lifted his head to consider the court. Gasps sounded from around the court, a few of the petty nobles standing in their messy groups in front of the throne, and, notably, the Rivers Baron herself, Cantria Shade, lank hair hanging to her jaws, eyes wide in shock and dismay.

"Yes," Faineant said, nodding at Cantria, his face creasing into worry. "The prophecy is clear to those who can read it. Seas on fire, ancient adversaries sailing entire—what is this moment if not the fulfillment of Laire's promise?"

"Is it truly the Supplicant Few, my King?" Cantria said, rising from her chair, reedy voice piping high in concern.

King Faineant did not chastise the Rivers Baron for speaking out of turn as he had Flitch and his family. Instead, he let her words fall into the silence of the court like seeds that burst wide in the imaginations of everyone present.

"What?" Flitch whispered, although so quietly as to make almost no noise. The Supplicant Few were a bedtime story Idyll used to tell him. Five sailors who got fed up with life on the Mainland, and so they set off to find the edge of Forever. In some of Idyll's tellings, the Few would land in a place run by animals who could talk and sing. In others, they were lost at Sea or devoured by wyrms. When they really wanted to scare Flitch, they would tell a version in which the Supplicant Few found a land almost exactly like the one they had left, except everyone there wore blindfolds and spoke in riddles. The story would end with one of the Supplicant Few reaching out to pull down a blindfold and finding horrors beneath it.

But that's all they were. Stories. Silly ones most of the time.

So, why were the adults in the room acting as though their own shores were on fire?

"It is indeed the Few," King Faineant said, nodding soberly. "My own loremasters have checked and rechecked the prophecy, cross-referencing it in the most reliable tomes, and the answer is clear. What we have seen are signs of certain doom, each frightening in its own right but nothing when set against the true threat. The Supplicant Few are returning, and the Mainland must rise in defense, unified and strong.

"To this end, we have conscripted those pirates who were willing to join the crown's cause. We have taken their vessels and will use their might against all who would stand in our way."

A horrified gasp hissed through the room as those present imagined pirates sailing along in their fleets. While pirates were a regular plague on Arcadian grasses, they were lacking closer to the Mainland, so they existed only as myths and stories to most sailors. Blackened hearts and pus-filled eyes; vessels that burned captains alive for their fuel and sails knitted together from human skin; casters of impossible cunning and inhuman strength; captains more evil than any villain or wretch known in the wider world.

At the Borders table, though, they gasped at a different meaning in the King's words: a pirate armada absorbed into his own and set loose on *all who would stand in our way*. There was that faux-communal usage again. While many in that room heard the King to say these pirates would attack all who stood against the Mainland, Flitch and his family heard something different, something truer: the pirates would attack all who stood against the King.

Faineant let his gaze wander the room before landing on the Borders table.

"So, too, do we call upon the Borders barony, traditional defenders of the Sea. Borders Baron, your King asks you now to throw the whole of your might into our defenses. My ships have saved us from the fire—and saved your ilk from the deeps this very morning—but with your sizable fleet aiding us, we might save our people from a greater danger yet."

A sick twist pulled in Flitch's stomach. Something was wrong there but he couldn't quite find it. The King was asking for their help—a great honor any other time, and more so when it floated to them on such sweet, airy praise.

But Faineant looked as though he'd landed the final blow in a game of psalmers and was savoring the realization washing over his opponent's face.

Flitch's father stood, his back straight, face flushed behind his dark, thick beard. He was angry, Flitch could tell that much, his hands flexed into tight fists behind his back.

"As the King commands," the baron said, bowing slightly. "Borders will join you in defense."

King Faineant's smile was a near-sneer.

"Very good. Let the other barons remain ready to pledge similar service should it be required. My councillor, Nab, shall join you, Borders Baron, to ensure our fleets might work best together, each bringing our own *special* talents."

King Faineant winked once, and with that, the meeting was dismissed.

The silence as the storyteller pauses is restful, and already those listening have begun to doze, hands clasped over bellies, feet splayed toward the fires, limp and relaxed. The story is no longer a spectacle held in front of them but a path they are walking together.

They have begun to listen *with* the storyteller, watching and hearing the story he is telling as if it were a fire around which they all sat, a growing, wild thing, giving heat and comfort, stealing breath. These people—Kindred and Flitch, Ragged Sarah and Jest, Awn and Idyll and all the rest—they have begun to populate the minds of those listening, and the inhabitants of Twist have constructed the story around them, each person dreaming the tale in vivid colors and wild shouts, constructing Sea and sky in their minds, drawing the smooth lines of a cheek or chin with their imaginations.

Even as they have begun to forget the teller of it, they have taken a hand in building the story itself, each in their own way, even the children. Especially them.

A few, though, resist the magic of the story and the lull of the telling.

Two men, lovers with the happy glow of their own story still upon them, sit close together and whisper small truths to one another, giggling and grinning, unaware of the quietude that has descended on the other listeners.

A child on the cusp of adulthood sits with her back straight, staring off into the darkness. The storyteller can see her past as though it were written on her face and hands. A mother taken by predatory vines growing along their home. A father who fell from one of the grass bridges while his only daughter watched, her hand gripping so tight to the braided railing that it would leave marks on her palm for days. She thinks of her parents every day, every moment, her thoughts swilling violently around and naming the world around her "enemy." The dark, the Sea, this world and everything in it—she will set herself against them until they overcome her.

Praise, too, is untouched by the story, as he was on the last visit. His mind is consumed entirely by the storyteller. How long can they keep him imprisoned? Will the storyteller try to escape? To break out?

But Praise has grown clever in his old age, and a suspicion has grown from a hard seed at the back of his skull into a bright, blooming flower.

He thinks: *Certainly, others have tried this. Those other communities visited by the storyteller are not fools, and they must have tried to keep this relic of safety by any means.*

He wonders: *Why did they fail?*

Praise meets the storyteller's eyes and feels, for the first time, real fear prickle his skin.

What have we imprisoned?

The storyteller smiles at Praise, and there is nothing human, nothing kind, nothing good left in the expression.

I have chosen correctly, the storyteller thinks, holding Praise's eyes for a moment too long.

Deep in the darkness beyond Twist, well beyond the range of hearing, something is nearing, and the storyteller can feel its pleasure growing with each step closer.

Long past, the storyteller found dread and terror in this part of the cycle, but now he finds a kind of solidity in it. Stability in the repetition. Soon the forgetting. Soon the arrival. Soon the taking.

And soon the leaving.

"Kindred below and Flitch above," the storyteller says, letting his voice thrum again with power, his skin aglow. "Both experiencing courtly life in a different way, and each contending with the loss of one world and the too-fast arrival of another. So much forgetting, and so little remembering. The longest story. Perhaps the only story."

He steps down from the dais, walking with slow, measured steps among the listeners, most of whom take no notice of him. Even those who have resisted the gravity of the story until now find their muscles sluggish and weak, bodies fallen under the spell even if their minds have not.

Praise watches the storyteller, concerned, but his muscles have also grown sluggish and weak, and though he tries to stand, tries to speak, perhaps to tell the storyteller to return to the dais, to not walk so freely among these people, to remember who is in charge—though Praise tries to act upon his world, he cannot.

"We tell stories of change," the storyteller says, looking around at his drowsing audience. "Which is to say: we tell stories of hope. Let us trace the changes now and find hope where we may."

The storyteller, who stopped changing in any real way a long, long time before, lifts his eyes from the people of Twist to the darkness beyond.

CHAPTER SIX

None spoke until they had emerged from the castle's darkness into the early-afternoon air. Flitch was starving, having not touched any of the food or drink arranged on their table.

The guards had run ahead to get their horses, and they were ready as the Borders party emerged, each of them clinging tightly to their silence. Petty nobility dispersed around them, most heading out into the city to the nearest tavern to dissect and analyze the contents of the council they had just witnessed, though some were most likely racing to find the nearest news-shouter to sell their information at a premium price. When information was your primary export, you needed to move fast to sell.

Unsurprisingly, Aster was the first to speak when they had reached their horses and were far enough away from anyone else to be heard.

"Well, that was a cow-shit council," she said, stepping into one stirrup and rising up onto her horse's back with ease. She had always been comfortable riding, second only to Idyll, who seemed most at home astride a horse.

"Indeed," Zim said, the creases of his forehead making a map of his frustration.

"A cow-shit council run by the Mainland's biggest, dumbest cow," Idyll said, moving so fluidly and easily onto their horse's back that they seemed to simply fly up.

Flitch cast a worried glance at their father, who had said nothing as they stood and left their table, not even returning the quiet greetings from friendly nobles and merchants.

He spoke now, his voice low and restrained and furious.

"*Enough*," he said, the clench of his jaw somewhat obscured by the morass of his thick beard. His eyes were hard as he looked around at them.

"Father—" Aster began, but she swallowed the rest of her words when she saw the baron's face.

"You lied to me," he said simply. "When you told me of your trip down to the dock this morning, you left out the part where you took a ship and sailed out into the harbor. Where did you go?"

The siblings looked between themselves, searching for and not finding the one brave enough to speak.

"*Where?*" their father said between gritted teeth.

"The Paths dock," Flitch said finally. It had been his idea, his attempt at re-braiding those connections that had so long before begun to fray. "We wanted to hear the news from the ships coming in."

"And you couldn't wait? You couldn't ask our own captains? You couldn't even ask me whether it was a good idea to sail to Paths this morning?"

"You would've said no," Aster said, cutting in.

"And what a good decision that would have been," the baron said, rounding on her. "It might have saved me finding out from that supposedly dumb cow that my own children were almost killed this morning! You didn't think to even warn me that you were leaving. Not a word, not a whisper—nothing."

"You were downstairs," Idyll said. "It was a stupid, rash decision. We know that. We might have told you, but you were . . . busy."

The baron opened his mouth, the fury still in his eyes, but he said nothing, and after a moment, he took a breath. And then another.

"Tell me what happened."

In broken, fragmentary snatches, each of them dancing awkwardly around the central, childish reason for their going in the first place, the siblings told the story of their morning.

By the time they had finished, most of the minor nobles and assorted moneyed persons had cleared out of the courtyard, leaving the great, open space eerily quiet and still.

The baron spoke little during the telling of the story, and now he glanced around at them all, one hand plunged into his beard to find his chin in the depths. He did not look happy, but Flitch knew his father well enough to see that this was a cantankerousness tinged with humor. A set, frowning mouth juxtaposed with an arched, wry eyebrow.

They would be okay. It would be okay.

"Don't ever do something that dangerous or stupid again without telling me first," the baron said finally.

The siblings nodded and mumbled their contrite agreement.

"And don't ever make Zim sail again."

More nodding, this time accompanied by quick, bright smiles.

"And if you find yourself in a situation where you can go down heroically or be saved by the King's ships, think of your poor father and take the dive."

That elicited some chuckles, and soon they were all laughing together, the madness of the morning not forgotten, and perhaps only starting to be forgiven, but worked into the reality of their lives. This was the quiet grace their father had always offered—a feeling that the world would go on regardless of whatever messes they had made, whatever incidental or intentional errors they'd created, whatever sadness or tragedy that had occurred.

Struggling to get astride his own horse, a spotted mare, Flitch said, "Can someone tell me what is going on with the King and that stuff at the end of his speech, please?"

"King Faineant is beginning the long, laborious process of fucking us, Flitchy," Aster said, her voice bitter and ugly.

"Aster," the baron said, frowning at his daughter's language before turning to Flitch. "But . . . she's not wrong. The King has long hoped to consolidate the power of the baronies under his own crown, and he's finally found a situation dire enough to do it. This is the first step of the dissolution of our individual power; make no mistake."

"But . . ." Flitch looked around, feeling even more confused now, as though he couldn't a hear a song everyone else could and was trying to imagine it from the tapping of their feet and bobbing of their heads. "But the Supplicant Few are just a story! They're not real!"

His siblings gave Flitch uneasy looks, and even the baron could only shake his head.

"They're not just a story," Idyll said finally. "I used to tell you the first part of their story before bed because you liked it and it was fun, and I would change the ending to make it scary or magical. When you were little, you only wanted to hear stories about adventurous sailors doing the impossible and never returning."

Flitch nodded at that. He remembered that boy, could feel himself again in those knobbed elbows and knees drawn tight to his body, the weightless excitement of listening to Idyll describe such adventure and wonder.

They arrived at the end of the Sea, Idyll used to say at the end of the story, *to find a deathless city filled with every plant and animal that had ever existed or ever would. They, too, became immortal and spent the remainder of their days worshipping the world they loved.*

"But the story is based on truth. I've seen the documents in my time at the Rose," Idyll said, looking around at the few nobles still standing about, some staring at the Borders group. "In the actual story, the Supplicant Few gain enough power to lay waste to the city at the end of the Sea. The people there, they find, are just like those they left behind—no concern for the Sea or nature. They kill some, and the rest they transform into mindless, powerless worshippers in their new faith. The Supplicant Few make the population of that city into nothing more than eyes to see the world and ears to hear it, a congregation for the majesty of the Sea."

"I can see why you didn't tell me," Flitch said, shaking his head even as he felt that same thrill of excitement at hearing Idyll tell a story. It was what they were best at, shaping the world around them into a tale to be told.

"That's not the end of it," Idyll said. "We have little scraps of evidence, some of it from Laire himself, that say the Supplicant Few are waiting on the other side of the Sea for a sign that they should return home and right the wrongs of this place. When that comes, they will make a bridge over the Sea and bring their justice back to the Mainland."

Flitch felt his mouth open as if he would speak, but no words came out for a long moment.

"But prophecies aren't always accurate, right?" he said finally, clinging to the last bit of sanity that he could.

"Some aren't, and some are," the baron said, nodding. "And although Laire has always been the most trustworthy of the old prophets, this one seems terribly convenient for Faineant. I'm sure some in that room believed what he said completely, and it's certainly possible the prophecy is accurate, but I don't think so. I think he's using it as a cover to take over the baronies."

Idyll was nodding too, although their eyes were far away, lost in some thought.

"I can't be sure without checking, but I've read most of Laire's work—

his treatises and poetic inventions as well as his prophecies," Idyll said, still staring off, as though peering at the shelves of their library off in the distance. "He has a very distinctive style, and the prophecy Faineant read contained almost none of that. None of the inversions, no asyndetic coordination, not even the parataxic remediation. It also had—"

"Yes, yes, the book stuff tells us what we already know," Aster said, cutting in with a wave of her hand at Idyll. "Faineant is using a false prophecy for his own purposes. You don't have to show off to prove it."

Idyll stared at Aster until the irony of her statement became clear.

"So, he's just—" Flitch began, but his father put a hand out to silence him.

"I agree, my son," he said, speaking just loud enough to let Flitch know they were not alone anymore. "The King is certainly wise in his assessment."

Ravel, emissary of the Paths Baron, stepped into their circle, looking small since the rest of them were already on their horses and he still afoot, though if he felt unease, he showed no sign of it. His eyes moved slowly across the members of their party, including the Borders guards, in casual assessment. One of his hands rested on the handle of a throwing knife, one of the many in his bandolier.

"Greetings to the sentinels of the Sea," Ravel said.

"Greetings, walker of the Paths," Flitch's father said, nodding at him. "We were just about to ride for home. We have much to arrange if we are to help prepare the defenses as the King has asked."

"I understand," Ravel said, his eyes holding the baron's for a moment with a look that said he did, indeed, understand what had just happened. "If it's not too much of an inconvenience, I have been asked to accompany you back to the Borders estate."

Ravel removed that same bit of paper from which he'd read his prepared statement and held it out to the baron. Flitch angled forward on his horse to read it around his father.

Let the boy ride home with you, please. He's shit on a horse, so be careful.

Flitch looked down at Ravel, who was smiling pleasantly at them. This was the same sheet he'd read from to deliver his statement from Paths to the court. Flitch was sure of it. But as the baron turned it over, apparently thinking along the same lines, the paper revealed itself to be empty of any other text, official or not. On the back, someone had left a few multicolored smudges, like a child's painting, done with grubby fingers and wild, uncoordinated ambition.

"All right, then," the baron said, one eyebrow raised as he handed the paper back to Ravel. "Do you have your own horse?"

———◆———

"So, tell us how you two got to know each other," Aster said, leaning forward in the saddle and looking between Idyll and Ravel. The baron rode just a little ahead with his guards, having a quiet, terse conversation.

"Yeah," Flitch said, edging his horse forward a little. "I'm also very curious about the nature of your relationship."

Idyll and Ravel, for their parts, had studiously avoided one another's eyes and rode on opposite ends of the party, speaking little save for noncommittal murmurs or grunts.

But what is the role of siblings if not to take the secrets of one another and bring them, wailing like babies, out into the sunlight?

"We—" Idyll began as Ravel said, "They—"

Both stopped, meeting and then dropping the other's gaze before falling silent.

A baker stood at the window of his shop as they passed, calling out the breads he was offering, and Flitch felt his stomach churn and groan with hunger.

"Ravel and I," Idyll said, still keeping their eyes forward, "have worked together occasionally at the Rose. We have similar interests in the various archives there."

Ravel, who proved Gwyn quite right and rode his horse awkwardly, watched Idyll with a mixture of confusion and humor. After a long moment of silence, he said, "Yes. We both like reading."

The look on Aster's face had moved from glee to pure wickedness, and she nodded as she looked between them.

"Hi, I'm Zim o' the Borders," Zim said, leaning over to shake Ravel's hand, completely missing the tenor of the conversation. "It's nice to officially meet you."

Ravel nearly fell as he reached for Zim's hand, but he managed to steady himself at the last moment. On foot, Ravel had moved like a wraith, silent and quick and easy. On horse, he sat like a stone, stiff and promising a fall.

"You, too," Ravel said, his hands tight on the reins. "I hadn't expected our first meeting to involve lying for you to gain entrance to the Paths docks."

His words might have been cutting, but Ravel softened them with an easy smile and a roll of his shoulders.

"Sorry again about that," Flitch said. "And thanks for letting us in."

Ravel nodded, as if it had been nothing, a small favor for favored friends, easy as a late-morning sail on calm grasses.

"We're all very thankful and grateful and sorry," Aster said. "But I want to know how long have you two been—" She paused, letting the brief silence and the licentious waggling of her eyebrows do the work of conveying her meaning. "Reading books together?"

"Oh, shut up, Aster," Idyll snapped, leaning over to swat at Aster, who had already nudged her steed out of reach amid the swarm of her cackling.

Flitch waved at Ravel while Idyll and Aster chased one another through the street, their abilities at riding on full display as they wove their steeds through the congested street, one screaming her laughter out, the other murmuring indistinct violence.

"Siblings," Flitch said with a shrug and an apologetic smile.

"This is normal for siblings?" Ravel asked, turning to Flitch as Idyll and Aster passed out of sight and the sounds of their dispute melded with those of the city.

"It's normal for our siblings," Zim said, pushing his steed—a chestnut stallion he'd named Pebbles for the spots of white on his flank—up to the other side of Ravel. "Those two are always poking at one another."

"Idyll did mention something once about their sister being . . ." Ravel began before stopping, maybe realizing he was speaking out of turn.

"A massive pain in the ass?" Flitch offered.

"A torturer of the innocent?" Zim suggested.

"A lovable, ill-behaved psychopath?" Flitch tried again.

"The world's worst, most chaotic ally?" Zim ventured.

"Complicated," Ravel said, looking between Flitch and Zim as if he couldn't tell if they were joking.

"You could put it that way, too," Flitch said, grinning broadly. "Anyway, we're just surprised. Idyll hasn't said anything about having a . . ."

He left the end of the sentence hanging in front of them, hoping Ravel might fill it in, but he sucked in a breath between clenched teeth, shaking his head.

"Library friend," Zim said, pulling at the stiff neck of his shirt with one hand. "Idyll didn't make any mention of having a new library friend."

"They're so private," Ravel said, shaking his head again. "It took more than half a year of seeing them almost every day just to get them to join me for a meal, and then another handful of spans to hear anything about their family."

Some of the excitement drained away from Flitch. Idyll had been seeing this man for most of a year? And they hadn't said anything about it to him? Aster and Zim he would understand—Idyll had never been as close with them. But his relationship with Idyll was different. At least, he'd thought it was.

"They talk about you three all the time, you know," Ravel said, misreading Flitch's silence as concern for their discussions. "Aster and her casting. Zim and his bookkeeping. Flitch and his plans to save the whole family. The baron and his hard work, too. And . . . your mother."

Ravel stopped and Flitch was glad for it. Even Zim, who could be thick as stone when it came to the emotional color of a moment, looked away. Their mother, Amain Windress, Lady of the Borders, hung heavy on all of their shoulders.

"I'm sorry about her passing," Ravel said, catching Flitch's eyes for a moment before looking down. "She sounds like a wonderful person."

"The best," Zim said, staring blankly ahead.

Flitch opened his mouth to respond but was saved by the return of Idyll and Aster, one looking grumpy, the other chastised. No mention was made of their antics.

"Hello, Ravel," Aster said after a moment, her tone carefully neutral, holding out one hand. "It's very nice to meet you."

"Your hands are just like Gwyn's," Ravel said, looking down as he shook Aster's hand. "Burn scars all over."

Aster pulled her hand back, speechless for the first time in recent memory.

"Idyll told me about your fourth ring," Ravel continued, his eyes flicking to Idyll for confirmation or encouragement. Idyll, however, was looking straight ahead, apparently oblivious to the entire conversation. "Congratulations," Ravel finished with a small smile.

"Thank you," Aster said, eyes narrowing. They were reaching the out-skirts of the new city now, and she took the opportunity to guide her horse off the road proper, taking advantage of the new space and fixing Ravel with a calculating look. "You seem to know a lot about us."

"Too much," Zim said, nodding seriously.

"We probably shouldn't let you live," Flitch finished, the joke arising in him almost automatically. This was a script and role he knew well, and it felt good to fall into it.

"Leave him be," Idyll said, frowning over at their siblings before look-ing at Ravel. "Just ignore them. They're starved for attention."

"You owe a debt," Flitch said, nudging his horse up to place himself between Ravel and Idyll, blocking their view of one another. "You know all about us, but we know nothing of you."

"Well said, dear brother." Aster clucked disapprovingly. "Such things cannot be borne."

"Imbalance is the father of failure," Zim said, echoing one of the guid-ing principles of the Borders bookkeepers, who wrought balance and or-ganization out of the chaos of Border's finances and operations.

"Just—" Idyll began, but Aster, after flashing a questioning look at Idyll, searching their face for a moment to make sure all was still in good fun, held up a hand.

"Our dear sibling, eldest among us and most respected, cannot simply become . . ." She stopped, looking around for the correct term.

"Library friends," Flitch supplied grimly.

"*Library friends*," Aster continued, speaking the words as though they tasted better than any sweet she'd ever had in her mouth. "Our eldest sib-ling cannot simply become library friends with any prairie dross blown in from the Sea."

"No offense, of course," Zim added.

"No, no," Aster said, holding up her hands in mock worry. "It's not that we believe you to be below our sibling's rank or requirement! It's simply that we don't know anything about you, and our deep love for Idyll bids us be protective."

"For their own good, you understand," Flitch said, frowning as though this were a hard but important truth.

"Idyll," the baron said from ahead, turning to the eldest sibling and ges-turing for them to join him.

"I hate each and every one of you," Idyll said, looking between the siblings before turning their gaze to Ravel. "I'm sorry for them. If they get out of hand, you have my permission to kill them. Slowly."

They rode ahead, casting a final look back before joining the baron and his guards in conversation.

Aster threw an arm around Ravel's big, muscular shoulders.

"Idyll promised they'd let a jarful of spur bugs loose in my room at school if I told any stories of their childhood or made any reference to your, umm, *reading activities*." She smiled and looked at Zim and Flitch. "But that just means we have plenty of time to get to know you."

Ahead of them, the Borders estate was a pile of stones on a distant hilltop.

━━━◆━━━

Between the edge of the city and the steps of the Borders estate, Flitch learned much about Ravel.

He was the head of the Paths guards and accompanied the baron—whom he called only "Gwyn"—wherever she went. He was twenty-two, three years younger than Idyll, had no immediate family, lived at the Paths estate as a kind of adopted child of Gwyn Gaunt. His primary jobs were gardening, taking care of Gwyn's dog, whose name was Adventure, and accompanying Gwyn to the few events she actually attended.

He seemed at ease talking with them, only occasionally bowled over by Aster's persistent questions or the game of concerned siblings that they were all playing.

"I always wanted siblings," Ravel said as they all cantered up to the Borders house. "When Idyll said they had two brothers and a sister, I was jealous."

"Don't be," Aster said, dismounting with careless ease. "Siblings are more trouble than they're worth."

But Flitch caught the slant of her smile as she turned away, and felt himself grinning, too. The complaints they sometimes threw at one another, the bitter fights and joyful celebrations, the annoyance bred by proximity and the sadness bred by distance—different melodies in a hymn about love.

As they approached the house, Idyll detached from the conversation they'd been having with their father, and though their smile came easily enough as they rejoined the siblings and Ravel, Flitch could see something uneasy in their face. Trouble moved in their eyes, and Flitch wondered what the baron had told them.

The door to the Borders estate—old, thick wood dulled by time and use—swung open, and Flitch looked to see which of the servants would emerge to greet them.

Only it was not one of the Borders workers who stepped out into the thick afternoon sunlight.

It was not someone from Borders at all.

Gwyn Gaunt, the Paths Baron, stepped out of the Borders house with a cup of steaming tea in one hand, looking as if she were emerging from her own home, coming out to greet the day and welcome visitors. She was small, short, and waifish, with too-big eyes set in a narrow, well-lined face.

Idyll had told Flitch once that the Paths Baron was not actually as old as she looked; as a child she drank a potion made by a wandering herbalist that had given her great wisdom at the expense of aging her prematurely.

Despite managing an area on the other side of Halcyon, the capital, Gwyn Gaunt kept her house beside the Sea, just down the coast from the Borders estate, conveniently located next to the very docks Flitch and his siblings had visited that morning. The Paths and Borders estates were close enough to be neighbors, and yet Flitch had never really known Gwyn Gaunt. Each time he'd seen her, the Paths Baron had been far too still for his liking, often saying nothing to the rest of the assorted party regardless of their rank or status, her wide brown eyes settling on whoever was speaking with unblinking intensity.

Once though, when Flitch was in attendance with his father, who had needed to drop some items by the Paths estate, they had encountered Gwyn Gaunt on her way out, and she had looked away from his father, who had been talking about trade or shipping or some adult thing, and winked at Flitch before returning her wide-eyed gaze back to the baron.

The stories about her were myriad: a caster of unmatched ability, so efficient at drawing power from burning plants that with even a tiny blaze and the smallest flower petal she could devastate entire groups of armed warriors. A gardener so skilled at her arts that even the captains of harvesting vessels coveted what she could grow in the secret fields behind her estate. A leader who came to power by poisoning her father, by pushing her mother off a ship, by burying both her parents alive and tilling her garden over their tombs, by being the only one of her siblings capable of passing an arcane test her father had given her, by besting a roomful of Paths warriors in unarmed combat, by drawing enough power from a burning wreath of blue gramma to light a room in the Paths estate for nine entire days, meting out the magic of the plant in a steady, golden glow.

The stories couldn't all be true, of course, but the bones of them certainly could be: Gwyn Gaunt was a mystery; Gwyn Gaunt was powerful; Gwyn Gaunt endured.

And yet here was the Paths Baron, tiny and unassuming, a wide smile lighting her face as she waved at them hard enough to spill tea down her front.

"Oh, piss," she muttered, flinging the cup into the grass and holding her robes away from her body.

"Paths Baron," Flitch's father said by way of greeting, favoring her with the same look of mild amusement he used with his children. "I had not looked to host you today, and I'm sorry to say you have caught us in a moment of urgency."

"Oh, yes, yes," Gwyn said, flipping a small, tanned hand at the baron, as if he and not she were the silly one. As if he, and not she, were standing with his robes pulled away, the herbal tea soaking deep and staining them brown. "You're very busy and important. But we two children of the crown, furthest from its warmth and light, have much to discuss, I think."

She spoke like the council of that afternoon and the power dynamics at play at court were a joke, one she found almost too funny for laughing.

"I expect we do," the baron said, "though our King has blessed Borders with a visit from his first whisperman, Nab, and my children and I must prepare for it. Perhaps you might have attended the King's meeting today if you wanted to discuss important matters."

"I wanted to take a nap instead," Gwyn said, dismissive.

Flitch let out a small, huffing laugh. Could she be serious? Ignoring the King's call to take a nap?

"He's going to get you eventually, Gwyn," the baron said, dropping finally his formal tone. "You can't continue to snub him so."

"Nonsense," she said, letting the robes fall back to her body for a moment before hissing and pulling them away again. "And if he's sending that sallow-skinned, fiery-haired, friendless weasel your way, it should be yourself you're worried about."

This time, Flitch wasn't the only one who laughed. He couldn't help himself. No one talked about Nab, the King's favored whisperman, like that. Not only because he commanded more power than most in the King's court but because it was his job to traffic in information, and he was sure to hear of someone speaking like that.

"You should not speak so ill of the King's honored—" the baron began, disapproving, but Gwyn cut him off again.

"He's a twit," she said, leveling a glare at the baron. "You and I both know it, and your kids know it too."

"A powerful twit," the baron conceded after a moment.

"Quite," Gwyn Gaunt said, smiling and nodding.

The morning had been full of confusions and concerns for Flitch, excitement burning away into anxiety, joy souring into fear, but this was strangest to him—his father and the mysterious Paths Baron talking like old friends, casual and easy. Flitch could see around his father's court mask, which meant he was letting it down for this woman, as if they were more than political acquaintances.

"I have much to do before we play host to this twit," the baron said, looking around at his kids. "We can speak but it must be quick. I can tell you briefly what happened at the council meeting."

"No, no," Gwyn said, shaking her head. "I've known what that fool was going to talk about for days. He's neither clever nor interesting. I want to talk about the real problem here."

Flitch became aware that his mouth was hanging slightly open as he listened, his wonder at Gwyn Gaunt only deepening with every word she said.

If the baron was surprised by Gwyn's statement, he showed no sign of it, only nodding and following her.

"Very well," he said. "As I understand it, the King is using a fake prophecy, through either complete fabrication or manipulation of something extant in Laire's work, to justify a takeover of the baronies and a consolidation of power. He will begin with Borders but will not stop there. Rivers is already under his power, which leaves only Paths to be conquered once he has fully taken over Borders. Nab's visit is the beginning of his efforts. And none of that even touches on the pirate armada Faineant has absorbed into his own fleet."

"A many-headed monster we face," Gwyn said, nodding, serious and focused despite the continued ridiculousness of her tea-soaked robes held out. "And you've said nothing of the Greys nor the creatures rising from below. But Faineant's petty political ambitions aren't the problem I'm talking about, and neither is the band of blackhearted villains he's recruited to his service."

Gwyn surveyed the group with her large, lamplike eyes.

"When I wish to kill a plant in my garden, I do not pull its flowers away one by one." She mimed plucking away the flowers meant to symbolize each of the threats. *Faineant's power grab. Pirates. The Greys. Nab. Creatures from below.*

"Instead, I go for the root, and though it may take some digging and some searching, I always find it."

Gwyn's hand plunged into the imaginary dirt in front of her and clasped around a root, which she viciously ripped free and tossed behind her.

"That," she said, smiling around at them, "was a lesson about gardening, which is to say life, which is to say gardening."

The baron frowned, his thick eyebrows stretching toward his beard and threatening to cover the whole of his face in dark hair.

"And what is the root we should be seeking, Gwyn?"

She let out a short, bright laugh and said, "I have no idea."

The baron's response was a weary laugh of his own, and Flitch had the distinct impression, shocking and sudden, that his father and the storied, mythic Paths Baron were not just sometimes-allies or colleagues in the slow war with the crown but honest, actual *friends*.

First Idyll and now the baron—Flitch looked around at his family and wondered how many other lives they were leading, how many other friends and family they were finding and founding, how many paths they walked without him. They were like Gwyn's plants, and while he had been mistaking flowers for the plant, their roots had been growing deeper and further away from him, their stalks reaching away, budding and flowering elsewhere.

"I have some books that might give us some answers," Gwyn said, pulling at one earlobe and looking around thoughtfully. "And we need to make plans for dealing with the King's immediate threats. But you need to stay here to deal with the King's stooge."

She turned to survey the Borders kids, squinting at them one by one.

"Give me this one," she pointed a finger at Idyll.

"What?" Idyll and the baron said at the same time, the family resemblance playing out all the way down to the particular melody of their confusion.

"Not for keeps," Gwyn said, laughing and shaking her head. "Just for the evening, maybe a bit longer. You have to stay for Nab, and young Idyll here should learn the ways of speaking for a barony if they're ever going to lead it after you've passed along your title. Am I wrong?"

Flitch felt more than a little disappointment knocking around inside him. So many mornings and afternoons of his childhood had been spent playing in the fields around their house, oftentimes in full or partial view of the Paths estate and the strange, wondrous house that served as its center. The siblings might have spent hundreds of mornings wondering idly about the Paths Baron, swapping stories and speculating about her true origins, but they had spent just as many spinning their imaginations around the wheel of that house, creating richer and richer fictions about it. Rooms filled with fantastical monsters chained in gold and silver links. Hallways that curved gently down into the earth and terminated in doors without locks or handles. Fountains that dribbled gems and demanded sacrifices.

Idyll used to tell Flitch stories at bedtime of the great labyrinth inside the Paths estate, ways and tunnels littered with magical impossibilities, caverns filled with rushing winds and whispering ghosts. And along the paths of this labyrinth, Idyll would say as Flitch snuggled deeper under his covers, walks a creature more terrifying than any other alive or dead. Older than time and capable of magical feats that made the casters of old look like children in comparison, this creature—nameless, faceless, empty of all but a strange, inhuman curiosity—moved among the labyrinth, seeking others with whom it might make a bargain. Perhaps it would offer immortality for the lives of everyone a person had loved. Perhaps it would offer riches in exchange for a person's dreaming. Perhaps love in exchange for hope.

Or perhaps it would simply take without giving, its actions governed by a higher, stranger logic.

Many of the stories Idyll had told Flitch grew fuzzy over time, losing their distinct edges and moments, but these stories—the ones of the labyrinth that sprawled across one floor of the Paths estate—were bright and crisp in Flitch's mind because they were the stories Idyll told him after their mother died, and for many days, Idyll would tell no other tales. Flitch and his oldest sibling, his oldest *friend*, both mourned their mother in those stories, softening the blow of her leaving in those strange rooms and infinitely long hallways, in the slow step of an ageless creature who might give, who might take, and who might act senselessly.

"Stories are the world's way of explaining itself to us," Idyll had once told him, the moonlight glowing gently against one side of their face. *"All we can do is listen and hope to hear its voice behind the words."*

"I'm not sure that's a good idea," the baron said. "I had hoped Idyll would be here to . . . help with Nab."

"Oh, you'll be fine," Gwyn said, letting the stretch of her robes fall finally back to her skin. She hissed and said, "It's cold now."

"What do you think?" the baron said, turning to Idyll, who had gone still and thoughtful. They looked first to Ravel and then, surprisingly, to Flitch before answering.

"They'll be okay without me," Idyll said, turning to the baron. "I can go with the baron and help however I can. She's right that I should learn to speak for the barony at some point. Why not now?"

"There we go!" Gwyn said, clapping her hands before turning to Ravel, her face going suddenly serious. "This isn't a romantic interlude for you two. It's all business right now; do you understand?"

Ravel, who had not flinched even a bit at any of Gwyn's antics or sudden shifts in conversational direction up to that point, choked on the air in his lungs at this and spent a long moment coughing, his face blotchy and red once he could finally breathe again.

"Understood," he said finally, his eyes flicking between Gwyn and his own feet.

"Wonderful," Gwyn said, turning to Idyll. "Can I ride back with you? Riding with him is like courting death."

"Of course," Idyll said, eyes flicking between Ravel and Gwyn, their alarm at the mention of their relationship fading.

"Idyll, a moment," the baron said, pulling Idyll away to have a quiet, whispered conversation.

Which left Flitch, Aster, and Zim standing in silence with Ravel and Gwyn Gaunt. Aster kicked at a rock near her feet.

"What do you think they're talking about?" someone whispered beside him, and Flitch was surprised to see it was Gwyn, who had taken a few steps closer to him without a sound. Her head was cocked to one side as she watched Idyll and the baron speaking.

"I . . . I'm . . ." Flitch had never felt more off balance in his life.

Gwyn regarded him for a moment before patting his arm gently.

"You're Flitch," she said, her voice kind. She leaned even closer, and Flitch felt the strain in his back as he arched away. "Nice sailing this morning, by the way. That was excitement worthy of the Laughing Queen herself."

If Flitch had struggled to speak before, he was completely speechless now. Gwyn gave him a wink before stepping back, just as the baron finished his conversation with Idyll.

"Ravel, we're leaving now," she said without preamble. "Let's go, Idyll. I want to ride ahead of Ravel. It's embarrassing to watch him ride."

"Of course," Ravel said, nodding and turning to the siblings. "It was great to meet you three. I hope we can talk more soon."

"Oh, there'll be time for that during the wedding planning and afterward," Gwyn said with a wave of one hand and not a hint of a smile despite the levity of her tone. She turned to the remaining Borders kids.

"Downy painted cup," she said, her wide, bright eyes moving between the three of them, holding their gaze one at a time for what seemed just too long to be comfortable. "The stems grow hairs so white and fine that they look to be covered in ash. Do you know it?"

Flitch, who thought he couldn't be any more surprised by the Paths Baron, said, "Yes."

"He doesn't," Aster said, frowning over at Flitch, who was still wondering why he'd spoken at all. "But I do."

"You do," Gwyn said, as if this were the answer she'd been looking for. She reached into her robes and pulled out three cut stems of a plant, presumably the one she'd mentioned. Its flowers were a series of spiking blooms, soft green lined by white, yellow, and currents of muted red, all covered in the soft, ashy hair.

She gave one to each of them.

"The downy painted cup is a parasite," the baron said, still speaking with grave seriousness. "A hairy, beautiful visitor that clings to native prairie plants. It works in secret, strange ways and only for itself."

"Burns like a rock, too," Aster said, holding up the plant Gwyn had given her. "Can't cast with it for shit."

"Yes," Gwyn said, smiling broadly now, as though Aster had said the most amazing thing she'd ever heard. "That's exactly right. It's useless, malicious, and startling to see. And, ultimately, from the correct perspective, powerless. Let's all reflect on this, shall we?"

Flitch nodded, with no idea what he was agreeing to or what had just happened, but spelled by Gwyn's voice and presence. She riddled with every word, and the shadow of her mystique spread, and he was happily, completely lost in it.

"Let's go, you besotted bump," she said to Ravel, raising one eyebrow to him as she turned toward home. "The roses need tending, and your future family needs to prepare for their guest."

The Paths Baron left, already chatting amiably with Idyll, who gave them all a smile and a wave before following. Ravel followed just behind them.

"What just happened?" Flitch asked, turning to his siblings.

"She's incredible," Aster said, staring after her.

"Incredibly odd, maybe," Zim said, looking down at the spear of downy painted cup in his hand. "What am I supposed to do with this?"

"I think it's a metaphor," Flitch said, peering at his own.

"I hate metaphors," Zim said, dropping his on the ground as he got down from his horse and handed the reins to one of the stable workers. "Why can't people just say what they think?"

"No appreciation for the finer arts," Aster said, looking at Zim with disgust, following him into the house.

Inside, the baron turned to his remaining children, his face serious and uneasy.

"We will need to be on our guard during his stay. The King has sent his cleverest spy to stay with us. I want him to get *nothing* while he is here. Do you understand?"

The siblings exchanged looks and nodded, knowing exactly what his father was talking about.

What would Nab give to find the door to the Borders treasure below? What would King Faineant offer his most trusted weapon for such success?

"They won't get anything," Flitch said, trying to give his voice that same steel his father's had, the same steel he imagined in the voices of the heroes from Idyll's stories. Mila Cloud-Walker and the Rilenius Brothers and Lyza Rightwell and the Fiend Queen and all the rest—the titans who had peopled Flitch's imagination as a child, built up and given color by Idyll, made to move and fly and triumph by his own dreaming.

The baron nodded at his youngest child.

"Good. Get yourselves something to eat and then meet me downstairs at the arch."

<hr>

The first Borders Baron—Flitch's great-great-grandfather—had made his fortune after the Silent Men of Arcadia had given up their business of crafting the runic masts necessary for any ship on the Forever Sea. As the first whispers of the Silent Men's retreat began to permeate, Flitch's great-great-grandfather saw an opportunity and immediately bought up every library and archive he could find. Books in any and every language, scrolls and tablets and grass-sheaf texts and everything else. The only commonality was the age: every text he bought was ancient, often rescued from the bottom of long-forgotten chests or pulled down from dusty attics. The man who would be the Borders Baron bought it all and built for himself a stronghold on the edge—the Border—of the Mainland.

As his estate neared completion, the baron began filling its upper floors with his treasures, his builders barely able to put up the shelves before they were filled with strange and wondrous texts. The baron would stand in the empty shell of his home, the shouts of workers echoing against the stone and wood as they trundled about, carrying tools and lumber and stone and metal. And amid this chaos, the baron would read, poring over every new book and scroll, hunting for some sign or symbol that might be used to recreate the success of the Silent Men. Days and nights he worked in those unfurnished, incomplete rooms, whispering strange words to

himself or scratching curious symbols into wood to see if they might im-
bue the necessary magics.

The Silent Men had never taught their secrets to the world, and so the
baron hunted for their footsteps in the thousand thousand texts he had
begun to surround himself with, his eyes growing strained by too much
reading, his cheeks hollowing with too little food.

He brought in every shipbuilder he could find, every sailor with any
experience; he studied functioning masts, bought a few and brought them
back to examine in his hollow home, ignoring the constant work of the
builders around him.

But his studies led to only frustration. The runes were impossible to
replicate—the wood curled and shifted around them, the haze of bluish
light flickering like a living thing, and the baron would watch in rage as a
rune changed before his eyes once, twice, over and over, until he couldn't
say what it had been or had turned into.

Flitch's great-great-grandfather had been born into wealth, but he spent
much of it acquiring his estate and his archive—squandered, many said.
He began to fire servants, to sell his belongings—everything from ships
that had been in his family for generations to the beautiful, crafted furniture that he'd hoped to populate his home with after it was finished. Whispers of his failure began to seep around the edges of Halcyon, ugly, delighted
whispers at the impending dissolution of yet another of the great baronies.
The baron retreated further and further from society, spending more and
more time in the shell of his still-incomplete home. In the darkness, he
whispered ancient words to wood and stone and heard only his echo in
response—the builders long gone, pausing in their work until their pay
resumed.

One day, the talk in Halcyon changed. The mad baron of the Borders
had found something. He had discovered a way to mimic the power of the
Silent Men. They were not the same runes, but they worked. They shone
with other colors—greens as true as the Sea, yellows bright enough to
hurt—but the masts he had carved would keep a ship afloat, it was said.
The production of new vessels that had halted so thoroughly after the Silent Men closed their gates could suddenly begin again.

Shipbuilders and sailors and workers of all kinds held their breath in
anticipation. Even the monarchy sent a delegation out to the empty, unfin-

ished house at the edge of the Sea to discover whether there was any truth to the rumors.

Soon the news rang out, leaping from house to house, city to city, lip to lip: the Borders Baron had given the sailors of the world their Sea back. Production of new ships—each fitted with a set of Borders masts—resumed.

And so, too, did the work on the baron's house. He filled his empty home with furniture and family to use it, advisors to pace the halls, staff to work in the kitchens and stables, and messengers to walk the increasingly worn trail from the Borders estate to the castle.

Finally, the home was completed and the Borders barony had a seat of power and grandeur again, but when the baron went down to pay the final wages to the builders, he found their leader waiting anxiously outside for him, the tall, powerful man casting curiously frightened glances at the house.

"There's something you need to see," he told the baron, and wouldn't say more, just took Flitch's great-great-grandfather by the arm and walked back into the house, down the stairs to the huge, open basement, and down another set of stairs to the root cellar.

The foreman stepped past the rows of wine bottles and meats packed away in storage, his breath fogging the air slightly, and finally held out the torch he'd been carrying to show the baron what had been scaring him.

"We didn't put it in," the foreman said as the baron stepped forward and peered through the darkness. "We built these walls, the shelves, every bit of it. I was down here not a span ago and that wall was blank. And I come down here today for this last inspection and . . ."

He trailed off, his voice becoming a whisper.

An archway had been cut into the wall, rough and lined with jagged stones embedded haphazardly around its edges, like broken teeth in a howling maw. It was uneven and crude, the stones of varying sizes but all wickedly sharp at their edges, thinning to points of glittering translucence.

Across the top of the arch, a large, flat stone had been wedged in among the others, its face strung with the accumulated spider webs and dust of centuries, and a single word carved there in a child's scrawling hand.

Sing.

Beyond the arch was darkness, thick and still. It might have been a small cavern or a huge theater; it might have extended out and down into the stone foundation, burrowing deeper and deeper until it reached the Sea, or its wall might have curved to a close just beyond the point where a fearful eye peering from the archway could see.

None of the workers, including the foreman, ever went inside, and none ever spoke of it. Instead, nightmares of that oily blackness beyond, of the rough, mouthlike cut of the arch plagued their sleep until they died.

Once the workers had left him alone in the house, the baron stepped through the archway.

Days later, he emerged and, without a word to the household staff who had begun to panic in his absence, the baron moved the whole of his archives into whatever lay beyond that archway, forbidding any to follow him and keeping the truth of its size and wonders to himself. Some claimed that he found a vast cavern there, always dark but full of impossible magics. Others said the baron met the ghosts of his past in that darkness and begged them for favors or forgiveness, for help in finding whatever other benefits his archives might hold for his fortunes.

The archway and the space beyond occupied his mind day and night, and soon he spent more time below than above. He would eschew afternoons outside in favor of the cool quiet below, hunting among his texts, perhaps, for some rune or phrase that might give a ship more stability, that might better catch or conjure the wind, that might grant speed or lift in endless amounts.

And when he did come back above, he talked in furtive, odd whispers of *below*, the darkness lit only by the floating pool of light cast by his torches. *A gift waits for Borders*, he would say. *A gift and a curse.*

He died down in the darkness below, but not before passing the secret to his children and wife, who, in turn, kept it, clutching tightly their family's new heirloom.

Each new generation of the Borders family found the story of their inheritance collecting in the corners of their minds like snow, gathering and growing from nothing, cold and beautiful. Each new generation learned of the archway, of the darkness beyond, and finally, when it was time, of the gift.

And always, the archway was a millstone hanging around the neck of Borders. A secret to be guarded, a shame to be hidden, a mystery to be avoided.

Flitch stood before the arch, his eyes tracing around its jagged edge before fixing on that single word shadowed with time's accumulated dust.

As kids, they'd snuck down to stare at it, catching glimpses around the tall cases that once contained fine wines and precious artifacts and now contained stacks of papers, carefully filled-in ledger books, stray coils of rope and folded sails. They hadn't dared to approach, both for fear of the guards standing watch at all hours of the day around it and also because of the archway itself.

It was cold and empty and dark and old—older than anything else in the house. And somehow, every time Flitch saw it, the archway seemed hungry, as though the rough, sharp stones lining it were stretching just so, widening out to consume him.

"Nab cannot find this," the baron said, putting his back to the archway, which was free of guards for the first time in Flitch's memory. "He cannot know it is here. He *cannot* step inside."

A pause as their father looked over the siblings, shaking his head slightly.

"Idyll should be here for this, but we can't wait. It's time for you to see."

Flitch sucked in a breath as goosebumps broke out over his skin in warm waves.

"What are the rules of court?" their father said, the words snapping out like a whip, at once familiar because of how often he had asked his kids to recite them and jarring, too, for his asking now, on the precipice of Flitch's *finally* knowing what lay beyond the arch.

"Do not laugh if the King is not laughing.

Do not find enjoyment in something the King does not enjoy.

When you enter a room at court, step first to your left and bow.

Do not speak unless the King asks you a direct question.

Do not speak to the King's whispermen, especially Nab, the one with long red hair.

If you must speak, speak only in sentences totaling an odd number of words.

Do not eat any food.

Do not drink anything.

Keep one hand hidden at all times."

The three siblings recited these together, their voices falling into a well-worn monotone.

"Good," their father said. "Remember these below."

And with that, the Borders Baron turned, picked up a torch from a stack beside the archway, lit it, and walked through, gesturing once for his kids to follow.

"It's finally happening," Aster whispered as she stepped forward, Zim mumbling something anxious and unintelligible behind her.

"Idyll should be here," Flitch said, echoing his father and feeling the pull of guilt. Idyll had dreamed of this with all of them, longer since they were the oldest.

Flitch followed in through the archway, shivering as he walked by the rough, jagged stone teeth that were finally devouring him.

CHAPTER SEVEN

Kindred told the whole of her story to the Lost Monarch's Traveling Court.

And why not? The world above felt like a past life, troubles and concerns and worries that she shed in the telling, a too-tight skin sloughing from her shoulders and knees and chin in opaque skeins.

It was like narrating a dream, one that had already begun to slip away. Cora and Captain Caraway and Little Wing, Mick and Cantrev and Morrow Laze and The Word—the people who populated her memory were still there, of course, but the events and the reasonings, the motivation for this or that, it was like smoke from a dying fire, expanding in the air until it became nothing at all.

In the telling, Kindred saw glimpses of a truth about herself, one that she had never known consciously but, in the discovering, found she had understood all along. It rang like a bell inside of her, the sound a tolling she had been hearing for a long time.

She saw herself as a young girl, left alone in the world by the death of her parents, sent to a grandmother she didn't know who lived in a part of the world she had never known, a life that forced a new present upon her.

She had become—or maybe she had always been—a smooth, perfect sphere, metal gleaming and untouched—untouchable—passing through her life, events and moments sliding across her, reaching with fingers that could find no purchase on her slippery surface. Leaving nothing of themselves behind. Forward was all she knew. Ahead, down, away—always movement, always.

Sarah was different—life stuck to her, memories and experiences left fingerprints on her skin, clung to the delicate span of her wrists and garlanded her shoulders. She had forsaken her home and her family and her past, had left it all behind, and still it clung to her, inflecting her words and resonating in her actions.

Awn, too, carried his past with him and in him.

As she told the story of the above world, and as she watched Sarah grimace at what they had left behind, Kindred felt a hollow where that past should have been. Absent were the hooks that memory and experience had so clearly buried in her crew.

Instead, Kindred felt only the pull of what lay ahead, the movement forward.

The Sea, infected and dying. The Marchess, somewhere below.

Sarah's life continued to change her; all she had known and experienced continued to work on her.

Kindred, though, felt that life had changed her once, finally and completely, and all else had been a slipstream passing by, unable to reach a heart buried so deep.

Sarah and Awn supplied what Kindred couldn't remember, and together they told the tale of *The Errant*, the fight for water, and a Forever Sea burning.

The Traveling Court were wonderful listeners. Jest gasped as Kindred described their first dive below the surface and laughed and held up her long braids in tribute to Captain Caraway's bravery and cunning. Madrigal clapped with joy when Sarah told of besting the wyrm, and even Wylf nodded his head and thumped his feet on the ground as Awn described their flight through the Once-City.

Only Fourth-Folly remained aloof, returning to the Court's curious vessel almost immediately as the tale began and remaining passive and stone-faced throughout.

The only time they showed any interest was the end when Awn was describing the sinking of the Once-City. They jerked their head up and made him repeat his descriptions of where they had been and how fast the Once-City had been traveling, all of which they wrote down in the margins of a hastily produced book.

"After that," Kindred said, putting a hand on *The Lost*—now just an empty shell, "we dove down. It must have taken the better part of a day, but we're here now."

"Indeed you are," Jest said, smiling and gesturing around, the tail end of a braid in each hand. "What luck we have to welcome you. We saw your craft descending and thought it great fortune to have ruins to scavenge in a clear-sky expanse, but what better luck it is to welcome visitors from the other side of the Forever Sea!"

Sarah still wore a guarded look, as though she were waiting for the knife to appear, for the kind look to be revealed as a ruse, but Awn had dropped to the ground next to Madrigal and was drawing pictures in the dirt with her, talking quickly, joyfully about how the ships above sailed and the various roles aboard a vessel.

The two exchanged questions with an almost unintelligible rapidity, and Kindred yearned to fall onto the dirt with them, to not be the leader making decisions but the wandering wonderer, curious about everything.

"What do you eat?" Awn asked.

"All sorts of things!" Madrigal said, lifting a handful of dirt and letting the gold-flecked grains fall in a shower. "Mostly stuff that grows out of the ground or the obelisks. What about you?"

"Not much recently, in fact," Awn said, grinning and rubbing at his stomach. "But before we departed, we ate plants and seeds harvested from the Sea, some grubs and bugs, too. Things like that."

Madrigal cocked her head to the side and frowned, but Awn was moving forward with his questions—*Are there many of you? How long have you lived down here? Did you come from above or were you born down here? But how long have you—you all, all the people—been here, really?*—and soon her confusion faded and was replaced with the same look of dazzled curiosity that Awn wore. Middle-aged man and child, both delighted by the sheer wonder of it all.

That's where I should be, Kindred thought as she and Sarah explained for Jest and Wylf how they had sailed down in *The Lost* and how the ship was different from the others that sailed above. Jest, it seemed, had as many questions as Awn, though all were about the ships above, and especially about captains—Where did captains sleep? Was it true they were the only ones allowed to steer the vessel? Were they born magical or did that come later? What was so special about their bones?

Nearly all of her questions came back to the legendary captains of myth: Timma Silverbark, the Guessing Two, Karana Bell and the daughter she called only Cloudless. Jest asked about all the old stories, but she asked as though the stories were true, as though they were histories of another place instead of stories swapped by kids standing on the docks, watching sails disappear on the horizon.

Wylf, it seemed, had a habit of standing just outside of a conversation, close enough to hear but not close enough that anyone would expect him to speak, and there he would stand, one arm crossed over his chest, one hand splayed across his cheek. It gave him the look of a person always half paying attention and half caught in thought. His eyes were the bright blue of a sky he would probably never see, and they held nothing but intense curiosity. His lips, Kindred noticed, moved constantly to shape words she could not discern.

Finally, Jest followed up an explanation with not another question but a sagely nod.

"I've learned much from you, Kindred Captain and Ragged Sarah," she said finally. "Thank you."

"Thank *you* for such a warm welcome," Kindred said, smiling with relief at these three members of the Court, Jest and Wylf still standing beside *The Lost* and Madrigal still chatting amiably with Awn, before looking past them to Fourth-Folly, who sat on the edge of the strange ship, legs dangling down halfway to the ground, their focus on whatever they were cramming into the margins of the book in which they wrote.

"Pay no mind to our dear Folly." Jest followed Kindred's gaze with a frown. "They have good reason to be suspicious of outsiders, but they mean no harm."

"They play tragedy in the Court," Madrigal said, breaking away from her conversation with Awn for a moment before leaping back in to ask whether there were kids above or just big people.

"Indeed," Jest said.

"Were you attacked?" Sarah asked, gesturing to the shield on Wylf's back, the metal face just as cracked as the rest.

"Attacked?" Jest asked, confused, looking at Wylf's shield and then at Wylf, who shook his head blankly, speaking silently to himself again. "Who would attack us? Oh! You mean because of the shields!"

She pulled off her own shield and held it out, the motion far too fluid and practiced for Jest to never have seen combat.

Pay attention to what a person can do without thought, the Marchess had once told Kindred. *In that thoughtlessness is their whole history.*

Jest held and handled the shield with careless ease and mastery, slipping its two well-worn straps casually from one forearm to the other while they spoke.

"These aren't for fighting," she said. "What a waste that would be! Not to mention the difficulty of finding someone to fight and something to fight about."

Madrigal, who watched this conversation with interest and had left Awn staring out into the infinite halls of the Sea, giggled at this thought.

"You could fight Tesser Cobb!" she said through a hand held over her laughing mouth. "I bet he would gladly fight you, Jest!"

Jest turned an arch glare on Madrigal, though her lips did twitch in the ghost of a smile.

"If they're not for fighting, what *are* they for?" Kindred asked.

"For when the sky falls," Jest said. Wylf cast his eyes upward, as if looking for a bit of falling sky, and even Madrigal nodded, the humor gone.

When *The Errant* had crashed into the Once-City, their arrival had been met by prison and tests, meetings with the Hanged Council and the breaking up of the crew. Their arrival meant conflict and violence, or at least the looming shadow of it.

Looking around at the Traveling Court—even Fourth-Folly—Kindred saw no sign of any of that. The old impulse of suspicion still worked in her, and Sarah, too, judging by the set of her jaw and the flick of her eyes. A fear, bone-deep and braided into the fiber of her, pulled at Kindred, whispering worries about enemies, about violence, about taking before being taken, about more and more and more.

But something in the vaults below the Sea was different. The slow, gentle *shush* of the wind gliding around the vast plants sang peace. The dirt pressed into the soles of her feet and caught in the space between her toes felt like contentment.

This was a place where everything small in Kindred felt suddenly burned away, and everything that might be big in her, every hope and goodness and kindness, was given substance and form.

"So, Kindred Captain," Jest said. "You have made it to the bottom of the Forever Sea. What will you do now?"

The question seemed to lift in the air above Kindred, flying with a levity and freedom all its own. She could do anything she wanted, she suddenly understood, suddenly felt all the way down in her bones, but beyond that, she could *be* any way she wanted there. In Arcadia, the desire for *more* was the beating heart behind every word and action, and if it required violence or theft or manipulation, then wasn't that simply how the world was supposed to work?

So much of her life—decisions and uncertainties and lies and joys and moments good and bad—took on a strange otherness in these wide, empty halls and in the face of this way of being, there all along but overlooked or ignored by so many.

What will you do now? Jest asked, but Kindred heard inside those words another question.

Who will you be now?

"I'm going to find out what happened to my grandmother," Kindred said, the words coming out with more certainty than she'd expected. "I don't know where she is or how to find her, but I'll figure out a way. And after that, I'm going to cure the Greys."

"*We,*" Sarah interjected, giving Kindred a pointed look. "*We* are going to find the Marchess and then save the Sea from this strange and evil sickness."

"Yes," Awn said, looking up from his conversation with Madrigal and sounding a little hurt. "We're a *crew*, after all, aren't we?"

Kindred flushed and nodded. "Sorry, yes. I'm still getting used to that. Yes, *we* are going to do those things."

"That's a lot," Fourth-Folly said. "Maybe too much." They'd hopped down from the ship and walked closer while they'd talked, and they stood now with the book in one hand, and with a jolt, Kindred realized it was a book she'd seen before. *Ten Sea Adventures* by an author named Tommia. She'd read it when she was just a teenager; it was all nautical derring-do and beasts from the deep. Kids' stuff, mostly. Even as a teenager reading it, Kindred had been mocked, sometimes gently and sometimes not, by those who saw her with the book.

"No need for pessimism, Folly, dearest friend," Jest said, turning a mildly reproachful look on Fourth-Folly. "We all must have journeys, and you know that the bigger the journey, the better it is." Jest turned back to Kindred with an eager grin. "Besides, our new friend's journey will be off to a quick start, since we know where her grandmother is!"

Kindred stared for a moment, sure that she had misheard Jest.

"You know where the Marchess is?" she asked after a moment, trying and failing to keep her voice even. "She's alive?"

"Very alive," Jest said. "Assuming we're talking about the same person, of course—she did not use that name when we met her. She walked down from the surface without the aid of a ship many sleeps ago; does that sound right?"

"Yes," Kindred said. Sarah stepped close and slid a hand around Kindred's back, and Kindred leaned hard into Sarah's strength. "Yes, that's her."

"She taught me how to play a game with coins and dice," Madrigal said, standing up and brushing herself off. "It was really hard, but I liked it. It was called—"

"Scatter throw," Kindred whispered. It had been the Marchess's favorite game, a complex competition involving dozens of odd, antiquated rules, including requirements for how a player could throw the dice or flick a coin, what words a player was and was not allowed to say and when, how to keep track of the seven distinct score lines, and more. Every type of toss was named after some long-dead master of the game—the Nell skip or Ludo's underthrow or the Otto blitz.

Scatter throw was a game that required a lifetime to learn and master all on its own, but playing with the Marchess was especially difficult for a single reason: she cheated.

Sometimes in obvious ways, sometimes in subtle ways, and sometimes in subtle ways masquerading as obvious, she would con and cheat and swindle her way to victory, laughing uproariously the whole way.

Tears stung at Kindred's eyes as memories flooded through her—giggling with the Marchess as they played doubles scatter throw against Red Alay and Maggie, the steady stream of cursing from Red Alay as the Marchess winked at Kindred before blatantly cheating; sitting with her grandmother on the deck of *Revenger*, evening giving way to night, flicking coins and sharing memories about Kindred's parents; winning her first game of scatter throw against the Marchess and basking in the look of pride on her face.

"She's here," Sarah said, squeezing Kindred and leaning in close to kiss her cheek. "You found her."

"*We* found her," Kindred whispered, turning in to Sarah and letting the moment take her—the fear and hope and certainty and doubt all coalescing into sharp relief.

Awn gave a whoop of joy and tossed handfuls of the glittering dirt into the air.

"Don't cheer yet," Fourth-Folly said, their pale face set in a gloomy frown. "We saw her ten sleeps back with the Fell Company."

Jest opened their mouth and then immediately closed it with a *hmmph* and a nod.

"What does that mean? Who are they?" Kindred asked.

"Caitiffs," Jest said, flicking their hands as if they were dirty. "Cowards."

"The Fell Company are another group of scavengers," Fourth-Folly said, shaking their head at Jest, who took a few steps back and turned away from the conversation. "They have territory north of here, on the other side of the canopy. A few days' journey away."

Fourth-Folly stopped, their eyes flicking to where Jest stood before speaking again, this time slowly, carefully, each word a sharp stone they were avoiding.

"They're not a group you want to tangle with. They've been known to steal—never from us, but from some others, I've heard. And they . . . they're just . . ."

The angry, annoyed countenance Fourth-Folly had worn since their arrival slipped for a moment as they looked again at Jest, but it was Madrigal who spoke.

"Evil," she said.

"They're not!" Jest said, voice stripped of playful airiness and sharp now. "They're not evil—they're not villains or enemies. They're just *people*."

It was not anger but sadness that moved under Jest's words—the Fell Company were *just* people, as if they might have been more, could and should have been more.

"*Bad* people who have done *bad* things to some of us in the not-so-distant past," Fourth-Folly said, returning again to curmudgeonly carping.

"Enough, Folly," Jest said.

Wylf stepped over to Jest and placed a hand on her shoulder, offering a moment of wordless comfort, which seemed to revive her somewhat.

"It's true that I have a history with the Fell Company," Jest said, turning around and studiously avoiding looking at Fourth-Folly. "I thought they were my friends. And then I thought they were my enemies. And it turned out that they were neither—simply people living a different myth than mine."

"Have they done something to the Marchess?" Kindred asked. "Is she safe?" Echoes of her time in a Once-City prison moved through Kindred's mind, and she imagined the Marchess held by the people of this Fell Company, trapped and frightened.

"Oh, she was safe," Fourth-Folly said. "She was one of those who greeted us as we passed through."

"Your grandmother is safe," Jest said, nodding and still ignoring Fourth-Folly. "She seemed involved in some new project when we passed by them. And we can certainly bring you to her without delay."

"Absolutely, we're ready to go," Kindred said, looking around at Sarah and Awn. "We didn't bring much with us."

"We have plenty of food and drink if you need," Jest said, already beginning to walk back toward their vessel. As they passed over the spot where the braided reins disappeared in the ground, they dropped more food from their pocket, and it again disappeared before Kindred could see what had taken it.

Kindred joined Sarah and Awn as they climbed back into *The Lost*, but she had spoken true—there was little left inside the ship. They had brought themselves, and that was it. A few scraps of plants, the spare grass Sarah had been braiding, now burned—there had been little time to grab anything else.

Would they return to *The Lost*? Or would it sit there as the Sea slowly unraveled its braids and undid its form, the soft, steady work of time laying it to rest?

Kindred followed Awn and Sarah over to where the Traveling Court were preparing to leave. Madrigal and Fourth-Folly were perched up on the deck of the small ship, which was big enough to have a tiny cabin below, probably capable of sleeping two, maybe three. As they approached, Sarah asked Awn about what Madrigal had been telling him, and Kindred was just about to ask what the young girl had said about how many people lived down there when she heard a faint, sweet song trilling in her mind.

She jerked around, staring back at *The Lost*, which looked like an empty husk now, tipped on its side slightly, empty cabin dark and still. The hearthfire was gone, put out and cold.

The melody in her mind twinned with one in her ears, and she turned again, back to the strange ship pulled by whatever creatures were below, floating just above the dirt, its keel the only point of contact.

On the small deck, Fourth-Folly had taken the reins.

And Madrigal was keeping the hearthfire.

Her voice, so soft and playful when she spoke, had taken on a formal, stilted quality, stentorian and ringing somehow. She sang without any of the cultivated rigor and lifelessness of the Arcadian keepers, but it was also not the random, scattershot melodies of the Once-City, pieced together by dangerous experimentation.

This was something else, something older.

In her short stint in the schools of Arcadia, Kindred had taken a class with a shriveled old bookmaven, hair like silver-spun wire knotted tightly at the back of her head, skin turned to jerky by countless afternoons of sun and wind. She was mean—mean to students, mean to her fellow mavens, mean to the administrators of the school, and mean to passersby on the street. She hated everything new and could frequently be heard in the hallways of the school, her weathered, ragged voice rising above the general din, bitterly criticizing this new ship design or the new build pioneered by one of the other faculty members. The past was a prize she clutched to herself, guarding it against every novel idea and practice the present might offer.

Kindred had loved her.

It had been this woman, Psallein Knoll, who taught the only class Kindred liked—History of the Hearthfire—and though Kindred failed out of the school before finishing the class, she could remember one section early on when Psallein Knoll discussed what she called "The First Forms," which were the practices of the very early hearthfire keepers. Builds that children could have constructed, rudimentary not only in their forms but their abilities to deal with anything beyond a perfect day: low, steady winds; flat, monoculture Sea; perfect, cloudless sky.

"The First Forms held the bones of all that would come after," Psallein Knoll had said from the front of the classroom, glaring out at the students. "Were they perfect? Only a fool would say such things. But they were functional, without any of the frippery and fiddling of keeping today."

She'd slapped one chalk-dusted hand flat on the desk, sending up an explosion of dust and a sound that cracked the air.

"Straight lines! Space for heat! Contained builds! Simple, stepped melodies!"

These had been her commands, barked and shouted at them nearly every class, and it was the last commandment that Kindred remembered now, listening to Madrigal's voice climb a stepped melody, every note precise and planned, dictated by the larger form, which prioritized symmetry and perfection. A soaring melody necessitated a plunging one later; speed promised sluggishness; discord would always resolve into harmony and home. It wasn't music—it was math, and Madrigal's voice moved through the equations with practiced ease.

Kindred stepped closer, giving a wide berth to divots in the ground where the reins disappeared, and peered onto the deck. The hearthfire looked like a sketch from old Psallein Knoll's books, the flames flicking up to an even, steady height, an ever-changing range of colors flashing through the fire.

"It is the hope of the Sea in miniature," Psallein Knoll had said, tracing a line of chalk across the top of a diagram sketched out on the board. "A wild thing tamed and ordered, every strand of the flame reaching the same height, contained neatly—*perfectly*—by the work of our hands."

She had jabbed the chalk at the basin—a square construction in those early days—and the build, which both worked to standardize the fire. It was the dream of those early sailors—a dynamic, beautiful thing, full of life and color and power, all chaos and disorder and wildness but contained in a box.

"But it's not really wild," Kindred had said one day. "If it's contained, how can it be true chaos and wilderness?"

Psallein Knoll had nodded at her as one might nod at a child who has learned a new word but has not learned how to use it correctly yet.

"We allow the fire to flourish in these old forms. In the safety of our build and the basin, the chaos of the fire is given the space to roil and burn as it sees fit, just as the Sea itself grows wild and chaotic within the lines of our spellwork, which keeps it flat and sailable. Contained wildness."

Kindred had raised her hand again but Psallein Knoll either ignored or didn't see her, because the old bookmaven moved ahead with her lesson.

But how could something be wild if it needed permission to do so? Could chaos really exist if it needed to first be given a contained space to do so?

No, thought that younger Kindred. *Wildness contained wasn't wild at all. Chaos couldn't be given, couldn't be allowed. A wild thing gave itself permission.*

Madrigal made her hands into flat lines on either side of the fire, fingers tensed, and as she sang, she moved the planes of her palms into the fire, straightening the structure, which was a simple box. With a craft that sailed across the unchanging dirt of this place, and one pulled by whatever waited on the other end of the reins Fourth-Folly was holding, they wouldn't need much more than an elementary build—just something to keep the ship up and steady. A wind cut through the Seafloor, a low graveyard moan, but without a mast or sails, a keeper wouldn't have to worry about it.

"Where did you learn how to do that?" Kindred asked, leaning against the solid steadiness of the ship. Even floating off the ground, held only by the force of the hearthfire and the length of the keel digging into the dirt, the vessel didn't move with her weight on it. Such was the promise of the First Forms—strength above all.

"Books," Madrigal said with a slight shrug.

"How old are you?" She looked much younger than Kindred had when she'd first stepped aboard *Revenger*, and she was definitely younger than Kindred had been the first time she'd kept the fire.

"I've seen Tylaean's Hall four times," Madrigal said, smiling at the thought and returning to her work.

"Leave her alone," Fourth-Folly said, turning back to glare at Kindred. "She needs to focus if we're going to get moving."

Madrigal gave an apologetic tilt of her head to Kindred as she began singing again, lifting her voice up the rungs of melody one at a time.

Kindred walked back to where Sarah was talking with Jest, who was fiddling with a few bags strapped to the gentle curve of the hull. One bag, much-patched and bright red, was packed full of looseleaf pages. Another held scraps of cloth, every shape and color, many of which looked to have already been used to fix the clothing of the Traveling Court.

"No scarcity of water *or* food?" Sarah asked.

"Correct," Jest said, looking over at Wylf, who perched on the side of the ship, his legs dangling. He shook his head and returned to his work, which involved painting a wooden plank—salvaged from a ship, by the looks of it. Using the end of one of his long braids as a paintbrush, Wylf added color from a set of small pots nearby to a simple sunset rendered in greys and blues. It was carefully done, and Wylf blended color and form with the smooth assurance of someone who had done this many times before.

"None?" Sarah asked, pressing and dubious. "What about clothing? Or supplies? You don't lack anything?"

"The Monarch's lands provide that which we need and much of what we might want," Jest said, gesturing about herself with magnanimity.

"What do people kill each other over, then?" Sarah asked, though she muttered it mostly to herself.

"Captain!" Jest said as she spotted Kindred. "Some of us will have to walk, but we have saved a space of honor for you on the deck." She gestured up to what looked like a small, woven cushion set on the deck behind Madrigal, butting up against the tiny gunwale running around the ship.

It was a place of privilege, where a captain might normally sit or stand, missing only a wheel to complete the picture.

"I'm okay to walk," Kindred said, looking around, the low-grade confusion she'd felt since meeting these people spiking suddenly.

"As you wish," Jest said, nodding. "I only thought it might befit royalty to ride, but I am the first to admit the deficiency of my knowledge regarding hierarchical expectations. Your grandmother, after all, didn't even wear a crown!"

Jest shook her head and gave a baffled chortle. She had an odd tendency of placing one hand on her hip and gesturing with her braid held out in the other, as though she were a captain holding a sword and preparing her crew to fight, or a politician mounted on some stage, holding forth in pontificatory peroration.

It should have made her buffoonish somehow, pompous and unlikeable, but there was something so genuine in the act, so unaffected even as it was practiced, done with such love and joy, that Kindred found herself liking this woman.

"What are you talking about?" Kindred asked, falling into step beside Jest as the vessel began to slide through the dirt with a smooth whisper. "I'm not royalty. And why would my grandmother wear a crown?"

"Modesty," Jest said, nodding and turning to Wylf. "Just as it is in the tales."

Seeing that Kindred wasn't going to take the seat on the deck, Awn had climbed aboard, and he sat now, cross-legged, back straight, face an open page on which the glory of the Seafloor was writ.

"I was surprised," Jest said, finding Kindred's eyes again, "that you chose to take the title of *captain*, though maybe it is more prestigious than *princess*?"

Sarah choked and then coughed, and Kindred's face must have given enough of her confusion away that Jest hurried on.

"It's only . . . well, your grandmother, she was not introduced as the Marchess—surely a famous name above, I have no doubt. When we passed through their territory, the Fell introduced her by her official title, one we had all heard and read about many times. Countless tales written about her bravery and courage, her feats of derring-do and power. We count ourselves as somewhat well-read among those who live on the Seafloor, but surely there are few if any down here who haven't heard of your grandmother's great victories, brought into being by her child warriors and the strength of her own magics."

Something was deeply wrong there, laughter that echoed and sounded too much like sobs, a sliver of darkness hiding a cold knife.

"Who do you think she is?" Kindred asked.

"The Queen Who Laughed," Jest said, cocking her head slightly, mirroring Kindred's own confusion. "The Fell introduced her, but she was gracious in accepting our tribute and gifts. I'm sure you know all about such things, having grown up with her!"

CHAPTER EIGHT

"**I**s your grandmother secretly a long-dead, probably fictional queen who commanded an army of vicious warrior children?" Sarah asked as the group got moving. Kindred had found nothing to say in response to Jest's revelation, which they apparently took to be confirmation.

"No," Kindred said, turning to find Sarah grinning at her. "Not that I know of."

"Damn," Sarah said, leaning in to kiss Kindred on the cheek. "I thought for a moment I had fallen in love with a princess from myth and legend. Instead, it's just a lowly keeper who dropped out of school and sank the first ship she was made full crew on."

Kindred gave Sarah a shove even as she let loose a peal of laughter. Somehow, this was perfect—smiling and laughing with Sarah as they traversed the empty-sky openness of the Seafloor, walking along behind a vessel pulled by unseen creatures and held aloft through the power of a fire kept by a child.

The vast arcades of the Seafloor devoured Kindred's laughter and echoed back nothing but silence and the wind.

Into that unchanging chiaroscuro of vast darkness and brightly limned columns, Kindred and her crew walked with these strange, new people. And as they did, life below the Sea came into focus, described in a medley of the Traveling Court's voices and punctuated by the occasional grunt and nod from Wylf.

Other groups—most just a few members and some only one or two people in total—lived below, all of them scavengers. Some, like the Traveling Court, were nomadic, moving around in search of newly fallen artifacts from above. Others were more sedentary and chose instead to dig for their relics, down to where remnants from ancient societies and cultures perhaps lay buried.

Some ate only the glowing fungi that unfolded along the banks of the various rivers, while others cast lines into the rivers themselves, pulling up various fish and water-bound plants. Some grew their own foods on the Seafloor, guarding their perimeters from beasts that roamed on legs or wings.

"And some hunt and eat the pluralities," Jest said, pointing with one braid toward the ground ahead of the ship, where the reins disappeared into the soft dirt.

"Those people are monsters," Fourth-Folly said over their shoulder.

"No, just people," Jest said again, her voice quiet.

"What are the pluralities?" Sarah asked, squinting at the ground ahead of the steadily moving ship. "Animals of some kind?"

How long had it been since Sarah had summoned her birds?

A memory broke inside Kindred as they walked: Sarah waiting for her on the dock, the Marchess's unopened letter in her hand, sparrows winging tawny orbits around her head. The rest of *The Errant*'s crew had been off in Arcadia, drinking or eating, buying or gambling, availing themselves of all the city had to offer.

But Sarah had eschewed all of that in favor of darkness and what had looked at first like solitude but had, in fact, been her community—the one consistent line throughout her life. From her time in the Once-City to her beginnings in Arcadia, bouncing from job to job until she found *The Errant*, her birds had been there, her own connection to the world outside of her.

She had followed Kindred below, but had she cut her own throughline to do so?

Kindred cast a glance back to where, distant now and out of sight, *The Lost* lay, still functional.

"They might be animals, yes," Jest said, nodding, thoughtful. "The pluralities are beings that live entirely below the ground, eating mostly bugs and other subterranean creatures they find. They're entirely peaceful and content to leave people alone, save for the occasionally stolen bit of food."

"What do you mean, 'They might be animals'?" Sarah asked, walking a bit more quickly to overtake the ship and study the ground in front of it. There may have been a slight mounding to the dirt, as though something tunneling underneath, but it was impossible to say for sure.

"Just that no one knows *precisely* what they are. The pluralities don't have any distinct form when they're below the dirt," Jest said, jogging to get out in front of the ship, too. "They exist below as potential—pure and endless possibility. Some have written that the pluralities actually hold many different and distinct shapes at once while they're below. Others say they are constantly changing. Whatever these many-beings do under-ground, all of that potential collapses into a single form when they rise fully above and are seen."

Jest clapped her hands together to emphasize the point, worlds of could-bes and maybes slamming together into a single point.

"That doesn't make any sense," Sarah said, though it wasn't criticism so much as awe. "How could a living thing do something like that?"

"How indeed," Jest said, nodding and smiling. "There's a group nearer to Forever who hunt and study the pluralities exclusively. I'm only repeat-ing the little that I've heard from them, or that I've heard from someone who heard it from someone who heard it from them. What was that group called again, Folly?"

"The Many Forms of Being," Fourth-Folly said, grimacing. "Absolutely idiotic name."

Jest frowned but didn't disagree.

"Very little is known about the pluralities," she continued, "but every-one agrees on a few things. First, the form they take when forced above the ground is not their true one, if indeed they *have* a true form at all! These bodies they occupy when above are varied and strange, as though put together from random, chaotic pieces of other beings, but none of them are the pluralities' true forms. I've even heard speculation that the first humans were pluralities forced aboveground and into these bodies, but there is little evidence to support such a claim.

"The second bit of truth about the pluralities is that once they have collapsed into a form above, they can never be released from it, even if allowed to burrow beneath the ground again. Once forced into place and form and being, they can never again achieve their previous existences."

"You're saying these ropes," Sarah said, lightly touching one of the reins, "are currently tied to an animal that exists in a form no one has ever or can ever see, and as soon as that animal is forced aboveground, it takes on a permanent form that isn't its true one?"

"Perfectly stated!" Jest said, casting a smug-muddled smile toward Fourth-Folly. "See, Folly? It's not that complicated."

Fourth-Folly rolled their eyes and didn't respond.

"Couldn't you just dig below and see what the pluralities look like underground?" Sarah asked, keeping pace with the three shifting divots where the reins disappeared below.

"If you wanted to die and leave no trace of yourself behind, sure," Fourth-Folly said, a curl in their lip.

"The pluralities fiercely guard their domain," Jest said, nodding, a look of dismay on her face. A childish energy animated Jest whenever she spoke, bright and genuine and unguarded. She was like a kid trying on emotions and actions, play-acting a daring warrior, a fearless leader, a consoling friend, a sage advisor. In another person, such a chaotic spirit might have been annoying or dangerous, but in Jest, it burned like a bright, warm fire, filling the space around her with something good and right.

"But they're quite peaceful so long as you don't venture below," Jest continued. "We've had these three for some time, and they've never been any trouble."

"Did you catch them?" Kindred asked, staring at the braided reins disappearing below and trying to imagine where they terminated and how. Were the pluralities entangled in the ends? Were they trapped by them somehow? Hooked by some barbed curve of metal?

She imagined the dark, packed space below her feet haunted by these creatures of possibility, saw them as pale ghosts floating through sand, forms shifting against every new grain of dirt touched, fluttering and morphing in response to each muffled sound from above. Underground, the pluralities were everything, endless, and they were nothing, too, their existence itself a flickering, trembling thing. Wing-arms parted dirt, teeth-hands grinned and grasped, mouth-spines moaned out prayers to gods not yet imagined and others lost to time.

Above, people walked and scavenged, lived and died, while below, these creatures braided and unraveled being itself, every moment, always, unendingly.

"Oh, yes!" Jest said. "They're not overly difficult to catch. It simply takes time and patience and some luck. They eat the ends of the grass, you see, but so slowly that one needs only tie a new braid on the end every so often."

"I had a dream that I burrowed underground and saw the pluralities and they all just looked like me," Madrigal said, smiling up from where she worked the hearthfire, her young eyes dreamy and far away. "They let me stay with them for a whole day but then I couldn't come back."

"Incredible," Sarah murmured, looking as though she wanted to kneel down and investigate the ground but couldn't because she would be run over by the ship. She asked Jest more about calling and capturing the pluralities, and soon both Jest and Fourth-Folly were talking and arguing about the various strategies and techniques involved in luring pluralities, which turned out to be somewhat similar to some aspects of how Sarah called her birds above.

Kindred watched Sarah talking excitedly with Jest, returning Fourth-Folly's surliness with some of her own until they both cracked a little, grins flashing for a moment before disappearing under general distrust and wariness again.

Nearby Kindred, Madrigal had returned to the fire and her archaic but effective style of keeping.

"Wonders upon wonders," Awn said from where he sat aboard the small ship. He caught Kindred's eyes and grinned, gesturing around.

⸻ ◆ ⸻

"Fall!"

Kindred had been listening to Jest explain how they were nearing the edge of the Lost Monarch's lands—with many digressions and explanations of the history of this mighty Monarch's lands—and what they called "a canopy run" when the shout erupted from Wylf, who had not uttered a single word until then. Just before shouting, he'd leapt up, as if seized by a great pain. His voice shook the air, so deep and loud that Kindred felt it in her bones and joints.

The Traveling Court of the Lost Monarch leapt into well-practiced movement. Fourth-Folly hauled hard on the reins and tied them off on the small, smooth spar extending from the bow. Wylf took a series of long, beaten-up boards from the deck of the ship and laid them in a crisscrossing pattern over the approximate place where the pluralities were. Madrigal stepped her song quickly down the scale until settling on a calm, steady note. She leapt belowdecks for a moment before emerging again with a large metal bowl riddled with holes and attached to a long wooden handle. This she placed over the hearthfire, which continued to burn evenly.

"Belowdecks, if you would," Jest said to Awn, gesturing with urgency to Kindred and Sarah, too. With her free hand, she had removed her shield. "It will be tight down there but much safer."

Awn obliged without a word, disappearing below in a clatter that described his ungainly fall a moment before his voice emerged. "Ow." And then a breath later, "I'm okay."

"What's going on?" Kindred asked, stepping closer to the ship but not yet climbing aboard. Sarah, too, had moved closer, one of her knives glinting in her hand.

"Get up here!" Fourth-Folly shouted, pulling a battered stretch of wood up from where it had been serving as a second deck under their feet. They propped it up against one of the poles they'd used earlier and formed a kind of slanted roof over much of the foredeck.

The ground exploded, throwing starry stretches of dirt high into the air, filling the emptiness and dashing away the silence of the Seafloor.

It's the pluralities, Kindred thought, fear rushing along behind the adrenaline as she imagined formless horrors writhing and wriggling and screaming and flying and clawing up from the dirt, reality shoving bone and fiber and muscle and teeth onto them. They were attacking, rising in anger from their variable existence below, reaching up to drag Kindred and the others down into the potential of what lay below.

This is what you wanted, they whispered in their many-tongued voices. *Come and lose yourself.*

A shout of dismay came as if from far off, and still the ground churned and roiled, tearing itself asunder as possibility collapsed into a single, brutal reality.

Hands reached, fingers and claws closed, and Kindred was hauled off her feet suddenly, her eyes snapping open—when had she closed them?—to watch the world around her jolt suddenly, not as she was dragged below but lifted up. Kindred writhed around and saw Wylf, his hair wild, half-pulled from the confines of its tails as he lifted Kindred with one arm up to the ship, harboring both of them below his shield.

Jest was already aboard, as was Sarah, and they were already moving toward the ladder to go belowdecks. Sarah had put her knives away and was gesturing for Kindred to follow them from beneath the protection of Jest's shield, which she held up, just as Wylf did for Kindred.

For when the sky falls, Jest had said about their shields, and Kindred looked out now at the erupting ground around the ship, seeing the explosions for what they were—not impossible beasts rising from below but the collision of falling detritus from above, the pieces of whatever it was dropping almost too fast to see, shrouded by the near-darkness of the Seafloor, every impact throwing up stretches of star-streaked ground.

The bits of the falling sky made almost no noise as they dropped—the space between the huge stalks of grass was too far, and they had nothing with which to collide as they fell, and the constant, slow sigh of the wind covered any whistling or slithering sounds they might have made.

One piece slammed into the shield Wylf held above their heads, a reminder that this was not a phenomenon happening only off the boat, and Kindred pulled her body into as tight a space as she could manage below the shield and hurried forward, dropping down the ladder after Jest and Sarah.

Wylf pulled a cover closed behind him as he followed her down, lips moving silently again, as though repeating some mantra to himself.

Below, the ladder deposited Kindred in what had once been a kitchen area with space for a table and a small stove, cabinets for spices, plates, forks, and the rest along the walls. It was a recognizable space—the same as thousands of other small ships of its size, even though every bit of furniture and storage had been removed.

A single candle burned steadily in the center of the small kitchen, showing at first the faces of the others standing shoulder to shoulder. Madrigal gave Kindred a tiny wave as she made it down.

Books ringed the walls around the tiny kitchen, taking up every bit of space they could on the floor-to-ceiling bookshelves, standing upright and shoulder to shoulder, just like the people in the room, but stacked atop one another too, wedged in spine-out or spine-in, with scrolls filling the few spaces where books wouldn't or couldn't be made to.

The room was small, but with the added layer of so many books, it was tiny.

And enormous, too.

Through the doorways on either end, Kindred saw berths in much the same state—a bed in the middle of the room large enough to fit two comfortably, three in a pinch, and walls perfectly insulated with books. On a ship above, it would have been madness to see something like this, and not only because so many texts all together could only be found in one of the libraries. The movement of the Sea and the constant dangers of sailing—harsh winds, rough grasses, and pirates—made such carefree constructions hazardous. Kindred had had her own small, prized bookshelf in her room on *The Errant*, and they'd been strapped in tightly to prevent them tumbling free and smashing her head while she slept.

These books, though, were not contained or confined in any way. She might right now pluck one from a shelf. An attack from another ship might knock every single one of them down. A change in the pitch or yaw of the ship could wrench whole shelves of books from their standings.

What an enormous change to live with such trust in the permanence of the world around you.

The sound of impacts, muffled by the wood of the hull and the inner hull of paper, was continuous outside, the occasional report sharper and nearer as the falling relics from above hit the ship itself.

For their parts, the Traveling Court seemed unbothered by the chaos outside. Madrigal immediately lit a candle for herself and sat down with a book she pulled seemingly at random from a nearby shelf.

"Nothing to do but wait it out," Jest said with an apologetic smile before gesturing to the aft berth with one of her long braids. "You're more than welcome to rest until it's over." And with a sleepy wave she stepped through the door to the other bed and dropped onto it. Wylf followed her a moment later, unhooking a coiled curtain to give some sense of privacy as he did.

Fourth-Folly remained, and they glared around in curmudgeonly silence, which seemed to be the base state from which they occasionally emerged with a smile or kind word.

"A rest would be nice," Awn said, lighting a spare candle and grabbing a book on his way back. He smiled as he went. "It almost sounds like rain outside."

Madrigal had fallen asleep already in the chair where she'd been sitting, the book open in her lap, head lolled back. Fourth-Folly huffed out a sigh and covered Madrigal with a blanket they pulled from under a shelf.

"How long does this usually last?" Kindred asked, sitting in a well-worn chair next to Sarah.

"Depends on what it is," Fourth-Folly said. "Parts of a single carcass? Pretty quick. A whole swarm of roaches? We'll be here for quite some time. A sunken ship? Somewhere in between. If it were that city— What did you call it? The one that sank?"

"The Once-City," Kindred offered.

"If it were something like that? We'd be down here for several sleeps." Fourth-Folly blew out a breath and sank down into a seat with thinning cushions. "I didn't see much, but I think it's probably a wyrm coming down, so maybe we will be out soon. There'll be a big boom and then we'll know it's over."

"Will you scavenge anything from the wyrm?" Sarah asked, revulsion clear in her voice.

Kindred grimaced at the sudden return of the memories: the wyrm slithering up from below to wrench *The Errant* down, draping its huge, stinking bulk around the ship, stunted arms flailing in the air. Its hide had been like calcified cobwebs, hard and porous and smoothed by its endless surges through the press of the Sea. The craters in its skin, so dark inside, promising and inviting and repulsive all at once, and still Kindred could imagine herself reaching a hand at first, and then her whole arm inside, deep into the wyrm and whatever made it move, down to where blood hummed and muscles thrummed and whatever poison and bile the wyrms held inside them pooled.

"No," Fourth-Folly said, and a wave of relief rushed over Kindred. If she never saw another wyrm again, alive or dead, she would count herself lucky. "There are two groups I know of who hunt and scavenge the wyrms, but that's not our myth. They're inedible and gross, anyway—good only for trophy collection or possibly building materials."

The rhythm of impacts outside continued, holding firm in its scatter-shot rapidity.

"What do you mean when you talk about myths?" Kindred asked, leafing idly through a book she had taken from a shelf. "Are you talking about stories?"

"Or is it to do with that nonsense Jest said about the sky falling?" Sarah asked, letting out a laugh that was both not unkind and not shared by Fourth-Folly.

"Don't," Fourth-Folly said, their voice deadly quiet as they nodded back to where Jest was sleeping. "Don't mock her."

"I . . ." Sarah began before stopping. The smile slid from her face and left confusion behind. "But they know, right? They know it's not really the sky falling?"

"It's their way of seeing the world," Fourth-Folly said.

"Just leave it, Sarah," Kindred said. The libraried cabin grew close, the air suddenly dry, oppressive.

Sarah paused and then plunged ahead.

"I'm not trying to insult anyone," she said, raising open hands to express her innocence. "But you know it's not the sky falling. You just told us all the things it could be. You know what it is. Just like how you clearly know Kindred's grandmother is not some legendary queen who never really existed."

There was no condescension in Sarah's voice, nor any hint of scorn or ridicule. Instead, she spoke as one bewildered and baffled.

"Keep your voice down," Fourth-Folly said, leaning close and looking anxiously at Madrigal's still form. The young girl slept in the way only children can: limbs casually contorted into ache-inducing positions, legs and arms bent and twisted torturously. And somehow asleep, happily so. Amid the flailing, chaotic energy of youth, peace.

"This place goes on forever," Folly said, gesturing in a circle around them. "And it's filled with endless mysteries. Jest will tell you all about them, I'm sure. The Locked Caverns. The Wild-Run Herds. Crown's Last Uttering. Tylaean's Hall. Gaunt's Unmeasured Depths. The Moonless Shore. On and on, so many stories and myths and legends down here. That's the endlessness of this place—not that you can walk and never reach the end, but that you can solve mysteries and live fantastical lives and never come close to reaching the end."

Folly had lost their gruff edge and just sounded tired now.

"That sounds *amazing*," Kindred said, trying and failing to speak quietly. This was why she had come; this endlessness, this forever, was what had sounded the caverns of her imagination. To know the place beneath her feet, to linger over what was here instead of longing for what was there. Every new mystery, every new story and myth of this place uttered by Fourth-Folly was a promise.

"It's not," Fourth-Folly said, bringing their gaze to Kindred and staring for a long time. They had dark brown eyes, with puddles of purpled skin beneath, and up so close, the lines on their face were clear, stretching like webwork from the corners of their eyes, along their jaw, spidering across their forehead.

They were exhausted.

"Everyone down here deals with this place in different ways. Some scavenging crews have adopted religions to give them purpose. Some chase after those mysteries and myths. Some hope to reach the sunlit world above and work always to that end. Others follow darker paths.

"The emptiness of this place can drive a person mad, and so, too, can the endlessnesses of it. Jest lost herself a long time ago, and it was only through stories that she found herself again. We scavenge books and scrolls and texts, anything from the people above, not because of some casual desire to read but because, for some of us, we need them to survive. Jest and the others live in those worlds because this one is too hard for them."

A thought moved in Kindred, sliding through her mind like a wyrm as she thought on Jest's talk of myths, of Wylf's voice, of Madrigal still not having found her myth.

"Jest said that you all are the Lost Monarch's Traveling Court. Who is the Lost Monarch? We don't have any myth or legend above about a monarch, not any that I've ever heard, anyway. Does the Lost Monarch even exist?"

Fourth-Folly smiled, and it was the saddest thing Kindred had ever seen.

"I met Jest a long, long time ago, when it was just her, before we found Wylf, and long before we found Madrigal. She was looking for the monarch then, and I told her I'd join the search. I thought it would be a few days of travel, maybe some things I could steal, and then we'd separate, or I'd slip away. One day, while we sheltered inside the ship just like this, some fall or another pelting down outside, Jest was sleeping, and I started looking through her things. I'd been living up until then by stealing and, sometimes, killing, and I thought I would just take what I could from this story-sick, eccentric, crazy woman while she slept and sneak away before she woke up.

"But I found her journals. She writes all the time, you know—while we travel, before she sleeps, when she wakes, always writing. And while she slept that day, I read her journals, all of them, all the way back to the pages that were stuck together from disuse, pages written in a different hand but with the same ink that Jest always writes in.

"I couldn't tell what happened, what caused her break from reality, but I did see that in those early entries, she always signed her name differently. Not just a *J* like she does now, but her full name and title: Jest, First Monarch of the Shadowed Lands."

Kindred let loose a long, slow breath.

"Jest's myth, her purpose, is to find the Lost Monarch, but Jest seeks herself. Whatever trauma she endured, whatever caused her to break from that old life is lost to her, pushed behind a wall she has no interest, maybe no ability, to look behind. She doesn't talk about it and will grow distant and quiet if you ask anything close to it, so don't."

"So, Jest is . . ." Kindred began, unable to imagine something so self-shattering as this, so heartbreaking.

"Jest is the Lost Monarch," Fourth-Folly said, nodding grimly. "She lost herself and seeks that person, oblivious to what it would mean to find her."

"Couldn't she just read her old journals?" Kindred asked. "Put it together as you did?"

"She could," Fourth-Folly conceded, nodding, "but I burned them a long time ago. Whatever happened to Jest was obviously something she wanted to forget. And beyond that, to know your own myth and to do the work of getting outside of it are two very different things."

"You burned them? But she'll never . . ." Kindred began, but trailed off again. This was not her fight, not her crew, not her *myth*, to use their term, but something about it pulled at her nonetheless. Was it mercy or malice to destroy Jest's only chance to find the person she was looking for, even if that person was a self she had tried or been forced to forget? Was Fourth-Folly protecting her? Was it even their choice to make?

"She'll never find the Monarch?" Folly asked, bitterness twisting her face. "Some things are meant to stay lost. A myth isn't a race to be finished; it's meant to be run while you've got air in your chest. No, she'll never find the Lost Monarch, but she will live a life of purpose and be protected from that past all the same."

Kindred nodded, troubled and unsure.

CHAPTER NINE

The air beyond the archway was warm and sweet, like a breeze carrying summer's missives. Sun-soaked bluebells and cloud-scattered skies, all the siblings home for a day or two, their laughter lighting again the dark, empty halls of the Borders estate.

Wind like breath crept along Flitch's arms, around the soft flesh of his neck, against his face, and through his hair. He put a steadying hand out and found the stone wall warm, almost hot, as though it had baked unshaded for an afternoon, pulling in the warmth and, like a miser, holding it.

The space was large but not overly so—a dim cavern covered in bookshelves and piles of scrolls, layers of rugs stretched over the stone floor to give it some sense of comfort. A few chairs and a small desk emerged in the torchlight.

It was strange, certainly, to see something so domestic in a rocky cavern, but Flitch couldn't help but feel disappointed.

This was the secret? A room full of books and moldy furniture?

"This is Grandfather's Library," the baron said, having stopped at the back of the space and gesturing around at the sagging shelves and scattered furniture. "Those are his books—your great-great-grandfather's— each one a stone on which our fortune was built."

"Idyll really should be here," Zim said, shaking his head and looking over the rows of books.

"Yeah," Aster said, already pulling a text from one shelf. The front was covered in dried, pressed leaves arranged in a swirl around the title: *The Ghost in the Grass.*

"All of his books?" Flitch asked, looking over the shelves with a poorly concealed frown. In the stories, the baron's textual acquisitions burst from tunnel to tunnel, taking up more and more space, piled against walls and propped up against stalagmites, hung from bags hastily nailed into the stone and tossed on haphazard heaps. It was a library to rival even the King's, and it spread through the huge caverns below the baron's estate like a slow-growing plant, roots reaching always farther into the darkness.

"Good," the baron said, a quick smile breaking through his anxious expression. "I wondered how long it would take you to notice."

He gestured around the cavern.

"The stories of this place are necessary fictions to protect the truth, and like all good lies, they have a heart of truth. Yes, your grandfather collected texts from around the world, and yes, he discovered the new runes to rebuild our fleet here. But something else drew him below, and you need to understand that nothing beyond Grandfather's Library—this room—is of his or any other relative's doing."

From a nearby shelf, the baron pulled several small books, each one bound in rough hide and tied around with string. He passed one to each of them.

"Over the generations, our family has added what little we can to these maps, keeping careful copies. If you are to step beyond Grandfather's Library, you must take a map with you. The tunnels are dangerous enough even if you are to walk known paths through static rooms."

Their father shook his head and blew out an exasperated breath, scratching hard at his jaw through the thick bristle of his beard.

"This is all wrong. I had planned to introduce you to this place more slowly, as my mother did before she passed, one room at a time, one step at a time. But I can't, not with the King's plans moving so quickly."

Flitch opened the book and found pages of thick paper covered completely in carefully drawn maps, each one of a single room, complete with tiny details—a chair drawn with meticulous strokes, a shelf of books inked in myriad vibrant colors, a set of footprints pacing in an endless circle. At the edges of the paper, arrows showed the path to other rooms, each carefully labeled and accompanied by dates and check marks, the full map of the room represented a page or two later.

What Flitch had at first taken to be thick, rich pages of paper were revealed instead to be pages covered by years and years of hands drawing over previous maps, adding thick corrections and new colors, each change covering over the previous draft like a new skin, until every page carried its whole history inside it. His father's perpetually ink-stained hands made sense suddenly to Flitch as he looked down at the marvel that was this map book, one of several, apparently.

"What are we doing down here, Father?" Zim asked, drawing their collective attention back to the operation of the moment, as was his wont. "What do you want us to do in this room?"

The baron nodded.

Here we go, thought Flitch, feeling that same excitement from the morning rising again in his gut. Here they were, together—or nearly together, anyway—and in the middle of change, characters in a story someone years from now would whisper to their little brother, delighting and distracting him from the flash of lightning, the crush of thunder outside.

As he spoke, the baron gestured toward the back of the room, and Flitch was surprised to see another doorway there, this one smaller and easier to miss than the arch at the entrance. Beyond this simple doorway he could see the beginnings of three different tunnels leading off in different directions.

"Beyond this room is a labyrinth—a maze. It has no end, so far as I know, and only one beginning. The rooms beyond change from time to time, and as we walk them in search of the gift, we update the maps. This is the work of our family, and when even one of us steps beyond this tunnel and into the labyrinth, the archway closes, sealing shut as if it had never existed, nothing more than smooth wall with a strange, unreadable word carved into it."

"What's the gift?" Aster asked, as breathless and wide-eyed as Flitch, as Zim, as Idyll would have been to hear the answer to their most cherished and well-handled question, one they had passed back and forth between themselves over dinners and sleepovers in one another's rooms.

"Something walks the labyrinth," the baron said, his voice deep and resonant. "Your great-great-great-grandfather saw it, as did a few other relatives and one of your great-aunts, too. It is a beast, dangerous and powerful and old, old as the world. It lives in the labyrinth and walks the paths, leaving traces of itself occasionally. If you can find it, this thing—beast or creature or person or whatever it is—it may offer you a gift.

"For your great-great-great-grandfather, it was directions to find the correct text to discover the right runes for shipbuilding. For your great-aunt, it was an answer to a question that had been burning inside her for many years. This gift has been the hand that might lift us from our fall.

"We call it Quietus, and it is a capricious creature, motivated by odd customs which I have tried to teach you through our nonsensical rules at court. The food Faineant provides may be tasteless slop, but I am sure it has always been safe to eat. I instilled and insisted upon these odd requirements to prepare you for this place, and you must follow them now unless you wish to draw the attention of Quietus."

He paused for a moment, and when he spoke next, it was with no small amount of fear in his voice.

"I have seen glimpses of it only a few times, never close enough to catch or confront, and each time I felt as though every bit of terror I'd ever experienced in my life had come back to haunt me." His eyes fell on each of them in turn before he continued. "Quietus is nothing to play with. It has hurt some who sought it, killed a few of your relatives, maimed others, and broken the minds of more than a few. My own father was killed in the labyrinth by the creature. It built a small home out of his bones next to his body and left him here in Grandfather's Library for someone to find. I was young—too young to be down here—but I was the first to see him."

The baron dropped his head to stare at the ground, lost for a moment in memories that Flitch could only glimpse the shape of, the sharp edges that worked at his father day and night.

Flitch had a thought then, a dark, horrible thought. It hurt to even consider, and when it worked its way slantwise through his mind, he shuddered.

They had been told their mother had died, tragically and horribly, in "an accident below." That's what their father had told them, and they had accepted it with the childish trust that only the young and mourning can offer. Flitch could remember little from that time, only bare memories of his mother from before—her quiet laugh and the way she hummed with pleasure while eating—but he could remember how hard it had been for the older siblings who had known her more, Idyll especially. They had refused to talk about what might have happened, and even years later, as the harsh sting of their loss dulled into something deeper and more profound for the siblings, Idyll would never join in their speculations about what their mother might have been doing with their father during her "accident below."

And now, it seemed, Flitch had an answer.

"That thing—Quietus—killed our mother." No need to make it a question, with the answer so obvious. The real question, the one rising on a wave of anger inside Flitch, was—

"Why didn't you tell us?" Zim asked, beating Flitch to it and surprising everyone with the harsh, ragged tone of his voice.

"I wanted to protect you," the baron said, and when he looked up at them, the pain of his decision was plain on his face. Eyes made for kindness and laughter filled now with tears, and his large, callused hands spread and clenched at his sides. "Your mother and I explored it together, and when I lost her here, I couldn't bring any of you kids into this more than I already had. I knew if I told you more, you would want to explore, maybe for vengeance, maybe for knowledge, maybe for some other reason entirely. But I couldn't do that."

He shook his head and swallowed, the sound loud in the sudden silence.

"The Borders family has always maintained a mystery around this place for those outside the family and for those too young to explore its ways," he said finally. "When I lost your mother down here, I simply let that mystery continue. Maybe I would have shown you the secret at some point. Maybe not. To be entirely truthful, I have often considered sealing the archway up and being done with the whole thing. But I couldn't."

"Why?" Flitch asked. This thing had taken their mother. It had taken their father's father. And all for some vague promise of a gift? Something that could restore their barony or bring them even lower? Something that he might never find after spending his life searching for it?

"Because . . ." their father began, but Aster cut in, and Flitch was surprised to hear the ragged edge of tears in her voice.

"Because you were going to find this thing and get it to bring her back."

Flitch felt as though he'd been kicked hard in the chest. The air whispered in and out of his open mouth, his lungs barely moving as his heart pounded frantically against the walls of his ribs. Those early days after losing their mother rushed through his memory, the sudden tears, the questions going unanswered, the long silences and sharp surprise of speech. Finding Idyll still in bed at midday, their eyes puffy and distant. Watching Aster rage over the smallest of things. Peering in at Zim in his room, folding and refolding his clothes with shaking hands.

What would Flitch have given to have their mother back in those days?

What would he have done, even at so young an age, even with so little knowledge of the world or how it worked?

His father was wrong—in those years just after the loss of their mother, the siblings wouldn't have rushed below to enact vengeance or seek knowledge. They would have been there beside him, seeking this creature in the dark, each one of them carrying the same hope. The same demand.

"Yes," the baron said, voice gruff and quiet.

Flitch swallowed a sob and moved forward, reaching his arms around his father's torso, and after a moment, he felt Aster and Zim join him, all of them embracing their father, who sighed deeply and draped his heavy arms around them in return.

It took a long time for them to disentangle, and they were each wiping at their eyes as they did.

"There will be time later to talk of this," the baron said after a moment, sniffing once and blinking away the remnant tears. "For now, let me say only: I am sorry to have kept this from you."

In his mind, Flitch heard Idyll, as though they were standing beside him, saying in their soft, measured voice: *I'm sorry you've had to bear this alone.*

Idyll really should have been there.

"Do not let this sad story take away from this truth," their father continued. "Quietus is more dangerous than anything you will ever see or meet or experience in this world. Its gift is tinged with violence. It is rose and thorn both. I have spent many, many days and nights seeking it."

Flitch had a sudden vision of his father, one hand buried in his beard, eyes wrinkled in thought, nearly lost in the labyrinth below his own crumbling home, seeking not the fame his barony might need but the wife his family did. His children happily ignorant above, racing about and playing in the sunlight while he labored endlessly in the dark.

To carry the weight of a failing legacy was enough, but to search for salvation like this, hoping and praying for something that sounded worse than chance, more failing than fortune? To carry a secret, hopeful and shameful, all alone for so long?

"Faineant knows of Grandfather's Library, but he does not know what is beyond. The stories of your great-great-great-grandfather's sprawling archive persist, but Faineant is clever enough to suspect something hidden from him. Nab cannot find this place, and I cannot be inside it to keep it closed while he is here."

"So, you want one of us to stay in the labyrinth while Nab is here?" Aster asked, balling a fist into the corner of one eye as she looked at the splitting paths beyond Grandfather's Library. Flitch was reminded of how she used to look when, the four of them playing outside together, Aster would crow her bravery to the sky before leaping from a tree branch or plunging her hand into an ant hill or stuffing a worm in her mouth. Aster acted, confident and sure.

"Yes," the baron said. "It is easy enough to say my children are at their work in the country or city. He will think nothing of it. But for me to be absent would arouse more than a little suspicion."

Noise from upstairs filtered down to them, muffled and distant.

"That will be Nab arriving," the baron said, shaking his head before stepping closer to the entrance to the labyrinth. He picked up several well-packed bags slung from a peg on the wall.

"Food and drink for you," he said, passing them out. "Follow the rules of court. Follow them exactly. Assuming the rooms haven't changed since I was down here this morning, you should be safest going to the left, then up, then to the left again and waiting there. *Do not explore.* If a room is different *in any way* from what is on the map, do not engage with the change. Do your best to not even look at it. Touch nothing. Eat and drink nothing but the food from your packs. If you see Quietus, turn and walk away. Do not engage. Do not speak to it. Flee carefully and quickly, even if it has not yet been long enough."

He stepped back toward the archway leading to the rest of the house, hands clasping and unclasping in an anxious rhythm.

"I'm sorry. I wanted to introduce you to this slowly. Carefully. I'm sorry. Left, up, left, wait. Give it your best approximation of three-quarters of a day. That should be enough time. Left, up, left. Remember the rules. All of them. Stick together. The labyrinth is odd and frightening and cares nothing for us. Do not explore it. Do not treat it like a home. It is more dangerous and fickle than ever King Faineant could be."

He was stepping back now, through the archway and into the house, and it felt as if he were suddenly a world away, standing there beside an old bookcase and a few empty barrels, his eyes concerned.

"Remember the rules," he said, speaking in a low, fierce whisper now. "Stick together. Left, up, le—"

A dark, dull wall suddenly existed where there had been only an archway, the stone cracked with age but still sturdy.

"What happened?" Zim said, stepping toward the space where their father had been. They could hear nothing from the outside now, no more sounds from the house, no urgent advice from their father.

Flitch turned to see Aster, one foot over the threshold into the labyrinth, her smile wide and mischievous.

"Oh, come on," she said in response to the looks of shock her brothers gave her. "You know how Father is with goodbyes. He would have stood there, saying the same thing over and over, incapable of just letting us fly free, until Nab came down, bid him hello, and asked to join us on our trip into our family's most sacred and secret heirloom. Someone needed to move us along."

Flitch laughed through his surprise and shock. The moment was marred by Idyll's absence and the revelations from their father, but it shone nonetheless.

He opened his map book again, flipping to the page for the room that should be to the left. It was labeled *The Low Place* in a hand Flitch didn't recognize.

"I still think we should have at least let him finish his sentence," Zim said, shouldering his supply bag and opening his map book, his irritation barely covering the thrum of excitement in his voice.

Aster scoffed and brushed his words away with a flick of one hand. She had lifted the torch and already hidden a hand. Zim and Flitch would hold the maps then.

"Are we ready?" she asked, looking between them, mouth hanging just slightly open.

"Let's go," Flitch said, and Zim nodded.

"Idyll is going to be so fucking jealous," Aster said with a cackle.

Flitch followed her into the labyrinth.

The path to left narrowed quickly, so much so that they had to walk single file for a short time, before it widened again on to a cavernous room filled with what first seemed to be tiny toys littering the floor, which was itself covered in a large rug stretching to the walls on every side, perfectly tailored to fit the odd, oblong space.

Aster walked into the room first and was about to step forward when Flitch hissed, "Aster, the rules!"

Aster brought her extended foot back, nodding. She stepped to the left and bowed, just as they had always done at court, a curiosity about which their family was regularly mocked.

Flitch and Zim followed, each dutifully stepping to the left and bowing before walking forward into the room.

The toys turned out to be tiny models of houses and stores, towers and castles, arranged with perfect precision to create a small version of an entire city, bigger than any Flitch had ever seen, including Halcyon.

As he bent down, he saw with surprise that many of the homes were inhabited by people, each one smaller than his little finger and carved with bewildering accuracy, faces full of expression, tiny hands held aloft in greeting and textured with wrinkles and the fine growth of hair on knuckles and wrists.

"This is incredible," Flitch whispered, peering into a tower where, on the tallest level, two men were frozen in the steps of a dance, their arms curved gently around one another, eyes caught together, lips curved into soft smiles that were so intimate that Flitch felt somewhat voyeuristic to be seeing them. The swirl of their cloaks, the lightness of their feet—it was all captured in the carving of them, so real that Flitch had to blink several times to make sure they weren't actually moving, stepping through the form of a dance slow and unending as time itself.

"This is bone," Aster said, kneeling down. She had stowed her torch in a wall bracket and was reaching for a two-story house, but she stopped herself, perhaps remembering their father's cautionary notes.

"It's so orderly," Zim said, looking at the layout from above. "The flow of horse and foot traffic, the sectioning of residential and business. Even the architectural styles shift in clever ways from neighborhood to neighborhood. I should take notes on this . . ." He searched for another word before adding, ". . . stuff."

Odd-numbered sentences. Flitch nodded at him.

As Zim flipped through the map book for an empty page, Aster stood up and laughed.

"Be sure to tell your precious First Pen that you got the idea from a city model made out of bone and located in the magical, uncanny labyrinth below your family's ancestral home."

Zim offered her a wide, fake smile that came nowhere near his eyes.

"We should keep going forward," Flitch said, standing up and looking around the rest of the Low Place. Apart from the thick rug and the miniature city, the room had nothing else in it, which matched perfectly with the map of it.

Aster nodded and moved to the end of the room, where two archways led away, one angling down slightly and to the right, the other sharply upward thanks to a set of stairs carved directly into the rock, each one labeled in a unique and seemingly random way. The first step had *penultimate* carved deeply into it, the letters ornate and curled, while the second had a word Flitch didn't recognize carved in simple, straight lines—a word he had never before seen, could not pronounce or identify, and yet seeing it brought a memory into his head of the soft-claw clutch of a lark sparrow clinging to a stalk of big bluestem bowing in a gentle wind. It was a memory that did not belong to him, he was sure of it, and yet it surged forward in his mind at the merest glimpse of that strange word.

Steps three, five, and eight all had numbers carved into them, too many to make sense of, the digits all crammed in at odd angles, and one of the steps—Flitch wasn't sure which—had a word that had been crossed out and chiseled over to the point of illegibility, though it was clear *something* had been carved there.

Up and up they walked, Zim checking off the stairs as they climbed them, each of them having been carefully labeled and described in the map.

After perhaps fifty or sixty of them, Flitch stopped and looked around.

"How can there be this many stairs?" he asked.

"We still have sixteen more," Zim said, holding up the map in his hand. Of course he had counted them out.

"If this many stairs are tiring you out," Aster said, turning around and grinning down at Flitch, "then you should really be taking more exercise. This is nothing."

"No," Flitch said, shaking his head, trying to stay focused on his words to ensure he spoke in odd-numbered sentences. The word carved into the next step ahead of him was *belletristic*, and reading it brought a wave of something sweet-tasting into his mouth even though he had neither eaten nor drunk anything. "With this many steps, we should have been inside the house by now. We should be standing in Idyll's room or maybe even higher."

Aster and Zim looked around, the truth of Flitch's words dimming their excitement and purpose. They climbed the last sixteen steps in silence.

At the top, they were met with two paths, one leading left and the other right. To the left, the path was dark and silent, and a cold wind slithered out from it. To the right, a gentle light shone, warm and flickering, as though a bonfire waited there, crackling out its invitation.

"The Merry Demise," Zim said, peering down at his map and gesturing to the room to the right.

"Father said we go left and wait," Aster said, mostly to herself, as she turned away from the Merry Demise and whatever was making the light.

Flitch flipped to the map for this place and found a square-shaped room with a circle of green grass fitted into its center surrounded by a ring of seven chairs, one of which had a large X over it, the two lines drawn and redrawn.

The Green Pool, the room was called.

Flitch followed Aster inside and, after stepping to the left, bowing, and taking the measure of the room, fought the deep, powerful urge to turn around immediately and let his feet fly down the stairs.

It was a square room, as shown on the map. At its center, a circular recess had been cut in the stone floor, the line perfect and smooth, and from this recess, a stand of grass grew, one Aster could probably identify but to Flitch looked pretty in a banal kind of way. The grass grew perhaps to his chest and bounced gently in the cool wind cutting through the room. A mote of light, cold white and constant, hung over the grass, its illumination barely reaching farther than the edge of the pool and ending in ragged tatters of light.

The chairs surrounded the grass pool, just as they did on the map. Simple wooden things, unpainted, the slats twisted by age and bleached by a sun that did not shine below the earth.

All of that was normal, as it should have been, identical to the map in his hand.

Except . . .

"There are only six of them," Flitch said, his voice hushed. He looked at the map again, mouthing the numbers as he looked at each chair—seven, including the one with an X drawn over it. "Here," Flitch added in a rush, realizing the folly of his sentence. "There are only six of them here."

"Shit," Aster said, her eyes flicking between her open map and the room.

"What did Father say to do if the map was wrong?" Zim asked, his nostrils flaring as he stepped back to the wall, aligning his spine with the safety of the rock.

"He said to avoid the change in the room," Flitch said. "We aren't even supposed to look at it if we can help it."

"How are we supposed to avoid something that doesn't exist anymore?" Aster asked, throwing out her free hand.

"What do you think the *X* means?" Zim asked, holding out his map so that Aster could see.

As Aster studied the map, Flitch studied the room, letting his eyesight go fuzzy and unfocused as it moved past the absence where the seventh chair should have been. He couldn't have said why, would have been at a loss to explain why that chair's absence affected him so deeply, but it did. Every bit of excitement and joy, every bit of pleasure at walking these tunnels and rooms with his siblings, at finally knowing his family's secret, vanished into the nothing where that chair should have been.

The labyrinth is odd and frightening and cares nothing for us, their father had said, and Flitch felt suddenly the attention of this place turning toward them, watching with alien expectation to see what they would do with this bit of change. Every crack, every stone, every puff of air and film of mildew hummed with a silent, impossibly other attention, and Flitch felt like he might burst.

The six present chairs were exactly where the map said they would be, and the wall still had scuffs and scratches in the places noted on the map. He wasn't going to do it, but Flitch was willing to bet that even the hairline cracks in the floor that someone had carefully noted down on the map would be the same if someone were to follow them out around the room.

Gentle tufts of moss dotted the walls and corners where they were supposed to, and the frame of a window hung askew high on one stone wall precisely where it was shown to be on the map, the thing's wooden pieces holding only the broken-teeth remnants of glass.

Only the chair was gone; only that had changed.

It looked as if someone had stepped into the room, grabbed one of the chairs, and left with it.

But who? The baron on his last time through? Had he moved it and forgotten to tell them in his haste to get upstairs to Nab?

Or maybe it was the thing, Quietus, that walked the labyrinth, dangling its promise of a gift in front of generations of Borders Barons and their families. The thing that had taken their mother and, in taking her, had in so many ways taken their father, too.

"Do we go back or stay here?" Aster asked, handing the map book back to Zim and taking the torch from him, which she held like a club, ready to swing.

"Father told us to wait here for most of a day." Zim had dropped his head and was staring at his feet, the absence to be avoided completely out of his field of view.

"Father also thought this would be a safe place to wait," Flitch said. "Is it still?"

"Yes," Aster said at the same time Zim said, "No."

"It's one chair," Aster said, adopting the voice she often used with the siblings younger than her—never for Idyll, of course. It said she was annoyed at having to explain something so simple to them, but she was willing to do it out of her love for and duty to her family. Despite being only a year older than Zim and three older than Flitch, she managed to find a voice that sounded world-weary and tired.

"Father said we should avoid any changes and didn't know this room would be changed when he told us to wait in here," Zim said, slowing down at the end as he counted out the words on his one free hand.

"We can't leave the labyrinth yet," Flitch said, speaking for the others as much as for himself, working slowly through the logic and his own sentences, "and we don't know of any rooms that father would have considered safe to stay in while we wait. Grandfather's Library is clearly safe but would leave the archway open. We shouldn't explore further, and we still have most of our time to wait inside. I say we wait here."

"Maybe we could just stay here against the wall and ignore *the space where it's supposed to be* until it's time to leave," Zim said, his head still down, although Flitch could see the rapid movement of his eyes. Ever since he was a little boy, Zim had not dealt well with this kind of confusion. He liked clear choices and order, his toys put away in their correct locations, his room neat, and his world sensical.

When they were younger, Flitch had seen other kids mock Zim for his fastidious tendencies and think it permissible because Zim would never stand up to them, preferring instead to let his gaze wander away from their insults and to the sky. He kept a cloud journal, noting down all the new shapes and textures he noticed throughout the day.

But what those kids missed were the mornings and nights Zim spent working tirelessly to make his world ordered, the books he filled with numbers and charts and graphs in the hopes of making sense of every new thing he experienced. What they missed were his furious tears when things didn't make sense, his rage and helplessness at the banal chaos he encountered.

And though Aster would poke fun at him in the safety of their own home, she would be the one leading the charge to serve Zim's antagonists the beating they earned, Flitch and Idyll close behind.

Flitch stepped closer to Zim, putting his shoulder against his brother's. "I agree that we should stay here."

Silence bloomed into the room then, neither comfortable nor easy, and as he moved his eyes around the room—carefully avoiding the space where another chair should be—a strange thought struck Flitch.

Their father had been preparing them for the labyrinth in his own way—the rules at court, the insistence that they be followed at all times. But he had said something in his quick explanation of this place, something that echoed in Flitch's mind now.

I couldn't bring any of you kids into this more than I already had, he'd said. But he hadn't brought any of them into this until now, right?

Flitch remembered suddenly the stories Idyll told him after their mother died, the tales of a vast labyrinth in the Paths house, filled with mysterious rooms and a strange, fickle creature that walked its ways. They told the same stories of that place to Flitch for many nights, and though he'd thought it a wondrous and fantastical possibility then, he saw it for the truth that it was now.

Idyll had been down there, perhaps with their father, perhaps with their mother. Maybe with both. Whatever process existed in Borders to introduce the young to the wonders and horrors of these tunnels had already begun for Idyll when their mother died.

More than I already had, the baron had said, and he'd meant Idyll.

Idyll who had seen this place, had known of the family secret and said nothing to the siblings.

Had said *nothing* to Flitch save for the stories, perhaps their way to prepare him indirectly, to speak of this place without speaking of it.

Could the baron have forced them to keep it secret?

Of course. As he'd said, he wanted to protect his children, and this was how Borders protected its own: secrets and untold truths.

Betrayal twisted inside Flitch's gut, and as he leaned back against the wall, he felt as though he might vomit.

He worked these thoughts over and over in his mind, searching for something that wouldn't make sense, anything to make it clear that his sibling and closest friend hadn't kept this from him, but it became more and more obvious with each consideration.

"Let's at least be comfortable while waiting," Aster said, pulling Flitch from his thoughts and, before anyone could stop her, dropping into a chair.

The wood groaned a little, old as it was, but the chair held, and Aster's smile resurfaced.

"See?" she said, gesturing with the torch in her one free hand, her bravado rising valiantly to cover what Flitch knew to be her own fear. "They're chairs, fools. They're meant to be occupied."

Flitch opened his mouth to respond but stopped, sure that he had heard something in one of the tunnels leading away from the Green Pool. It was light and bright, like someone dropping bits of metal on the stone floor, but it might just as well have been drips of water, and Zim was wiping his face after taking a drink of water from the bottle in his pack. Had it just been that?

"I don't think so, Aster," Zim said, shaking his head, still not looking up. He sank down to the ground, letting his legs cross beneath him and keeping his back to the wall. He pulled out some of the food next, and sitting there like that, he looked so young again, just like Flitch remembered him. As young as Flitch still thought himself to be.

That was the problem with his siblings' growing up—they changed before his eyes, growing into adults even as the Flitch inside his own head never seemed to change, left behind in adolescence by siblings who wouldn't wait for him.

"I'm not even looking at the gap," Aster said, nodding toward the place where there should have been a seventh chair. She shifted in her own chair so that her back was to the gap. "See? Easy. And I get to look at this pool of . . . bluestem, maybe? It looks like bluestem, but not any strand I've cast from. The coloring is all wrong even though it has . . ."

Of course Aster knew the plants, but Flitch lost the thread of her words as he heard a noise again, this time coming from the stairway, a kind of slithering, hissing noise, quiet and hushed, and his heart thudded against his ribs as he saw Zim turn that way too, his eyes wide. It hadn't been in Flitch's head, which meant the first noise probably hadn't either.

"Did you hear that?" Zim asked as Aster continued to wax botanical.

"Yes," Flitch said, feeling the pull in his gut as he realized Zim's sentence had only four words, but the noises were coming from every direction now, shivering down through the cracks in the walls and huffing up from the tufts and hills of moss, which had begun to expand and contract as though each one were a tiny green lung heaving for air.

A song, airy and broken, sounded behind the noises, a melody to their rhythms, and though Flitch could not discern the words, he knew—in that deep-down place where real knowing happens—that something bigger than anything he could comprehend was coming his way. Gone were the anticipation and the joy at a day spent with his siblings.

Terror like nothing else, terror bright and whirring and whining, terror unconquered by metaphor or simile, took hold of Flitch. Every part of him went cold and still save for a small voice in his mind that screamed endlessly, breathlessly.

It was coming. The giver of gifts. The beast that had driven Borders children to madness, that had killed his own grandfather and played with his bones.

Quietus, who walked the labyrinth, was coming.

Aster had stopped and was staring, open-mouthed, at the passage leading to the stairs, the torch dipping closer and closer to the grasses, which bent and arced for the flames, straining at their roots for it.

The noises, hissing and whispering and clicking and tinkling and dripping and singing and—was that laughter ringing out?—converged into a single point in Flitch's head, and perhaps he screamed, too. His mouth was open, jaw straining to release the pressure, and through his slitted eyes he saw Aster writhing on the chair, the torch now lost in the burning grasses, the flames black and speckled with tiny flickers of bright white light.

Zim had dropped into a crouch and had pressed both of his hands to his ears, the map book open on the floor in front of him, pages cascading back and forth as though flipped through by an invisible hand.

The tumult ended abruptly, the mess of noise disappearing and leaving just one behind: footsteps, too many of them for the lone figure that stepped into the room.

Quietus had found them.

Twist sleeps, and its people dream a world of sun and sky and Sea, a world that was, with people who were. One by one, the listeners have dropped off, abandoning their tenuous hold on waking and falling totally under the storyteller's spell. Here is the world's true magic: a story of what was and the promise of what will be.

Seeds grown in light and dark into a Sea, weaving and waving in hopeful green.

A child grown into a woman willing to chase wonder and seek in darkness.

A child watching the world change around him and grasping for what he has already lost.

The storyteller has placed a hand on every cheek and arm, a ritual he moves through with solemnity in each community he visits.

Perhaps, he offers with each touch. *Maybe. Perchance.*

Hope, he gives them. Simply that. What he struggles so hard to find himself.

Twist sleeps.

Except for Praise.

The man who saw in the storyteller a safety for his community sits still and silent, the muscles of his face and body gone totally slack. He breathes in panicked huffs, and his eyes roll and widen in fear.

Terror, the storyteller thinks, as he always does, his mind falling into the thoughts and movements this cycle demands. Praise fears what he does not know, cannot know. It is not the horror of watching and understanding a violent act.

Just as the rest of Twist dreams of possibilities fired by hope, Praise dreams of possibilities thrumming with mights and maybes of fear. His own mind imagines endless terrifying paths he might even now be on.

The truth, as he will soon come to know, is in the story itself.

The plants and animals of the Sea that have stayed back during his visit make tentative moves to enter Twist now, growing in spastic reaches forward or careful leaps. Slithering and swinging, pawing and flapping, they come into Twist for the first time, moving among the people there without ill intent, abiding by the storyteller's peace.

Roaches scuttle between the feet of a child and stare with unblinking, inky eyes.

Vines split and split until they form a watchful canopy over the two lovers, sending out gossamer leaves that shift and move with their breath.

Creatures descended from birds, feathers long ago replaced by sticky scales, soar through the air and land on the shoulders of the sleepers, cocking their heads in deep, careful consideration.

They do not need hope, these beings of the Sea. It is there in their every movement and breath. The same might be said of the people of Twist, but they forget so easily, look outside when they ought to look inward or— better—not look at all. Why search for hope when you have been singing it with every word, sounding it with every gesture?

Praise's eyes widen with shock as the first creatures of the Sea come into view, and he watches them, first with concern and then with confusion, as they move among the sleeping. He is looking at these creatures, and so he does not see that which walks among them.

The storyteller does, though, and he watches as that pool of shadow, shrouding some inscrutable form, approaches along with the creatures of the Sea, every plant and animal, every bird and insect keeping its distance. Even the lowest, simplest creature of the Sea understands that whatever walks in those shadows is not to be crossed.

"Him," the storyteller says, the word accusation and edict all at once. He raises one glowing hand and points at Praise, who stares back at the storyteller in panic now. Praise understands that *something* is happening, something important going on just outside his line of sight.

Those shadows swirl and writhe, and the storyteller has come to think of that movement as something like anticipation. Not excitement, exactly, and not happiness, either—never happiness for this being.

But anticipation of a pattern once more completed. Of a debt once more settled.

The Sea gets its fill of looking and, slowly, retreats again, roaches skittering back into the dark, vines retracting, creatures climbing or flying away. They leave almost nothing of themselves, and when Twist wakes, it will be to a curious wondering at the odd footprints pressed into the ground around them, the strange feeling that something has happened, something important, but it has gone too quickly and left only the feeling of its absence.

They do not go far, though. Even these beings of the Sea wait to hear the end of the tale.

The storyteller nods at these creatures and plants as they leave, nods as he has so many times before and as he will so many more times. Once, he longed for change, for disruption and growth and death and all the rest. He hungered for it deep down, where the smallest, truest parts of him existed.

Now, the thought of variation is a fantasy so distant, he cannot even laugh at its impossibility. He walks. He speaks. He offers what must be forgotten. And he walks again.

Only his book, his wild, forgotten forever, holds that last whisper of possibility.

Perhaps, a small voice whispers in his mind—the same voice he spent the night resurrecting, digging its melodies and music up from the hard, fallow ground of his memory.

The storyteller climbs again the dais and looks out over his audience, all but one deep in slumber.

All but *two*.

Praise is not looking up at the storyteller but is, instead, breathing rapidly through his slack mouth as he stares to the side, able only to glimpse the thing that has settled in beside him, the folds of shadow like delicate cloth caught in a gentle, playful wind. The hint of a form inside is just visible to Praise, and that hint, that *maybe*, is what captures the older man's mind as the storyteller, looking between the two members of his audience, resumes his tale.

CHAPTER TEN

No one moved or spoke for a long, long moment.

The figure stood in the entrance, static in a pool of darkness.

The grasses continued to burn in their steady, silent way, black flames climbing toward the ceiling.

Flitch thought Zim was whimpering and was surprised to find it was actually himself, the sound a weak, mewling thing.

Only Aster moved with any confidence.

She stood, both her hands free now, their father's rules forgotten, and raised herself up onto her tiptoes, arms stretching out to either side in a movement Flitch had seen from her a thousand times. It was the limbering movement she did before beginning her casting practice.

And suddenly her writhing in the chair made sense. *A caster of the fourth ring is always prepared,* she had said, clicking the bones together in her pocket. As Flitch and Zim had struggled to even stand and breathe amidst the storm of sounds, Aster had fought back and made of the green pool a casting fire.

Flitch felt a surge of pride as Aster pulled a handful of casting plants from a pocket and tossed them into the fire, her hands already flicking through the complex movements of an expert caster. Compared to the everyday casters hired on to ships leaving Borders docks, Aster was an artist, painting with a full range of colors while they labored with blacks and whites. She had been so excited when she was accepted to the academy, one of only a few, prouder still to have gotten in despite her name, because no one with any knowledge of it would see Borders as a barony of leverage and power.

Aster got in because she was talented, and she excelled because she was more driven than anyone else.

What she had done on *The Laughing Queen* that morning was nothing compared with this, a meek-mouthed preamble before a stirring epic.

The words of her casting rang in the air, a brilliant staccato song that flared into pinpricks of light almost too bright to see, each one bursting like a sun from the end of her fingers and flung toward the creature with a practiced, almost careless flick.

Like stars cutting through the night sky, tossed by a bored child stranded in space, Aster's spell careened through the room and broke against the figure in the tunnel, erupting into sprays of light and color and heat so intense that Flitch was thrown back against the wall.

But Aster was not finished.

Her song changed, inflected by the wide, manic smile on her face and the boisterous laughter bubbling through her voice. She shouted and leapt into the air, tendrils of red and gold power pulled from the wild fire in the pool and coalescing now around her, encasing her body in a sorcerous fire.

Aster slapped her hands together, arms straight, shoulders bunching around her ears as the pent-up power poured forth, rushing across the space between her and the creature and engulfing it in a bonfire of spell-work that lit the chamber and threw odd shadows across the walls—many-fingered hands reaching out and writhing, wriggling snakelike things; blocks of darkness that tumbled against one another like dice across the walls and out of sight.

It was magic like Flitch had never seen before, and his sister had done it. Aster, who used to pilfer sweets from the kitchens and bring them up to her siblings late at night, mischief lining her face.

Aster, who screamed endlessly at their father before leaving for the academy on her first day, tears of rage and embarrassment and shame and sorrow coursing down her cheeks, and Aster, who returned half a year later with tears of a different kind, apologies running thick from her lips.

Aster who could love fiercely and hate fiercely and who had no use for any emotion that didn't burn hot and fast and bright.

Aster had gone away and found the power she had so wished her own father had, and she used it now, pulling every mote of magic from the paltry handful of plants she'd had in her pocket.

Her last spell was a lance of sunset red that drizzled a steady crimson trail onto the ground, the droplets hissing and smoking as they burned away to nothing. The attack hit and cut through the shadowed creature in the doorway, showing for the barest instant a face buried in the folds of darkness. The skin was an array of tiny leaves, perfect reds and hopeful goldenrods and deep browns, veined in bright sapphire, all overlapping and shivering at their edges, an autumnal palindrome writ endlessly across its face. A mouth cut through the foliage in a single slash, off-kilter and hanging slightly open to reveal a darkness inside that, even in the single moment he saw it, Flitch felt sure went on forever. Stars and moons and suns twinkled and burned distantly inside that slantwise maw, galaxies spiraling inward and outward forever.

Its eyes were closed, but they flicked away beneath the leaf-scale eyelids, dreaming, moving and wriggling like a child beneath a blanket.

Aster finished her movement—her one, long movement, every piece connected and continuous—in a crouch, her head down, shoulders and back rising and falling rapidly as she sucked in breath.

Quietus, no bigger than a person, stood statue-still, outline just barely visible now that the light of Aster's spells had faded.

A cold sweat broke out along Flitch's back and neck a moment before Quietus spoke, not with a voice, not with any utterance, though a deep, husking noise did emanate from the somewhere well inside its folds of darkness.

It spoke with light.

A lazy wave of golden light drifted from one slowly extended hand, gentle and soft as a butterfly cutting its whirligig way through a long morning sky. The light split and converged, tracing a web across the space between Quietus and the Borders siblings.

In those threads, Quietus spoke and Flitch heard, an array of confusing, overwhelming information crashing through all of his senses.

Words cascaded through his mind, the voice his own. *Welcome children of the first, branch of the branch of the branch of the branch, full-flower grown and growing.*

Living stone filled Flitch's hands as he climbed through his home, burrowing deeper and farther, each space an artwork, shaping the air trapped for so long into things, approximating the dreams and hopes of those beings above, so loud and destructive, all mouths and eyes and fists.

The smell of green growth in the dark, of creatures old as dirt and air, of beginnings and their promised endings filled Flitch's nose, pulling him along a line of memories that broke and reassembled his mind with each turning century.

Fresh water sparkled against his tongue, the bounty gathered in the holy temple of dawn's first chamber, the taste pure and wide, the horizon in a droplet.

He heard the song of all things, the mighty Sea and the holy Beings below, the Seven Rains to the east and the Eidolons' sad, silent wails, the tiny voices of people dotting a world they pretended to own and the world itself, its endless grey-sky song of love, love, love.

He saw and smelled and felt and heard and tasted everything time and a slow life could offer. It was all inscribed somehow in the light released by Quietus, a name that soured in Flitch's mouth as he blinked and returned to himself.

This thing wore the name like an ill-fitting garment, tattered and loose, slipping from it with every movement and gesture. It had lived long enough to have many names, each another partial thing, a fragment. Some were words: Quietus, End-speaker, the walker of the ways, and long, long before, the Broken Shield.

But others were names of a different sort.

The light in the air after a thunderstorm in summer, and the sweat-coddled feeling of it, too.

The sound a stone makes after being tossed by a young, bored child late in the day, its hard, round edge striking another stone and clicking just so.

Love that has grown old and, in its age, has begun to fracture.

Loss so great and deep that it cannot be understood or overcome, cannot be rent or beaten or worked through.

All of these described this creature too.

As the light of its message faded, any hope of this creature offering a free gift to the barony evaporated from Flitch's mind. In its memories, he had seen the favors granted to his relatives, paltry nonsenses offered by a creature curious about these people traipsing through its home, standing and bowing and speaking so oddly in its creations.

It would not have brought his mother back, not if the baron had found it, not if anyone had found it. Such a request would have been a curious absurdity to this being who existed in ways no human could ever fully understand.

The deaths had been nonsensical bibelots, too, accompanied each time by some disgust as it looked deeply into these people and saw seekers who had lost their way, too far from their path to find their way back. Quiet had been the answer. Quiet and return.

"Oh, no," Zim whispered, almost certainly arriving at the same conclusion as Flitch.

Aster, who had remained in her crouch throughout all of this, pushed herself up, readying for a fight despite what she now knew, what they all now knew.

Quietus was not a creature to be found and begged for a gift. It was not a creature to be handled by adherence to flimsy rules only tenuously attached to its predilections.

It was not a creature to be sought. It sought you when it desired to do so, or when it tired of your footsteps in its home.

Flitch was suddenly desperately, profoundly grateful that Idyll was not there. One Borders sibling would survive, live on to—

A thought clutched at him, brave and stupid in the way that all brave things were. Running through every story Idyll used to tell him, holding them all together like a bright, golden line, was one truth about the heroes who won out in the end: they were willing, always, to give themselves up for others. Perhaps it was their time, perhaps the strength of their arms or the cleverness of their minds, and perhaps, last of all, it was their lives.

Somehow, in the maelstrom of terror and confusion and anguish and certainty running through Flitch, he found that bright, golden line and grabbed hold, feeling Idyll's pride prickling along his neck.

"Get out of here!" he shouted to Zim and Aster. "Go get Father!"

And Flitch, abandoning his map and barely slowing to grab the handle of the torch sticking out of the pool, raced further into the labyrinth, knowing Quietus would follow, curious and odd.

Though he swung the torch hard at a chair, smashing it to kindling as he passed by, just to ensure he had the creature's attention.

Flitch passed into a low, wide chamber where three small squirrels were chasing another up and down a vibrant blue tree, swollen fruits bowing its thin, pliable branches nearly to the ground. The squirrels paused as Flitch entered, glaring at him with the single, large eye each had in the center of their heads.

After that was a room with waterfalls cascading upward and sideways and slantwise around the room, all gushing out from the air itself and disappearing back into nothing. The water swirled and swilled on its way down, and Flitch had the certain knowledge that, had he stopped to touch it, it would have been warm and fuzzy.

He ran through a room that was a single bridge suspended over a chasm with no bottom that he could see, with bats winging the air above him.

A room with a campfire set against one wall, the smoke leaving oily smudges along the stone that slid and squirmed in the low light. Next to the campfire was a young boy, sitting too close to the flames, laughing quietly to himself. As Flitch entered, the boy began to turn, and Flitch screamed and ran ahead, desperate to not see whatever that face held.

Room after room he passed through, looking back over his shoulder to ensure Quietus's pursuit. The beast came for him, and though it could have caught Flitch at any point, it didn't. It followed as if to say *Please look through my work. Explore what I have wrought before the end.*

Most rooms were odd, fantastical, horrifying things—spaces where the walls convulsed and sweated, alive and in agony; great cathedrals with otherworldly music shivering through them; caverns filled with trees that shook with something inside their foliage; vast spaces swaying with homages to the Forever Sea, Flitch's feet pounding across a wooden boardwalk set just at the tip of the shifting grasses; tables bowing under the weight of foods known and unknown to Flitch, soups that boiled and burbled, roasts small as his fist and big as a person, vegetables in every color strewn across tables chaotically and arranged with courtly precision on plates and trays of jewel-encrusted silver.

Most of the rooms were completely alien and new to Flitch, but as he ran, he found some that stirred the depths of his memory, and the images evoked by Idyll's stories rose in him, matching with a space that flashed in bright colors and held far-off figures or a room that had doors lined up, frame to frame, along the floor, the wall, and the ceiling—a whole room made of closed doors.

Idyll's stories became for him a guidebook in this strange, distant land, reminding him to step over that strange glowing fern or to plug his ears when that tangle of snakes began to hiss in rhythmic pulses.

And though a sense of betrayal at Idyll's having kept the truth of this place from him still burned inside of Flitch, he felt grateful in those moments, too. Not for the first time in his life, he gave thanks for Idyll's stories.

Inhuman bodies arranged in beautiful patterns; plants that crawled across the floor, trailing their roots and mumbling of greed; motes of light that swam through the air and spoke of futures; two birds beside one another on a branch, each slowly eating the other; rocks stacked precariously atop one another, their shapes a language forgotten; caverns so still and empty that Flitch wept to disturb their tranquility with his footsteps.

It was the work of a lifetime that knew no end, and Flitch might have marveled had his mind not gone slowly numb with each passing wonder and horror.

His feet carried him forward, lungs rasping for air, until he finally stopped, not out of exhaustion—though he was exhausted.

He stepped across the threshold of a room and found himself in his own bedroom, the recreation of it perfect in every way, down to the blankets heaped haphazardly at one corner of his bed, the desk piled with books as unfocused as his own mind—tomes of shipbuilding lore sat next to thin texts on captain's exams, which leaned against piles of books ranging in topic from the great rulers of the past to speculative assessments of lands to the west, known plants of the Forever Sea to economies of the southern islands.

A testament to your possible futures, the baron used to say about Flitch's desk, never prodding him to choose a role but reminding him always that it must be done eventually.

The rug was faded and tattered, though still showing the rich, complicated pattern that must have once stood out so beautifully. The chair had been left leaning against the desk, just as Flitch liked to leave it, to the chagrin of his siblings and father and anyone who ever saw him do it. Dressers and bedside tables and inkwells and clothes and all of it, exactly as Flitch might have found it upon entering his own room.

On the bed, facing one another, were Idyll and Flitch himself, frozen, Idyll's eyes wide, their hands splayed around them, rendered, no doubt, in the act of telling a story to Flitch, who sat cross-legged, hands clasped and shoved down between his legs. His shoulders were pressed up around his ears as he leaned forward, mouth open slightly, eyes wide and locked on Idyll.

It was a scene played out almost every day in Flitch's room or Idyll's, the two sharing space and sharing stories.

It could have been his room, and Flitch, shocked as he was by his time in the labyrinth, might have convinced himself that it *was* his room, that he was dreaming and watching himself, or perhaps that self was dreaming and he was really here—he might have been spelled by all of it if it weren't for the window.

The windows of Flitch's room above, his real room, looked out over the Sea, three big frames surrounding what Idyll liked to jokingly call their "untamed backyard." It was Flitch's favorite part about his room, the thing that, no matter how faded their house became, no matter how in tatters the family's reputation was, how many invitations to court or formal events Borders did not receive—no matter how diminished the barony and his family had become, Flitch always had that view, high up in the Borders estate, looking out over the vastness of the Forever Sea.

He used to sit on the window ledge and stare down at the Sea, a shabby blanket pulled up over his shoulders, imagining that the ripples and lines in the Sea's surface, etched by the wind, were a living language that only he could read, a message from the deeps or from the far side of Forever. He dreamed of sailing his own vessel across those windswept plains, shouting out orders and grabbing at lines tearing free in storms, fending off pirate attacks or beasts from the deep, sword in hand and a grim smile on his lips.

Those windows had been doorways for him, the future waiting on the other side.

These windows, though, showed a scene of horror and destruction. The Sea thrashed and roiled in chaotic winds, veins of greyed, diseased grasses bursting up in uncontrollable growth, choking out healthy plants.

And on their noxious waves rode monstrosities—wyrms and roaches and edge wasps boiling up from the darkness as if driven mad and sent by a vengeful god. These Flitch saw and recognized from the stories he'd heard from his father's sailors and a few of the books on his desk.

But others were strange to him: scuttling and slithering things, creatures with too many eyes or burning with unquenchable flames or leaping from stalk to stalk, some big as ships and others moving in swarms composed of tiny bodies.

Vessels sailed out from the harbor to defend the Mainland, but they sailed to their deaths. The creatures were too many, too powerful, and though the ships burned and buzzed with magical attacks, lashes and lances of power that scorched the Sea and blinded Flitch with their brilliance, it was not enough.

The defenders were overwhelmed, and the nightmares birthed in the dark below the Sea approached the shore.

Footsteps rasped against the stone and then disappeared as Quietus stepped into the room, feet padding into the rug it had recreated.

More rooms lay ahead, doorways and doorways leading ever on, but Zim and Aster would be out by now, and what was the point? What better a place to end this than his own room, standing beside Idyll as they spoke one of their spelled stories into existence, wrapping Flitch up in the possibility and wonder of a tale that might be lived.

Even in the well-lit space of Flitch's faux bedroom, Quietus remained in a shadow that pooled and lapped around it, obscuring its form and body.

"I'm ready," Flitch said, fighting to keep his eyes open. If this was truly the end, he wanted to see and know every bit of it.

This time, when the light emerged from Quietus, it was not the diaphanous golden webwork full of memory and meaning, every stray sparkle and glow bursting with information.

Instead, a single speck of light, blue-green and burning, floated out from Quietus, bobbing gently as though floating on water and making its slow way to Flitch. A manic voice in his head began to keen and urge him to run, flee, to not let that bit of fiery light touch him, but Flitch could not have moved even if he still had any energy, even if his legs didn't feel like mud, his lungs like empty wineskins.

The light neared and neared and neared, and just as it was about to touch his chest, it stopped, and he felt Quietus's attention, a fraction of its mighty, cosmic attention, settle on him.

When the voice spoke, it was in his head, distinctly his own voice, his slight nasal pitch, his way of rounding off certain vowels and sliding through others. Quietus was using his voice, his mind, to speak to Flitch.

You seek a storied life, the voice—*his* voice—said. *You wish to become the star so that you might shine on your family.*

"Yes," Flitch said after a moment, his face tingling and numb. He had a feeling that even if he'd wanted to lie, he wouldn't have been able to. And why lie there at the end? What use were such things when all else was gone?

You yearn for a life made for memory, full of power and glory, adventure and mystery. You want to be the key unlocking all your family's problems, those of the here and now and those of the long-suffered. All this I offer you for a price.

"What price?" Flitch asked, his lips barely moving. A distant part of his mind wondered if this was shock or if he had already died, but then Quietus spoke through him again.

That you will be forgotten. That your deeds, worthy as they may be of stories, will never be remembered by any but you. Your memory will stretch toward infinity even as you drip like water from a cupped hand from the minds of those nearby. A fragment you will be. The husk of a tale, half-remembered and easily lost again.

"Idyll will remember me," Flitch said, the certainty so overwhelming that it brought tears to his eyes. "I'll tell them my story and they'll remember me."

No. I will be your only audience. Should you try to spread the seed of your story, it will find dry, cracked ground and will die away before blooming. If—when—you speak your story into the world, I will be there, and I will take from your audience.

Flitch had a sudden vision of himself, sitting in a thickly padded armchair, a fire burning low nearby, his own children sitting at his feet as he spoke of his own life, his great defeats and greater glories. The upturned faces were open and amazed, and if they whispered occasionally among themselves, it was not distraction but a necessity for the story, the call-and-response of a tale well told.

They would be enchanted that way, rapt and wrapped with wonder, when Quietus came, moving among them without their knowledge to collect its debt. They would not see it coming, and that would make it all the worse.

Yes, that voice said, pleased by his understanding. *You will have a hand in the grand goings-on of this world. And you will be forgotten.*

That speck of light still hovered there at his chest, waiting for his decision, and Flitch realized on some level that he really could say no to this bargain. Perhaps Quietus would play with him some more, or perhaps it would let him go. Perhaps it would kill him where he stood or let him wander the labyrinth for the rest of his life, but he could say no, and whatever strange intelligence fired inside the shadows around Quietus would respect it.

But in the end, that didn't matter, because Flitch had already made the decision. What danger was there in being forgotten to a boy whom the world had already forgotten? A boy whose family had long since passed into the dusty tomes of history.

The decision to accept was like a well-prepared path for Flitch, and he took it with little hesitation.

"Yes," he said, and the speck of light was inside him then, burning there, a heat that radiated out along his veins, scouring away impurity.

Flitch saw only the barest shape of what this would mean for his future and present, and he bore down against the heat with the knowledge that he had made the right choice. His life, whatever was left of it, would fold unevenly around this crease, a divide between Before and After.

His hands were still his hands, his arms still his arms, and a cautious survey of his body revealed it to be unchanged save for perhaps the slightest luminescence in his skin that could have been from the room itself.

A single hand emerged from the shadow around Quietus, gnarled and with too many fingers, each layered with more leaves, clutching a book.

Flitch took it without thought, the movement as natural as a child reaching for the hand of a parent.

Sing, memory, a voice said, and it might have been from Quietus and it might have been from Flitch. His vision was going fuzzy and dark, and the floor was pulling him down, and the last thing he saw were the two people on the bed turning to watch him fall with looks of profound sadness on their faces.

———◦◆◦———

"Flitch? Come on, come on, Flitch!"

"He's breathing, right?"

"Back up, Zim! Yes, he's breathing!"

"*You* back up, Aster! You're as bad as him!"

"I think he moved! Should we take him further out?"

"Father said to leave him here. He'll be back soon with the medicker."

"Who knows how long that could take!"

"And what would you like to do instead?"

"I . . . I don't know. Something. Anything!"

"The best we can do is wait here for Father to return. Hell! I wish Idyll were here. They'd know what to do."

"Yeah."

"Are you okay? Don't tell me you're going to be sick again."

"Just thinking about it all is making me queasy."

"Let's stop talking until Father returns. You've already thrown up way too many times, Zim."

"I can't help it!"

Flitch rose from unconsciousness to the clamor of his siblings' bickering, each soft barb and gentle jab music that he thought he would never hear again. He lay with his eyes closed for a long time, listening to them, the curve and rhythm of their voices, committing each one to memory as best he could, holding them close.

In one hand, he still held the book from Quietus.

Aster's brash directness, blunt and honest, a voice made for laughing. Zim, his hesitant, quick voice, his words so often floating on a half-hidden smile. Only Idyll was missing, their soft, gentle voice, given to questions more than answers.

Flitch breathed in the melodies of his siblings, and only after soaking in them did he finally shift and groan, opening his eyes and looking up at their worried faces above him.

"Thank you, every god who has existed and might exist," Aster said, slumping back as the relief snapped the tension in her body.

Zim stared at Flitch, his face a mess of sweat, and he absolutely looked close to vomiting.

Their arms were around Flitch before he could even react, his siblings wrapping him up in a hug, and Flitch leaned into it, smiling, feeling their relieved weeping and surprised that he wasn't crying in return. It had become a well-chewed joke in the family to remark on how easily Flitch cried.

"Don't drop that carrot," one of them might caution at dinner before gesturing gravely toward Flitch. "We wouldn't want Flitchy to weep at such misfortune."

Tender, his father called him, though never as a pejorative. To be tender was to be open to the world and all its wonder, according to the Borders Baron. He would smile and hug his son, whispering, "Come here, my sweet, tender boy."

"What happened?" Aster asked as she sat back, wiping at her eyes and peering at him.

They were just outside of Grandfather's Library, the first room Flitch had seen, and it seemed impossible now that any of them had thought that simple, banal space, full of its dead books, could be the labyrinth itself.

Above them, the central stone said *Sing*, a quiet command.

What *had* happened?

Flitch told everything he could, stopping mid-description of a room that had been filled with pigs sprouting bushes and vines and trees from their backs, half-animal and half-plant and, somehow, Flitch realized in the telling, completely beautiful. He saw how his siblings responded—in disgust and horror—but he found suddenly that he would be happy to see those beings again.

But before he could go on, his father arrived with the medicker.

And Nab.

The medicker, whose name was Marr, set about checking over Flitch in a businesslike manner, flicking open his eyes and peering into them, his mouth and ears, too, running hands along his skin, prodding here and there.

Right beside them, the baron kneeled and, as soon as Marr allowed for it, wrapped Flitch in a great, lasting hug, and Flitch did cry a little this time, a few tears into his father's shoulder.

"I was so scared," the baron said, murmuring the words into the hug, perhaps for Flitch and perhaps for himself.

"Me, too," Flitch said quietly.

"You had us all scared, young master o' the Borders," a slick voice said behind the baron, and as Flitch was released by his father, he saw Nab, his luxurious hair untroubled by any fear he might have been feeling, his eyes flicking around the room before returning to Flitch. He offered an obviously fake look of concern and regret. "What luck that you have returned, and what a strange space to be found in beneath the Borders estate. Our King, whose love and attention we are all lucky enough to have, will want to know immediately that you are safe, I'm sure."

Nab's smile was shit glistening in the hot sun.

His siblings, Flitch saw, quailed beneath the insinuation in the whisperman's voice. Even the baron dropped his eyes.

How soon until Faineant himself stood in this room, leafing idly through the pages of Grandfather's Library, his servants traipsing into the depths of the labyrinth to find Quietus? They would begin with swords and axes, casters with rush pits and arsenals of casting plants, but Aster was the best of them, and her assault had had no effect whatsoever on the walker of the ways.

Faineant would begin with force, but cleverness would soon follow. Lives would be lost, Borders deemed unsafe for all but the King's own brave servants, and all would end for Flitch and his family.

As he'd touched consciousness again and found his way back to the present in the sea of his siblings' voices, a slim set of hopes had moved through him. Perhaps Nab had been too occupied to sense anything amiss. Perhaps the baron had Faineant's whisperman completely ensconced in a cage of papers and plans. Perhaps this was why only his siblings had found Flitch, why the whole of Borders was not packed into that room.

But the smile on Nab's face snuffed out what hope Flitch had had, and in its absence, he found a curious emptiness. Not apathy or ambivalence, but a kind of summer-sky freedom, unbound by that same fear of possibility that worked the anxious hearts of his family.

After fleeing through the labyrinth, after the terror and marvel of Quietus's creations, after Quietus itself—what was Nab, First Whisperman to King Faineant? A man, a bundle of ragged, twisted threads waiting to be unwound, pulled apart.

Flitch reached out and pulled.

"I discovered something in the labyrinth," he said, sitting up further and groaning, pressing one hand into the side of his chest even as he slid the book from Quietus carefully behind his back, making as though he was using that arm for support. "Something valuable. Something . . ."

Flitch let his eyes go soft, his voice almost reverent.

"Something impossible."

In every story that had captivated him, Flitch had loved most those moments when Idyll had gestured at a shape beyond the story itself, an evocation of something that words could not convey, a form in the absence.

What could Flitch offer to Nab that might get the whisperman to stay? Nothing firm would do, nothing solid. To tell him what lay in the labyrinth would be to rob him of his power, treat him like a child being told the truth of the world.

But to gesture at what might be? To speak and then fall quiet? To let the wonders of silence work on him, lighting again the fires of his imagination so that he became author, too, of the lie? That was the magic of a good story, lie or not.

Nab's face grew hungry for a moment, empty of anything but pure want. He had joined the tale, and even as a look of careful wariness took over again, well practiced and automatic for him, Flitch knew that the whisperman was under his spell.

"I shall inform the King immediately," Nab said, taking a step back, his eyes lingering on the dark archway leading onward. "He will, I'm sure, make all haste to join us."

"It won't . . ." Flitch said, hissing with pain he hoped looked real enough. Marr, the medicker, gave him a quick, confused look.

He closed his eyes a moment and gritted his teeth before opening them again. "I don't know how long it will stay. I carried it as far as I could but couldn't get it beyond the next chamber, just beyond that tunnel."

He nodded toward the tunnel at the other end of Grandfather's Library, the entrance to the labyrinth.

"Flitch, what are you—" Aster began, looking at him with confusion and anger.

"I'm sorry for my son," the baron said, standing and putting himself between Nab and the archway. "He is not recovered yet, I think. Nothing good is beyond that tunnel."

Brilliant, Flitch thought, watching Nab's eyes, shifting and flicking around as he considered the situation, every thought bare and obvious. Did he leave and give Borders a chance to cover up and hide their secret once more? Would the archway still be here when he returned? Or would he look the fool in front of his King, the whisperman who pushed too far, guessed at too much?

Flitch fought a smile down a moment before Nab's decision firmed into a resolute frown on his face.

"I think it best if I give the King a clear, knowledgeable assessment," he said, puffing out his chest slightly and looking up at the towering baron above him. "If Faineant is to make a good decision, he needs good information."

Nab stepped around the baron and walked under the archway, his eyes tracing along the carving—*Sing*—etched above for a moment. He passed slowly by the lines of books before stopping at the threshold to the labyrinth and turning around.

"Through here?" he asked, looking at Flitch, who fought to avoid the accusing glares of his siblings, each of them saying, in their own way: *What are you doing? Why are you giving up our secret?*

Flitch moved to push himself up and bit back the imagined pain with a grunt, falling back to the stone floor.

"Just in the next room, yes," he said, letting the discomfort seep into his voice. "I'll show you—just give me a moment to get up."

He tried and failed again to stand, and Aster stooped to help him.

"No, no," Nab said, the gallant man now, putting out a hand. "You have done enough and need tending to. I will look for a moment before reporting back to the King. Only a moment."

Nab stepped across the threshold and disappeared behind a wall of stone that suddenly filled the archway, smooth and seamless, as though it held nothing beyond it but more stone, more earth, more nothing.

"What was that?" Aster's voice was dull and dampened against the stone wall. She turned to Flitch with accusation in her eyes.

"You just gave him the labyrinth!" Zim said. "He's going to know everything!"

"Are you all right, Flitch?" the baron asked, leaning down to peer into his son's eyes. "What happened with Quietus?"

"Is that book the gift?" Zim asked.

"If it is, I think it should belong to all of us," Aster said, annoyance creeping into her voice. "The labyrinth is technically Borders property." She gestured around at them all.

"Did you escape from it?" the baron asked, and Flitch could hear the lifetimes of worry he'd experienced between being told that Flitch was still in the labyrinth and seeing him alive and well.

"Yes," Flitch said, and then, "no. I don't know." He'd been interrupted by his story, and he wanted to finish, but not yet. He was waiting for something, his intuition like a fire inside him, flickering with anticipation for he couldn't say what.

"Why did you let Nab into the labyrinth like that? He's going to realize there's nothing in that next room and then come back," Aster said, staring at Flitch as though he were a stranger.

"What if he finds Quietus like we did and gets . . ." Zim began, gesturing wildly in the air in front of him.

"A gift?" the baron finished for him, shaking his head. "I have spent years searching for Quietus and seen only traces of it. That you three found the walker is unbelievably lu—*rare.*"

Lucky. He'd been about to say *lucky* before looking to Flitch.

"So, he just gets to look around in the labyrinth—*our fucking labyrinth—* and then run off to Faineant to tell him everything?" Aster asked, gaining back some of her fire.

"What happened to your skin?" the baron asked, tracing one long finger along Flitch's arm.

But Flitch was focused elsewhere, listening with a part of himself he'd never accessed before, or perhaps had never had. Waiting.

There.

He felt the change deep down in his gut, as though a thorny problem he'd set aside for the day had finally been resolved by some latent part of his mind.

Two things happened almost simultaneously.

The first was a scream so loud and piercing that not even the thick stone of the archway and the layers of labyrinthine walls between could silence it entirely. It was a cry of terror quite familiar to Flitch, and his heart raced sympathetically with the feeling singing beneath the scream.

The second was the archway opening, the stone shifting for a moment, as though it had only ever been a curtain, still and waiting to be brushed by breath or the wake of a passing body. It moved slightly and then was gone, opening onto Grandfather's Library once more, the room unchanged save for something small and rustling on the floor in the center of the room.

"Don't go in there," the baron said, but Flitch was already pushing himself up, the feel of the book—his gift—comfortable in his hand.

"It's okay," Flitch said. "He can't hurt us anymore."

The labyrinth was tension and release, he saw now as he stepped inside. Quietus was at once its creator, curator, and custodian, tuning it as one might a fine instrument, every string perfectly tense, every lever in careful working order. All so that it might sing when struck.

Every new footstep traipsing along the darkness, every new room made, every new Borders dream filtering in—each was a new twist, a new tension to be understood and resolved, not for the sake of efficiency or ownership or authority, but for the sake of beauty, of elegance.

Quietus unmade and remade that which came inside the labyrinth into something more.

"Is that . . ." Aster's voice was a whisper that trailed off in horror as Zim retched back at the entrance to Grandfather's Library.

"I don't understand," the baron said, turning it into a question. And then, a breath later: "Oh, no. Now I do. Oh."

Set in the exact middle of the room, almost like a gift waiting to be found, was a bird's nest, three bright blue eggs already cracked open, their tenants standing atop their small, bowl-shaped nest or nearby, chirping and attempting to fly. Each bird was colored a bright, icy blue, and when they extended their tiny, fledgling wings, they revealed markings like cats' eyes.

The nest itself was made of fine-spun hair, red and beautiful, woven together with expert precision.

"Leave it," the baron said as Flitch kneeled down and extended a hand. His father's voice was hard and harsh, holding back his own retching.

"It's okay," Flitch said. "It's a gift."

"I said *leave it*," the baron said, putting an arm around Flitch and guiding him out. "All of you, out. Now."

Flitch looked over his shoulder once as he passed under the archway and thought he saw, for a bare moment, a figure looming in the far entrance, cloaked all in shadow, looking on its good works with satisfaction. The three birds took flight and disappeared into the shadows, the eyes on their wings beginning to open.

CHAPTER ELEVEN

When it became clear that the sky would continue to fall for some time, Kindred fell asleep in a chair beside Madrigal, and she didn't wake until much later, when Sarah's hand on her shoulder pulled her up from a dream in which she and Jest had been racing to see who could climb one of the stalks of the Sea first. Kindred's own stalk had spoken to her in a deep, booming voice, mocking and deriding her attempts to climb it, and soon Jest, crowned in a circle of scintillating silver-green light, was lost to the glowing vaults above, while Kindred scrabbled about in darkness.

"It's over," Sarah said, her voice soft, her smile sweet. She bent down for a kiss, and Kindred turned her face up into it, closing her eyes and feeling, for just a moment, that the world had contracted into the rough brush of Sarah's lips meeting her own. Everything stilled around her and in her, the memories and anxieties suddenly remembered upon waking held for a breath as she lived for a moment on Sarah's lips, on the smell of her, on her closeness. If she could wake every day in that way, nothing could stand before her.

Fourth-Folly was already gone, become a pair of footsteps leaping from the deck above, and Madrigal was soon to follow. The young girl had woken at the same time as Kindred but rose with impossible vigor, unfurling from the constricting angles of her sleep and springing from her chair straight to the stairs and up, a breathless giggle accompanying her.

Awn was close behind, running a hand across the wayward growth of his beard, sleepy but no less excited than Madrigal. He even let out a little giggle of his own to match hers.

Jest emerged from her berth, already talking to Wylf about what treasures or wonders they might find outside, how they might be clues to the

Lost Monarch's whereabouts, and while she spoke in the same grand manner as before, the words sounding as though they had been lifted from
some archaic text, she was changed. Grown deeper, wider—a thin stream
sounded and discovered to be hiding deep rivers below, waters icy and
unrelenting and rushing ever downward where few cared to look or know.

"Perhaps a message from the Monarch?" Jest said to Wylf, tipping her
head to the side as if, yes, it might be unlikely, but perhaps it wasn't impossible. "Or a message *for* the Monarch? There is simply no reason to believe
our Monarch did not have a foothold in the sunlight seas above. No reason at all."

She waved to Kindred and Sarah with a braid of hair as she passed by,
and there was something in the gesture—so casual and easy—that told
Kindred she belonged.

Jest seeks herself.

Fourth-Folly's revelation whispered through Kindred's mind as she and
Sarah followed the others up onto the deck. Jest had turned the Monarch
into a figure of legend, equal in every way to the legends Kindred had grown
up reading—the Queen Who Laughed, the Supplicant Few, the Gilded
Port, burning hides and Running Ones and the Sea Lords' graves and all
the rest. Jest had broken from herself and made that person into a myth,
at once wonderful and unattainable.

And now she led a group of people in search of that myth, armed with
stories from above, each a narrative of how life might go, of what heroes
are, of what bravery looks like. Jest had built herself a castle of tales from
which she could look upon her old life and find it beautiful and worthy.

Kindred thought she might love her just a little bit.

"Did you sleep too?" Kindred asked Sarah as they emerged onto the
deck.

"No, I was reading," Sarah said, shaking her head. She had pulled her
hair back into a messy tail at the base of her neck, and it revealed the dark
brown growth coming in around her scalp, evidence of how long she'd
gone since coloring it in the ways she liked. "Folly showed me a few scrolls
and a handful of random pages with information and sketches of the creatures down here. Some of them were familiar—wyrms and mid-Sea bad-
gers and that kind of stuff, but some were totally strange to me. Did you
know none of them have ever even seen a bird? I told Folly I would try to
do a calling sometime, but . . ."

Sarah said more, but Kindred didn't hear her, because the Seafloor had become a battlefield.

What had been smooth, untouched fields of starry dirt were now scenes of stilled chaos. Small craters pocked the ground to mark the places of impact, the dirt shoved up into uneven humps or scattered in haphazard waves. In the craters and out of them, curled tightly into balls and stretched out, bleeding and already bled out, but savagely broken regardless, were the remains of what had been a massive army of Antilles roaches.

Their smooth, red bodies, like stones half-buried along a beach, covered the Seafloor around the Traveling Court's ship, littered out as far as Kindred could see. Antilles roaches traveled in huge swarms, thousands of bodies clicking and whispering against one another, the sound of their approach said to be a deep, profound buzzing that, instead of striking fear and horror in the hearts of those who heard it, lulled those nearby into lolling stupor. Limbs went slack at the fanfare of their approach, muscles relaxed, minds wandered, and eyes looked to the horizon.

> "When red swarm ascends and croons sluggishness to
> sailors near,
> Find the broken-hearted and give her to the grass,
> It's lovestruck grief that makes Antilles' brood appear,
> With their due given, the roaches will let you pass."

The old rhyme slipped from Kindred's lips without much thought. She'd never seen Antilles roaches like this, not in such a huge amount, not so recently alive. Sailors lucky enough to live through an attack sometimes brought a few carcasses back, shiny red carapaces the wonder of Arcadia for a few spans while everyone got their look. Younger sailors and foolish sailors alike would remark on how the roaches didn't look so tough, each body—curled up in death—no larger than a child of six or seven years. "A few hammers and strong hands to guide them would take care of such as these," the sailors would say as those around them, wiser and older and more fearful of things meant to be feared, would shake their heads in pitying condescension and move on their way, giving the carcasses a wide berth.

Kindred had only seen such a roach once in her time above, but the memory of it had never left her. Its body had been curled up tight enough to leave its inner workings entirely to the imagination, and its shell, cracked and broken though it was from the desperate defenses of the sailor who had killed it, shone in the sunlight, glowing a red bright enough to be almost aflame. Even in death it had been a thing of power.

Beside her, Sarah drew back a pace and put a hand on Kindred's arm, taking in their surroundings for the first time.

"Roaches," Sarah said, the word almost a growl, and Kindred remembered the stories Sarah had told of ships she'd crewed on before *The Errant*, the ill-considered voyages charted by their greedy, inexperienced captains—voyages into contested grasses, into grasses rumored to have seen wyrm or badger or roach activity. Her first sighting of an Antilles roach had not been on the safety of land while staring at a corpse.

"Yep," Fourth-Folly said from where they squatted at the edge of the deck, casting a baleful glare out at the field of bodies ahead of them. "Just roaches. I thought it might at least be something interesting."

"Oh, come now, dearest Folly," Jest said, a hint of reproach in her voice. She had already gotten down to the ground and was walking slowly among the bodies, bending down now and then to inspect one. "We have, none of us, cause to offer injurious thoughts to those claimed by death's swift hand. Think on the wind, my friend."

That seemed to mollify Fourth-Folly, and as Jest wandered farther out among the unconcealed graveyard this patch of Seafloor had become, Kindred and Sarah stayed nearer to the boat, by Fourth-Folly. Madrigal, Wylf, and Awn had walked in the other direction but to the same effect. Myriad bodies in myriad positions all describing the same fall, the same death, the same reclamation by the Sea.

Kindred raised a hand to the sites of her own reclamation, feeling the small, tight coils of plants broken through and resting against the skin of her hand and her neck, wondering where the Sea would make claim on her body next.

"What did she mean, 'Think on the wind'?" Sarah asked as they all examined bodies near the ship.

"It's her way of saying all things are connected," Fourth-Folly said with a shake of their head. They bent to inspect the body of a roach, turning it over with an effort. "The wind down here is always blowing. It connects every part of the Seafloor to every other part, and even connects us to the people above. Jest is always talking about how interconnected we are—

one big system, everything in it important. She hates when we say anything to the contrary."

"So, these aren't *just* roaches," Kindred said, squatting down beside one and finding herself caught on that sublime line between horror and wonder. As if these creatures could ever be *just* anything.

"Exactly." Fourth-Folly wrapped their arms—thin but run through with taut muscles—around the body of the roach and lifted it with a grunt. When they spoke next, it was with a surprisingly accurate affectation of Jest's speech. "The roaches, dearest Folly, are merely one such thread in this myriad tapestry which we here call life, and whose tune is plucked by that very same wind that will, someday, play misery upon our own."

Sarah let out a laugh that filled the vast arches with joy, and even Fourth-Folly's grim facade broke for a moment.

But Kindred did not laugh, and she did not smile. After a lifetime sailing above, being told in every way that the world was made of discrete, disconnected parts, some important and others worthless, such a sentiment as Jest's was at once strange and familiar to her. Like the roaches, which both drew her close and repelled her, Kindred felt dread fascination as she imagined the wind that stirred lifeless antennae there in this death field was the same wind that ruffled alien feathers some great distance away, or that stirred living sands elsewhere.

The same wind that filled sails above, that carried rain to Arcadia on fortunate days and dust every other. The same prairie wind—*in and out, in and out*—that Kindred had breathed as she left behind everything she'd known and sailed for something wilder.

Above and below, Sea and land, Roughs and tamed grasses, Arcadia and Mainland—divisions had been the archaeology of her life, of everyone's life above, and the belief in the fundamental disconnectedness of it all had given spark to the very life that Kindred had sought to leave behind.

See the world as broken, that life seemed to say. *Draw lines in your mind and fix them in place. In crossing them, bury them even deeper.*

In the prairie wind, out the prairie wind. Kindred breathed, and the air in her lungs came from every stretch and strand of the world, skeins of wind pulled from the mountains of the Mainland, from the dried crust of Arcadia, from the far ends of forever and every place in between, and from every mysterious and magical and terrifying and wonderful place on the Seafloor. For a long moment, Kindred held this breath and did not move, did not think beyond an image of herself as a mote of light caught in the wind that was everything.

She thought on the wind, on the hidden truth carried along it across borders: it's all important, every one and every thing, significant to the webwork world.

As the group continued to inspect the roaches, taking a few for meals, Kindred moved little and said less.

After a time, she moved back to the ship, having gotten her fill of examining the roaches, which, underneath their glossy, hard shells, were segmented, chaotic things—all legs and antennae and stalks on which eyes and mouths were mounted. They were horrifying and alien.

On the ship, Kindred watched Sarah mingling with the members of the Monarch's Traveling Court—of Jest's Traveling Court—and felt a flicker of joy light the heaviness of her mood. Sarah was smiling and laughing as she held up a lifeless roach, hefting it like a barrel. Madrigal had come over to join her and was laughing too.

"Amazing, aren't they?" Awn said as he climbed aboard next to her, breathless from running around. "I've seen them in motion before— terrifying! But they're so different in death. Still scary of, course!" He held up his hands, eyes wide as he sucked in a breath, pantomiming terror. "But amazing still."

"They are," Kindred agreed, nodding.

When he didn't respond, Kindred looked over at Awn and was surprised to find him studying her, his normally busy eyes fixed on her.

"What's wrong?" he asked, the words quiet and kind.

Kindred shook her head and opened her mouth, struggling to find the words.

"Nothing," she said finally, and then quickly, as if that one word had knocked free the rest, "Was it insane to come down here?"

"Absolutely," Awn said, nodding. He gave the word no emphasis, as if he were agreeing that it was a pleasant day. "But that doesn't make it wrong. And your intuition was spot on! You found your grandmother, or will have when we arrive, and you were right in thinking the Seafloor would be full of wonders! That young singer, Madrigal, was telling me that a stretch of the Seafloor near here is a constantly swirling whirlpool that emits a foul wind. Isn't that incredible? I want to see it."

Kindred nodded along to the now-familiar patter of Awn's excitement, but some part of her had been spun off kilter by what Jest had said. When she spoke, it was as a confessor, each word putting name to a guilt twisting her gut. She found her way through each sentence, discovering what it was she was feeling as she spoke it aloud, relief and shame singing through her.

"I left behind a crew, destroyed our ship, helped ignite a water war and bring about the destruction of the Once-City, and set fire to the grasses around Arcadia, all because none of that was important enough to me, not as important as the possibility of this place down here or my grandmother being found. I was every sailor chasing the horizon, enamored with something out there and ignorant of the importance of all that I already had."

Awn watched the others walking about among the field of roaches, Sarah laughing at something Jest had said, Madrigal riding atop Wylf's broad shoulders and hooting her triumph to the sky. Even Fourth-Folly was smiling in response, just a little, one side of their mouth giving way grudgingly to a half-grin.

"You have big dreams," Awn said, smiling at the action in front of them. "Saving the Sea. Finding your lost grandmother. Understanding the secrets of the world. There's nothing wrong with that. It's part of the reason I was happy to follow you below, and part of why I wanted to work with you in the Once-City from the start. My son was like you. Full of dreams so clear and strong that they seemed to pull him right on through life."

"I didn't know you had a son," Kindred said, startled. How many conversations had she had with Awn while they worked the hearthfires of the Once-City? He'd never mentioned a son, or any family.

"His name was Brey," he said after a moment, voice quiet and strained. He gestured toward Madrigal, still laughing atop Wylf's shoulders. "He was around her age when he died. He and my wife both, sunk on the Sea in an accident."

Kindred put a hand on his arm and said, "I'm so sorry, Awn. I had no idea."

He nodded and smiled at her, eyes shining. When he put his hand on hers, it was steady and warm.

"Thanks. I thought for a long time about following them." He straightened and took his hand back, his eyes dropping to stare down at the ground below them. "I didn't have any big dreams like Brey did, not after he was gone. He *was* my dream! Him and his mom, they were my life's adventure.

And they were gone. Without a goodbye. Without a hug. Just gone. And I wanted to be gone too."

As he paused, the sound of Sarah and the Court came back to them, their joy and fun a strange background for Awn's grief.

"My boy didn't get to do all the wonderful things he dreamed of, and he didn't get to have any of the big adventures he wanted to. So, I decided to see all the wonder I could for him, not by going off to the horizon but by finding it around me. And if I couldn't find it around me, I would make it around me. I couldn't have his big dreams, but I could have small ones, not handed down from whatever magic makes us who we are or from fate or whatever else. I made my own small dreams. I woke up every morning and decided on them."

He looked up and fixed Kindred with a clear-eyed look.

"It's good to have dreams, Captain," he said with a sad little smile. "But not all of them need to be big ones."

Awn hopped from the edge of the ship with a glance back at her, and when he rejoined the rest of the group, he was back to himself, chattering happily and quickly, awed by every little thing.

<hr />

When the ship shifted slightly under Kindred a short while later, she sprang up, alarmed, thinking with irrational fear that the earth itself had shifted. It was no longer so easy to imagine whatever existed below the Seafloor as distant or distinct. *Think on the wind*, Jest had said—a sentiment not so different from one the Marchess might have offered—and Kindred found something of fear and something of awe in it. She was a stranger in this place, and she could take nothing for granted, nothing for true, nothing as a given.

"Jest!" Kindred called as the ship moved again on its own, but even before the erstwhile Monarch had joined her, Kindred saw the cause.

The pluralities had begun to pull at their tied-off reins, yanking the ship forward little by little in their pursuit of the roaches, which they were disappearing below the ground at frightening speed, yanking the roaches under with no sound, no flash of power, their reach almost completely obscured by the small explosions of dirt. Again, Kindred spied flashes of many somethings—an arm that might have been hairy and glowing gold, a pair of mouths with one tooth each, a butterfly's wing dripping a viridian liquid, clawed tentacles spasming and undulating—every moment of clarity gone before it could be confirmed and fuzzing at the edges in her mind, as if even her memories of the pluralities were subject to the same possibility and uncertainty as the many-beings themselves.

"What is it?" Jest cried, running to the ship and leaping aboard with an impressive show of agility. She looked about with wide, concerned eyes. Wylf also loped over, though he didn't join them aboard.

"The pluralities," Kindred said, gesturing. "They're moving."

Jest stared for a moment at the pluralities hunting around for roaches, the small divot of their reins disappearing into the ground the only marker of their movement apart from the occasional disappearance of a body.

"They're hungry," she said after a moment, her tone confused, the words no longer arched by gentility.

"They're not being held in place by anything?" Kindred asked. How had she missed this? A ship pulled by wild many-beings, impossible to know or see, capable apparently of eating anything, and nothing held them in place?

"I know of nothing in the Monarch's lands or beyond that could boast of confining the pluralities," Jest said. "And for what need? The many-beings have never in my lifetime run or sought other lands than these, and what's more, they have no need of escape, for they are not, in fact, imprisoned!"

Jest laughed at this, delighted at the thought of something clearly so ridiculous.

Fourth-Folly had drawn close by this point and said, "The pluralities can let go of the reins at any point they want, but they seem to like being with us. We feed them much more consistently than they would get otherwise, and Madrigal reads to them almost every day."

"They're part of the Court!" Madrigal said, her piping voice emerging from a tiny fortress she'd built from roaches, cute and gristly all at once.

"We do not impose our will upon them," Jest said, smiling down fondly at the pluralities. "And they do not impose theirs upon us."

"It's a community," Sarah said, standing near the pluralities' shifting reins. She rubbed a hand across her face, accidentally smearing it with dirt, her long nose smudged a dark grey but sparkling with whatever starry

grains were in the ground here. She was sweaty and messy, her face a play
of shadow and light, clothes covered in the glistening slick of roach blood,
and she glowed with happiness. Her smile was a bright cut across her grubby
face, and her eyes were wide and joyful as they found Kindred's.

"Perfectly said." Jest nodded and watched Sarah for a moment before
looking around, one of her braids held out as she gestured to the members
of the Court. "I believe we've gathered enough of this bounty to feed us for
some time, yes? Shall we press on?"

Wylf and Fourth-Folly both stooped to pick up another roach carcass,
slinging them both onto the deck to join the pile already gathered there.
Madrigal made a face of disappointment before grinning and bursting out
of her roach fortress, playing the monster as she tore down her walls and
stomped forth, her growls turning to giggles as she accepted Jest's boost
up to the deck.

The Court busied itself—Madrigal took up her post at the hearthfire
and began again her stentorian song; Wylf set himself to a task Jest called
"shucking," which involved using thin strips of metal—each looking to have
been salvaged swords repurposed and dulled over long use—to peel back
the carapace of the roaches to gain access to the meat within; Fourth-Folly
stood once more at the bow, reins in hand, casting one quick glance around
the field still littered with roach bodies. Then, with a quick flick of their
wrists that sent shivers down the reins, Fourth-Folly had them all moving again.

Kindred, Sarah, and Jest walked along beside the ship, and as Sarah
and Jest began to talk about the roaches and the pluralities and all the
other creatures to be found below, Kindred felt a smile on her own face,
the mirror of Sarah's, as she recognized the ghost of a thing she had thought
lost forever from her life. Behind all of this, every sung note and shucked
shell and banal utterance aboard the ship was the same shared spirit that
moved feet and hands and bodies across the ships above. It was the same
ghost Kindred had fallen in love with aboard *The Errant*, one that made
itself known equally in the quiet mundanity of regular tasks as it did in
the heroic leaps and wild battles any crew would face.

Among these people and creatures, and in this strange place, empty
and full all at once, Kindred found that same community that lit Sarah's
smile and excited words, the same shared purpose that had connected

sailors aboard *The Errant*—that same purpose that Kindred had betrayed to follow her heart.

Here it was again, tying this Court, this crew, together, and as she walked, Kindred felt herself falling again under its spell.

⬤◆⬤

"Welcome, new friends, to the canopy," Jest said, rousing Kindred from where she'd been dozing, stretched out on the deck with Sarah. The Seafloor had seemed cold and empty, beautiful in an icy way, before they'd met the Traveling Court. But in their company, this place grew warm and familiar: listening to ancient songs trilled out in Madrigal's youthful voice, watching Fourth-Folly grump from one task to the next, none of them critical or crucial, sitting near Jest as she told those same stories as above but reimagined, myths and tales held up and examined, gaps filled in with speculation, heroes questioned and criticized, villains rehabilitated in reflection and deeper consideration. It all felt like family, somehow. Like crew. Like community.

Kindred sat up and looked around, squinting to see what might be different and finding nothing. The Seafloor continued in every direction, glowing stalks and starry ground, empty archways leading away. On one nearby trunk, its head and torso bursting from the plant, was a lantern bearer, shining with pink light, one arm extended as it held out its lantern. Without warning and with no clear catalyst, it rose up the plant, shooting upward in irregular, spastic movements, still half-in, half-out, its body swaying with the motion.

As it rose, Kindred followed it, and that was when she saw the canopy.

"Oh," Sarah said beside her, eyes already locked above them.

"Are those . . ." Awn began before gulping noisily, head tilted back, mouth falling open.

"We're too small for them," Fourth-Folly said, casting a quick look upward before returning to their task, which involved cutting up the roach meat and tossing it into small barrels that they had untied from the side of the ship.

High above them, connecting the surrounding stalks of grasses in thick, fuzzy beams of cloudy white, was a web, though one bigger and more solid-looking than anything that had ever existed above. It was a ceiling-city of alabaster, tunnels and platforms and nests all reinforced by so much webbing that they had the look of solid stone.

The canopy covered the whole sky above them—it *was* the sky above them, a whole landscape etched in the space between pure white and darkest black. It was overwhelming to look up at it. It rendered its observer small and insignificant, a nothing next to it.

Trundling and traipsing along and through it were spiders, the smallest of them bigger than most vessels Kindred had seen in her life, and the largest too big for comparison. They moved in concert, some working together to form new bridges or repair sections of the canopy, while others spun thick webbing around objects Kindred couldn't make out and didn't want to know about. They scuttled through huge tunnels and emerged from them, leapt impossible distances with no effort, clustered together and scattered to individual tasks.

It was bustling and alive, too much activity to take in at once—too much to take in *ever*. And yet Kindred wanted nothing more in that moment than to look and look and look, to see forever, gone from herself, sitting in adoration of a thing that had probably always been and would probably always be. What work of people above or below could change this?

"These are the Silent Gods of this place," Jest said, gesturing around. "We are allowed to travel through their land because of their grace. We have only to offer our thanks in passing."

She raised a hand and nodded at the creatures above, who took no notice of her, a thing too small and insignificant to warrant their attention. The others did the same, and so, too, did Kindred, because why not? If gods existed, they would be like these spiders. Silent, busy, glorious, uncaring.

As the undersea wind moaned through the vast spaces, and the Silent Gods above busied themselves with their work, Kindred found herself mesmerized by the Sea, the song of its breath and the lights of its life. Above, the Sea was chaos and color, endlessly changing and reinventing itself.

But here, forever took on a new meaning, not just of space but of time. This place, its huge arcades, its enormous creatures and wondrous stillness—all of it lacked the energy and ecstasy of the surface. Instead, the Seafloor sang a song of age and epoch, its vastness unchanged. A person could dream infinitely down there, staring at the shifting, scurrying lights of the lantern bearers as they climbed and fell along the lines of forever, like blood coursing through an ancient body.

Just as she had upon landing, Kindred felt suddenly kin with the Sea. As a sailor, she'd often felt the Sea's presence, heard its voice, while keeping the hearthfire, and this was similar but somehow closer to the source, as though all her life, she'd been hearing the Sea from a great distance, its voice obscured by some barrier that was no longer present.

If the Sea had a heart, it was there, beating an infinite steady rhythm to set the world in motion above.

And inside that heartbeat, in the thick, ubiquitous light emanated by the stalks and trunks and boles of the Sea, in the air and in the wind, was a magic deeper than anything Kindred had ever experienced. Not the sharp shock of a casting fire yielding up a plant's magic, and not the calm steadiness of a hearthfire burning away at bone and build.

This was different, more profound. It was the magic of staring at the world in wonder. It was the magic of love's sighing joy. It was the magic of a laugh and a sob. It was elemental and primal. It was first, the magic of a seed sprouting, the magic in the tiny stand of golden grasses even now unfurling from Kindred's skin.

A dizzying, terrifying thrill ran through her then as she understood that this magic was a river flowing all around her, and that she might, at any moment, scoop a hand into it, dip a toe into it, fall into it entire, and let it carry her where it might.

"Are you okay?" Sarah asked from beside her as Kindred shivered in both fear and excitement. Here was the wild daydream of the Sea, and she was in it, walking its ways and running its paths.

"I'm great," Kindred said, planting a kiss on Sarah's cheek before looking back up at the spiders above.

"I want to know everything about them," Awn said, speaking like someone just woken up from sleep and stunned by the morning.

"Very little is known about the Silent Gods," Fourth-Folly said, pointing upward with the knife they held. "They're scavengers like us, but they catch whatever falls in their webs. At least that's our best guess. They never come down to the ground. And no one ever goes above, not if they want to keep breathing."

"Incredible," Awn said, as if Fourth-Folly had given him the answer to his most pressing and cherished question.

"What are those?" Sarah asked, pointing up to a series of long, spiraling structures extending out from the bottom of the canopy. Some spiders moved along them, stopping occasionally to examine something before shuttling onward.

"Art," Jest said at the same time Fourth-Folly said, "No idea."

The two stared at one another for a moment, Jest's arched eyebrows weighing on Folly's scowl, until finally Folly relented and continued with their work.

"Those structures serve no purpose beyond beauty," Jest said, pointing up with one braid at an example directly above them, its spiraling tendrils bursting out in all directions, like a tangle of snakes or worms all frozen mid-writhe. "These structures have, at times, fallen from the canopy and crashed down to the ground, there to be examined by any with an interest. I, myself, have seen such a one cut open—a blasphemous act under the eyes of the Silent Gods above, but some know no shame."

"What was inside?" Awn asked, awestruck.

"Nothing," Jest said simply, shaking her head. "They are structures made and maintained for *no purpose*. We simply have no evidence, gathered or speculated, that they can be anything other than the art of those above. Their wondrous attempts at rendering emotion and experience in beauty's service. We should count ourselves lucky, each and every one of us," she said, eyeing Fourth-Folly, "to be in the presence of such high art."

"*Or*," Fourth-Folly said, decidedly not meeting Jest's eyes, "they have a function and utility beyond anything we've figured out yet. I know nothing of art or beauty, but just because we don't know what something is doesn't mean it must be created *in beauty's service.*"

Wylf, who had been watching this exchange with interest, leaned down and put a heavy hand on Fourth-Folly's shoulder.

"We all work in beauty's service," he said, each word spoken slowly and carefully, given the full weight of Wylf's consideration before living on his breath.

Fourth-Folly gave him an annoyed look but said nothing, and the staccato chop of their knife seemed to soften somewhat.

"I thought about making the Silent Gods' spiralwork webs my myth,"

Madrigal said from the fire, looking up with a pleasant smile on her face. "But they weren't right for me."

"A myth is like a goal; is that it?" Awn asked.

For a moment, no one spoke, and the only sound was the ship skimming through the dirt, soft and smooth, a complement to the gentle wind combing out Kindred's hair and ruffling the plants along her hand and throat, which had stretched and now moved lazily in the breeze.

"Yes. No," Wylf said. It was the most he'd talked—the only bit he'd talked—since they had joined the Traveling Court.

"A myth is a map," Jest said, having hopped down from the deck of the ship and walking beside it now. "With it, a person can navigate the world. A goal gives a person direction but not understanding. A myth allows its believer to make sense of all they experience."

"Your myth," Fourth-Folly said, pointing at Kindred, "is finding your grandmother and saving the Sea from the Greys. A dumb myth, I think, but it's yours and not mine."

"Folly!" Jest said, looking up at them, horrified, but Fourth-Folly continued.

"Your myth lets you know who and what matters, what to do in any situation—so long as you understand it well enough. The world has so much in it, but a myth tells you who you are and what you could be in that world. Jest's myth is finding the Lost Monarch, and it's about more than just the *doing* of it. It's about the life a person leads to walk the path that may reach that end. Goals are meant to be accomplished. Myths are lived. They offer something to do, yes, but more importantly, they offer a way to *be*."

"And you say you know nothing of art or beauty," Jest said, shaking her head, the look of horror replaced now by admiration and a love Kindred had seen before on the face of crew members grown close over many long voyages and through many hardships. It was a look that said *I see you and I know you and I am here with you*.

"So, all of you have myths?" Kindred asked, looking around at the rest of them.

"Not me," Madrigal said, grinning over at her. "I haven't picked mine yet."

"The rest of us do, yeah," Fourth-Folly said, though they offered nothing more. Kindred was going to let the topic die there, feeling as though she were peering in to something private and quiet, but then Sarah asked.

"What are your myths, Wylf and Folly?"

Sarah had a way of speaking that set those in the conversation at ease. Her voice, which could be so animated and wild, sarcastic and biting, at times, could also be gentle and curious. No matter the character of it, though, she always sounded genuine, as though she saw through the thicket of habitus and affect to the person beyond, peering in at them with a kind, earnest interest.

So, when she asked the question Kindred couldn't imagine asking without pushing too far or receiving prickly responses, Sarah opened them up.

"Wylf's myth . . ." Fourth-Folly began, looking up at the man, who nodded down at them solemnly, giving his permission, "is the Windrake."

"*Windrake*," Wylf intoned, giving the word a weight and importance, hissing out the first half and allowing the second to explode against the roof of his mouth, smiling the whole time he said it. He drew the word out, and even after he'd spoken that last syllable, it seemed to hang in the air around him, sharp and persistent.

Fourth-Folly returned to their work—stabbing the knife into the block of wood they'd been using as a cutting board and using their hands now to shuck a new batch of roaches free from their shells, prying the meat free with quick motions and bright *cracks*.

"Should we know what that is?" Kindred asked, looking around uncertainly.

"Be thankful you've had no occasion to know the Windrake," Jest said before casting a meaningful glance at Wylf, who continued to smile in a garish, awful way.

"The Windrake exists closer to Forever, off to the East, or at least that's where Wylf found it," Fourth-Folly said, casting occasional glances up at Wylf, making sure they weren't overstepping. "It comes from a plant that grows out that way, the only one of its kind, thankfully. It has a simple, unassuming name—blue miracle—and it has flowers that stay curled up in buds down near its base, each about the size of a little kid, like Madrigal."

"Hey!" Madrigal shouted, looking up from the fire. "I'm not little!"

"Like a big kid, then." Fourth-Folly grinned over at the hearthfire keeper before continuing. "Every hundred or so years, one of the buds opens and out comes a new Windrake. There are a few books about them down below that you can read if you want, but they're full of nonsense guesses. No one really knows what the Windrake is or why it does what it does. All we know is this: a Windrake emerges from the blue miracle and fixes upon the first person it sees. It's a hunter, the Windrake. It needs no food, no water, no sustenance of any kind, and it's tireless. If it touches you, it will begin consuming you, starting with your thoughts and memories. Every hope and happiness you've ever had is slowly and excruciatingly pulled from your mind until only the barest bits of you remain, enough to recognize hurt, enough to feel pain.

"Only then does the Windrake turn to your physical body and consume that, although that part is nothing by that point. Probably a welcome release."

Wylf nodded through all of this, his lips moving in silent speech, and now it was clear what he was saying—what he had been saying to himself all along.

Windrake. Windrake. Windrake.

"It can't be killed and only dies when a new Windrake is born from the blue miracle. Slow but persistent, and always it knows where its prey is. It could be across the entire Seafloor from the one it hunted, and it would know the shortest path to reach them. Even now it is pointed toward us, toward Wylf, seeing him and smelling him from wherever it is."

Kindred sat up, shocked at the thought. She pictured a slimy creature belched forth from a balled-up bud, mewling and searching for its prey, its bright, wicked eyes falling on her, its many hands reaching out, many mouths opening wide as it set about feeding on what lay inside her mind.

"Why aren't you running?" she asked, looking with horror at their unhurried pace, the lazy state of the Traveling Court. "Should you—should *we*—be running away?"

"The Windrake is relentless in its pursuit, and it can only be stopped by one thing," Fourth-Folly said, continuing their slow, steady dismantling of the roaches. "If its prey—Wylf—thinks of it, really holds the Windrake in its mind, then the Windrake stops and remains still, wherever it is, whatever it's doing. Totally still. So long as Wylf keeps his thoughts on the Windrake, seeing it and all it can do in his mind's eye, then it will make very little progress in reaching him."

Wylf's constant whispering to himself made sudden sense, not just what he was repeating—*Windrake. Windrake. Windrake*—but why.

"That's horrible," Kindred said, looking to Wylf. "You're never free of it. Either you let it consume your thoughts to remain safe from it, or you live free of it and then it consumes your thoughts in a different way. It's a curse no matter what you do."

Wylf nodded, though he seemed unperturbed by it.

"Why would anyone go near that plant if that could happen?" Ragged Sarah asked, frowning. "Why wouldn't you just avoid it? Or cut it down?"

"Many have tried destroying the blue miracle, but like the Windrake, it can't be killed, at least not with anything anyone has attempted to use on it. As for its appeal . . ." Fourth-Folly trailed off, looking at Wylf, who smiled broadly.

"The blue miracle blooming is the most beautiful thing a person can ever see." It was the longest single sentence Wylf had said since Kindred and the others had joined them, and he spoke the words with almost no inflection. No attempt to convince them, no overconfidence or haughtiness. He said it as one might look at a ship and say, "*That is a ship.*" A simple truth about the world.

"Seeing it bloom gave him some abilities," Fourth-Folly said. "He can sense a fall before it happens, and he barely needs to sleep at all. Not much, maybe, and I don't know if it's worth it or not, but it's something."

"So, you have to spend every moment of every day thinking about a horrifying creature whose sole purpose for existing is to hunt you down, and if you stop thinking about it for even a moment, it continues its life-long pursuit?" Sarah asked this with more than a little dubiousness, and then asked the question Kindred was wondering about. "Was the beauty of a flower blooming worth it?"

Wylf, apparently done speaking, only nodded. The smile on his face had an inward turn, as though he was giving himself a break from thinking of the Windrake, allowing it to take a few steps his way, so that he might once again remember the blooming of the blue miracle.

"That is horrifying and wonderful all at once," Awn said, staring at Wylf, wide-eyed, mouth slightly open.

"And what about you, Folly?" Kindred asked, trying to mimic Sarah's easy, disarming tone.

"Fourth-Folly plays tragedy in the court," Madrigal said, repeating herself from the day before.

"My myth is atonement," Fourth-Folly said, looking up, fixing their eyes not on Kindred but on the vast alabaster colony of Silent Gods above them. "Beyond that, my myth is my own."

They said nothing more, and Kindred didn't ask.

CHAPTER TWELVE

———◆———

Kindred heard the Greys first.

It was a melody whined in pitches almost too high to hear, giant and echoing in Kindred's mind. Dissonant one moment and perfect harmony the next, the song trilled and tripped along without clear direction or purpose, and Kindred had no doubt that it would drive her to madness if she listened for long enough. She began to cast about for its source, first looking out along the arcades in every direction and then at Madrigal, thinking perhaps she had let the fire go wrong, but it still burned in its stately, even way, built on solid, unadorned foundations.

But Madrigal had clearly heard the shrieking song too. She broke off her work with the hearthfire and looked up with a sharp snap of her head, eyes focusing on a spot off in the distance that looked, to Kindred, like every other stretch of space.

"Folly," Madrigal said, her voice bereft of its usual youthful levity. "Right there." She raised a hand and pointed with one finger, off in the direction she'd been looking.

"Got it," Fourth-Folly said, squinting that way. "It's spreading fast here. Shouldn't be this far along."

"What is it?" Kindred asked.

Fourth-Folly shook their head and frowned, a look that seemed at home on their face. Sharp chin rounding as their lower lip pushed up in displeasure, eyebrows drawing down across their eyes in a firm line. They looked as though everything and everyone in the world around them was, on some level, deeply suspicious.

"Just look," they said. "You should be able to see it right . . . now."

As the pluralities pulled ahead and the ship veered around one of the huge, perfect plinths, its sides smooth as the horizon, its skin emitting that ubiquitous glow, Kindred saw the Greys.

Above, they had been tangles of grass, dead or dying or perhaps born again as something awful and else. Oily and wet, the Greys had spelled disaster for ships sailing into them, and disaster, too, for those plants nearby. Flower or nettle, prairie smoke or fire thistle, all fell to the unctuous spread of the Greys, which turned plants slick and grey and heavy. Dead without dying, living without life.

But there, where they erupted from the ground, the Greys were plants grown chaotic and vast. The clean, straight lines of the trunks all around Kindred were gone, distorted and bent and covered over. Like a skeleton taken over by mosses and vines, made into the home of rats and snakes, the plants sick with the Greys still had a central trunk almost visible at their core, but a huge, winding, brittle mass grew up around it, expanding out like a city. Crumbling grey branches—spindly and weak in areas, thick and strong in others—grew in looping hoops and stretching arcs around the trunk of the plant, bursting through it at points, tearing out of the central trunk, a passenger exploiting the inactivity of its host.

They were like the gnarled, shaking hands of an old woman, half-closed and clawed, all tangled and twisted in great messes. Bright, harsh light shone in a quivering inconsistency at the heart of the growths, filtering through in spears and lances at odds with the soft light of the Sea.

More than anything, it reminded Kindred of the coral she had seen growing once in the watery Seas on the other side of the Mainland. Impossible, alien, enormous, unknowable. The Greys were like a city, with animals flittering and skittering and slithering in and around it. Around *them*. It was hard to see if it was a single organism or many growing out of and around the trunk of grass.

Discs of the calcified material extended out, great plates like half-moon steps climbing up the plant, fungal and tenebrous. They might have been red or blue or white or black or yellow once, vibrant and diverse as the corals Kindred had seen as a young girl, but they were faded, greyed over, wrong somehow.

The Greys were a living creature drawn by an unpracticed hand, an attempt at life gone terribly bad. This was not a healthy thing become sick. It was a wrong thing birthed into the world.

And it sang a melody of imperfection and dissonance, tripped through a rhythm always a little too slow, like a heartbeat lagging behind.

"What ails the Sea," Jest said, gesturing ahead toward the Greys, which Kindred could see now clustered around several trunks of Seagrass in front of them. A whole clutch of them, probably resulting in a huge patch of oily, grey grasses on the Sea's surface.

"And there's your grandmother," Fourth-Folly said, pointing to a group of people—tiny figures from this distance—standing next to one of the massive grey structures.

Kindred sucked in a breath and started running.

Heart beating like a thunderstorm in her ears, breath ripping from uncaring lungs, feet a rushing mess in the dirt below, Kindred ran. Tears stung her eyes and traced lines back across her temples and into her hair, blurring her vision and turning the Seafloor into a vast, wavering mess of glowing stalks and endlessly dark corridors.

But at the center, clear, in focus, unmoving as she watched this woman sprinting near, was the Marchess.

Memories of their last meeting, the shouting and bitterness, the words that felt like stones tossed on the grave of who they had been—all of it gone in a wind that scoured Kindred clean and brought her there, to this moment, the long-lost grandmother found at last.

She had no breath to call out but shouted a wordless cry anyway, chest on fire with the effort of running so quickly. One hand in the air, waving around, fingers splayed as if she might catch the Marchess then and there, keep her still and safe.

A stack of something huge and white rose beside the Marchess; two people stood around her, loading or unloading items from a ship similar to the Traveling Court's, the telltale lines of braided grass dipping into the ground and pointing toward the pluralities below. Something was going on, some operation or procedure, but none of it mattered, none of those other people mattered, because the Marchess was looking up from her work with the white stack—were those bones?—and seeing Kindred, and it was too far away to hear what she said but she was speaking, first to those around her and then louder, to Kindred, too far to be anything more than an inarticulate shout that gave new speed to Kindred's legs, new vigor to her laboring heart.

The Marchess ran to meet her, a laugh on her lips, and Kindred nearly fell those last few steps, relief and exhaustion making her legs sluggish and heavy. She toppled but her grandmother caught her, arms still strong, and the two of them went down into the dirt, laughing and crying and screaming in a joy wordless and wide.

"You're here!" Kindred said finally through her tears, running her hands over the Marchess's face and arms, every touch another stone in the monument to now, to this moment, to this small dream come true. "I found you!"

The Marchess wrapped Kindred in a hug Kindred had never thought to experience again, and she leaned into it, breathing in her grandmother's scent, spreading her hands along the Marchess's back. She closed her eyes against the future, knowing that soon Sarah and the others would join them, that soon the goings-on of the Marchess's life there would be revealed and continued—that the world would spin again soon, but wanting to drop anchor in this moment for as long as she could.

The Marchess pulled back, holding Kindred out at arm's length, and Kindred got her first good look at her.

Her grey hair had grown long, and she'd pulled it back into a loose knot at the back of her head. Cuts and bruises and burns marked her face and neck and arms, most of them recent, small but numerous. She looked old, somehow. Not just older than she had been, which she did, but as though age had finally caught her. The woman Kindred had known aboard *Revenger* had carried life with her, worked into her breath and sewn into her movements, threaded into her every sentence and arcing along her smile. Her teeth clicking together said *alive* to those who knew how to listen. Her hands shaped it from air, and her brown eyes, so keen and clever and full, carried it for all who could see.

But something had changed in the Marchess. She was smaller somehow—not physically, not by any metric a medicker might measure, but diminished, like a night empty and longing for its moon. Enormous, vast, and incomplete.

"I found you," Kindred said again, just as the Marchess spoke for the first time, her voice a rough, scratchy shadow of what Kindred remembered.

"What are you doing here?"

Kindred's joy staled at the question, and she shook her head slightly, confused.

"What do you mean? I came here looking for you, like you told me to."

Now it was the Marchess's turn to blink and look surprised. The crunch of boots on the ground and the slow slide of the ship skimming toward them felt like a boulder falling toward Kindred, bringing this moment, which should have shone and sparkled but had grown dim somehow, to a close.

"Like I told you to? My girl, what are you talking about?"

"Your letter," Kindred said, disentangling herself from the Marchess to reach inside her robes and pull out the folded sheet of paper, now worn away and torn, having gone through so much. The paper was dark from sweat and grime, from being taken from her pocket and put back in too many times, clutched in oily, dirty hands. But it was intact, and Kindred gently, almost lovingly, unfolded it before passing it to the Marchess.

"Oh, my," she said, taking the letter and peering down at its contents. "I had forgotten about these, all of those farewell notes. You can forgive an old woman her bit of melodrama."

"What do you mean?" Kindred asked now, gesturing to the letter. "You told me to come and find you." She pointed to the line of text: *If you seek me, look below.*

"Oh, no," the Marchess said, shaking her head and looking more closely at the letter, her eyes narrowing at the words there. "Kindred," she said, "I didn't think . . ."

Her expression was one Kindred remembered, a birdlike curiosity, quick and intense. But it was changed somehow, different from what Kindred held in her memory. Sharper, colder, with something like laughter in her eyes. Had it always been like that?

No, Kindred thought, her gut twisting uncomfortably. The Marchess was just too big for the world, too wild and joyful and free for others to understand. Even Kindred had felt she didn't truly understand her grandmother at times. But she had never been mean, never cruel. Never.

Never.

"Kindred," the Marchess said, her voice full of disbelief and wonder. "You came down here—left behind your whole life, your future, everything you wanted and could have had—because of one measly line in your grandmother's farewell letter?"

This was wrong—all of it hummed dissonance. Where was the reunion? Where was the Marchess's knowing nod upon seeing Kindred? The look that said: *Of course you're here. Of course you left the world behind as I did. I called and you came, as I knew you—you alone and above all others—would come. You and I are the same, drawn to the overlooked and the misunderstood. I left you a guide to follow, and you did, and it is all I wanted.*

"You . . ." Kindred began, but stopped, staring at the letter. Shame held hot coals to her neck as an errant thought crept into her mind: *You did all of this for nothing and no one.*

But before Kindred could continue, the Marchess laughed, loud and rough, her eyes open and crinkled with that same joy Kindred had seen and longed for and imitated as a child and adult both.

"It is done, no matter the reason," the Marchess said, waving around the letter as if it were an insignificant scrap. "You're here, and I'm so glad for it. Welcome, my girl. Welcome to the center of *everything.*"

She pulled Kindred into another hug, this one softer than the first, and Kindred clung to it, letting her shame and fear and worry vanish in the encircling pressure of her grandmother's arms, the feel of her breath on Kindred's neck.

"I missed you," Kindred said.

"I missed you, too." The Marchess pulled back and gestured at the plants growing along Kindred's neck and jawline. "And what is this?"

"I . . ." Kindred started, trying to figure out where to start, how to start, and giving up with a laugh. "It was an adventure getting down here. The journey changed me in some unexpected ways."

The Marchess let out a big belly laugh at that, and for a moment, it was all as it should have been—joy overflowing.

"Everyone thought you were dead," Kindred said, "that you'd leapt to your death in the Sea, but I knew that couldn't be true. I knew that you were still alive."

"You always had faith in things no one else was willing to," the Marchess said, shaking her head, eyes flicking past Kindred to the approach of the Traveling Court.

"I got that from you," Kindred said, grinning and moving to catch the Marchess's eye. Just a little more time there, just another few breaths of this. "The prairie holds worlds, and the wind beneath the Sea is unceasing."

The Marchess cocked her head.

"What's that? One of the old poets?"

Kindred laughed and said, "No. *Yes.* That's from your letter. That's *you.*"

The Marchess huffed out a chuckle and was going to say something else, but the moment broke and Sarah appeared next to them, breathing hard from having run the last bit of the way. She looked between Kindred and the Marchess.

"Another topsider!" the Marchess said, pushing herself to her feet and staring at Sarah in amazement. "How many of you did my grandchild bring down with her?"

The others from the Traveling Court arrived and approached.

Sarah let out a laugh and said, "Just two of us. We were her crew, kind of. I'm Ragged Sarah, Kindred's . . ."

"Kindred's?" The Marchess rounded on Kindred, one eyebrow raised, eyes sparkling with laughter. "You forget to tell me you're a captain now *and* that you have a . . . ?"

"Girlfriend. First mate. Best friend," Kindred said.

"I thought I was your best friend," Awn said, hopping down from the ship and walking over.

"You're not even in the top five," Sarah said to him, though it was with a smile.

"The Lost Monarch's Traveling Court!" the Marchess said, looking them over as they got down from the ship, too. "Good to see you again, Jest. Fourth-Folly. Silent-fellow-whose-name-I-can't-remember. Little, loud person."

Wylf only nodded at his descriptive sobriquet, lips moving rapidly as he silent-spoke the name of his pursuer, but Madrigal gave a shout and corrected the Marchess, who held up her hands in defense and promised to remember next time.

"They brought us here," Kindred said, gesturing to Jest and the others. "We came down back that way and they found us."

She nodded back the way they had come, or the way she thought they had come, but Fourth-Folly shook their head, pointed in a slightly different direction, and said, "We found their ship back by the Mite Stretch."

"It was our deepest honor to find the grandchild of one so esteemed," Jest said, offering a deep bow from the waist.

"Even if that person of great esteem is running with a group of black-souled bums," Fourth-Folly said, lofting their words beyond the Marchess and to the people approaching.

"It's the big-bad-boom story-sick players!" said the man walking in front, the light skin of his face all smudged over with ash, probably from the hearthfire burning on their ship, its distant song playing just at the edge of Kindred's consciousness.

"Lurch!" Fourth-Folly said, their normally grumpy expression growing almost hostile. Their smile, when it appeared, was sharp and edged. "Any success in thieving recently?"

"Oh, Folly," Lurch said, his accent thick and strange, like nothing Kindred had ever heard before. "From one old-mold thief to another, I'm surprised you would even ask about my lit-light ventures."

"*Former* thief," Folly corrected. "And I never stole more than I needed before moving on."

"Former, nothing," Lurch said, offering his own predatory grin, a yellow line through the ash-grey of his face. "You're still a trip-trap thief. You're just else stealing something now-wise."

Folly opened their mouth to respond, but it was Jest who spoke next, directing her words to the other person from the Fell Company, an unremarkable man of perhaps thirty or thirty-five years, balding and with a thin mustache. If Lurch was dirty, this man was filthy—his clothes had dried mud creating topographies along them, mountains and valleys of brown gunk. His hair, what little was left of it, swirled into a nest atop his head, cracking with crusted mud.

"Hello, Tesser Cobb," Jest said, tipping her head back so she could stare down her nose at the man. Braid in each hand, she crossed her arms and fixed the man with a cold stare.

Tesser Cobb sucked in a breath at the sight of Jest, trying to run a hand through his hair and managing only to get his fingers briefly stuck.

"Jest," he said in rushed exhale. "It's wonderful to see you."

"Do not attempt to work your wiles upon me, Tesser Cobb," Jest said, narrowing her eyes. "You are wind upon my face, easily forgotten and bearing an unpleasant odor."

If Tesser Cobb was insulted by this, he showed no sign of it. If she hadn't heard Jest, Kindred might have even thought she'd complimented Tesser Cobb by the broad smile on his face, the way he looked down at his feet and hunched up his shoulders.

Kindred was reminded of Jest's advice from before: *Think on the wind*.

"Oh, Jest," he said, crumbling the dirt on his hands into dust. "It *is* good to see you again so soon. We didn't get a chance to talk properly last time."

"It is my suspicion that a proper talk is beyond you." Jest turned her head away from Tesser, though her eyes darted back.

The Marchess had been watching these exchanges with open curiosity, and she now turned back to Kindred, a familiar mischievous light in her eyes.

"The people down here are strange," she said. "I like them a lot."

She stood and then reached down to help Kindred up.

"Come on; we were just about to eat," the Marchess said. "You can join us."

"What about—" Lurch began, but the Marchess waved him away.

"We're eating. My granddaughter has found me beneath the Sea! If that doesn't call for a celebration, then nothing does!"

<hr />

They ate—a spiced soup that left Kindred's mouth feeling numb and pleasant. When she asked what was in it, the Marchess shook her head and said, "It's better not to know with this dish. Just enjoy it."

Despite the Fell only having two members—three with the Marchess—their boat was much bigger, though still a simple vessel. The groups joined on the deck, unencumbered by masts or sails and bare of anything save a few oddments—barrels and clothing and water skins.

The groups ate on the deck, plenty of room for them all to sit or stand as they pleased, spread out but still organized by allegiance—the Traveling Court clustering roughly near the bow, the Fell Company sitting aft, with the Marchess, Kindred, and Ragged Sarah arranged somewhere between. The deck was well worn, and Kindred found herself thinking of sailing in the sunlight for a moment as she sat down with her food in this dark, quiet place.

Looming over them, their play of sharp light a constant invitation to reverie, were the Greys. So close, they were a civilization, overrun with wild growths of half-dead plants, every shelf and spear of growth playing host to a panoply of insects and animals, some winged and some slithering and some skittering, each flickering in and out of light, washed in the sickly glow before disappearing into the folds of shadow worked in and around the Greys.

And stacked beside the strange growth was a tower of clean white bones, arranged in a chaotic build, taller and wider than a person, built like a chimney with a wide shaft of nothing in its center. It was enough bone to keep a single ship above going for thirty, maybe forty days of hard sailing.

The structure sat on a massive pile of thick, dark ash.

No one spoke of it, and no one asked.

Despite the initial hints of hostility between the groups, they behaved amiably during the meal, laughing at jokes and poking at one another in fun. Fourth-Folly avoided Lurch, who seemed happy to reciprocate, and Jest and Tesser Cobb stepped through what could only be a strange courtship. It was as though two children, both gifted with adult vocabularies and advanced conversational skills, were flirting. Jest offered veiled barbs and eloquent insults, and Tesser Cobb responded with bottomless kindness, smiling and nodding at every slight, blushing—though it was hard to tell through the dirt and ash—with each bit of disrespect.

They began with Kindred's story, and for the second time in as many days, it was told. Kindred began but found herself unable to find the excitement in it, and so Sarah and Awn took over, only too happy to add their perspective on the events that had brought the crew of *The Errant* to the Once-City, and the Once-City to Arcadian grasses, and *The Lost* below.

The food was delicious, the conversation rich and interesting, the dynamics full of history and mystery, and Kindred watched it all through what felt like a mask of joy. Her grandmother sat beside her, regularly putting a loving arm around Kindred and smiling at her, leaning close to say again what a wonderful surprise this was, a gift she couldn't have hoped for and was given anyway.

"I thought I had done with seeing familiar faces here in the twilight of my life," she said, whispering the words.

It was all happy and pleasant and wrong.

How many nights had Kindred imagined this reunion? How many daydreams given over to the look on her grandmother's face when she showed up, when she found her?

I knew it, she would say in those reveries, putting a hand on Kindred's shoulder, every dark moment in their past, the fights and bickering and awful final goodbye gone now, no longer final, washed away with this single act of a woman's love for her grandmother. *I knew you would find me. You and I are alike, and it is this likeness that has brought us together again.*

Instead, it was a surprise.

The Marchess laughed and listened and spoke exactly as Kindred remembered, the Marchess of this place lining up with the Marchess of so many afternoons and mornings and evenings sailing the grasses of the Forever Sea, leaning into the grass to let it skim past their outstretched hands. This was the same Marchess who sat before the fire with Kindred, demonstrating the builds and the songs, encouraging Kindred always to steal her techniques, to do the work to find the answers for herself.

This was the same Marchess.

Almost.

While she ate her food, while she leaned back against a barrel and listened to Lurch tell a story about a place called the Wanton Ruins, while she leaned in close to listen to her grandmother whisper something about Lurch or Tesser, about a memory that had just occurred to her—throughout it all, Kindred watched the Marchess and saw *almost.*

Did she smile less? Did her eyes dart like that before, flicking around as if to mark everyone around her? Had she ever eaten so little at a meal before?

"What have you been doing down here?" Kindred finally asked, speaking quietly.

The Marchess nodded and smiled at that, chewing her food before responding.

"Good work." She lifted a finger and pointed to Lurch and then Tesser Cobb. "I came down here to understand this sickness killing the Sea, and I found two people who care just as much as I do."

"You know what's causing the Greys?"

"They are." The Marchess let that same finger point up. "The people above. The Sea is a beast to be broken and made profitable to them. That magic they use to keep the grasses flat and ruled? This is the effect."

She swept one arm out toward the massive tower of corrupted plant rising above them.

"It was us all along," Kindred whispered, letting her eyes follow the Greys up, but her grandmother's hand on her shoulder stopped her.

"*No,*" she said, emphasizing the word with a sharp shake of her head.

"Not *us*. You and I, Tesser and Lurch, even the Traveling Court, feckless as they might be—all of us understand the magic and spirit of the Sea in ways those above never will. The people who see the Forever Sea as a vast field to be plundered are the ones to blame here, them and all the rest who profited from it."

"Do you know how to fix it?"

The Marchess grinned at that—the same knowing, confident grin Kindred had seen her whole life.

"I do. You'll see, once we're done with dinner."

When the Marchess got up to relieve herself, Kindred moved over to Ragged Sarah, who was eating a second bowl of the soup and talking with Tesser Cobb.

"Hi, you," Sarah said, shifting to lean slightly against Kindred. "Tesser Cobb was just telling me that parts of this deck are actually scavenged from a ship I used to sail on. Apparently, the Fell used to scavenge near where the Once-City had been when I was just coming up. Feels like I'm going back to the beginning again, somehow."

She put a hand to the battered wood of the deck, eyes staring briefly into memory's distant pastures.

"I salvaged the deck myself," Tesser said. He sat with his legs folded beneath him, knees pointing forward, legs parallel. From a small bowl, one edge badly mended, Tesser drank his soup. He had made no attempt to clean himself up for the meal.

Kindred nodded but said nothing, and when Sarah looked at her again, it was with weight and intensity.

"Is everything all right?" she asked, leaning close and bringing the conversation into the space between just the two of them.

"I . . . I don't . . . I'm fine," Kindred said, struggling to think through a numbness that was sweeping across her body. The golden shoots growing from her hand had curled into tight, hard, painful swirls, and the bud at the base of her neck clicked uncomfortably every time she swallowed.

"Hey, come here," Sarah said, wrapping her arms around Kindred and pulling her into a tight hug before helping her up and saying "We'll be right back" to Tesser Cobb.

Down in front of the ship, where the pluralities—only two for the Fell—shifted around under the dirt, Sarah turned to Kindred and said, "What is it?"

Kindred sucked in a breath but again managed to say nothing at all, sputtering quietly.

"You're scaring me," Sarah said, leaning close and peering into Kindred's eyes with the look of a medicker examining a patient. "Is it the food? How much did you eat?"

"It's not that." Kindred waved the suspicion away even as some part of her mind clung to the spirit of it, using it as a rope to climb out of her confusion and hurt. "It's the Marchess. Something's wrong with her."

Back at the ship, the Marchess was climbing aboard again, her throaty voice thrumming with the beginning of a story as she sat down beside Lurch. It took her only a moment to spring up again, acting out some antic from her past.

"She seems all right to me," Sarah said, dubious. "I've known sailors half her age who couldn't move like that."

"No, no. I don't mean physically. She's different somehow. Do you think . . ."

The Marchess stood now, arms outstretched, holding her audience's attention, the same big personality that had commanded her ship, *Revenger*, for so many years. She cut her eyes to Lurch and Tesser Cobb often, her smile mirrored on their faces.

"Do you think they did something to her? The Fell Company?"

"Kindred, what's going on?" Sarah put a hand on her shoulder, pulling Kindred's attention away from the deck of the ship and back to her. "What did she say to you? Did something happen?"

She wasn't waiting for me, Kindred wanted to say.

"She's changed," Kindred said. "I can just tell. And I think it's from the Fell. Jest and Fourth-Folly both had bad things to say about them. It has to be from them. They did something to her. She wasn't like this before. Above. She wasn't like this then."

Sarah was watching Kindred, one foot in the conversation and one foot out of it, peering at her from just outside.

"What happened, Kindred?"

I broke everything in my life above to follow her, and she wasn't even waiting for me. She didn't want me to come.

The words sounded childish even in her own head. The letter had made no promise, nothing explicit, nothing clear. This was always how the Marchess had been.

Stealing the technique of the hearthfire. Speaking in riddles and almost-meanings. Every action a metaphor and every syllable a simile.

Hot and heavy in her gut, hanging like an anchor from every thought in Kindred's mind, was shame.

"Nothing," she said, absent-mindedly brushing the coiled growth on her hand with a finger. "Nothing happened."

"It's time!" someone shouted from the ship, and Kindred and Sarah turned to see the Fell Company, the Marchess included, climbing down and walking toward the stack of bone and the Greys. The others, Awn and the Traveling Court, were following, though with just as much curiosity and uncertainty as Kindred felt.

"That's a lot of bones," Sarah muttered as they approached the tower. "Do you know of any build that would use so many bones?"

"No," Kindred said, keeping her voice down. She was watching the Marchess, who was laughing at something Lurch had said, laughing with her head thrown back, eyes cast skyward.

Had she laughed like that above? Or was there a sharper edge to it? The Marchess had always been the kind of person who squeezed her eyes shut in joy, wanting to feel every bit of it. Did she leave them open now?

"Kindred?"

"What?" Was that touch, the Marchess's hand on Tesser Cobb's shoulder, something?

"I asked how much you thought that many bones would go for in the Captains' Exchange."

"Oh," Kindred said, shifting to peer around Awn, who walked ahead of her, and see the Marchess. "I don't know."

The closer they walked to the stack of bones, the louder the song of the Greys became in Kindred's head, a jangle of melodies all caught and catching. When the song surged into splintering discord for a moment, she winced and saw the Marchess did too. At least there was still this shared sensitivity to the world around them. At least the Fell hadn't changed that, too.

When she spoke, the Marchess raised her voice enough to speak over the clang of the Greys, though to those who couldn't hear the discordant melodies, it must have simply sounded like the Marchess was shouting for no reason.

"You're lucky to catch us today," she said, looking small beside the stack of bones. She kneeled down, setting herself as she used to when keeping

the hearthfire, her knees sounding like rocks clicking and clacking together. "This should be a treat to see."

"Another one of your plans, Tesser Cobb?" Jest asked, glaring at Tesser,
who stood near enough the Marchess that he might have offered help,
though it seemed as though there was nothing he could do.

"A bit," he said, smiling and nodding, looking like a fossil recently
pulled up from the dirt. "Lurch and I provided the materials, but it was all
her idea. She sees much more than I ever could. She's a lot like you, actually."

"Flattery is not in your limited skill set, Tesser Cobb," Jest said, looking
at him out of the corner of her eye, though Kindred saw a slim smile play
across her lips for a moment.

"She's a knower, a sip-sop certainer," Lurch said, bobbing his head and
pulling at one ear.

"You don't make any sense," Fourth-Folly said in a muted grumble.

"Sense is—you don't din-dan don't make it," Lurch rejoined, glaring at
Fourth-Folly, who ignored him and looked to the stack of bones.

Jest said more, and so, too, did Tesser Cobb. Madrigal and Awn were
talking as well about Madrigal's favorite books and whether Awn had read
or even heard of any of them.

"Kindred," Sarah said, putting a hand on her arm, trying to get her attention, but Kindred couldn't give it, couldn't give it to any of the conversations or dynamics at play.

Because the Marchess had begun singing, and tears were welling in
Kindred's eyes. It was the song that played across the deck in all of her
memories of those early years aboard *Revenger*, the Marchess sculpting
the words of the hearthfire melodies. There was no deck, no sails, no
hearthfire, no ship or crew or Sea without the Marchess's voice singing in
the background, husking out the syllables in deep, resonant tones.

On some level, in some dark, quiet part of her mind, Kindred had
feared—or believed—that she would never again hear her grandmother
sing.

None of the religions practiced on Arcadia or the Mainland had ever
appealed to her. Her parents had believed in the Morning Gods, and They
had offered nothing when Kindred's parents needed Them. It had all
seemed overly manufactured to her, the oaths and prayers, the buildings
and false promises of faith—all attempts to recreate what waited in the

play of the Sea. It wasn't until Kindred sat on the deck of *Revenger*, her life gone still and cold behind her, the future a vast horizon of possibility ahead, that she had found something like religion, and it had been in the colloquy of song and bone and flame and ash. Somewhere in the magic of a song become flame become lift, Kindred had found her religion.

In the winding corridors of her grandmother's songs for the Sea, Kindred had found something holy.

This, though, was no song Kindred had ever heard before. She caught clusters of phrases and sounds she recognized, but it was run through with strange words and turns of the tongue, something like the language of the hearthfire but not. It rankled and itched, the slight wrongness of it. Listening to that song felt like returning home to find everything almost exactly where it had been left, clothes nearly in the same place, food nibbled and put back.

It spoke of intercession, of another voice hiding in the sibilants and plosives, of a hand guiding this hand.

It was wrong, and even as Kindred felt the waves of nostalgia and memory crashing against her and pulling her back to that skinned-knee, hole-in-the-heart kid she had been, some part of her recoiled at the wrongness of the Marchess's song.

It twinned with and threaded through the music of the Greys, and the fire that bloomed beneath her hands was an oily, thick thing, brown and black and sludging up to engulf the stack of bones. Tongues of flame leapt out and splashed to the ground around the Marchess, sizzling and popping as they met the dirt.

A noise like the ground itself crying out sounded behind them, and Kindred turned to see the pluralities racing and pulling about, their lines straining and slackening, tangling together as the beings below moved chaotically.

"Folly," Jest said, but Fourth-Folly was already running back to the ship. Madrigal had started to follow them but had stopped, wincing at the broken melodies working inside her head, just as they worked in Kindred's.

"Don't worry," Tesser Cobb called out to Fourth-Folly, kindly concern on his face. He took a few steps back from the viscous fire roaring up from the tower of bone. "They don't like it initially, but they calm down after a bit. We just give ours some food for this first part."

Fourth-Folly offered him a scowl that said quite clearly what they thought of his suggestion and advice, but they dropped handfuls of food from their pockets on the ground nonetheless, and the pluralities began to settle, the noise of their distress fading.

The Fell's pluralities, Kindred saw, were clustered together beside their boat, where a small bounty of food had been scattered across the ground for them.

"Hush-a-hush-a," Lurch said, putting a three-fingered hand out behind him, the skin a swirl of badly healed burns. "Let her work now-now."

The Marchess's song grew louder and faster, the syllables slipping quickly from her mouth, and streaks of bright colors began to slip across the surface of the fire, oranges and reds, silvers and whites, each one mirrored and magnified in the towering Greys rising behind the stack of bone. Whatever the Marchess was doing with the fire, whatever strange magic her song was conjuring, was happening in the Greys, too.

Creatures living among the calcified growths scattered at the sudden change of light, disappearing inside the myriad holes pocking the plant or pressing themselves into seams between strands of the growth. Some climbed high, and Kindred found herself wondering how high they would go. To that dark middle of the Sea where plants completed the archways begun below?

Or did they flee all the way to the surface? Legs or wings or lined limbs carrying them alongside the lantern bearers rising up and up to the light?

That thought was pushed away from Kindred's mind as the Marchess's work reached its purpose.

"Stand back, everyone," Tesser Cobb said, taking several steps toward the ships and gesturing for the others to follow.

The Marchess, Kindred's grandmother and legendary captain of *Revenger*, raised an arm above her head, fingers straight, and brought it down like a blade into the mess of flame and bone, cutting a trail through the tower and leaving a line which held in the swirling rush of viscous fire and burning bone.

A sibling slash appeared in the Greys, first a thin scratch of black but soon a widening gash, pulling apart in uneven tugs, mimicking the one before the Marchess, which she had worked her hands into, spreading her fingers wide and pulling it open, bone snapping into jagged fragments as she did so.

Madrigal had begun to cry, and her wail was a perfect harmony for the

Marchess's melody, which spun wilder and wilder, every sound and syllable now a thorn pricking and tugging at Kindred's mind. She found herself
leaning forward despite the revulsion of it all, teeth gritted and bared, one
hand clamped hard on Sarah's, which Kindred hadn't even realized she'd
grabbed in the first place. A low, guttural moan was sounding in Kindred's
throat, and the muscles in her jaw were clenched tight enough to hurt.

People had begun to shout, Fourth-Folly demanding to know what was
happening and Lurch shouting obscenities back as he demanded they be
quiet. Jest's voice, too, was a strand in the maelstrom, her cries of concern
met by Tesser Cobb's banal reassurance.

Awn's cry was a wordless one, too near to pain and wonder to be dis-
tinguishable as either.

Sarah wrenched her hand from Kindred's grip and stepped forward, a
knife held up as though she would throw it, eyes trained on the person
kneeling at the altar of all of this madness.

The Marchess.

Panic surged through Kindred, pure and cold and more actionable than
the fear and confusion that had been crowding her thoughts and memories. She had lost her grandmother once, and she would not again.

"No!" Kindred growled, staggering forward and slamming into Sarah,
driving her shoulder hard into Sarah's even as she grabbed for the hand
holding the knife. Sarah's grunt was more surprise than pain as she fell
forward, Kindred clinging to her.

"What are you doing, Kindred?" Sarah hissed, writhing until she'd
burst free from Kindred's grip.

But Kindred was looking beyond her, beyond the Marchess, and beyond the fire.

Starless black, the Marchess's spell was a tear through both the fabric
of the Greys and the space before it. A cold like nothing Kindred had ever
felt emanated from that vast, widening chasm, the dark of it like a well to
be fallen down.

Arcs of light moved in that way-down darkness, and it took Kindred a
moment to realize it was a single form moving closer, its enormous size
catching bits of illumination in whatever that other place was, for surely
the Marchess's work had been in opening a doorway.

Sarah uttered a low, urgent cry of fear as the creature neared and came
through.

A wide snout, split top to bottom and lined with a tumble of teeth, emerged first, wide eyes on either side of its head open and blinking. A thick neck dripping a thin, foul-smelling liquid came next, and then the body, which looked at first to be thick as the neck and head, long and serpentine and riddled with holes, but then the creature twisted and Kindred saw the truth: its body was flattened from the neck down, impossibly thin. Its head was round and wide enough that it could swallow everyone present and have room to spare, but its body, down past its neck, wouldn't have been wide enough for even one of them.

As it emerged fully, the drip of liquid from its neck turned into a steady drizzle and the creature, its tail end still beyond the doorway the Marchess had opened, coiled in on itself, eyes rolling in their sockets, mouth opening with a wet, tearing sound to reveal more teeth covering the inside of its mouth in a hypnotizing spiral pattern.

The Marchess shouted her song, melody and rhythm all but forgotten in the moment, and the beast looked down to her, snapping its head to the side to glare with one eye.

The fire, sludgy and thick as it was, leapt up at the Marchess's command, a thick glob of it, bigger than a person, splashing up and across the creature's snout. It hissed and sizzled against the black, close-grown fur.

A bellow of rage rent the air as the creature reacted to the fire, its head thrashing about in agony, body coiling and uncoiling, before it leapt away, extending itself fully and flying up, away from the Marchess's fire, its eyes mad, mouth open. It climbed the Greys in an ungainly motion, coiling and uncoiling like a spring against and around the plants of the Sea.

With only a lingering smell and the quickly fading sound of its escape, the creature was gone.

In its wake, several more came through, all in a rush, as though the first had shown them the way. Each was unique and horrifying in its own way.

A collection of arms, furred and scaled and smooth, each wide around as a person, terminating in wicked claws or grasping fingers thick as Kindred's arm, their center a bolus of bulging skin.

Creatures half-animal and half-plant that Kindred would dream about later, their skin bursting with vines and flowers like her own. One had nightmarish blooms that rose from its heads on stalks and swiveled around like eyes.

A person, naked and featureless, skin striped over with bands of baleful yellow and perfect-sky blue, who, when the Marchess flung her flames onto him, laughed in a voice that sounded like the growling of a beast too big and too close to have come from him.

Birds with skin like tree bark and mouths like wounds on their heads, wings made of bone spanned by stretches of ragged, fluttering cloth bearing strange sigils.

The Marchess's doorway spewed monstrosity into the world, each one huge and angry, bigger than any natural creature in the Sea, big enough to devour the wyrm that had terrorized *The Errant*. On and on they came, each one a horror, faster and faster, as if rushing to make it in time, and soon enough, the gash in the Greys began to close, and the Marchess moved quickly, working at her build to salvage the burning pieces of it, keeping it upright for just a little longer.

"Kindred!" she shouted over one shoulder. "Help me!"

The parade of monstrosities had come quickly after that first creature, and Kindred had fallen into a stupor as the seemingly unending line of nightmares continued to emerge and then flee in the space above her. But her grandmother's call, so achingly familiar, jarred Kindred enough to bring her back to the present. She was standing and lifting one foot to approach when a hand clamped on her arm, and Sarah's voice, urgent and hard, sounded in her ear.

"What are you doing? You're going to help her with that?!"

Jest and Wylf sat together on the ground nearby, staring up at the slowly closing tear. Folly remained by the pluralities, one hand open at their side, frozen in the act of giving them some food. Awn and Madrigal had retreated to the ship, both crouching just behind it, peering out at the spectacle.

Only Tesser Cobb and Lurch moved and seemed at all comfortable. Lurch lay on the ground, one hand pillowing his head, the other holding a half-eaten stick of burnt root. He might have been watching the stars on a quiet night.

Tesser had out a small book and was writing something down in it with a stub of coal, muttering to himself.

"Kindred!" the Marchess shouted again, but Sarah didn't let her go, and a moment later, the burning tower of bone collapsed, its integrity challenged by the Marchess's initial slash and finally giving up its ghost.

The doorway in the Greys slammed shut, cutting off the enraged howls of all those creatures approaching their freedom.

"Fucking shitlicking wastrel!" the Marchess shouted, turning around looking with a wild, enraged look, which finally found Kindred—and Sarah, who still held on to her. "We could've had more!"

"Is this what you've been doing, Lurch?" Fourth-Folly shouted from the ship. "This has been your big plan to save the Sea?"

Lurch responded, but Kindred paid no attention, because the Marchess had stood and walked over to her, eyes wide, teeth grinding together in anger.

"What is this?" She gestured down at Sarah's hand on Kindred's arm. "You can't help your grandmother because your *first mate* won't let you? I thought you were a captain."

A flush of heat burned along Kindred's neck as she pulled her arm from Sarah's grip.

"What's going on here, Grandmother?" she asked, looking over the Marchess's shoulder at the smoldering remains of the fire. "I thought you were saving the Sea."

"I am."

"By . . . what? Pulling monstrosities from the Greys?"

"Yes," the Marchess said, nodding, as though the question weren't an insane one. "They're a gift from the Sea, Kindred. They're nature's attempt to set things right, and all they need is a doorway to come through and the fire to go above."

"And do what?" Kindred asked, but she knew the answer already. Not *us*. Them.

"Those above have thought for too long that they can break the world around them," the Marchess said, speaking in a quiet, sad voice. "It's time they were broken in return."

CHAPTER THIRTEEN

Silence filled the dining room despite all four siblings and their father occupying the chairs. Flitch couldn't remember the last time they'd all been there together, the kids and their father, and knew that there had never been a time when they'd all been there and been silent.

Idyll had been sent for as soon as the emergency below had been made clear. They'd ridden back in haste to find Flitch alive and well, the house in an uproar, and Nab dead.

The baron had said little on their way up from the labyrinth save to tell Tally, captain of his guards, to lock down the house and to "continue preparations."

As Flitch and the others walked up the stairs, Tally was instructing two of her guards, each holding a massive maul, to seal the archway as permanently as they could.

Shortly after that, Twyllyn Tae, first captain of the Borders fleet, had come down the stairs, stopping to pull the baron to the side and have a hurried conversation with him, one that Twyllyn looked none too happy about. Twyllyn was a one-eyed sailor, as experienced and hard as any who sailed the Forever Sea but cleverer than most. The baron had once told his children that Twyllyn only pretended to be crass and rough to fit in with the rest of the sailors on the Mainland, but they had a keen mind working under their mat of shaggy golden hair.

At the end of the conversation, Twyllyn had nodded to the baron, clasped his arm, and said goodbye to each child before hurrying down the stairs.

"What was—" Aster began, but the baron shook his head firmly and said nothing.

As they walked up the stairs together, each walking the labyrinth in their own mind, Flitch examined the book from Quietus.

It was a thick volume bound in dark blue cloth, hefty but surprisingly light. It felt good in his hand, as though it was meant for him, or him for it. A title cut across the cover in flaking, golden script: *This Wild, Forgotten Forever.*

Flitch wanted to open it right then, to drop onto the stairs and rush through the pages, but the family moved with purpose, and it would have to wait.

Finally, they made it to the dining room and sat down, and with the sounds of the servants and guards bustling about echoing into the room, the Borders siblings looked around at one another anxiously, waiting for their father to speak.

The baron ran one large, callused hand across the wood of the table, spreading out his fingers to reach each crack and divot, every one a story of some moment in their lives. When he spoke, his voice was quiet.

"We need to flee. It is not safe for us here, or it won't be once the King discovers that Nab has disappeared."

"Excellent plan on that one, Flitch," Aster said, putting one elbow on the table and nodding at him. "Now Faineant can hate us for existing *and* killing his favorite whisperman."

"Enough," the baron said, holding up a hand. "What Flitch did was rash and dangerous, but it will not matter in the long view. Nab's presence here was only preamble to Faineant himself arriving. The whisperman would have found and fabricated enough reason for the King to send more people and take Borders, regardless of our attempts. Faineant is making his play for Borders, and Nab's visit was only the first move of many. Flitch may have sped up the game, but the trajectory is unchanged."

Flitch looked across the table at Idyll, and the betrayal he'd felt down in the labyrinth reared its head. All the stories they'd told him, the quiet aloofness they'd maintained while Flitch, Aster, and Zim speculated about what mysteries could wait for them below their house—all of it was a kind of quiet lie, and even as Idyll looked at him with real concern, Flitch felt the beginnings of anger rising inside.

A memory of Idyll telling him a story of the supposed Paths labyrinth played in his mind, and he saw Idyll's room in startling clarity, the white of the sheets crisp against his hands, the bunched pillows firm behind his neck and head. He saw the titles of books leaning precariously against one another on Idyll's desk, could pick out the individual names, the stamp or swirl of text; he could count the number of loose pages splayed like a fan on the floor nearby. The wind coming in through the open window, bellied forth on the wide expanse of moonlight, felt cool against his cheek, and he smelled the flowers from outside—the sweet, light fragrances that he could never identify but loved all the same.

His anger suffocated beneath the immensity of the memory, his petty feelings gone as he marveled at every detail of the memory presenting itself to him, as though the whole of it was simply waiting for his attention. As if he were really there, really snuggled in Idyll's bed, listening to their story, the smells and sounds and sights of that room waiting for his consideration.

He heard the delicate timbre of Idyll's voice as they described that room, and the words—the *exact* words—rang in his mind as if they were ringing, too, in his ears.

There's a room in this labyrinth, shaped like a teardrop and filled with small, woven baskets. In each is a smaller basket, and in those, there are smaller baskets still. The baskets are made of cloth and smell of sunlight. To open one is to know sadness. To open two is to know dread. No one has ever opened three.

It was not a memory like any he had ever experienced. It was a doorway back to that perfectly preserved moment.

It was wonderful.

A gift.

Flitch let his eyes fall to the book in his hand, his true gift from Quietus. *This Wild, Forgotten Forever.* He let his fingers trace the title, watching as bits of gold flecked away.

"Borders has few remaining friends and, of those few, almost none with any real power." The baron grimaced as he said this, as though it were a personal sin of his instead of a truth known and acknowledged by everyone in that room, in that house, and on the Mainland. Borders and all of its traditions and finery and history had become the specter of spectacle, once grand and now only a memory of grandeur, a body moving and slumping on despite already being dead.

"So, we leave the Mainland," Idyll said, gathering their papers into their bag. "We run west and hope to escape before Faineant discovers what has happened."

"We won't make it," Zim said, speaking matter-of-factly. "I've seen the reports of how many whispermen the King employs to watch the roads. He would know before we had made it past Halcyon, even if we took roads through the country."

The baron nodded, one hand scratching at his jaw.

"We cannot flee, at least not yet."

"But we can't stay," Aster said, sounding suddenly young and petulant, a child cornered and caught. "You said it right: we have no friends with any real power."

"No," the baron said, his face grim. "I said *almost* none."

"Paths," Flitch said, his mind firing with the clarity of it. The Paths estate was close by, and Gwyn Gaunt held a special power around her, one even King Faineant was leery to press and test. She had already suggested they join forces against Faineant's power play; perhaps Paths would offer shelter to the people of Borders as well.

"I had a suspicion that our time in this house would not last," the baron said, nodding around at his children before looking to Idyll.

"While there," Idyll said, "I asked Gwyn Gaunt about the possibility of our people joining her at the Paths house should it come to that."

"And what did she say?" Aster asked.

"She said, 'Sounds fun. I love sleepovers,'" Idyll said, cracking a smile.

"We leave immediately," the baron said, rising from his chair. "Take only what you can carry. I do not expect us to return to this house."

"*Now?*" Zim asked, looking around. "Right now? I'm not prepared."

"I'm sorry, son," the baron said, putting a hand on Zim's shoulder. "This is not how I hoped to leave our house. But Faineant will know of Nab's demise soon, and his response will be swift. We cannot be here when that happens."

He left, his deep voice resonating with authority as he directed staff and guards.

For just a breath, no one moved as the meaning of their father's words took effect. They would flee to the home of the Mainland's strangest, most ascetic baron and throw themselves upon her mercy.

They would not return.

Zim was the first to go, speaking quickly and to himself about "records" to collect. Aster was just behind him, her fear already transforming to charged anxiety and emerging as a string of curses filthier and angrier than anything Flitch had ever heard, most of them describing or directed toward the King.

Idyll went more slowly, packing up a few papers they'd been carrying and eyeing Flitch.

"You didn't finish your story," they said.

Flitch looked up from the book, *This Wild, Forgotten Forever*. He'd been thinking about his room, about running around in it, loading up bags with clothes and books and tools and models. What an impossible thing, to gather up a life in a moment and run away with it, as though he could carry the Flitch that had walked through these halls and laughed in these rooms and dreamed big dreams.

He had the sudden wild urge to take only the clothes on his body and the book in his hand. Why not? Whatever was ahead was new and would require a new Flitch. Perhaps Quietus had given him everything he would need between the covers of this book.

"I'll tell the rest later," Flitch said finally. In the mess of the moment, it had seemed so unimportant.

Idyll quirked a smile at him, surprise showing on their face.

"You finally get to be the hero and you're going to wait until later to tell the story?" they asked, shaking their head, long, dark hair playing around their face. "The labyrinth really did change you."

"As it changed you, I suppose," he said, trying and failing to keep a bitter note from his voice.

Idyll sighed and said, "I wanted to tell you the truth, but I couldn't. Father forbade it."

"You should've told me," Flitch said. "You should've told all of us."

"I couldn't," Idyll said again.

"Because Father said not to? How many of his rules did we break as kids? You should've told me anyway, instead of sliding in the truth sideways through stories."

"I couldn't tell you," Idyll said, closing their eyes to speak over Flitch, "because *I* couldn't do it. Father forbade it, yes, but it was too much for me to share. I had nightmares about it every night for at least three spans. Stories were the only way I could tell you. The only way I could tell myself."

Flitch said nothing for a moment as his anger gave way to a deep melancholy. His memories of Idyll in those days after their mother died had grown just as crisp and true as the rest, and he watched them now, struggling through meals and conversations in ways that a younger Flitch had completely missed or attributed to simple chance of the day, a bad night sleeping or an upset stomach. He saw Idyll's eyes, red and puffy from crying, as they put on a smile and performed joy for their youngest sibling.

They had carried this burden alone, and stories had become their only way of making sense of what they'd seen and come to know. Whispering these slantwise, sideways truths to their younger brother who wouldn't understand.

"I'm sorry," Flitch said finally, stepping forward and wrapping Idyll in a hug. They might have stayed that way for longer, but the bustle of people outside pulled them apart. They needed to move, to pack what they could and leave their home, probably forever.

"One good thing about those stories," Flitch said as they separated. "They helped me make sense of the labyrinth in a way I couldn't have otherwise. I thought it would have been scary, and it was, but it was also amazing. I kept thinking about how much you would have loved some of those rooms and caverns, each one like a little set piece from a story."

Idyll gave him a long, studying gaze.

"You almost died down there, Flitch, and Mother *did* die down there. There's nothing I can love about that place," they said. And then, after a moment: "What really happened to you?"

Flitch thought about waiting for the others, whispering the events of the labyrinth to them as they fled down the never-used sea-side road between Paths and Borders, but somehow, this—just the two of them, leaning over the dinner table and telling a story—somehow, this seemed right.

It was as it had always been, except this time Flitch had the story and Idyll listened, rapt and attentive, eyes growing wider as Flitch described his attempt to run from Quietus, the rooms he'd seen, and the final room— an impression of his own—in which Quietus had caught him.

"I woke up back in the entryway, still holding this book," Flitch said as he finished, lifting the thick book, which Idyll took with interest.

They turned it over, letting their hands move smoothly over the cover and binding, their fingertips brushing across the page edges. Flitch had always loved watching Idyll hold books.

Everyone worships something, he had once read in a book given to him by one of the tutors who had tried to wrangle the children when they were young. *See what they worship, and you will see who they are.*

As he watched Idyll inspect the book, opening it and turning the pages with the care of a parent holding their newborn baby, Flitch saw his sibling.

"It's beautiful," Idyll said quietly, reverently. "All this fine work on the cover and spine. They look like stalks of grass in gold, but they're very faded."

"What do you mean?" Flitch asked. The cover had seemed a uniform blue to him save for the title, so faint as to be almost impossible to actually see.

"Look here," Idyll said, leaning across the table and holding the book to the light, angling it until yes, Flitch could see the barest outline, skeletal, like dust trapped in the wrinkles of the cover.

"Have you heard of it?" Flitch asked, but Idyll shook their head almost immediately.

"No, but that doesn't necessarily mean anything. There are loads of texts that— Oh, no, never mind," Idyll said as they cracked open the book and found hundreds of empty pages, yellowed with age. "I've never heard of it because it isn't a real book, I guess."

Idyll laughed and flipped through the pages quickly, and they almost missed it—Flitch, too. A page buried in the emptiness, maybe two-thirds of the way through the book, contained writing. Dark ink and a steady, stylistic hand.

Flitch moved instinctively, his hand cutting through the air like a javelin, fingers burying into the book to save the page. He couldn't say why and was just as surprised that he'd moved as Idyll, who let out a yelp of shock. But the desire to read that page was stronger than anything he had ever experienced, and he felt Quietus's influence working through him and on him, as though Flitch were yet another piece of some vast, grand instrument.

"Sorry," Flitch said, grabbing the book and wedging it open to the filled page. "I didn't want to lose the page."

Idyll shrugged but continued to look at him with the same calculating consideration.

"What does it say?"

Flitch looked down at the page and found a short note, only a few lines.

I don't know who will get this missive, but it comes with gravest urgency. The monsters climbing up from the Sea and attacking are being let loose and sent above by a crazed ex-captain named the Marchess. She is pulling them through the Greys and means to send enough of them to kill many, many people. Perhaps everyone on the Mainland. If you can break the spellwork keeping the Sea flat and tame, then the power of the Greys will diminish, and so, too, will the monsters. Let the Sea grow wild, and there may be a chance.

Ragged Sarah, of The Lost,
formerly of The Errant,
first mate of Captain Kindred Greyreach

"What?" Idyll said, confusion mingling with something very like anger as they reached across the table for the book, scanning the page and jabbing a finger at the last line. "Kindred Greyreach. She's the one who set Arcadia's grasses on fire! I heard Father talking about her."

"So, she must be alive," Flitch said, his mind turning at the magic of that, the seeds of rumor flowering into fact. Finding the Once-City, escaping it, setting fire to the grasses around Arcadia, and disappearing below. She had really done it all, and now she and her crew were actually down there! It was like no story Idyll had ever told him; it was messy and complicated. People had died. Lives and livelihoods burned up in this woman's pursuit of . . . what? What had she wanted? In Idyll's stories, someone wanted to stop evil or right a wrong or defeat the faceless hordes of some wicked king. But there was nothing like that here.

Why had she done it?

"This can't be real," Idyll said, closing the book and pushing it back across the table to Flitch. "How could this book only have one page with text that references events from *right now*? It's not possible, not if it really is from the labyrinth."

The sounds of bustling and packing outside the room had grown louder, and voices could be heard urging speed. They should really be going, but Flitch found a strange calm inside of him at the whole thing, as though it was all happening as it was meant to, the song Quietus was playing on its grand instrument perfect and harmonious.

"I think it is real, Idyll," Flitch said, smiling a little. "It's the gift."

Idyll stared at him for a long moment before smiling, wide and bitter.

"This is all a joke, isn't it? You found a blank book down in Grandfather's Library after escaping from that beast and filled it out with this stuff before waiting for the rest of us to find you. Right? It's good, Flitch. Unbelievable, maybe, but good."

They laughed at the thought, but their laughter curdled as they saw the look of placid confidence on Flitch's face. The Flitch of even a day before would have protested, explaining again everything that had happened to him, saying more, and in saying more, giving less. He'd been the loud one, comfortable in his role in the family, among the siblings. Every interaction was like a play where he knew the script and his character.

"It's real," Flitch said, his voice quiet, his smile untroubled.

"What happened to you?" Idyll asked, their voice a bare whisper, no longer curious.

They were afraid.

Borders did not boast the same numbers of staff and guards, servants and cooks, stablehands and advisors as other baronies. Like the house and the lands and the position at court and the wealth, the population of workers laboring for the sake of the barony had declined over the years. Only the Borders sailing fleet remained strong in number, the jewel Faineant hoped to add to his own crown.

Still, even with the reduced number of people, it was no quick or easy feat to flee.

Some refused the safety of Paths and instead chose to flee to the homes of relatives or friends. They fled in the near-dusk, eschewing the main road and running across the wild, untended country lands.

These the baron let go with some sadness, but he did not attempt to stop them.

The rest, the family included, raced down the narrow road, barely visible in the low light, leading to Paths. A few horses pulled carts laden with only necessities and anything else that could fit.

To one side of the road, thick shagbark oaks grew, providing a gnarled, overgrown barrier between the Seaside path and the rest of the Mainland. It formed a kind of corridor, cut off from the rest of the world.

To the other side was the Sea itself, down below the sharp, high cliffs on which Borders and Paths had built their estates. As kids, Flitch and his siblings used to walk that road, never far enough to get near to the Paths estate, but far enough to get away from their own and feel like they were alone. They would climb the trees and run along the road and toss rocks and sticks down into the Sea, watching as the projectiles fell and fell and fell before disappearing into the green mess.

Now they all rode, eyes ahead, speaking very little. No one in the train of Borders people, it seemed, knew what the plan was beyond seeking refuge with Paths, who had, reportedly, returned the Borders Baron's urgent request for sanctuary with a note that simply read, *Delighted!*

Flitch rode with his siblings, just behind the group of people around his father, all of whom were in a quiet, intense conversation, probably deciding how to best run from King Faineant and his swarm of power-obsessed lackeys.

"What was that game we used to play on this road?" Flitch asked, turning to the others. "Something about being winged warriors whose homes were in the trees?"

It was warriors who had lost their wings and needed to climb the trees to talk with a tree spirit who could regrow them, actually—Flitch could remember the feel of that shagbark on his palms as if he were climbing one of the trees right then. But he wanted to hear the rest of them talk and remember, and Idyll was still not saying anything or even looking in his direction.

"Tree Spirit!" Aster said, her face brightening at the memory. "That game was fantastic. Zim hated it."

"I hated it," Zim agreed, nodding, voice dull. They'd had to pry him away from the careful records he'd been trying to pack. None of the siblings or their father could imagine a scenario where they would need numbers tracing the average growth cycle for their garden's vegetables over the previous ten years.

"But Idyll loved it," Flitch said, smiling at the eldest sibling, who rode a little ahead of them, their face turned out toward the Sea. Idyll gave a non-committal grunt and did not turn around.

"Sometimes, I think about all the dumb stuff we did as kids and feel amazed that none of us died," Aster said, standing up in the saddle and stretching, her back giving a series of satisfying *pop*s.

"I did break my arm once," Zim said, still gloomy. "I had to learn to write with the other hand. Father had to help me bathe!"

Aster chuckled darkly at that.

"If you'd taken the route up that tree I recommended, you wouldn't have fallen," Aster said, speaking the old lines and falling into the old character as easily as anything.

"It was a rotted tree, Aster! Do you even know what that means? There were no safe routes!"

"Oh, no? Then how did I get up there?"

It was an argument the two of them returned to regularly, and Flitch looked past them to Idyll and the Sea beyond.

"Are you okay?" he asked, nudging his horse up beside Idyll's. The Sea beyond was a play of dark colors, purples and crimsons, the sun's fading glory played out in the feather-fine grasses.

"Five," Idyll said after a moment, finally turning to Flitch. They had gathered their long hair into a braid once more, smooth and put together, their Borders robes clean, posture stiff and upright.

"Five?" Flitch asked.

"I've seen five eruptions of creatures from the Sea since we left our home. Five, and we're not even a quarter of the way to Paths yet. That's five more than I should have seen."

The movement of the Sea, wind-carved and shadowed, seemed a promise, and Flitch fought to keep his eyes on Idyll's face instead of staring, waiting for a sixth sighting.

"I remember playing Tree Spirit, but I also remember spending whole days out here, hoping to see a Sea bird or a cloud of ants. We could have stayed out here fifty days, keeping constant watch, and we wouldn't have seen five sightings of anything that actually lived that far below the surface."

That same anger from before animated their words, an anger Flitch saw but did not understand. It was unlike Idyll, who was always so even and calm. How many times had Flitch come to them, incandescent with anger or devastated by despair, only to be eased by Idyll's tranquility?

How many hurts and slights and dashed hopes had been made better by their careful, considered, calm ministrations?

"It makes sense if Ragged Sarah's letter is right," Flitch offered, cautious, feeling as though Idyll might break or snap at any moment. "That person—the Marchess—is down there, sending the monsters up. They're being forced to rise."

Idyll nodded, their mouth a thin line, and muttered, "It makes sense."

Flitch huffed out a breath, confused and frustrated.

"Six," Idyll said a moment later as, out on the Sea, a great swell of plants gave way to a creature breaking the surface, a splintered beak opening in a noiseless cry, head and long, sleek body dotted by patches of feathers that glowed in the darkness of dusk. Long, ropy arms exploding from several thick knots of skin at random points on its body, each one waving about in the air as the creature's momentum took it up and up and out of the Sea, a long arc of monstrous flesh, big as a house—big as ten houses—hanging in the air for a long, long moment, sounding its soundless yawp.

Thankfully, none of the ships in the harbor were anywhere close to the creature, and it sent up a spray of seed and chaff as it dropped back into the Sea, disappearing before any of the fleets might have had a chance to prepare anything against it.

When it broke again, it was nearer the shore, and the telltale flash of casting magics answered its rise, lashes of red and gold power from the King's casters, driving the monster back, cracking against its sides and face, an onslaught of power.

Whatever force from the Marchess moved the creature to act flickered and died in the face of the King's casters, and when it dove below the Sea this time, it did not return.

"What was that?" Flitch asked, awed. It had been like nothing he'd ever seen, and in a flash he remembered a similar wondering confusion, down in the labyrinth in that room that was his and not his, staring out the window at a Sea boiling over with nightmarish creatures that had no names, no descriptions, no knowledge shared by sailors old or new. More than ever, Flitch felt like he was on the right path, was moving toward and with something beyond him.

Maybe this is what heroes feel, he thought with a smile.

"I don't know," Idyll said. "I've only been able to identify one of the six."

They fell into silence after that, both scanning the Sea in the increasingly dwindling light, and just as Flitch was trying to figure out how to unravel the mess that their relationship had turned into, Idyll spoke.

"You're different since coming back from the labyrinth," they said, not meeting his eyes. "I thought it was perhaps just shock at the outset, but a change has taken place in you, Flitch. You talk about that creature below, *Quietus*, as if it couldn't or wouldn't have killed you and our siblings if it felt the need. Father, too, it could have killed on any of his thousand nights spent below, each new exploration of his undertaken without telling any of us. It's a curse, and you're acting like it's the greatest blessing a person could receive, all because it chased you through room after horrifying room, gave you a book that has an impossible message in it, and knocked you out before bringing you back to the entrance."

They finished with a quick gasp, as though they would say more but didn't.

Idyll had always been a careful, conscientious speaker, never given to outbursts or ill-considered communication. They'd once told Flitch in confidence that they practiced almost everything they said in their head before speaking, carefully building the sentences in their mind, connecting words and phrases inside before actually talking.

"I used to get nervous speaking," they'd told Flitch, sitting cross-legged on the floor of their room and working on a wooden puzzle, trying to fit the various shapes together into a whole. "So, I just slowed everything down and practiced. It was hard at first, but I didn't care if I spoke too slowly. I wanted to be perfect. It's only with family that I don't feel the need to recite and construct my words before speaking."

Flitch had felt such gratitude and pride in that moment, knowing that he was part of this group, this privileged few, with whom Idyll felt comfortable enough to not practice their words.

But this speech had the patter of practice about it, each pause measured, each word chosen and spoken with precision.

Idyll was speaking to him like a stranger. *This* was the source of their anger, that somehow he had taken a step outside of that small circle. He had gone from being a brother whom Idyll understood and loved to a brother speaking and acting in strange ways. Idyll wasn't angry at the complications of the book or the message or Quietus or even their flight to Paths.

They were angry that Flitch had gone into that labyrinth and perhaps would never come out again.

The pleasant warmth of the purpose granted him by Quietus was suddenly shot through with fear and worry, and Flitch fought back a gasp of shock.

"Idyll," he said, guiding his horse close enough so that he could reach out and put a hand on Idyll's arm, and waiting to speak until they met his eyes. "Idyll, I'm okay. I'm still me. I can't explain what happened to me down there, and I honestly have no idea what Quietus intended in giving me this book and leaving me to live. I ran because I wanted to save Aster and Zim, and I ran because I thought it was the kind of thing that would make you . . ."

Proud, he thought.

He stopped, blinking away the tears and watching Idyll do the same.

"I'm still me," he said again, emphasizing the words of the lie.

Idyll's nod was enough to break his heart.

Behind them, beyond the slow-curving line of the trees, the Borders estate exploded.

CHAPTER FOURTEEN

The Borders estate, ancestral home to the barons of the Sea, burned like a pyre, flames reaching higher than the trees, flicking up to welcome the stars as they came out.

There had been shouts at first, cries of surprise and despair as the train halted and turned to see what the great noise had been, but now they were silent and still.

"The King has found out about Nab, it seems," the baron said, his voice a calm counterpoint to the chaos of flame and light and explosions still coming from the Borders estate, or the place where it had once stood. "They will find our trail soon if they haven't yet. Move quickly. Two to a horse if needed. We bring everyone at speed. *Everyone.*"

Some had been walking until this point, easily keeping up with the steady but relaxed pace of the group, but now there were no feet on the ground save for a few guards who would bring up the rear and run.

Flitch took on one of the old cooks, now retired, helping the old man up and getting him settled before urging his horse into a trot and then, after a short time, a canter. Before long, they were galloping.

"Oh no, oh no, oh no," muttered the old cook, whose name Flitch was surprised to remember was Ivor. Flitch cast a glance back and saw the rear guard, black-and-gold clothing dull in the low light of torches and the moon, arranging a quick defense to stop the riders coming their way, the coloring of the King clear even from that distance.

Flitch turned back and urged more speed from his horse, wishing he had trained at riding as much as Idyll or Aster had.

The night turned nightmarish, the trees dancing oddly in the fast-moving torchlight as the horses ripped up the long growth on the road. The sounds of the fighting faded but did not go quiet behind them as they rode, and Flitch tried not to think of what was happening back there, who was winning and who was dying. He looked ahead, hands clutching the reins, the world all shadow and flickering light now, every tree a ghoul dancing in the night, the Sea waiting to catch him should he lose control—he, Ivor, and his horse all tumbling from the cliff, free for a few long moments and then wrapped tight in the Sea's green embrace.

Idyll was ahead, long hair untied and flowing behind them, two young children crammed together in front, and even amid the rush and terror of the night, Flitch could see that they were speaking to the children, telling them something calming, something to let them know that, yes, this was scary, and yes, there were some bad people trying to get them, but it was going to be okay.

Listening to Ivor's maddening mantra, Flitch wasn't so sure it would be okay, especially as lights began to near on the other side of the trees, lights that could only be the glint of sword and shield, the dull burn of rush pits—the closing of King Faineant's pincer. Some forces behind, and some ahead.

Only the trees were saving them, but even those huge shagbark oaks were distinctly less gnarled and overgrown than before, their underbrush and branches neatly trimmed, the grass around them clipped away to make a series of doorways between the trees through which Flitch could see the enemy now—thirty, perhaps forty of Faineant's soldiers, riding on horseback, and two casters, each feeding kindling into their rush pits, preparing to unleash devastating magical arsenals.

And were those Rivers warriors riding with them, too? Flitch thought he could see the white and red of Cantria's house, but he couldn't be sure.

He had the oddly banal, quiet thought of surprise that Borders could afford to have anyone trimming their trees like this, and then the realization hit him—these weren't Borders trees anymore.

This was Paths land, which must mean that the Paths estate was near.

Flitch tore his eyes from the warriors riding on their course to intercept the Borders group and looked ahead, past and through the riders bent low over their steeds, through the churning, thundering horses, to where the Paths estate waited at the end of the road, growing nearer and nearer, its every window lit, a small welcoming party standing outside the wide front door.

Gwyn Gaunt stood at the end of a short walkway leading from her front doors to the road. To either side of her were two short pillars in the shape of flowers, though from each of their stone petals burned enormous fires to show the way.

She was a small, still figure at the center of a growing storm—Borders flying toward her down the road, pursued by Faineant's soldiers behind and to the side, all converging on the same point.

Behind her, the Paths house rose wide and tall, lit by vining glow-stalk that had been trained to grow along its lines, limning the entire building with a deep, low orange light. Flitch had never been in the estate, but he had seen it often enough, both on the siblings' braver and braver dares to get just a little bit closer to the home of the mysterious baron and in the books Idyll was once infatuated with about famous architecture of the Mainlands. The Paths house made regular appearances in such texts.

Three stories tall, built of wood instead of stone, with a porch that wrapped most of the way around each of the three levels, the Paths house was an architectural curiosity.

Two small towers spiked high on either side of it, and the front of the house sloped down and out to the front door, which was impossibly wide, easily the size of three or four doors set beside one another.

But oddest was the roof, which was made out of glass banded through with thin lines of metal to add structural integrity. The King himself had apparently laughed at Gwyn Gaunt's decision to make her roof of such breakable, fragile material, but she had shrugged his decision away and done it anyway.

How easily would the King's forces shatter that roof if Borders did indeed manage to secure themselves within Paths? How quickly would Paths fall to the might of two other baronies, one of which was led by the King?

Of the group who fled with Borders, only a handful were capable fighters, and most of those were currently fighting the rear attack. And of those standing behind the diminutive Paths Baron, most looked old, dressed in loose robes, no weapons in sight, their expressions as pleasant and unperturbed as the placid smile on Gwyn Gaunt's face.

Flitch's father shouted something about a charge, his deep voice lost amid the rush and roar of the warriors on the other side of the trees and his own horses. He pulled a sword from the scabbard on his back, a weapon

Flitch hadn't seen him wear for a long, long time, and held it up, ready to die for his people.

Ivor had halted his mantra and was simply breathing in quick, ragged breaths, hot in Flitch's ear as the older man clung to him. Flitch had no weapons, had brought nothing but his book, which rode securely in the saddlebag. He could not cast like Aster, could not ride like Idyll, and was not valuable to any business ventures like Zim.

Faineant's warriors were streaming through the gaps in the trees now, coming into the lane in ones and twos, threes and fours, riding hard to keep up with the Borders party. Close as they were now, it was easy enough to see Cantria at their head, a wolfish smile on her face as she swung her ball-and-chain flail around her head, the spiked orb at the end glinting dangerously in the torchlight.

A Rivers warrior, breastplate colored in white and red checkered squares, crashed through the space between two trees, her horse clearly exhausted from being pushed so hard. The warrior held a naked sword in her hand and wore a look of eagerness that twisted devilishly when she saw Flitch, unarmed and so close.

Without thinking, Flitch kicked out at the woman, missing her and planting his foot squarely in the side of her horse, which shied away for a moment before returning. The Rivers warrior swung her sword at Flitch, who pulled right on the reins and leaned over, shouting "Watch out" to Ivor and hoping the old man shifted to dodge the cut too.

Enemy riders crashed into their ranks everywhere, and they came not for battle but for a slaughter.

Flitch kicked out again and was thinking of pulling off a shoe to throw at the woman, anything for a little more time, just enough to reach Paths and whatever safety they might provide.

A chorus of whistles sounded over the noise, a barony of birds erupting into song, highs and lows, warbling and trilling and cawing and chicka-deeing and chirping, a world of sound that caused Flitch and his assailant to pause in their scuffle, both halting for a moment in confusion and surprise.

But instead of sparrows or ravens or chickadees cutting sky for their nest, disappearing into the night, arrows whispered through the air, plant-ing themselves in the bodies of Faineant and Cantria's warriors, appearing in rapid succession and sending riders toppling from their horses. Flitch's attacker had already raised her sword again, guiding her mount close enough to guarantee that this strike would land, when an arrow hissed close and pierced her sword arm, the sharp, glistening head, drooling blood from its point, protruding out the other side. She dropped her sword but did not fall, merely slowing her horse down and leaning over her injured arm.

A few of the arrows gleamed with an otherworldly light as they sliced through the night, moving almost too fast to follow, and these did not pierce the enemy in arm or leg but instead collided with shield or shoulder plates, flashing with light upon impact before slamming the rider to the ground, seemingly striking with the force of a boulder.

The birdsong took on a new tenor, streams of communication burbling through the noise, call and answer, and the volleys of arrows changed course, whispering in a high arc over Flitch's head, back in the direction of the Borders house, disappearing among the stars before crashing down to earth behind the bend in the trees, eliciting cries of pain.

Flitch brought up his mount, hauling hard on the reins, casting about for the source of the arrows as more birdsong filled the air, and that was when he saw the people in the trees, three or four high up in each shagbark oak, their forms barely visible in the night, obscured as they were by the branches and leaves around them.

They might have been totally invisible if it weren't for the fires burning on what Flitch first thought was the tree itself but soon realized was a small basin set into a large branch on each tree.

"Back! Back!" someone was shouting, and Flitch turned quickly in his saddle, almost knocking Ivor off, to see Cantria pulling her horse around to retreat, arrows bristling up from both shoulders. She had moved back to the other side of the trees and put some distance between herself and the road. Even injured as she was, the Rivers Baron was still a commanding presence, rallying those still astride their horses and gathering up those who had fallen. She was in charge, it seemed, of even Faineant's troops; those wearing the King's colors circled behind her, shields up, eyes on the trees.

The rear guard, faces Flitch had thought he would never see again, emerged around the bend in the road, their numbers somewhat diminished, clothing and weapons bloodied from battle. Tally, head of the Borders guard, led the group, jogging with a limp, her shield gone, the broken spear she carried repurposed into a makeshift cane.

"You're finished, Borders!" Cantria called. "You killed the King's closest advisor and whisperman. You can't come back from this." The last of her warriors grouped behind her, more than half injured, though, Flitch was surprised, none dead. The road, the trees, and the field on the other side of the trees held no bodies—no horses, no humans. The archers—Paths archers, Flitch surmised—were either terrible killers or had aim better than anything he'd imagined an archer capable of.

"When we return," Cantria said, the venom in her voice thick, "we do so in force. If Paths chooses to shelter you, then Paths will fall too."

Flitch's father, farther up the road, clutching one injured arm, his sword nowhere in sight, said, "Faineant already had plans to annex Borders. Nothing we might have done would have persuaded him otherwise."

Cantria said nothing to that, a confirmation as much as if she'd agreed. When she spoke next, it was to Paths.

"The King will not be happy to lose two baronies. If you refuse them now, I can guarantee the King's favor."

Gwyn, who had not moved during the skirmish and stood still, calm and easy, between her two burning pillars, appeared to think about Cantria's offer, her arms folded, her head moving in a slow, meditative nod.

Her big eyes blinked a few times in quick succession as she took deep breaths, totally at ease as the remaining fragments of the Borders barony and the warriors from Halcyon and Rivers who would kill them waited for her answer, the tension building with every moment she was silent.

Gwyn Gaunt, Paths Baron, standing in front of her impressive home, shook her head once decisively before looking to Cantria, cocking her head to the side, and saying, "Who are you, again?"

A moment of silence followed this before Cantria released a bellow of rage. She had worked for so long to curry the King's favor, ingratiating herself with every action and word, seeking his approval and wisdom on all matters associated with her barony, and now she stood, defeated by a woman who cared nothing for King or court, who so rarely attended formal functions that there were regularly rumors circulating about her death.

Cantria, who pushed and pushed for more, would be defeated and forced to return to her King to tell him that the Paths Baron had stopped them and was now housing the survivors of Borders. Everyone knew the King was afraid of Gwyn Gaunt, and the King knew that everyone knew. What suns would the heat of his rage rival when Cantria was forced to deliver the news of his defeat at small, silent, apathetic Gwyn Gaunt's hands?

Flitch found himself smiling even as Cantria reached for a spear, still screaming her rage. As she hefted it, Gwyn Gaunt moved, and if Flitch hadn't seen Aster make precisely the same movement down in the labyrinth that morning, he wouldn't have recognized the limbering stretch for what it was. Her arms spread wide, fingers splaying out and dropping a small, dark shape into the fires on either side of her, which roiled and twisted with their new fuel before turning a nauseating shade of green that hurt to look at.

Cantria Shade's wordless cry reached a climax as, still seated on the back of her horse, she hurled the spear, brute strength and searing anger sending the weapon in a dangerous arc that would terminate in the tiny form of the Paths Baron.

Gwyn's movement was lithe and quick, the words of a song on her lips, her eyes closed and head drooped slightly forward, as though she were a dancer working to remember the steps of her dance, blocking out the external distractions and going deeply into herself. She stepped and sang and reached.

And the power of her spell burned a ring of fire into the air around her, a torrent of that same green fire bursting into life around her, flames swirling and churning in a whirlwind of power like Flitch had never seen.

Gwyn leapt into the air, rising like a bird, up and up, to meet the incoming spear, one open hand extended, wreathed in green flame that burned bright and thrashed in the wind.

She met Cantria's attack, the spear that should have cut through her hand and buried itself deep into her arm, perhaps even ripping through the flesh and bone and spiraling out the other side—the spear exploded in a shivering rain of wooden matchsticks, tiny and thin and tinkling to the ground in a harmless spray.

Gwyn landed on the ground, still wearing a mantle of green, swirling flame, her eyes open now and staring across her yard at the Rivers Baron, who, to her credit, did not look as terrified as Flitch felt she should have.

Cantria stared her hate at Gwyn Gaunt and then at Flitch's father, gritting her teeth in anger before shouting out the retreat and turning her horse back toward her waiting King.

With a gesture and a word, Gwyn cut the work of her spell, the flames around her receding into themselves as though the air around them had been sucked away, and soon enough, even the flames in her pillars had returned to a cheery orange crackle.

She turned to the Borders Baron and said, "Welcome to Paths."

⸺◆⸺

"Idyll! Flitch! Zim! Aster!" Ravel pushed through the crowd of people as the Borders refugees got off their horses and moved, some still in shock, up the pathway to the big house. He looked disheveled and tired, but his smile when he saw Idyll made all of that fall away. "I was so worried about you all!"

"Aren't you sweet?" Aster said, though it was a shadow of the sarcasm she normally mustered. Like everyone else in Borders, she had the hollow-eyed look of someone who had passed near enough to death to see its teeth. She'd taken a glancing blow from a mace to her hip and walked with pain now, though she claimed it was nothing.

Zim, too, had been injured, and now that the initial pain had worn off and the blood stopped flowing, he was proudly and grimly showing off the long, shallow cut that ran from his shoulder to his elbow. He'd twice already asked the Paths medickers, with more than a little hopefulness in his voice, if they thought it would leave a scar. It would, they assured him.

As Ravel moved to Idyll, slipping free of whatever false formality the two had been operating under and running his hands over Idyll's arms and shoulders, checking them over for injuries before pulling them into an embrace, Zim stood up from his third examination from a medicker and said, pride gilding his words, "I guess it's going to leave a nasty scar."

"You don't say," Aster muttered, glaring at him as they all walked up the front steps and into the house, through that enormous front door. The wood was carved into a scene showing a single path, smooth-grained, lighter wood inlaid to set it off from the rest, surrounded by a vast swirling chaos of plants growing wild and tall beside it. It was hard to tell, and Flitch was herded inside before he had a chance to examine it more closely, but it looked as though a huge tree grew off in the distance, all covered in strange growths, tipped at an odd angle, as though it weren't growing up from the ground but floating on the surface.

"Just this way, please," a man at the door said, gesturing the Borders people inside, and Flitch was carried on the wave into the house, and the door was pushed from his mind by the grandeur there.

The door opened onto a huge open space that, even with everyone, seemed empty and cavernous. The glass ceiling above showed stars and moon in the sky, making the room feel as though it were open air. More of the same glow-stalk grew inside, tracing up along the columns on the wall and worked through the thin metal banded through the glass ceiling, though this was a different species apparently, because it shone with a warm, golden light instead of the deep orange of the growths outside. It had an odd effect, like soft bands of thick, summer sunlight growing through the vast, dark expanse of a starry night. Flitch found he couldn't look directly up into it for long without getting dizzy.

The floor was a tiled mosaic, grooved grass-green tiles to create the Sea, tipped by the purples and blues and reds and golds and whites of full-bloomed flowers. A single ship had been placed in the scene, barely more than a few white squares set against the dynamic color of the prairie, an approximation of full sails on the horizon.

Otherwise, it was Sea and sky and the chaos of color they created in their shared purlieu, all laid out in clean lines and squared angles that were growing obfuscated with mud and grime as each new member of the Borders party stepped inside and made room for more.

Along the walls were tall, arched doorways leading to other rooms, every door closed and blocked by a Paths worker standing calmly in front. On the other end of the enormous entryway was a tripartite staircase wrought in the same rich, dark wood as the walls. The side branches led to the second floor of the house, veering off to the right and the left, while the central stairs climbed straight up, higher and higher, until their ascent was blocked by the floor of the second level.

On this staircase, deep in conversation with the Borders Baron, was Gwyn Gaunt, who poked at the baron's injured arm, frowning and giving him a look that said, quite clearly, *Is it really that bad?*

When he shook his head and muttered something back, Gwyn smiled and turned out to the assembled members of the baronies.

"Welcome, Borders guests," she said, looking from face to face, as though making sure that everyone was accounted for. She wore the same plain robes as the rest of her people, simple brown, functional and informal. Her smile was that of a friendly grandmother, unassuming and easy. If Flitch hadn't just seen her working magics powerful enough to scare the King of the Mainland, he might have actually believed she was that quiet old woman.

"We have refreshments just through there." She gestured to her left at a pair of doors, and the man standing there, blocking their entrance, nodded and flung them open to reveal another cavernous room, this one featuring another mosaic floor showing a different scene—the pathways to the West that had brought this barony its riches and fame. Not only did merchants pay to travel the well-kept and -guarded roads that Paths maintained, but they also hired out Paths casters to protect their caravans through more suspect and dangerous travels.

"Please, go and rest, drink, and eat, and do not fear for your safety," Gwyn said, nodding around at them all, her smile all warmth and comfort. "King Faineant will not attack Paths, not until he has shored up more support."

"What if he attacks anyway?" came a shout from someone in the Borders group, and Flitch found himself nodding. Everyone knew Faineant to be a jealous, angry man, and what he shouldn't do often had little to do with what he wouldn't do.

"Then I'll kill him and see if that crown is really as heavy as he claims," Gwyn said, so matter-of-fact that a burble of anxious laughter went up from those in the room, though only from the Borders crew. Ravel, who stood with Idyll nearby, frowned and nodded, as though it were a hard truth that, should it come to pass, would have to be borne.

"Now just through there," Gwyn said again, gesturing once more to the open doors. "Couches and chairs, good drink and food, and a rest from this day."

Flitch's father caught his children's eyes and motioned for them to stay. Tally, too, he kept behind. The rest of Borders, though, moved through the open door, and Flitch heard the deep sighs and happy exclamations only possible in those who had found food and drink precisely when they needed it.

"Oh, look," Gwyn Gaunt said as the siblings approached the stairs, meeting her and the baron as they descended, "it's the children who started a war!"

Aster opened and closed her mouth, and Zim dropped his eyes to the floor. Flitch tried to think of what he could say, but his mind had become a simple, quiet place with not a thought to be found. He clenched the book, *This Wild, Forgotten Forever,* in his hands and said nothing.

"She's kidding," Ravel said, shaking his head at the siblings. He had received a similar "stay here" gesture from Gwyn and stood now, halfway between Idyll and the baron.

"Not really," Gwyn said, shrugging. She scratched at her head and left behind a tuft of dark brown hair standing on end. "But it seemed inevitable, based on what Uthe has told me."

Flitch blinked in shock. Uthe was his father's name, but it was one he hated and preferred to never use. Flitch had known him only as *Father* or *the baron*, and though Uthe made no effort to hide his name, neither did he regularly volunteer it to anyone.

When was the last time Flitch had even heard that name uttered aloud? Certainly among his siblings, who liked to tease their father with it, but only in the privacy of their house and never in the presence of any of their father's advisors or guards or staff.

How did the reclusive Paths Baron, who, as far as Flitch knew, had no relationships with anyone, professional or private, outside of her house, know his father's given name?

Idyll turned to Ravel, the two of them exchanging a look in their own language before leaning in close to whisper back and forth. Flitch stared at them for a moment before realizing that Gwyn Gaunt, too, stared, her look as curious and concerned as he felt his own must be.

Aster was the first to get over her shock and speak.

"I've never seen casting like that, not even from my teachers at the academy, and they're supposed to be the best on the Mainland."

"Those old babies," Gwyn said, rolling her eyes and shooing the very notion away with a curt gesture. "So concerned with telling everyone they're the best. They should be more concerned with *being* the best. Actually, they should be more concerned with something that matters. Like pickled beets! Oh, Ravel—get me some before they're all gone, will you? Quick as a rabbit."

Ravel nodded, which seemed to mean that such quick changes of thought were a normal occurrence for the baron. Gwyn watched him until he'd disappeared through the doorway, and then she turned to Idyll.

"If you hurt that poor boy's heart," she said, the kindly grandmother gone suddenly cold and hard, "I will remove every bone from your body and break them before your eyes with my ancient and arcane magics. Do you understand?"

Idyll, struggling to keep up with Gwyn's whiplash conversational style, could only nod.

"I'm serious; I could really do it, and it would hurt. A lot," Gwyn said, folding her arms and trying to look severe and authoritative, which was difficult, given that Idyll was at least a head taller than her.

But her attempt had its intended effect. Idyll bowed their head and nodded again.

"Of course, Baron. I wouldn't ever hurt him."

Gwyn's face softened into something sad, and she said, almost to herself, "We always think that, don't we?"

Ravel came back through the door, a small wooden bowl filled with the requested beets.

"Oh, good! They're still cold," Gwyn said, pushing away the fork he offered and beginning to scoop the bright purple taproots into her mouth one at a time, dribbling juices down her chin and front and erupting in a cooing wave of delighted moans.

The baron watched her for a moment before turning his attention to more-important matters.

"Tally, are you all right to continue leading?" he asked, gesturing to her leg, which had been worked on by the Paths medickers before being bandaged.

"Of course," she said, casting a derisive look down at her leg. "This is nothing. It took six of their shit fighters to do this, and I left every one of them on the ground."

"Good," the baron said, nodding. "I need you to gather what guards we have left and work with the Paths guards to offer whatever we can to their defenses."

"Nigh-Elyn there," Gwyn said, gesturing with a half-eaten beet in one garnet-stained hand to one set of closed doors and the woman standing in front of them. "She's the head of my guards. Watch out, though; she has a predilection for naps."

Gwyn winked and returned to her food.

Nigh-Elyn was a woman older than Gwyn and looked as though she'd been napping on her feet before hearing her name and perking up. With a questioning look at the baron, who only nodded, Tally set off across the floor to meet her counterpart.

"So many new friends this evening," Gwyn said, showing stained teeth in a garish smile. "Your kids should start wars more often, Uthe."

The Borders Baron *humph*ed but said nothing.

"You can have the rest," Gwyn said, pushing the bowl back to Ravel and wiping her hands on her robes as she turned to the rest of them. "We need a plan. Sooner or later, Faineant *will* attack us here with a force large enough to settle the matter one way or another, and I have no desire to commit regicide, not unless we have no other option."

Gwyn held up a fist, flicking out one finger at a time as she worked through the potential actions they might take.

"You can hide here, but it's not a sustainable plan. We could bring the fight to Faineant before he brings it to us, but I'd prefer not to go into the city. It's so dirty and loud there. We could get on our ships and sail off for Forever. But I really like my house."

"And Faineant already has the entire fleet out in the harbors to protect against his imaginary threat of the Supplicant Few," Flitch added, and Gwyn turned her bright gaze on him.

"You're the young one, the one who didn't know anything about downy painted cup, right? Flitch." Gwyn looked him over with a keen eye. "You're different than you were this morning, I think. Stranger. Less like yourself. Maybe more like yourself."

"I suppose so," Flitch said.

"I know so," Gwyn said, nodding and letting her eyes linger on him for another long, uncomfortable moment. The sounds from the other room were a swell of cautious laughter and quiet conversations; Paths people being welcoming and Borders people wondering what their futures held. Would Borders—the barony itself, not the house, even exist after all of this? Faineant had destroyed their home in his rage, but would their lands and responsibilities still remain?

"Before we fled from the house," the baron said, clearly trying to bring the conversation back to its supposed purpose, "I had the head of our fleet, Twyllyn Tae, send all of our ships, including those docked at home and those out on harvesting missions, to one of Paths' harbors. It earned us some time, perhaps, but the King would have known soon that our ships were not joining his in his fake defense of the Mainland. The Paths Baron has said we can keep our fleet in her harbor as long as we want, but we are waiting to be found and destroyed by Faineant's ships if we simply sit at port."

"Not to mention the creatures coming up from below the Sea," Gwyn said, frowning. "That's the *real* threat out there, and they don't care about the colors on your flag. They'll pull the ship and any crew under without a thought."

"Can we escape to the north or south?" Ravel asked, and Flitch tried not to stare at his use of the word *we*.

Gwyn, though, seemed to not notice or care. She shook her head, gaze wandering up to the ceiling in thought.

"The fires from Arcadia cut off both routes, and that area won't have grown back to anything resembling sailable grasses for forty, maybe fifty days. It grows fast after a cleansing fire, but not nearly fast enough for us to use it."

"Why don't you just kill the King like you said?" Flitch asked, knowing it was a blunt, uncomfortable question but seeing no other way around it. "We can't escape, we can't stay here, and if the charred ruins of our house are any indication of the King's feelings, there isn't any room for negotiation."

Gwyn continued looking up at the stars through her glass ceiling for a long time before bringing her gaze back down to Flitch, her eyes hard.

"If we fight, I will kill Faineant and all who stand between him and me. But many, many, *many* people will die in the doing of it, and that's not something anyone should want."

Flitch nodded and dropped his gaze, feeling chastised. Of course he didn't want people to die, not even Faineant's warriors, or Cantria's. Not that he would be the one doing the fighting or killing, anyway. If they were to fight, he'd be almost no use—never having trained in any of the martial paths, barely a competent rider. When had he last held a sword? Their father had wanted all of his children to practice with a weapon, but when their mother died, those sorts of plans faded. Tutors came and went, their father was a shadow of himself, and his dreams of his family following certain traditions or learning certain things or becoming certain people—all of that fell under the weight of his—of all of their—grief.

"Of course," Flitch said, feeling the blood rush to his face. "I'm sorry to have asked."

"Perhaps our business interests in the city can help us?" Zim volunteered, looking to the baron, who shook his head.

"The last report I had from our businesses told of Faineant's incoming raids. Some of our people made it out. Some . . ." He trailed off, his lips coming together into a tight line. "Faineant was too organized, and this whole thing was too well planned. I suspect we only escaped the house because he didn't expect things to go so bad with Nab so quickly."

Zim opened his mouth to speak but no words came out. His every effort over the past, what? Five years? Eight? Gone in a day, Borders businesses wiped clean by the King's authoritative fist. He would not become Third Pen or Second Pen, would never show his friends and coworkers the scar on his arm. Zim would stay forever a Callow Pen.

Flitch put out a hand and rested it gently on Zim's shoulder.

"There's more to consider," Idyll said quietly, darting a quick glance to Flitch and then down at the book in his hand. "Something Flitch found in the labyrinth."

CHAPTER FIFTEEN

The Marchess slept, saying she was exhausted by the casting and depressed by the state of things.

This last she said while staring at Kindred.

Lurch followed her into the ship, and Tesser Cobb, after some hasty apologies, went too.

"It's just that it took us so long to scavenge so many bones," he said, stepping back toward the ship but casting a pleading glance toward Jest. "Even with the Marchess's creatures pulling down ships laden with bones, it takes us an awful long time to find and scavenge them. It's just an inefficient use of resources that's upset her. That's all."

"I don't think *efficiency* or *resources* are the problem here, Tesser Cobb," Jest said to his retreating form.

But he was already climbing aboard the ship and going below, that same pained smile on his face.

Once the Fell were away, the rest of them sat on the deck of the Traveling Court's ship or on the ground nearby for a long time, all of them silent in the temples of their own thoughts. Kindred sat beside Sarah on the ground, a noticeable gap between the two of them, one that neither was willing to bridge.

"Did you know about this?" Sarah asked suddenly, turning to the Traveling Court. "Any of you? Did you know they were doing this?"

"We don't associate with the Fell Company," Jest said, her eyes still lingering on the ship holding the three members of the Fell. "On our last pass through this area, they were merely excited to show off their newest member, and I foolishly assumed their grand boasting to be nothing more than hot air on the tongues of foolish men."

"You were too fascinated by thinking that woman was the Queen Who Laughed," Fourth-Folly said, lifting themself up onto the deck and glaring down at Jest.

"I admit to a certain lack of clear-sightedness on that score, certainly," Jest said. She opened her mouth to say more but was stopped by a shocked cry from Wylf, who flung out his arms and spun about, looking in every direction and whispering the name of his pursuer to himself.

"Not that whole time?" Fourth-Folly said, looking down at him. Wylf, after carefully scanning the vast, empty arcades around and finding no sign of the Windrake, looked up to Fourth-Folly and nodded.

"You weren't thinking of the Windrake that whole time?" Madrigal asked, eyes going wide, mouth hanging open. She stood next to Awn, and she reached up, slipping her tiny hand into his.

Wylf nodded, continuing his feverish litany, head still swiveling around.

"What a disaster," Fourth-Folly said.

"Agreed," Sarah said, looking everywhere, at everyone, except Kindred, who had not spoken since the summoning.

"We should leave," Wylf said, speaking the words quickly and then returning to his whispering.

"Yes," Fourth-Folly said, already moving to the bow and reaching for the pluralities' reins.

"Absolutely," Jest said, nodding. "Tesser Cobb and the others do not deserve a proper goodbye after such a thing."

"I can't go," Kindred said, looking up and feeling a weight settle into her stomach at the thought of these people leaving, of watching them sail off into the darkness.

But she couldn't leave with them. Not now.

"Me neither," Sarah said, and Kindred exhaled in a rush of gratitude. Sarah understood, at least.

"You want to stay with them?" Fourth-Folly asked, raising an accusatory finger toward the Fell boat.

"No," Sarah said, looking at Kindred now, her eyes hard, mouth set. "We have to stop them." No one spoke, and as Sarah's eyes found hers again, she said, her voice smaller, "Right?"

"I . . ." Kindred began, but stopped. This was her grandmother. The woman who had raised her, who had been the strong shelter when the whole world seemed an endless storm.

"I won't be staying," Awn said, venturing into the conversation tentatively, his eyes flicking up to Kindred and Sarah before dipping back down to his toes.

"What?" Sarah said, sharp and hard.

Awn looked as uncomfortable as Kindred had ever seen him, and he shifted from foot to foot as he spoke.

"There's more I want to see, and I came down here to leave behind everything above. I'm glad Kindred found her grandmother, but I don't want anything to do with her. She seems scary to me. Sorry, Kindred."

Gone was the excitable, awestruck man Kindred had gotten to know. This was Awn, sad and down.

Madrigal leaned into him and looked up with an encouraging smile.

"We can't just let them unleash a horde of monsters to kill the people above," Sarah said, looking around with mounting frustration. "You're all okay with that? You're okay with the people up there dying in droves? The same people who drop the things you scavenge and write the books you read?"

"Tesser Cobb is famous for his unfulfilled goals," Jest said dismissively, her eyes wandering toward the Fell ship again. "Even with their newest member, I see no reason why we should fear their success. Who's to say those creatures don't die on their way to the surface or crawl back into the sickened grasses first? We simply cannot know."

"We have our own myths," Fourth-Folly said, the reins already in their hands. "And this isn't part of them."

"Where will you go?" Kindred asked, already feeling the connection between her and the Traveling Court severing, each word a new tear in the bonds holding them together.

Fourth-Folly looked to Jest, who nodded, and they said, "We'll see if we can find that city you told us about, the Once-City. Based on your description of where that fight happened, it should be straight that way, out near the Forgetting Hall."

They raised a hand, gesturing out past a stalk of grass alight with lantern bearers climbing along it.

"Can't you stay for a little bit?" Sarah asked, hands out, pleading. "You— We can't just let something like this happen. There are people up there— actual people, with lives and families and myths just like yours. Kindred, tell them!"

"They . . ." Kindred began, but she couldn't say anything more. Her grandmother's words moved through her, as they had always done, pulling and shaping her, guiding her own thoughts. Those above *did* gain from the exploitation and ruination of the Sea, turning natural beauty and diversity into monolithic wealth and power.

"Kindred?" Sarah asked, suspicion and accusation creeping back into her voice.

She was that child again, had perhaps never been anything other than that child, walking the decks and climbing the masts of *Revenger*, listening to her grandmother navigate the world and feeling safe and secure in that knowing. Whether it was the Sea or the civilization next to it, the hearthfire or the rigging, the path forward or the path behind them, the Marchess had always seen the truth in things. Kindred had grown and changed and done things she was proud of and ashamed of, and still she felt herself to be that little girl, watching her grandmother, trying desperately to steal what little knowing of the world she could from her.

She was still a child, certain that her grandmother knew more than she did.

"Maybe she understands something we don't," Kindred said finally, unable to look at Sarah. "We— I just need to talk with her. Make sense of all of this. It's all happening too fast. If I can just talk with her, we can sort it out."

Jest's smile as she nodded at Kindred was a sad, resigned thing.

"Of course we understand, Kindred Captain," she said.

Fourth-Folly's words followed Jest's, running through Kindred's mind unbidden: *To know your own myth and to do the work of getting outside of it are two very different things.*

Awn nodded at Madrigal, who let him go and climbed up onto the deck. He stepped over to Kindred and Sarah, the crew of *The Lost* together for perhaps the last time.

"I'm sorry about all of this," he said quietly, looking between Sarah and Kindred. His beard had grown longer and wilder since his time in the Once-City, and he seemed to hold himself differently now, less frantic. Steadier. When she'd first met him, Kindred had thought Awn might be the most frantic, erratic person she'd ever met. Kindly and well-meaning and earnest, certainly, but unstable, like a man constantly catching himself just at the moment of falling.

Now he walked and breathed and spoke with a calm ease. Still excitable and given to quick, enthusiastic questions and curiosities, but there was a steadiness beneath it all. Maybe this was how he had been with his family. Maybe he'd finally found a new one.

"You're really going to stay with them?" Sarah asked, a hint of resignation in her voice.

"Yes," Awn said, firm and gentle. "I think it's where I'm supposed to be. Madrigal said she could teach me how to keep the fire as she does. And there's only two books in their whole library that I've even heard of! Think of all the reading I can do! A whole world of mysteries and wonders around me, and I'm going to spend my days reading inside a ship!" He let out a laugh that was pure joy.

Kindred stepped forward and wrapped him into a hug that said more than she could manage.

"Thank you," she said. "For everything."

"No, no," Awn said, pulling back and smiling. "I'm the thankful one. You let me see the world in a new way. I needed that more than I can say. So, thank *you*."

Sarah gave him a hug too, muttering a goodbye too low for Kindred to hear. Awn pulled back and said, "Of course. Are you sure?"

When Sarah nodded, he climbed quickly up on deck, rustled about while whispering to the Traveling Court—of which he was now a part, apparently—and returned with a worn, patched sack for Sarah, which she took with a nod.

"Who knows?" Awn said, smiling in that bright, guileless way that he so often did. "Maybe we'll see each other again."

And then the Traveling Court were off, Madrigal waving before sitting down to her work, Jest and Wylf calling out their goodbyes, and Fourth-Folly giving a curt wave before returning their attention to the pluralities. The smooth hush of their vessel cutting through the soft dirt receded as they disappeared into the darkness of the Seafloor.

Kindred waved until she couldn't see them anymore, but when she turned to Sarah, Kindred found that she'd begun walking away in long, purposeful strides, looking back, not at Kindred but at the Fell ship. Kindred jogged to catch up with her.

"Where are you going?" she asked, and then, "What are you doing?"

Sarah had kneeled beside the remains of the Marchess's fire, which glowed and burned with a sullen, dying light.

"Can you get me a splinter of that fire?" she asked, not meeting Kindred's eyes.

"Yes," Kindred said, uncertain. "Why?"

"Can you or not?"

Kindred nodded and kneeled before the low-burning fire, its base nothing more than a divot scooped from the ground and tamped down. How long had it been since she had worked with a hearthfire? Madrigal had had the Traveling Court's hearthfire well in hand, and some part of Kindred had liked the idea of leaving the keeping behind, turning over a new page down below, no longer the hearthfire keeper but something else. An explorer. A seeker.

She sang again, reaching out with her voice and perception to the fire, which still wavered and shifted in a strange way, but Kindred found connection with it all the same and pulled out a small, stubby bone, unrecognizable to her after so much burning.

Sarah, meanwhile, had scooped out her own small basin, pressing the indent with her hands to firm up the sides.

"Right here," she said, gesturing to the center.

"Is this . . ." Kindred said, looking up at Sarah as she set the splinter of the fire down. "Are you going to do a calling?"

Sarah reached into the sack that Awn had given her, pulling out more bones and a few of the dried plants that the Traveling Court had in stock.

"Yes." Sarah moved with rapid precision, building the fire with the bones. "They need to know."

Kindred opened her mouth to ask more, but Sarah had begun to chant, her voice a fluid falsetto flung high, although quieter than any calling Kindred had ever heard from her. Sarah dropped plants onto the fire, which had started in that same viscous brown but quickly thinned to a vigorous, ghostly red.

As she worked, Sarah flicked glances back to the Fell vessel, which was silent and still save for the grazing movement of the pluralities.

"What are you afraid of?" Kindred asked as Sarah finished her chanting and began sifting through the plants Awn had given her, the fire burning steadily. Its song was a low thrum in Kindred's mind, a slight distraction pulling at her attention.

"Your grandmother," Sarah said, her head snapping to the side again as she looked at the Fell ship, still silent.

"What are you talking about?"

"Open your eyes, Kindred." Sarah had found the plant she was seeking and began ripping it into shreds, scattering the tiny flecks of leaf and stem across the fire, which broke immediately into a seething, rambunctious existence, flicking and flaring, its color shivering into a deep, thick blue that smoked slightly.

"The Marchess's plan to save the Sea is to kill the people above. You think she's going to be okay with me telling them what's happening?"

"She doesn't want to kill them," Kindred said, shaking her head. "She's not— That's just how she talks. Everything dramatic and overblown. She doesn't want to kill anyone—it's all about scaring people, showing them that the Sea needs to be treated with care."

Sarah finished sprinkling the fragments into the fire and finally looked at Kindred, really looked into her eyes, and it wasn't anger that Kindred found there.

It was pity.

"Oh, Kindred. Don't be such a child."

When she sang, Sarah's voice was no longer a whisper. A plaintive cry, loud and lasting, it was the brightest, sharpest thing in the Sea or under it, and Sarah crowned her call by dropping one last plant into the fire, its mass wadded into a ball in her hand.

Above, such a casting brought the birds that lived in the skies over the Sea, their clear eyes seeing more than any sailor could ever hope to. Certain species might offer a sense of what lay ahead or behind, what the winds would be that evening or the next morning, or even what plants grew nearby. Crow-callers could send and receive messages with the birds, too.

But what birds could Sarah call down there in the dark? The winged creatures they had seen were far cries from the birds above, leathery wings instead of feathered ones, teeth and tendrils instead of beaks.

The fire boiled with color and sudden heat as it consumed the pressed plant from Sarah's hand, blue breaking to orange and black and grey and pink and white, each vying for dominance before surrendering to the next, waves and waves of color that twisted Kindred's stomach to watch.

Shouts sounded behind them as the Fell Company emerged from their ship, led by the Marchess, who had the tousled, haunted look of one who was woken at the exact moment of falling into sleep. Her eyes landed on Kindred and then shifted to Sarah.

"No!" she cried, leaping down from the deck and stumbling from the drop. Lurch and Tesser Cobb dropped down next to her, reaching out to help, but she was already up, running for Sarah, who shifted to the other side of the fire but kept singing, speeding up her song, eyes hard and trained on the Marchess.

"Stop her, Kindred!" the Marchess shouted as she neared, but Sarah's song was ending, the final note hanging for a moment before Sarah stepped back from the fire, knife held up before her. A thick fist of heavy smoke shot up from the fire, up and up and up, leaving behind a trail of wisps that curled on themselves into a language unknown.

"It's done," she spat, looking from the Marchess to Lurch and Tesser Cobb behind her.

All of this was wrong: Sarah's blade held at the ready, the Marchess's rage, the crew of *The Lost* broken up a bare handful of days since their forming, the Traveling Court gone.

The Marchess blew out a long breath, steadying herself.

"She's worried about the lives lost, Grandmother," Kindred said, aware of the pleading whine in her voice and unable to do anything about it. "Those people . . ."

"They're killing the Sea," the Marchess said, weariness revealed as her anger burned off. She looked between Kindred and Sarah. "Do you think I want the death? Do you think I dream of the dead in scores along the shore?"

"You couldn't think of any other way to solve this problem?" Sarah asked, cautious in the face of the Marchess's emotional shift. "Calling or communicating with them somehow? Nothing?"

"None of us know how to call, and even if we did, I wouldn't have put any hope in it." The Marchess looked sad in a way Kindred had never seen before. "Before I left, I spent every day we were at port talking with officials and senators, trying everything I could to get them to see what they were doing. I knew even then—or suspected deeply enough to think I knew—that we were the cause of the Greys. The greed, the pilfering of the world, the certainty that we are above all of this."

She extended her arms, hands open, palms up, gesturing at the Sea around her, every bit of its majesty and magic. When she spoke again, it was in a flat, hard voice.

"No one listened. No one cared. I sailed for the Mainland and was met with the same response. Everywhere all the same—no one would listen or see, not without something to make them see. People care about what's in front of them, about the lives around them and the road ahead. If I can make them understand what's happening by threatening those things, by giving them a reason to respect the Sea, then I will, and I'll live easy with the knowledge of what I've done."

Kindred had seen so little of the Marchess in the time before she'd disappeared from the world above, and now it was clear why.

"There has to be another way," Sarah said, shaking her head. "There has to."

"There isn't," the Marchess said.

Kindred had come down there hoping to find her grandmother and do something about the Greys, and somehow she'd found herself in the center of an impossible situation again. The natural world squeezed between two opposing sides, each with their own claim to it, their own belief about it, their own moral certainty.

The Marchess looked up into the empty black above them for a moment.

"It looks like your casting didn't work," she said, bringing her eyes back to Sarah. "I'm not surprised, and I don't think it would have any effect even if it did work and you did send a message."

When she spoke again, it was in that same empty voice, bereft of any of the emotion Kindred had just been telling Sarah was typical of her grandmother. Instead, she spoke like a tired, sad, lost person.

"But if you try to stop or hinder this process again, we'll kill you. I don't care what your relationship is with my granddaughter. This is more important than any one of us. You get in the way"—she raised a finger, flicking it between Sarah and Kindred—"either of you, and it won't go well. I'm doing this. I'm saving the Sea."

It was only then that Kindred saw the blade in Lurch's hand, a rusted sword, held as if he knew how to use it, low and out of the way, but she could easily imagine it cutting upward, slicing the air and anything in its way with practiced ease and precision. Tesser Cobb held one too, and there, obscured but still visible, was a long, wicked knife held in the Marchess's belt, one of her hands resting on it.

Sarah would have no chance against them. Neither would Kindred, even if she had a weapon.

"If you were anyone else," the Marchess said, shifting her eyes from Sarah to Kindred, "this would have been different. I need to rest now after the summoning—really rest. When I wake, we'll do it again. You can either help me save the Sea or be gone with those others. Anything else, and I'll cut you down. I'm giving you a chance because you're my family, but this work is more important than that. Be with me or be gone. It's up to you."

And with that, she turned and walked away through the Sea, the rest of the Fell trailing along behind her.

The fire burned lower and lower, its flames returning to a banal, beautiful orange.

Sarah did not speak.

Soon the flames were gone, and the fire was nothing but ash and heat and the memory of something more.

And still Sarah did not speak.

She sat beside her makeshift basin, eyes glaring into the remains of the fire, mouth set. She had wrapped her arms around her knees, pulling her legs in and making herself small. The knife lay forgotten on the ground beside her.

Kindred sat next to her. She sat across the fire from her. She stood and paced.

"She's like you," Sarah said finally, not looking up.

Kindred sat again, close but not too close.

"Or maybe you're like her. I don't know."

"She raised me." Was it apology or explanation that Kindred offered? She wasn't sure. "She taught me everything—how to keep the fire and how to sail, what to eat from the Sea, how to spot the—"

"I'm not talking about that stuff." Sarah cut her off with a slice of one hand through the air. She took a moment, and then said, "When we left Arcadia and sailed for the Once-City, I saw something in you that excited me. You weren't like everyone else. You saw the world differently, talked about it as if it were the most beautiful thing that could ever be. You didn't move and jockey for coin or power like everyone else. I liked that about you. I *loved* it."

She let out a low laugh that twisted Kindred's stomach and made her body go cold.

"I was a fool. So was the captain. And the crew."

"Sarah," Kindred began, her voice small, but Sarah pushed on, heedless.

"You and your grandmother talk about the people of the world plundering the Sea for resources, using green leaf and golden limb for their own ends. But you both do the same with the people around you."

Kindred pulled in a thin, dry breath.

"You used *The Errant* and everyone on board—me included—like we were bones in the fire, positioning and manipulating us to get what and where you wanted. How many people died on that voyage, Kindred? There were real reasons for us to run from Arcadia, but you and your dreams were behind the push to go to the Once-City, and you maneuvered us all around to make that happen. Crew dead, ship sunk, probably already picked over for bones by those monsters—" Sarah pointed back toward the Fell ship. "The Once-City gone, Arcadia probably gone too, the Sea burned, all so you could walk the path you want to walk and chase the dreams you want to dream."

She pushed herself up, looking down at Kindred with wet, hard eyes.

"I loved you for that dream and for how hard you were willing to work for it, and I see now how terrible it all was. Your grandmother sees those people up there as *them*, something other, a field of bones needing to be stacked, arranged, and burned for what she needs to happen. She's like you, Kindred."

Kindred opened her mouth, but nothing came out. Nothing could come out. What could she say to such things?

How could she respond to the truth laid so bare and cold?

"Tell me you weren't going to go to her when she asked you to," Sarah said. "Tell me that. When she called for you, right at the end, when her build was falling apart and she wanted to pull through more monstrosities to enrage and send above, tell me you weren't going to go to her and help."

Kindred shook her head, mouth open. She felt like someone had struck her in the head. Her ears were ringing. Her jaw hurt. Her breath was a dry autumn wind scratching along the dusty, arid tunnel of her throat.

"Of course not," Sarah said, working her mouth for a moment before spitting on the ground. "You two care so much about this world that you've forgotten people are part of it, too."

She went quiet then, her eyes holding Kindred's, searching for something to prove her wrong, maybe. She was waiting for Kindred to say something, anything to pull her back.

"I'm sorry," Kindred managed finally, the words rough and scratchy as they emerged. "You're right."

Sarah nodded and looked ready to say more, but a whispering suddenly echoed through the space—impossible, given the lack of walls and structures around which the sound might bounce, and yet it echoed nonetheless. Many voices, thousands and thousands of them, whispering together and apart, coming together in choruses and diverging again. A tumult of noise, a chaos of it, slithering through the air and drowning out every thought in Kindred's head save one: fear.

It came down from above, covered in shadows so deep and thick they made the darkness of the Seafloor seem bright in comparison. Limbs of an indeterminate number moved beneath those shadows, covered in robes or clothing of some kind, a face cowled and hidden.

Leaping in steady, graceful arcs, it descended, jumping out from the stalk of the nearest healthy plant and returning to it, as if pulled ever back. Out and back, out and back it moved, and still that whispering.

Its final leap brought it close to Sarah and Kindred, and it landed without a sound, the whole of it caught in a swirling fog of black.

In one hand, extended so they could see it, the creature held a dead bird, feathers a brilliant emerald green, its wings and small body cradled in long, scabrous fingers almost reverently. Its neck had been broken, and it was easy enough to imagine those hands, those long fingers, doing the breaking.

Sarah's calling, it seemed, had worked up to the point of being intercepted by something else.

Kneeling, the being set the bird into the still-hot coals of the fire, and where its fingers touched, shoots of a thin, winding plant burst up, growing out of the embers and coals themselves.

Kindred could see now that they were not scabs clustered along the creature's fingers and hands but leaves, many leaves, placed or grown over one another until no skin could be seen.

The whispering that populated the air condensed into a single breathy stream, one voice made of many, all speaking in concert. It was overwhelming and there was no doubt that it came from or moved through the creature.

A message.

It gestured to the fire, where the plants growing from the coals had converged into a thick, vining mass, growing in tangled, loose curls that came together to form a huge, furled bud, the skin of its petals dotted and splashed with color, as if a child had flung fistfuls of paint at it.

It grew larger and larger, lifting off the coals on a single delicate stalk, far too slim to hold the massive bulb but holding anyway, and then the flower was blooming, colors coruscating along the skin of the petals, which opened to reveal two books, side by side, thick and hefty.

One of these, the creature lifted and offered to Sarah. The other, it lifted and held close to itself, the book disappearing into the darkness surrounding it.

The whispering coalesced again, too loud to be comfortable, too near to be safe.

Writ in one, read in the other. A debt incurred, a debt paid.

Sarah took the book, tentative and fearful, but before she could open her mouth to ask any questions, the creature was away, bounding up and up again, leaping along the stalk of healthy grass, arcing upward to the surface.

For a moment, neither Kindred nor Sarah said anything. The Fell ship was quiet, the deck empty. How could they not have heard the whispering?

"I guess it worked," Sarah said finally, running her hands over the dusk-blue cover of the book. She opened it on to fields of empty pages; a short quill of the same green as the dead bird's feathers had been cleverly worked into the inside of the cover.

"Can you trust that?" Kindred said as Sarah removed the quill and turned to the first page, "We don't even know what that thing was."

"Look around, Kindred," Sarah said, sitting down on the ground and readying herself to write. The tip of the quill shone. "We don't know what any of this is. The pluralities? The Silent Gods? Those mushrooms we picked on the way here, the ones with the spikes that we had to remove? Or the tiny, glowing fish swimming through that stream where we drank and filled the waterskins? All of this is a mystery. And this?"

She held up the book.

"This is all I have. Calling, at its heart, is the passing of knowledge from one party to another. This is new, but it's the same in some ways as how it works usually. If that thing was right, I should be able to see any response to what I write. Now let me send this message."

Sarah wrote, and Kindred watched, her eyes flicking constantly to the ship, sure that the Marchess would appear any moment, hair wild, eyes wide and searching, hands gripped into tight, angry fists.

But she didn't come, and Sarah finished the message with a sigh, slipping the quill back into place and closing the book.

"That's done," she said, voice low and quiet. She looked around, as if surveying this place one last time.

"I'll talk to my grandmother," Kindred said, nodding in the direction of the ship. "I can make her understand. She's always been—"

Sarah held up a hand, cutting her off.

"I'm leaving. I don't know if there is more I can do to help those above, but I know it won't happen here. I suppose I could try to sneak in there while they sleep and cut their throats"—Sarah fingered the knife at her belt—"but I can't bring myself to do that, because even now, after all this, I know what it would do to you to see your grandmother gone for good. And I'd probably die trying, anyway. I don't think the Marchess would suffer from such fears in cutting me down."

"You're leaving?" Kindred asked, brow creasing in her confusion. "Where will you go?"

"I don't know," Sarah said, her smile a brittle, angry thing. "I followed you down here and left the little bit of family and community I had behind, and now here I am, losing the one thing I thought would be constant. It feels like I took a leap and haven't stopped falling yet."

"Don't go," Kindred said. "Please. I don't want to lose you."

"Come with me, then," Sarah said. "You heard your grandmother. You're either with her in *destroying the lives of those people above*, or you're gone. Come with me, Kindred. We have this book. We can keep sending messages until someone on the other end answers. Please come with me."

Sarah's anger had gone and left behind a sad certainty. She was asking, but she already knew the answer.

"I can't leave her," Kindred said. "I just found her."

Sarah sighed, nodded, and walked away.

She followed the line the Traveling Court's ship's keel had left in the dirt, a rut running off into the low-lit dark.

Kindred thought to call out.

She thought to run after her.

Instead, she watched every step, silent and still, eyes following Sarah until she was nothing but a memory in the darkness.

CHAPTER SIXTEEN

Kindred slept, and in her sleep she dreamed.

Sarah ran ahead, and Kindred chased her, feet churning through sand and dirt that clung to her, dragging her down, pulling at each step. She called out to Sarah, but her voice had become a cracked, harsh thing, and she was capable only of a wild, wicked laughter.

Sarah turned at this, rage in her eyes, and she renewed her efforts to escape.

Kindred reached for Sarah, but it was not her hand that extended before her. A tentacle, tipped with a curving talon, lashed forward, catching Sarah across the back of the neck and drawing a bright line of red in her skin. When she cried out, Kindred did, too—a cackling, cruel laugh.

"Kindred, wake up," the Marchess said, jostling Kindred's shoulder and pulling her from sleep. She lay on the ground beside the Fell ship, on her side, the dirt around her disturbed by the movement of her dreams. "What are you doing down here?"

"I didn't know if I could come aboard," Kindred said, sitting up and taking a few deep breaths as the lingering grip of the dream faded from her mind. "I didn't mean to sleep; it just happened."

"Where's Sarah?" The Marchess stood with a load of bones gathered under one arm, spars of white poking out in a disorganized jumble.

"She left." A fine skin of star-strewn dirt covered Kindred's cheek from pressing her face into the ground in sleep. Kindred brushed it away and watched the grains fall.

The Marchess kneeled down beside her, putting one free hand on Kindred's shoulder and waiting until Kindred brought her eyes up.

"I'm sorry about her. None of this"—she nodded around them—"is easy, I know."

When Kindred said nothing in return, she dropped the bones in a dry clatter and said, "Pace with me."

It was a phrase Kindred had heard many times throughout her childhood. *Pace with me*, the Marchess would say, and they would walk back and forth on the deck of *Revenger* or stalk through the streets of Arcadia or, in the few instances that their work took them west, the busy roads of Halcyon.

Pacing, for the Marchess, was moving the body to move the mind. She paced when she needed to make a decision or consider a proposal, when she needed to come to terms with bad news or work through the rush of good news.

Pace with me, she would say to Kindred, and they might talk the whole time or say nothing; it didn't matter. The point was to let your mind pace with your body, every thought a step, every step a movement forward.

Kindred accepted the Marchess's offered hand, standing with a stretch, letting her cramped muscles lengthen, the aches of sleeping on the ground soothing slightly.

Lurch and Tesser Cobb had emerged on the deck, wiping at their eyes and yawning.

"Should we slip-slop start building the structure?" Lurch asked, leaping down from the deck and landing awkwardly.

"No," the Marchess said, shaking her head. "Bring the materials over but leave the structure. You're both awful at building them. I'll do it when we return. Prepare to fetch more."

"Where are you going?" Tesser Cobb asked, eating what looked to be a bowl of cold soup, slurping loudly.

"I'm pacing with my granddaughter," the Marchess said, setting off without another word, walking fast enough that Kindred had to jog to catch up with her. It was how she had talked to the crew of *Revenger*— brusque but not unkind, straightforward and to the point when the need to think was on her.

There was something in the Marchess's bearing and speech, some purpose, some vim and vitality, some deep knowing, that brought the people around the Marchess into line behind her. She cultivated loyalty in her crew and respect in her enemies.

"*She's looking at the horizon while we're all looking at our feet,*" Red Alay, the Marchess's next hand had always said, a mixture of respect and awe in her voice.

They didn't speak at all at first, and soon enough the Fell ship and the bustling, busy work of Lurch and Tesser Cobb were left behind.

Around them were the vast and distant towers of grass, bigger around than anything ever built by people, each releasing a glow of light that permeated the darkness, lining it with a fuzzy luminosity. Lantern bearers raced up toward the surface, every one an almost-person, a close guess at what made humans human—jagged smiles and broken bodies and bright eyes that looked and looked and looked.

The soft wind that moved always along the Seafloor brushed Kindred's cheek and played along her neck, smelling of something old and dry. Kindred thought of her grandmother's letter, folded in her pocket. How foolish she felt now to have labored over those words, excavating meaning and importance that had never been there in the first place.

The wind beneath the Sea is never ceasing, her grandmother had written, and Kindred breathed in that wind now, extended her hands and arms into it. It was only wind. Where Kindred had found intent and metaphor, a truth about the world and her own relationship with her grandmother, the Marchess had found nothing more than description and a slight turn of phrase.

Kindred walked through the rest of the letter in her mind, seeing anew each sentence and word with cold clarity. With each step she took, the letter in her pocket became less heavy, less important.

"It's lonely down here," the Marchess said finally, her eyes ahead on some unseen, fixed point. "Even with those two, it's lonely."

Their steps made a soft, rhythmic *shush* in the loose dirt. Kindred didn't say anything.

"I know I didn't say it very well, but I *am* glad you're here. I didn't expect it, and I didn't hope for it, but I'm glad nonetheless."

Kindred nodded.

"You left and you wrote me that letter, and I thought you were telling me to follow you." Kindred set her eyes ahead, too, both women looking into the glowing dark. "I broke almost everything I could break up there to follow you."

And now Ragged Sarah was gone, and that was broken too.

"It's lonely down here," the Marchess said again, without any inflection.

"Do you miss it?" Kindred asked. "Sailing and the sun and everything else. Do you think about it at all?" *Did you think about me at all?*

The Marchess made a small, noncommittal noise. "Some. But this is more important. If I don't do this, no one is ever going to be able to sail again. There won't be a Sea to marvel at."

Kindred wanted so badly to believe that it was this possibility that had brought her down—her love for the Sea tangled up in her fierce desire to protect it. It was clear that this was true for the Marchess.

And for Kindred. *No*, a small voice inside her said. *Nothing so noble.*

Their steps had brought them in a large circle, and the Greys were there to welcome them back, ugly and wrong and beautiful somehow. Even the natural world made unnatural could capture the eye and bewitch the heart, but Kindred heard its rotten melody, and the memory of the horrors pulled from inside it was fresh in her mind.

Tesser Cobb and Lurch had stacked another huge pile of bones next to the mound of ashes from the previous fire, and they were standing now on the deck of their ship, Tesser Cobb with the reins in his hands and Lurch tying down a barrel.

"Nearly ready," Tesser Cobb said. "Did you ask her?"

"Not yet," the Marchess said, frowning at him.

"Ask me what?" Kindred turned to her grandmother, who was already walking toward the stack of bones.

"You said the Once-City sank, right?" The Marchess began to sort the bones, her smooth, callused hands placing them in neat, orderly piles. She'd been the one to teach Kindred how to organize bones on a ship, where to put long, thin bones and how to stack some of the more ungainly pieces so they wouldn't move around on a journey. Seeing her handle these bones brought a flurry of small memories rushing back—the sound of bones gently clicking together, the rush of heat and power as a new build burned, the sound of the Marchess's careful breathing as she placed each bone in its proper spot.

"Yes," Kindred said.

"Where did you say it went down?" The Marchess didn't look up as she asked it, but there was a new note of tension in her voice, as though she were pretending at calm disinterest.

"I . . ." Kindred began, remembering how interested Fourth-Folly had been that first day, noting down exactly what Kindred and the others had said about the approximate position of the Once-City. "I don't remember exactly."

"We're running out of bones," the Marchess said, gesturing to the organized stacks around her. "Lurch, Cobb, and I have been scavenging these for some time now, and the creatures I send up bring down a mighty share of ships and their bones, but we're still starting to run low. There aren't many people out here in these grasses—I bet the Once-City hasn't even been touched yet."

She looked up, eyeing Kindred with more of that feigned nonchalance. "You didn't mention it to the Traveling Court fools, did you?"

Aboard the ship, Lurch was strapping a sword to his hip, and Tesser Cobb had two long knives in sheaths along one leg.

"We could use the bones," the Marchess continued. "I don't know if the Court would scavenge them—they're usually interested in other things. Books, clothing, *artifacts from the sunlit lands.*" The Marchess's Jest impression, mocking and overblown, was still somewhat accurate.

"Of course," Kindred said, nodding. She thought of the Traveling Court's shields, used as roofs during a fall. What use could they have for weapons, Jest had asked, surprised. For the Traveling Court, they had everything they needed, *would always* have everything they needed below the Sea. With so few people living down there and every need, every real need met, who could imagine wanting for more and wanting it so much that violence became a possibility?

"When did enough stop being enough?" Kindred whispered to herself, the words barely more than a stirring of breath deep in her chest. It was one of the last things her grandmother had told her above, back when Kindred still served on *Revenger.*

"What?" the Marchess asked, frowning at her. "Did you tell them where it fell?"

"No," Kindred said, shaking herself loose from her thoughts. "No, I didn't."

Kindred felt herself standing at the center of a vast storm, winds buffeting her from all directions, memories and selves and maybes, snatches of sentences and sentiments, hymns and songs, all lighting along her body and mind, filling her with the richness of who she had been and who she might be.

The Marchess, standing beside her at the bow of *Revenger*, the two of them staring off at the horizon, saying nothing, alone together.

In the prairie wind, out the prairie wind.

Sarah, taking her hand as they walked through the Once-City, smiling at her in that way that said simply, *Here, we are together now.*

Captain Caraway saying only "Be welcome aboard, Keeper" her first time stepping aboard *The Errant*'s deck as a possible crew member.

Her parents kissing her goodbye, casual and unknowing, that last morning. The way her father's rough, gnarled hands felt against her own as he swung her laughing around the room.

The citizens of the Once-City and Arcadia, crews of *The Errant* and the pirate vessels, all true believers in their lost causes, knowing and unknowing.

Jest shaking her head and saying, "No, just people." As though that truth were so much worse than anything else could be.

Look beyond. Look below.

Past and present and possibility collided in Kindred's mind, and she felt like the pluralities, moving underneath awareness all her life until this moment, when, regardless of her desires, she was being forced above, every maybe and might-be about her, every imagined future and past, every self she might have been collapsing together as fresh air struck her for the first time.

Kindred saw herself again as that woman going through life, unaffected by those around her, focused and driven, bare and rootless. A plant pulled in the world around it through its roots and leaves, made rough skin and long limbs with the gifts given by the community of sun and rain, earth and sky, plant and person around it.

She saw her grandmother, and Sarah's words ran through her mind: *She's like you.*

Kindred didn't want to go alone anymore. She wanted her roots to run deep and wide, her arms to grow leaves that pulled in the world around her, taking and giving back in equal measure. She let past mistakes and triumphs in, watching the plants growing along her hand stretch in pleasure.

In the prairie wind.

Who will you be?

Out the prairie wind.

"Kindred?" the Marchess said, frowning at her. "Where did the Once-City go down?"

"The northern border of Arcadian grasses," Kindred said, squatting down and tracing a quick map in the dirt with her finger. "Up near the Mists. Remember that run of seldom shoots we found that morning?"

The Marchess closed her eyes and smiled at the memory. "Those fuckers at the Trade said it was out of season and wouldn't be back until the next year. I'll never forget how wide their eyes were when we brought that harvest back. Big men convinced they knew everything."

The crew of *Revenger* had toasted their captain that night, sitting on the rocks on the Arcadian shore, backs to the city they despised, faces turned into the wind, exchanging smiles and stories until morning outshone the stars and moon.

"That's where it came down," Kindred said, nodding and smiling.

The Marchess stared down at the map on the ground for a moment, muttering quietly to herself, before nodding.

"You're sure that's where it went down?" Her eyes, when they met Kindred's, were empty of her usual fire.

"Yes," Kindred said, nodding.

"I'll tell Lurch and Cobb, and then we can get this structure built." The Marchess pushed herself up, rubbing the dirt from her hands.

"I'm leaving too," Kindred said, pushing herself up. The words came out calmer than she had expected them to. Her gut was a turbulent sea, and her hands shook with the revelation of the moment and the realization of what it meant.

"You're leaving? You just arrived."

Kindred looked around for the line cutting through the dirt, the line that would lead her back to the Traveling Court and back to Sarah.

This isn't my myth, Kindred thought, but instead she only said, "I'm going to find Sarah."

The Marchess didn't say anything, and when Kindred turned back, she was close enough to touch, eyes squinting in thought, fixed on Kindred.

"What's going on, Kindred? Is it the work?"

"No," Kindred lied. She had to be careful. If she was going to have any chance to stop this, the next moment was crucial. "It's . . ."

She trailed off, and the Marchess put a hand on her arm.

"You're in love," she said, her voice quiet but kind. She chuckled. "Here I am, saving the world, and you want to trail off after your sweetheart."

Kindred looked down, smiling. She was in love, that was true. And if the Marchess wanted to believe her to be a lovestruck fool, then good.

"She came down here for me," Kindred said, looking up. "And I forgot about her."

The Marchess squeezed Kindred's arm.

"You go find your lovey," she said, smiling for a moment before growing more serious. "If anyone from the Traveling Court, or anyone associated with them, tries to mess up what I'm doing here, it won't end well for them. Pass that message on, will you?"

Kindred nodded, and the Marchess squeezed her arm again.

"I'll come and find you after it's done and the Sea is safe," she said. "Maybe we can sail together again."

Kindred followed the line.

She imagined Sarah with each footprint she found, followed her as she wandered off to find water from a nearby stream or to pick some of the mushrooms Wylf had shown them to find and identify.

When Sarah's footprints grew heavy and led to an impression of her feet forming an angle, the imprint of the book pressed into the dirt in front of her, Kindred placed her feet where Sarah's had been and wondered what message Sarah had sent or received.

The black sky above her promised a fall with every step, and Kindred felt keenly the absence of the Traveling Court's vessel and its repurposed shields. But stepping out into the wild was an act of trust, of faith, and she clung to both.

She slept once for a little while, or maybe a long while, before rising and walking more. Sometimes she cried, and she couldn't have said whether they were tears of joy welling up from the vast freedom she now felt or if they were tears of sadness for what had been.

As she walked, Kindred saw a field off in the distance, its expanse broken by the remains of a huge creature she thought might have been a midgrass badger in life but was now a mountainous mass of broken flesh and bones, black-and-white fur sticking out at odd angles and matted down with blood.

Even as Kindred watched, the body shifted and moved, sinking slowly into the ground as the pluralities below it feasted, pulling more and more of it down.

On and on she walked, and soon she began to see signs of the Once-City's fall—huge shards of wood and sprays of rubble, walls and plants, pieces of buildings that were once homes. Long, thick, familiar branches lay strewn across the ground, like arms and hands reaching out for something they would never touch.

Fragments of architecture spiked Kindred's memory, pulling her back to those streets and passageways, the levels inside the tree that was the Once-City, the people who had lived there for so long, slowly losing their way, just as so many did.

She walked through the broken body of the Once-City and remembered what it had once been—a place living in accordance with the world around it, a sail caught and moved by the wind, minds and bodies humming in harmony with the song of the Sea.

The shell of the Once-City, the wall that surrounded the whole of it, had broken in the fall, and only a rough section—a quarter of the hollowed trunk—remained somewhat intact, looming over its spilled innards, a protective wall against the oppressive emptiness of the Seafloor. Its edges were long, ragged splinters of wood, uneven and jagged, and the inside of it bore signs of its life—interior walls still clinging to it, carvings and art etched and painted onto it.

The myriad mess of it all seemed strangely out of place on the Seafloor; its busyness a jarring contrast to the clean emptiness elsewhere.

In the shelter of this wall, the Traveling Court had found harbor.

Fourth-Folly and Wylf were prying a huge slab of wood—what had once been the wall of a home—up to get at the goods beneath it. Madrigal waited beside them, shifting from foot to foot, and when the wall was lifted enough, she darted in, calling out what she found and tossing it out.

Jest and Awn stood nearby, sorting through what they had already found—her lifting and presenting books and clothes, damaged art and handfuls of plants, him nodding excitedly and speaking quickly. He was too far off for Kindred to understand what he was saying, but the familiar tone—wonder and awe and excitement—brought a smile to Kindred's face.

Sarah, though, was nowhere to be seen.

"Kindred Captain!" Jest shouted as she neared, holding up the spoils of their scavenging. Her smile was one of utter joy, and Awn matched it. "You return to us, a treasure greater than any we might scavenge in this Once-City!"

"I didn't think we would see you again so soon," Awn said, cocking his head to the side. "Or ever, maybe."

"Kindred!" Madrigal's voice preceded her, emerging out from under the sloping wall a moment before she did, shedding the treasures she'd scavenged as she ran through the detritus to give Kindred a hug. She was covered in dirt and grime and looked incandescent in her happiness.

Wylf and Fourth-Folly dropped the wall, which made a deep *boom* against the ground and set the pluralities to scurrying around near the ship.

"Did your royal grandmother send you to fetch supplies?" Fourth-Folly asked, their surliness apparently having returned in full.

"Folly," Jest said, shaking her head in displeasure, but Kindred laughed it off, smiling.

"It's all right," she said, hugging Madrigal against her side. "My grandmother wanted me to join her work, and I said no."

That brought a moment of silence to them all.

"Well done," Awn said, offering her a nod and a small smile. "That must have been difficult."

"It was," Kindred said, nodding, "right up until it wasn't."

Wylf walked over and pulled Kindred into a gentle hug.

"Good," he said, before returning to his whispering.

"And she just let you go?" Fourth-Folly asked, examining a broken, jagged length of wood that might have once been the long handle of a shovel or axe. "Just like that? 'Thanks for coming and see you later, have a happy life'?"

"Not exactly," Kindred said, before briefly explaining her last bit of time with the Fell and her grandmother, including the threat she'd sent along at the end, which brought about a different, grimmer silence than the first one.

"She's a monster just like Lurch and Cobb," Fourth-Folly said, shaking their head before meeting Kindred's eye. "Sorry."

"They're just people," Jest said, though quietly and without any heat.

"It's okay," Kindred said, shaking her head. "I know who she is now. And who I am."

When Jest stepped up to Kindred, her eyes were shining and full.

"You found your myth," she said, huffing out a small, sniffly laugh.

"I think I did." Kindred took the Lost Monarch's hug with a smile. When they separated, she looked around at them and asked the question she'd had since arriving. "Where's Sarah?"

"She's on the other side with the trees," Madrigal said, still standing beside Kindred, one hand laid against Kindred's side, forgotten there. With her free hand, Madrigal pointed at the wall looming over them. "Fourth-Folly showed her how to catch pluralities, and she's been trying since."

"Badly," Folly said, though not unkindly.

"Yeah," Madrigal agreed, looking up at Kindred. "She's been crying, too."

Kindred nodded and left.

⸺ ◆ ⸺

On the other side of the wall, the remains of the Forest and the Gone Ways were intermixed, and Kindred stopped in astonishment at the sight of it.

The Forest in the Once-City had not been a real forest, the trees not really trees but simply the ingress of the Sea's power taking over the Once-City, approximations of real trees just as the lantern bearers were approximations of people. Kindred was caught suddenly by the memory of her leap into that Forest, crossing the line from the path that no one was supposed to cross and finding herself in a world of endless shadow.

Those trees had not been trees, and yet on the other side of the wall, trees had begun to grow in the dirt, some knee-high, others taller than Kindred, and a few reaching already up into the darkness. They were not nearly as myriad as they were in the Once-City, but they were the same, Kindred was sure without really knowing how she knew. The magic that had reached up to that city above and grown through it like a garden had followed its descent and seeded itself into the ground there, too.

Kindred even spied a few growths that looked like the plant that had healed her and given her the growths along her hand.

On the ground around the trees were the remains of the Gone Ways, bones and ash and plants and weapons laying in a vast chaotic mess.

Near one of the taller trees, the ground around her meticulously picked clean, was Sarah, a thin metal pole wound with grass in one hand, a fistful of food in the other. Moving carefully, Sarah stepped through a dance strange and wonderful, quick leaps and slow slides, and as Kindred neared—walking as quietly as she could so as not to disturb Sarah—she heard the words of a song, whisper-sung in Sarah's beautiful, cracking voice.

> *A-may a-may come dark and say,*
> *A-lee a-lee rise dark to me,*
> *Swim deep of sea, run dark of day,*
> *Could-be, could-be, could-be,*
> *Come near to me*

Kindred felt before she saw the fire nearby, a small blaze burning a mixture of plants strung together into a busy braid. The flames shifted and changed constantly, unable to settle into a steady burn or an even color.

Sarah sprinkled a few pieces of food on the ground in front of her, sweeping one pointed toe in an arc around them and driving the pole deep into the dirt.

She waited a moment like that, and Kindred couldn't help stare at the muscles bunched and corded along her shoulders and stretch of back visible outside of her tattered, ragged clothing. Kindred could imagine no future better than one in which she spent every day with Sarah, exploring the world and setting right what they could, and every night working away what she could of those tight, strained muscles.

It was a small life she saw for them, unremarkable perhaps. Filled with simplicity and bounded by enough. What could be better?

Something shifted in the dirt below Sarah, and she leapt back, letting out a strangled cry, half-laugh and half-sob. Quickly, she unstrapped the grass wound around the pole and pulled it taut, the end of it disappearing into the ground and shifting around, roving here and there to pick up what food it could.

Sarah's crow of triumph lit the darkness of the Sea better than any fire could have, and when she looked around, she found Kindred.

Neither spoke for a long time, and apart from the plurality shifting around beneath Sarah, moving like a dog sniffing around for treats, neither moved. The ever-present wind below the Sea brushed them both, connecting them to one another and to every other piece and person and plant of the Forever Sea. Kindred breathed it in and spoke.

"I'm sorry."

Sarah watched her but said nothing, expression unreadable.

"You were right. I am just like my grandmother. For a long time, I thought the parts of me that were best were the ones she had given me. She was a dreamer who caught everyone else around her in the dreaming, and I loved that. She taught me how to see the world and how to love it. She taught me so many good things that I never understood what she didn't teach me."

Kindred walked closer to Sarah, moving slowly through the steps of her own dance.

"She was always this person," Kindred continued. "She cared more about her ideals than any person or place. I never saw it. Or maybe I did and thought her all the better for it."

Next to Sarah now, Kindred yearned to reach out and run a hand along Sarah's arm, to clasp their hands together, braiding fingers through the other's. She wanted to kiss Sarah like Sarah always kissed her—wild and with abandon.

But she waited.

"I was so focused on my own ideals—the Sea, the people of the Once-City and Arcadia—that I forgot about this world and these people and this Sea. I thought of love, but I didn't think enough of *our* love. I lost my way."

The plurality below had gone still with no more food to find, and Sarah's heavy breathing was the only sound Kindred could hear, the only sound that mattered to her.

Sarah reached out, tentative, touching Kindred's hand where the golden shoots had grown through her skin and her neck where the flower had curled into a tight, hard bud, perhaps feeling Kindred's fear and uncertainty.

"I love your idealism, Kindred. You look where others won't and see a world of wonder and wildness where many see only profit and power. You're gentle and uncertain, simple in the best way. You see the beauty in things that no one else sees."

A small smile pulled up one side of Sarah's mouth.

"You saw me when no one else did."

Kindred smiled at the rush of memories—seeing Sarah for the first time, watching her with more than professional interest as she climbed to the crow's nest, listening to her songs and stories, marveling at the worlds inside her words and inside her silences.

She had begun as a wonder, and she had only grown more wonderful since.

"Your grandmother," Sarah said, pulling back from Kindred a little, "was there for you, Kindred, just like she was there for her crew at times. It would be easy to see her as purely evil now, capable of only great callousness and evil, but it's not so simple. I'm no great seer of people—I tend to fall for the melancholy mourners of the world," she said, nudging Kindred with a smile that pulled a thin, wet laugh from Kindred.

"But if your grandmother isn't solely the hero she has been in your memory, then she is not solely the villain she plays now. Like you, like me, like so many of us, she is full of the potential to be both."

Kindred put a hand to her pocket, thinking of the letter there. It had become a horizon for her, a light in the east to sail for, a goal and an assurance that she was on the right path.

Or, better, an anchor pulling her down to this place, this moment, this story.

Old conversations, ones Kindred had thought of hundreds of times to relish the twist of her grandmother's words or the calm assurance the Marchess had offered—these glowed with new meaning to be discovered, a snide smile Kindred had forgotten, a power imbalance unconsidered, a joke told in meanness and spite.

"I remember hearing stories about the Marchess," Sarah said, not quite speaking to Kindred but for her. "I was new in Arcadia and looking for a ship, working as a dockhand for a few coins a night, and I saw *Revenger* sail in one evening. I couldn't believe any ships that old were still in use. Even the pirates I'd left didn't sail anything so old. When I asked another hand, he told me all about the mad captain aboard, the old crew sailing the older vessel. 'Like the dead piloting a corpse,' he said."

Sarah smiled at the memory before shaking her head at Kindred.

"That guy was an idiot, of course. *Revenger* was a beautiful ship. But he told me stories about the Marchess, how arrogant she was, how she swaggered around Arcadia like she owned it, better than everyone she encountered, above it all."

As Sarah spoke, Kindred felt that old spike of defensiveness rise inside her, a gut instinct to defend her grandmother. Her ideas weren't bad, just old-fashioned. *The old ways are best. You just don't understand.*

All the tired, well-used phrases were sand and ash in her mouth.

"When I met you on *The Errant* and found out who you were, I didn't say anything about the Marchess and what some people—lots of people, really—thought about her. It was clear she had shaped you, that she meant everything to you even if you two had left off with a fight."

Sarah gave Kindred a small, sad smile.

"Your grandmother became a giant in your mind, a giant she only sometimes was—is—in life. But who she was for you—and what her letter became for you—is still important. You told me once that she never taught you how to keep the hearthfire directly, right? She made you steal her techniques?"

Kindred snorted out a laugh at that.

"Yeah. She would never tell me how to do anything. If I wanted to learn it, I had to watch and steal the technique from her. Callous, mean-spirited nonsense."

Sarah lifted Kindred's hands in her own, one thumb tracing along the golden plants curled gently against one set of her knuckles.

"You took the best of her hearthfire-keeping, but you also took the best of *her*, Kindred. You stole yourself from your grandmother. You took everything good about her and made it your own, and that says everything about *you*. That kind, passionate, dedicated person you were holding in your mind, the giant you've been chasing? That wasn't her, Kindred—it was you."

The storyteller pauses, letting his words sink into the dreams of his listeners. They will not remember this, not anything about Kindred or Flitch, not anything about the way it was, but perhaps his story can shift the foundations of their dreaming. Perhaps a story of hope might let hope flicker again.

Perhaps a story of the sun might pull eyes up in search of the light.

The storyteller looks down at a child, a girl of perhaps five or six, brown hair messed and tangled, face smudged by work she is too young to be required to do. And yet, the world, *this world*, requires it of her anyway.

In one hand she holds a small doll, its body and hair made of grassy detritus, belt and dress made of scraps of cloth. She has drawn a face onto the doll's wide, green face, and somehow, impossibly, this child has made her doll smile. The eyes are mismatched, one much larger than the other, and the line of the mouth is shaky, but the joy there, writ forever on this doll's face, is plain to see.

This, too, is a story, the thing, the being that once was Flitch, thinks.

To imagine happiness in something so small and insubstantial, to create it in this way, is a surprise to the storyteller, and that he can still be surprised is yet another surprise.

He looks at this child, small enough that she might be devoured by a hundred different creatures waiting out in that darkness and give none of them the slightest pause or trouble. She is all frailty and innocence as she sleeps, a flower waiting to be trampled, and yet that shaky smile spells resilience, and those clutching fingers, even now holding to the tail of a sunlit bird in dreams, are capable of something good and powerful and endless.

There, too, is a story, and it is the same one the storyteller has been offering.

Before he can stop himself, and before the echoes of his surprise fade to true dullness, the storyteller bends down, the motion quicker than any he has done in a very long time.

With a steady hand, he brushes tangles of hair from her face and, after a moment of timidity, mimics her breathing, pulling in air and releasing it in a rhythm grown foreign and strange to him.

For the span of several breaths, the storyteller does nothing but breathe in time with this child's lungs, his hand still held on her forehead, as though checking for a fever. He breathes with her, closer to this small, rebelliously happy person than he has been to anyone in a long, long time.

When he finally stands and steps back from the child, the storyteller has begun to doubt the ease with which he will be able to bury again these unearthed memories.

Lifting his eyes, he finds the two remaining members of his once-audience, his slumbering, dreaming congregation.

Sitting side by side, Praise and Quietus have listened in total silence, one because he can no longer speak, and one because it has no need to speak.

But now, as the end draws near, the heavy blanket of darkness around Quietus stirs, and the uneasy calm Praise has found, a product of exhaustion more than true peace, is shattered. His eyes follow Quietus as it stands before him, a fountain of darkness spilling around it.

"I am sorry," the storyteller says, the lie no longer leaving a trace of guilt behind.

Quietus, unmaker and remaker, end-speaker, walker of the ways, the Broken Shield of ever ago, reaches a single hand out from its cloak of darkness, the layered leaves shivering as though caught in a winter's wind. Its many-fingered hand reaches out to and *into* Praise, grabbing hold of his ribs, fingers hooking between bones, and with a slow strength, Quietus lifts Praise from his seat, the man beyond terror, beyond fear, beyond pain. He has become eyes to see, a heart to beat, and a spirit to tremble in anticipation.

Quietus pulls Praise into its dark folds, drawing him close, and only when he has disappeared from sight completely does Praise cry out, the note long and wavering, musical and beautiful, resonating against the tall shells of the buildings around them.

Silence comes then, inevitable, and the storyteller watches Quietus for a long moment, wondering what it will create from Praise.

Perhaps it will make him into a stand of crowned vervain, purple-blue flowers clustered in a wash of sunlight he never got to feel.

Maybe Praise will become a shrike, butcher of the sky, quick of eye and quick to strike, a grey blur against a blue-white sky.

Or possibly Quietus will create of Praise a new room for its labyrinth, a small space, decorated with chains and doors that lock, close walls and endless quiet.

The storyteller finds he does not care, and when he turns away from Quietus, his mind is occupied only by thoughts of a small smile, drawn by a quivering hand, and of breath moving in and out, in and out, steadily, profoundly.

Endlessly.

The storyteller moves outside of the circles of listeners now, reaching into his bag for the book. The cover is unchanged by time, still a beautiful blue. The storyteller does not open it. Not yet.

Instead, he carries it with him as he moves through Twist-that-was-Arcadia, looking at the slow work time has wrought on the buildings and structures. When he speaks to continue his story, he gives his voice reach and resonance, and while those dreaming can hear him, and while Quietus, too, can hear him as it unmakes and makes, the storyteller offers this final stretch of the tale to the architecture of a past world.

CHAPTER SEVENTEEN

G wyn called it the Sea Deck.

Before being sent off to sleep on the hastily arranged bedding on floors in various out-of-the-way rooms and hallways, they'd all been given directions to meet there first thing in the morning.

"I like to drink my tea on the Sea Deck in the mornings as the sun comes up," she'd said. "We can sip in peace and plan our destruction of King Faineant's iron grip on the Sea. What kind of floral notes would you like in your tea?"

The others had slept, Idyll and Aster along the length of a hallway, Zim curled into a corner of a nearby washing room, and the baron slumped over in a chair.

Flitch tried to sleep. He lay stretched out on the hard floor, feet pointing toward Aster, head toward Idyll, feeling like a link in a chain, but rest would not come. It wasn't the stone along his back or the sounds of servants and staff bustling about, dealing with the ramifications of a house's population almost doubling in size.

He wanted to look at the book Quietus had given him, but he'd allowed Gwyn to take it for the night.

"I promise I'll return it," she'd said, hugging it close as she left him to sleep.

Even when quiet finally came and the Paths house breathed gently with the prairie wind against its walls, Flitch could not sleep. He remembered footsteps behind him, fantastical and terrifying spaces ahead of him, an endlessness stretching all around. Walls that rose and fell with a beastly breathing, and a presence in the dark tunnels that waited, watchful and curious, unencumbered by anything remotely human.

Who could sleep when such thoughts played over and over in their head? Flitch wiggled his fingers and toes. He opened his mouth as wide as it could go, feeling the strain in his jaw and cheek. With careful deliberation, he pinched one arm and then the other, tracing the rise and fall of pain. He rolled over onto his side, facing into the wall, imagining the tiny shadows slivering the grains of wood were ships sailing against the wind, beleaguered captains ordering their crew to haul hard, prepare for a starboard tack.

It was a game he'd played as a child when alone, letting his mind float away into the bliss of pure imagining. He would see himself at the helm, wind pulling at his clothes, sunlight burnishing his face, captain of a vessel, leader of a crew who looked to him for wisdom and, should the moment require it, bravery.

This time, though, the doorways of imagining were closed to him. Flitch watched the ships in the grain of the wood and could see himself nowhere on them. The winds of that wondering world, always so near to him, felt impossibly distant now, and Flitch could feel nothing but the cold stone holding him up.

After waiting fruitlessly for sleep or dreaming to take him, Flitch rose, stepping carefully and quietly around his siblings, pausing to watch his father's sleeping form for a time.

He walked the halls, examining with uncomprehending intensity the works of art hanging from the walls, many of them little more than finger paintings done of the Sea, each tagged with a note explaining which child in the Paths house had made it and at what age.

Sheroo, Age 6 had made the Sea out of splayed, green handprints, each finger dotted with a bit of red or orange to make the flowers.

Tassi, Age 9 left the white of the page dominant, choosing to cut its center with a single stalk of bluestem.

Flitch laughed to find one by Gwyn Gaunt herself: *Gwyn, Age 195* had rendered the blue sky over the Sea in her small handprints, each one showing a different hand gesture wrought in bright blues and puffy whites.

He could picture Gwyn sitting beside the children at some table in the house, elbow to elbow with Sheroo and Tassi, chuckling and winking as she told them she was 195 years old, happily splashing her hands onto the plates of color, chortling along with the creative play.

He wandered the night away, stepping around sleeping bodies, propelled ever onward by a numb curiosity to see the house. When he walked back through the hallway where he'd started the night, he found Aster snoring loudly and Idyll conspicuously absent. Perhaps gone to find a bathroom. Or to find Ravel's room.

He helped a few servants pack away the remaining supplies Borders had managed to bring. In the kitchens, he passed one of the cooks scoop after scoop of flour to make the enormous flat loaves that Paths was fond of eating.

Through the glass ceiling he watched the night sky soften to shades of blue more beautiful than anything he'd seen before.

At one point, in that sacred quiet just before true-dawn has flushed pink on the horizon, Flitch found himself outside a room in which several of the guard captains and commanders were strategizing, standing in clumps around a large map of the harbor, pointing with stubby fingers at models meant to represent fleets or factions. The tactics and planning might have been interesting to him once, but he couldn't find the fire for it now, and instead gave Gwyn and his father—her bright-eyed and listening carefully, him exhausted and struggling to focus—a wave and left.

He let his feet lead him for another little while, stopping at the windows facing the expansive gardens in the back to watch the messy rows of plants waking to the morning.

When he finally made his way out the back door, along the winding trail, and up on to the raised wooden deck extending out over the cliff face and looking down on the Sea itself, everyone else was already there.

If the Paths house was a work of beauty and artistry, then the Sea Deck was a work of architectural daring. The wooden slats of the floor ran off the edge of the cliff, supported by fewer and fewer angled slats below, pushing farther and farther out until it ended in a circular pad, the wood curved into swirling patterns, nothing below but many, many lengths of air and then the Sea.

"I made you chamomile and sun-ray spar tea," Gwyn said, rising from one of the seats arranged in a rough circle around the oblong table on the pad. "Good for dreaming."

"Isn't sun-ray spar a cactus?" Aster asked from where she sat, sipping from her own mug of tea. "And also extinct?"

"Yes to both!" Gwyn said brightly.

Aster looked as though she wanted to ask another question but decided against it.

Gwyn passed the mug to Flitch.

"Isn't 'tea for dreaming' better served before bedtime?" Zim asked, sipping his own tea, which looked floral in the morning light, bits of brightly colored flowers floating along its surface.

"Some of us need dreams even during the day," Gwyn said, her voice friendly but the look on her face quite serious. Her eyes held Flitch's for what felt like too long before she turned and sat back in her seat, leaving Flitch to wander over to a rough wooden seat next to Idyll and Ravel, who were tangled in the soft whispers of infatuation.

"Good morning," Flitch said.

"Couldn't sleep?" Idyll asked, turning to face him, a smile lighting their countenance. "You weren't in your blankets when I woke up."

"That's funny," Flitch said, smiling in return. "I went for a walk, and when I came back, you weren't in your blankets either."

Idyll opened their mouth and immediately shut it again.

"I saw you get up, too," Aster said, taking a gulp of tea from a purple, glazed mug. "You weren't exactly subtle. Flitch is the one I didn't see."

"I saw, too," Zim said, meek and refusing to meet Idyll's eyes.

Idyll cast their eyes skyward and blew out a long breath.

"I don't know what you all are talking about," the baron said, frowning around at them. "And I do not care to."

The lie was obvious, and Idyll looked horrified as they stared at their father.

"It's no big deal," Aster said, leaning over with a leer. "No shame in engaging in a little—"

"Stop," Idyll said, their nostrils flaring, one hand held out like a blade. "Do not think of finishing that sentence."

It was the first real moment of normalcy with Idyll and his siblings since Flitch had emerged from the tunnels, and he let the small moment press itself into his mind, leaving an imprint there forever. The lopsided way Idyll smiled in their embarrassment, Aster's gleeful cackle, Zim's pleasant grin, the way Idyll looked skyward, as if seeking some godly wisdom in navigating the treacherous grasses of sibling relationships.

It might have been an insignificant moment, but what moment wasn't when such chaos and danger moved in the world? It was a small joy, and Flitch held it close to himself.

Ravel, for his part, said absolutely nothing, looking from Idyll to Gwyn, who shook her head and said in a quiet voice, "Just drink your tea, lovey boy. Some people are very odd about sex."

The slight blush coloring the high ridges of Ravel's cheekbones grew to a full flowering of red splotches. The Borders Baron coughed into his cup of tea—a delicate porcelain thing, small on its own but absolutely tiny in his hands. The rest of them, even the guard leaders and ship captains—all of whom were looking increasingly uncomfortable, their gazes locked firmly on the Sea beyond the deck—had thick, sturdy mugs.

Only the baron had a tiny cup, and Flitch could imagine Gwyn laughing to herself as she prepared the tea, each blend perfectly chosen for its recipient.

"Were those arrows shot by your people in the trees last night magically reinforced?" Aster asked, whiplashing to a new subject, a favorite pastime of hers, never able to stay focused on one topic in a conversation for long.

"They were!" Gwyn said. "Well spotted."

Aster asked about the plants they burned and the techniques they used, but Flitch let her questions and Gwyn's excited answers fade as he looked out over the smooth wooden ledge running around the outside of the platform.

The Forever Sea was an abstract painting below him, thick, oily swirls of color. Ridges of raised plants caught in the early-morning wind, mountainous and tossing shadows behind them. The smoke from the Arcadian fires had thinned away to nothing now, leaving the Sea once more holding up a wide blue sky. Ships could be seen in the harbor below, moving about in threes and fours, flags so distant as to be almost impossible to make out, although Flitch found he could still see them, could almost imagine the snap of the fabric in the wind, the call of captains, the songs of the keepers.

Winds from the east sent waves through the Sea, flipping leaves and collecting loose seedpods up into an accumulated being, a pixie that skipped and danced along the surface of the Sea, scattering itself and reforming itself with each breath.

From this high, the Sea was like a game board, beautifully wrought, with each vessel and patch of harvestable plants a point of strategy. Captain

Ever-Run and her ship *Benevolence* maneuvering toward that stretch of whorled milkweed, outpacing *The Truncheon*, captained by Lula Accoy until recently when she passed away. Who was captaining *The Truncheon* now?

Flitch searched his memory, frowning at the absence in his knowledge, but then he was frowning for a different reason, squinting down at the pack of three vessels sailing hard behind *Benevolence*, hulls and sails and flags strange to him. He knew every vessel in the Mainland fleet, regardless of barony allegiance or age, and he knew or knew of almost every vessel sailing out of Arcadia, not that there were many to be found in that group anymore.

But these were strange to him.

"I've never seen those ships before," Flitch said, not realizing he was speaking out loud until Ravel spoke.

"They're pirate vessels that Faineant captured."

"Our dear King," Gwyn said, nodding down at the vessels, "has apparently decided his fleet needed more vessels, and he has requisitioned the Once-City ships. Messages from my friends close to the King say Faineant kept the captains and crew who swore allegiance to him and executed all the others."

"He's a monster," Idyll said firmly, and the rest of them nodded.

"Sadly, I think he's quite a simple monster," Gwyn said. "Most powerful men are."

She let the silence draw out for a moment, and Flitch gave a last look to the pirate vessels, watching as they neared *Benevolence*—a vessel owned by one of the minor landholders and independent. When the pirates began to board, it became clear that *Benevolence* would not be independent for much longer.

"But now let us discuss our plans to dismantle this simple man's power— a slightly more complicated task, I believe," Gwyn said, settling back into her seat and nodding at Ravel, who sat forward, easily the youngest of the captains or commanders present, yet he spoke with a calm that suggested this was not his first time discussing battle strategies with his elders.

"We have many factors to consider," he said, pointing to a map on the table. It showed the eastern shore of the Mainland, with bright blue stars where the Paths and Borders houses were—though the star for Borders had a slim X drawn through it. Further inland was a red circle showing the castle. Roads and paths, each accompanied by tiny, tidy handwriting, webbed the landscape around those three major landmarks.

Atop the map stood small figurines, each painted with perfect precision, including shading for shadows and dust, age lines on the faces and details in the hair. Faineant was there, lounging in a pose of casual cruelty that captured him perfectly, not at the castle but near a small building labeled *Faineant's sleeping quarters*.

A tiny Gwyn and a tiny Borders Baron were currently at the Paths house, along with the commanders and captains of their fleets, save for Twyllyn Tae, the captain of the Borders fleet, his figurine a sailboat with his head attached to the mainmast.

His figure was out at the edge of Mainland grasses, as close as a ship could get to the burned Sea surrounding Arcadia.

The map expanded westward, though scaled down, the kingdoms and baronies and terrenes and enclaves of the west rendered in miniature, but even those places had figures placed in key locations. A figure standing beside a dog was placed over the Sorrowful Terrene, clearly meant to be Eightform, the never-elected leader of that terrene, her hound Bask always nearby. Flitch spotted Oelius Tartakower astride one of the mammoth goats famous in his mountainous region.

It was the most detailed map he'd ever seen, even the parts that were scaled back.

"First," Ravel continued, gesturing at Faineant and then the loose collection of figures clustered around the castle, "the King has begun to marshal forces with which to assault the Paths house. Our sources inside suggest that an attack could come as early as this evening, though we suspect Faineant's caution regarding Paths will push any such attempt until tomorrow morning.

"Second, our fleets—Paths and Border—are too far apart right now to orchestrate any joint defenses or attacks of our own on the Sea. Borders, as I understand it, has wisely sent its fleet well outside Faineant's scope, which has been limited somewhat by the creatures from below but bolstered again by the addition of the pirate fleet."

At this point, an older man, bald and sporting a thick brown mustache that flared out at the ends, spoke up.

"The Paths fleet has remained conspicuous in our positioning. We have hidden as many vessels as possible in our covert coves, but it is only a matter of time before they are found. Any plans involving an attack from our fleet should happen sooner rather than later if we are to make use of our advantage in surprise."

Gwyn nodded at this but said nothing.

"If I could speak with a crow-caller," the baron said, "I could get word to Twyllyn and coordinate something with my fleet, though we lost many ships before we could get away. Faineant's plan to combine his forces with ours to patrol the Sea for the fake threat of the Supplicant Few gave him perfect proximity from which to attack our vessels."

"I think our plan should rely on smaller points of pressure," Gwyn said, arching an eyebrow at the baron, "instead of large-scale attacks. Keep your people out near the edge, Uthe. Borders has lost enough."

The baron looked unhappy with this plan, but he said nothing.

"Right," Ravel said, "the third issue we face is the threat of the Sea itself. If Flitch's book is to be believed—"

"Which I believe it is," Gwyn said, passing the book back to Flitch across the table. As he took it, a muscle along his shoulders that he hadn't known had been clenched suddenly relaxed.

"And so," Ravel continued, "the appearance of monsters from the deep will only continue until the ancient magics flattening and controlling the Sea are broken."

Ravel touched a finger to the carved ship sitting in the middle of the Mainland grasses, huge and double-hulled, three masts rising from the deck, each festooned with myriad sails and flags, all carved and painted with meticulous care.

The Arcana. The King's favored vessel, on which the fires never went out, each blaze fed and monitored by a continuous watch, crewed at all times by the fiercest fighters and most accomplished casters the academy produced.

"You're going to attack *The Arcana*?" Aster said, sitting forward, incredulity plain on her face.

"It is an option we're considering, yes," Gwyn said.

"You know it's protected by a defensive vessel circling it at all times, right?" Aster said, reaching out to draw a wide perimeter around the miniature of *The Arcana*.

"I think it's actually two now," Gwyn said, turning to look at the mustachioed man who'd spoken earlier, who nodded.

"And so, you must also know," Aster continued, looking around, unabashed skepticism in her voice, "that there are twenty-nine casting fires going at all times on *The Arcana*, each one tended and kept by the best casters the Mainland has to offer, all of them trained and committed to protecting the casting fire at the heart of the ship, the one that maintains the spellwork keeping the Sea flat."

When no one, including Gwyn, responded, Aster continued, speaking as though she were addressing children.

"So, that means even if you can get past the vessels surrounding *The Arcana*—each of which is also loaded with warriors and elite casters—you still need to deal with the fiercest defenses imaginable if you want to reach the casting fire at its center. It's impossible. Actually, it's more impossible than impossible. It's a fantasy to even imagine attacking that vessel and having any success."

When Aster finished, the looks around the table suggested that most people hadn't considered the problem in such detail. The baron's eyes were wider than usual as he stared down at the ship figurine on the map, and even Ravel was looking doubtful.

"Agreed," Gwyn said, looking troubled for the first time that morning. She took a sip of her tea, which looked suspiciously like clear water, and leaned forward on one elbow, peering down at the map. "It is common knowledge that such an attack is both impossible and unthinkable. After all, who could benefit from the Sea breaking its bonds? No sailor would opt for such a thing—their livelihood would be ruined, and who knows if the resultant grasses would even be sailable? No lord, lady, baron, or person with any power could imagine wanting to do such a thing either. The Sea would surely creep inland even as it rose, and many would be forced to choose between living in the Sea itself and dealing with all the attendant dangers thus presented or retreating west."

Gwyn let that hang in the air for a moment before nodding and saying, "Absolutely unthinkable. Which is why neither Faineant nor his lackeys will see it coming."

The wind held up the conversation after that, its whispering and moaning the only sounds as everyone around the table chewed on Gwyn's words. None of the advisors around the table said anything, despite the preposterous suggestion, and Flitch realized they were already on board with this plan. The planning session he'd walked by in the still-dark period of the morning must have been the time when Gwyn convinced them all.

But if they were already behind the plan, why was this meeting happening?

Why did they need the siblings to be convinced?

"Why don't we deal with Faineant's forces on land first?" Idyll asked after a moment.

"Many will die if we do that," Gwyn said, shaking her head. "And solving that problem will not solve our other one." She gestured out at the Sea, where even now the grasses were stirring with movements from below.

"How can you be sure Flitch's book is telling the truth?" Zim asked before grimacing and flicking his eyes toward Flitch. "Sorry, Flitch."

"I trust the book," Gwyn said, nodding at where it rested on the table. "Though you are right to be suspicious. I should apologize now to Flitch. After looking carefully over the book, I tried to send a message in return to Ragged Sarah and her captain Kindred, but nothing I wrote on the pages, no matter the ink or coal I tried, seemed to stick."

What? Flitch stared at Gwyn for a moment before grabbing the book and opening it, past the message from Ragged Sarah to the next page, which had grown old and cracked, the paper yellowed and curling in on itself. The page before it and every one after were still a clean, perfect white, but this one, just this one, seemed to have aged a thousand years overnight.

"Nothing I wrote stayed on the page," Gwyn said, "and before I could try anything else, that happened. I am sorry for attempting this without your leave. Too much is balanced on this decision for me to leave it up to chance, and I didn't think such a thing would occur."

Flitch ran his hands over each blank page following the dead sheet, feeling the racing of his heart slow with each smooth expanse. Why did he care so much about this book? What was it about the worn blue cover that soothed him so?

Images of Quietus—its hands of overlapping leaves, its quiet, steady steps, the thick shadows roiling around it—filled Flitch's mind, and he felt none of the panic that had fired along his muscles as he'd run through those tunnels. Instead, he felt only a kind of emptiness, as though the memories weren't from a day earlier but a year, ten years before. He encountered the horror and terror from a distance, the memories unable to reach him.

Still, the book was a balm in his hand, and every unmarred page was another drink of cool, nourishing water.

"I wonder," Gwyn said, continuing in a tentative voice, "if you might like to respond to Ragged Sarah, Flitch. If, indeed, the book allows you to send a message, it would both soothe the fears of some here and allow us the chance to communicate with someone who may prove to be a valuable ally in our *unthinkable and impossible* scheme."

There it was. The reason why Flitch had been included in this meeting, and he was sure Idyll's, Aster's, and Zim's roles would be made clear soon enough.

"What should I say?" he asked, reaching for the slim length of charcoal Gwyn offered.

"Ask if she's real," Aster said before Idyll reached over and punched her hard in the arm, eliciting a hiss of pain.

"Not a bad idea," Gwyn said, bobbing her head back and forth, "but perhaps too obvious. I would suggest taking her missive seriously and letting her know we would very much like to help, but we may need some aid of our own if they can manage it."

Flitch stared at the blank page for a moment, trying to see his way into the letter, envisioning the words he might write. It took him a long moment, but finally he began.

Ragged Sarah and Captain Greyreach, he wrote before pausing, waiting to see if the page would reject his writing, too. When it didn't curl or crack or yellow in response, he continued.

My name is Flitch o' the Borders. We on the Mainland have seen the monsters, and we are working to break the spellwork keeping the Sea flat. But we need your aid to do this. Can you help us?

Flitch o' the Borders, with the Borders Baron, his children, the Paths Baron, her friend Ravel, and several captains and commanders of our joined forces.

Flitch finished and held a breath, still feeling as though the book would reject his message at any moment. But the words on the page stayed, and he breathed a sigh of relief.

"Let's see it, then!" Gwyn said, gesturing to the book, which Flitch spun around to let everyone else read.

A silence took the table as everyone leaned forward to look over his message.

"A very thorough signature at the end there, Flitchy," Aster said, grinning at him. "Are you sure you didn't want to say a little about where we are? Maybe a few words about the weather? What tea you're drinking?"

"Enough, Aster," the baron rumbled, giving his daughter a stern look before turning to Flitch. "It's excellent, son."

"It is," Idyll agreed, putting a hand on Flitch's shoulder and giving him a smile.

"Indeed," Gwyn said, nodding and turning the page. Flitch thought for a moment that a message would be there waiting for them already, but it was blank.

Gwyn, apparently, had the same hope. She let out a sigh and said, "Flitch, please let me or your father know immediately when you get a response."

Flitch pulled the book back, nodding and saying he would.

"So, now we wait for a person who may or may not exist below the Sea to let us know if our incredibly dangerous and impossible plan can go ahead?" Aster asked, smiling pleasantly.

"How have you not been kicked out of your school yet?" Idyll asked in awe.

"There are more than a few teachers who would love to see that happen," the baron said in his low voice, sounding pained.

"It's because I'm the best caster there and they all know it," Aster said, cocky as ever.

"I hope you are," Gwyn said as if this were exactly what she wanted to hear. "Because our plan proceeds regardless of whether our friends below can help, and for it to happen, we will need to bring all of our special talents to bear. *All* of you."

"I want to say this," the Borders Baron said, breaking in with a look of displeasure. "None of you need to say yes to these things. It is true that an attack must happen, but you have not signed up for service in our guard or fleet, and these roles do not *need* to be filled by you."

Here we go, Flitch thought. *The reason we're here.*

"What your father says is true," Gwyn said, looking at each of the Borders children. "Everyone else here is prepared to do what they must for this plan to work, and that may include giving our lives. It is a possibility that you should be aware of. I would not ask for these things if I did not believe in your ability to do them or if there were another, safer way."

Gwyn paused for a moment, looking around at the others there before sharing a wordless exchange with the Borders Baron, who finally nodded, weary.

"Idyll," she said, "I want you and Ravel to set the Rose on fire."

Idyll froze, and the gasp of air sounded like a dying person's last breath.

"I know, I know," Gwyn said, holding up one hand. "Books are precious and we must safeguard our stories of the past to be the bread of the future and all that—I understand. I want you to just set the top floor on fire. None of the texts on that level are in any danger of being hurt by fire, but Faineant won't care about that. The fire will be out before any real damage is done, and he'll be distracted enough by the ruckus to let us work elsewhere. You'll need to move quickly before you're recognized. You'll be disguised, but you shouldn't depend on that too much. Once you're finished setting the fire, you and Ravel will ride back and help in leading those not taking part in the attack from the house."

Idyll's eyes were wider than Flitch had ever seen them, but Ravel leaned in and said, "It'll be fine. Just a tiny little fire. Nothing will actually be damaged. Nothing of value, anyway."

Of course they were more worried about the fire in the archives than any potential danger from taking part in the assault.

"You have a key to the King's Door?" Idyll asked finally, their voice small and rough.

It was the door leading to the last room in the Rose, the room at the top of the tower where only a few—a very, very few, if Idyll's past statements were true—were allowed to go.

"Yes, yes," Gwyn said, nodding.

"But how?"

"I bought it from a man who cared more for money than for knowledge," she said, shaking her head and frowning. "So, will you do this?"

Idyll nodded and took a gulp of tea, which seemed to satisfy Gwyn, who moved on to Aster.

"Aster, goddess caster among mortals, arcane artist among fingerpainting five-year-olds, I would like you to join my assault on *The Arcana*."

"Yes, absolutely," Aster said, losing her lighthearted bravado for a moment.

"Good! And Zim," Gwyn said, turning again, "you and your prowess with numbers will be most valuable working with my accountants. If we're successful with this plan, we won't be able to stay in this cliffside home anymore, and we'll be moving two households much further inland. Your father has given leave for you to act as the household accountant as we make this move, and I'm hoping you will work with my people to make the transition go as smoothly as possible."

It would be a huge task—coordinating and organizing the supplies and resources and people for such a move. The midnight fleeing of the Borders household had been a chaotic, impulsive thing, driven by the impending attack from Faineant, but this would need to be done with more care.

Zim nodded and said, "I will do this."

"Very good! Then let us move on to how these various pieces will come together," Gwyn said, gesturing now to the map.

"What about me?"

Gwyn had already opened her mouth to speak when Flitch did so first.

"The book, Flitch," his father said, gesturing to the blue-bound tome on the table. "You're communicating with those below."

"My role is to wait for someone to send us a message?" His siblings were off to become vital people in the webwork of this plan, and he was left behind again, waiting for someone to write, waiting for something to happen. So much had changed in just a few days, but there he was again, watching his siblings go off to do important things, to become who they were in the wider world—all while Flitch watched from afar, hoping for news of them.

Flitch listened to himself speak and experienced himself having these feelings as if from far away, marveling with strange peace at the instinctual indignation with which he responded. The anger and frustration, the sadness and hopelessness—all there inside him, but muffled somehow, like rocks carried in a thick sack. He could feel them, but the edges weren't nearly as sharp as they had been.

"It's a very important role!" Gwyn said, looking up with some surprise. "You can communicate with them for us, and that may prove the difference."

A sudden thought struck him, and Flitch said, "You need me on the boat."

"No, Flitch," the baron began, but Flitch pushed on.

"What if Ragged Sarah or Kindred writes back during the assault? What if they can give us some key piece of information right before we attack? You need me on the boat in case we need to contact them at the last moment."

"I . . ." Gwyn began, letting the word trail off as she cut her eyes to the baron, who was shaking his head.

"You are too young for this, Flitch," he said.

"I'm not!" Flitch complained. "And you know I'm right."

"I almost lost you already," the baron said quietly, his brown eyes meeting Flitch's.

"The boy is right, Uthe," Gwyn said, watching Flitch with a calculating gaze but speaking to the baron, matching the low tenderness of his voice. "And I'll keep him safe if I can."

Flitch could see the pain in his father's face as the logic worked on him, pushing his resolve until it broke.

Flitch's distant surge of disbelief in being left out of the plans was already fading by the time his father nodded and said a quiet, defeated "Okay."

It was odd, experiencing the shadow of those old feelings, the rise and fall of them. That same indignation had fired in his gut so many nights, just he and his father left in the house, and his father downstairs, searching—Flitch now knew—for a gift that would never come for him.

Flitch felt now as though he wore clothes fitted for a different him, skin stretched for a slightly different frame, a smile made for another Flitch's face.

He felt *almost* himself, and his complete peace in the face of that fact was only further evidence of it.

"Fantastic," Gwyn said, sitting back in her chair. "It sounds like we have all the pieces we need. Now let's figure out how to put them together."

They talked long into the morning, those at the table all getting a chance to push a figurine or two around on the map, and by the end of it all, they had a plan.

Sarah's next message came as the group was standing to begin preparations for the assault.

> *Flitch,*
>
> *I don't know what help I can give. I am alone now. There is nothing I can do.*
>
> *Ragged Sarah*

CHAPTER EIGHTEEN

Kindred and Sarah stayed behind the wall for a long time, the plurality tied against one of the trees, their clothes tossed into a pile on the ground. Some things are best communicated without words.

When they emerged, holding hands and warming themselves in the slow, gentle heat that comes after such intimacy, they found the Traveling Court breaking from their scavenging to have a meal—dried mushrooms and seasoned roach slivers. The smell was inviting and warm, and Kindred found her stomach murmuring in response as they neared. The mushrooms she'd scavenged on her walk were a distant, digested memory.

"Oh, good, you found her," Jest said, smiling up at Kindred as they approached. "We were getting worried."

"Some of us were getting worried," Fourth-Folly amended, swallowing a mouthful of food. "And some of us were not worried at all." Their smile said they knew exactly where Kindred and Sarah had been, but it shifted into something more open and joyful when they saw the braid of grass clutched in Sarah's free hand. "You caught one? Yes!"

In a display of affection far beyond anything Fourth-Folly had shown up to that moment, they rushed over to Sarah and gave her a hug and a broad smile.

"Lots of dangerous artifacts around here," Awn said, nodding, picking the thread back up. "Not to mention the possibility of another fall. I wondered if we should come looking for you."

"You shouldn't have," Sarah said, smiling at Kindred.

"Sit by me!" Madrigal said, patting the ground on either side of her and smiling up at Kindred and Sarah. They took the bowls offered to them by Wylf and sat.

They talked of small things—bits and nothings they'd found among the wreckage, books and parts of books that were new to the Court, promising areas to search next. No one spoke about Kindred's return, or the Marchess, or the summoned monsters. It lurked behind their every sentence, and Kindred felt the push to bring it up, to ask what she meant to ask, but she waited until the right moment.

"Ah!" Jest sighed, sitting back and setting her bowl beside her. "That was delicious."

Everyone agreed, and into the satisfied silence that followed, Kindred spoke.

"I would like to ask for the Traveling Court's help in stopping my grandmother from killing the people above," she said. The slow, careful entreaties she'd considered had about them the quiet stench of manipulation, the same manipulation and maneuvering she'd done above to manifest her dreams and desires on *The Errant* and in the Once-City.

Instead, she would be direct. She would be clear. She would be honest.

It was Sarah's idea, discussed quietly as they lay together. She showed Kindred the message Flitch had sent and the despairing one she'd sent in return. Kindred wanted to stop the Marchess and had planned to ask the Traveling Court to help, but Sarah showed her how it might be done, and how it might work in concert with those attempting the same goal above.

Jest scrunched up her eyes and considered Kindred's request, making small *hmm* noises as she breathed. Beside her, Wylf continued his silent litany, but a slight nod of his head gave Kindred hope.

Fourth-Folly was the first to speak.

"Why would we do that?" They asked the question with genuine curiosity. "It doesn't matter to us what she does, and we have gotten by down here by letting the other groups of scavengers do what they want and receiving the same grace in return. I don't even think what she's attempting is going to work. And even if it was going to work, and even if we did want to stop her, Tesser Cobb and Lurch would kill us before we could accomplish anything."

Jest looked like she wanted to argue that point, but she said nothing.

"So, why would we do that?"

Even Madrigal seemed swayed by Fourth-Folly's question, a troubled look creasing the smooth lines of her face.

"Because a lot of people will be hurt or killed by this," Kindred said, looking around. "Because even if my grandmother's final goal is a good one, the way we do things is just as important as what we accomplish."

Doubt still lingered on the faces of the Traveling Court.

Kindred took a deep breath.

"And because of the wind," she said, looking from Fourth-Folly to Jest.

Think on the wind, Jest had told them, and Kindred found that she had been thinking of little else since. What did it mean to do good, to *be* good, when you were one note in the world's melody? What was a good life when a person could be nothing more than an empty cathedral built by the hands of everyone and everything they had ever encountered?

If the air in Kindred's lungs was the same air that moved and rustled in the Marchess's, then what song was she meant to sing?

"Because of the wind," Jest said in a hushed, satisfied voice. She nodded. "Yes, I think that is why we all must do this."

"Yeah," Madrigal said, clasping Kindred's hand.

Wylf smiled and said, "The wind."

"I'm not uninterested," Fourth-Folly said, giving Jest's beatific smile a surly glower in return. "But it doesn't answer the question of how we—without weapons or training in the use of weapons—could hope to overcome the Fell Company."

"It is a good question," a voice behind Kindred said, and her body went cold at the sound of it. She turned to find Lurch and Tesser Cobb standing there, weapons drawn, their vessel waiting some distance back. With all the rubble and mess from the Once-City, they'd been able to sneak up on the Traveling Court easily.

"You lied list-lost-list to us," Lurch said, taking a step forward and raising his rusted sword to point at Kindred. "Your grandmother, too-too-too. Right to-to-to her face."

Tesser Cobb ran a hand across his dirt-crusted forehead, grimacing as if all of this were the most awkward, uncomfortable thing he could imagine. He held the short spear in his other hand loose and easy.

"We ran for a bit in that direction you sent us, Kindred," he said, shaking his head, disappointment sounding in his voice. "But there was just no sign of anything."

"Tesser Cobb, put that weapon down right now," Jest said, rising to her feet and glaring at the grimy man.

For a moment, Kindred thought he might do exactly that, but a look of grim resolve crusted over his face and he shook his head.

"I'm sorry about this, Jest, I am. But there's no way around it. Kindred here lied to the Marchess, and we all, I think, understand why—we're not mad about it. But—"

"I! I am mad!" Lurch said, kicking at the ground and looking around with wild eyes. "You lying liar. Sent us snoop-slooping sailing in the wrong direction."

Wylf leapt up suddenly, spooked, perhaps, by Lurch's outburst. He looked around at the Traveling Court, whispering still the name of his pursuer, but under the attention of Lurch's sword point, which rose and moved in Wylf's direction, he sat down again.

"There are some hard feelings, certainly," Tesser Cobb admitted, bobbing his head at Lurch and holding out a hand as if to say *I'll handle this*. "But there need not be any going forward. We make it down here by tending our own gardens, and we can still do that. Lurch and I only need the bones from this crash. We won't get in your way while you scavenge everything else. We'll even let you take a few bones for your ship. We don't want to be unfair or cruel."

Lurch, who had resumed staring around at the Traveling Court, sword clutched tightly in one hand, looked very much as if he did want to be cruel.

Fourth-Folly got to their feet, flat eyes moving between the two Fell men, unimpressed by their weapons but not making any move to attack them.

"There are more of us than you," they said, voice empty and quiet, sinister in a way that raised expectant prickles along Kindred's skin and caused the plants along her hand to pull back into hard curls. "And we have something you don't."

"Your mess-mussed myths," Lurch said, shaking head. "That's nothing."

Fourth-Folly said only "Surprise" and pointed up.

For a moment, the black of the sky remained, uninterrupted and deep.

The first piece of the fall slammed into the concave wall looming over them all, splattering wetly against it. Kindred had time to see it clearly—a length of bone longer than she was tall and thicker than she was wide, swaddled with hunks of bloody meat and thick, spiky fur—before the world around her erupted into chaos.

The ground bloomed with sprays of star-strewn dirt with each impact, a messy, myriad rhythm played by uncoordinated hands beating wildly, throbbing like too many heartbeats in Kindred's head.

People moved around her, Fourth-Folly leaping forward and tackling Lurch in his moment of surprise, Wylf and Jest closing on Tesser Cobb. Madrigal was a small, fleeting shape, dodging and diving under the shelter offered by the Once-City ruins. An errant curiosity floated through Kindred's mind, completely at odds with the madness of the moment: was this Madrigal's first experience with violence? If so, it was better for her to hide herself.

Sarah leapt up beside Kindred, her blades out and ready, and she joined Fourth-Folly in their attack on Lurch, who had fallen back after having his nose bloodied by Folly. He was now running flat out for his vessel, sword still clutched in his hand. Fourth-Folly was close behind him, though they had no weapon with which to attack him, and Lurch stopped every few paces to menace the air behind him with his blade, keeping Folly at bay.

Kindred pushed herself up, feeling that familiar bone-deep fear when violence erupted around her. As keeper, it had been her job to ignore any fighting as long as she could, focusing only on the hearthfire and its maintenance. While other sailors learned to wield a sword or throw a knife as a matter of course, hearthfire keepers were told to focus on the fire, to rely on their crewmates to defend them should an attack come.

A chunk of carcass hurled dirt skyward just beside Kindred, stinging her eyes and blinding her until she had rubbed them clean, the shouts and *boom*s rending the air and screaming panic along her bloodstream. When she could finally see again, Lurch was engaged with Sarah and Folly at his vessel, swinging down at them from the deck, and Tesser Cobb had retreated to the Traveling Court's vessel, harried by Jest, Wylf, and Awn, who looked to be too much for him to handle.

Kindred ran for Ragged Sarah, grabbing the only thing she could think of possibly using to aid their side: Sarah's plurality.

The creature seemed to intuit her path, because it shot out in front of Kindred, almost dragging her at one point in its eagerness to go faster.

It was impossible to dodge the falling remains—they came too fast and too silently, and so Kindred ignored them as best she could, running in a straight line to the fight at the Fell ship.

Lurch laughed from the deck, fearless and cocksure. As Kindred neared, she saw why.

Fourth-Folly had wounds along their neck and abdomen, and one of their arms hung limp and useless, dangling around as they dodged Lurch's attacks and looked for a way in.

Sarah had stopped fighting altogether. Her knives were gone, and she stood a little behind Fourth-Folly, swaying slightly, feet spread apart to stay standing. Blood soaked her clothes, and her face had gone deathly pale.

Collisions bombarding the ground around them, and Lurch's mocking laughter cutting through the noise, Kindred watched Sarah stumble and fall.

With a wide, arcing cut, Lurch forced Fourth-Folly back, and he took his chance, leaping from the deck of the ship toward Sarah, his smile a wicked, rotten curve mirroring his sword. He was going to kill her. He was going to kill Sarah.

Kindred rushed forward and pulled as hard as she could, muscles straining and joints popping with the effort. She used her forward momentum and leaned into it, yanking at the braid of grass, imagining the creature on the end of it like a weight swung up and at Lurch. Perhaps a ravenous, mad creature of nightmare would emerge, something to make the Marchess's monsters seem banal and soft in comparison. A many-toothed, many-mouthed horror ready to devour Lurch slowly, painfully.

She felt the plurality resist for a moment before giving in, and when it exploded from the ground, it was preceded by an explosion of dirt darker than anything on the surface of the Seafloor, soil thick and soft as cloth, pulled up from some stratum well below where Kindred put her feet.

The plurality collapsed into form with a bright, sharp *snap* as it emerged, and for the barest, thinnest splinter of a moment, gone almost before it was there, Kindred saw its multiplicity—endless forms embodied and extinguished, constantly shifting and changing, existing myriad and wild, a multitude and a singularity, perfectly at peace in the many forms of its being.

A stab of regret cut through Kindred as she saw this many-being rise as a bounded, completed, finished thing, a creature lithe and long, packed with short, bristly fur glowing a burnt orange. Eyes wide and curious ran in a line from the center of its triangular face to its tail, spaced evenly and surrounded by whorls of that hypnotizing fur.

Big, well-padded paws splayed into the air beneath it, the fur wet and dripping a dark black substance. Its tail, too, was tipped by the inky liquid, and it traced a pattern behind it through the air, droplets hanging without falling, congealing together into something that might have been a map or a word or a picture—it was impossible to tell.

The plurality—no longer plural—collided with Lurch, its front paws landing on his chest and pushing him back, reversing his leap and hurling him back onto the deck of the ship, where he went sprawling with a cry of shock and fear.

With a howling, harrowing cry, the plurality launched itself up from the Fell ship, climbing higher and higher and leaving only the slowly evaporating trail of its work—*its art*, Kindred thought, remembering how Jest talked of the Silent Gods above.

Lurch's own screams grew pained as he sat up, the two huge paw prints, each made with that same inky black material, were smoking and burning on his clothes, and he wriggled and rolled to get them off, revealing faded imitations of the plurality's feet on his chest, too, the skin red and puckered and actively blistering.

But Kindred wasn't done. She looked quickly to Sarah, finding her eyes half-shut and rolling back in her head, breathing labored and loud, before reaching out with her mind to find the slow-burning hearthfire on the Fell ship's deck, finding its stentorian song, so like the ones built by Madrigal.

Burn, Kindred told the fire, a command and an entreaty and a hope all at once. *Please burn.*

She let her voice follow the steps of Madrigal's songs, clear in her memory, the simple and symmetrical melodies easy to recreate and powerful in their plainness.

With each rise in tone and tempo, Kindred begged the fire to burn, and it heard her.

Lurch rose from the deck, bare-chested and bawling a wordless shriek of anger, and behind him, a shadow wreathed in flame, the hearthfire rose too.

Fourth-Folly screamed their own battle cry at him, a wicked, bloody smile following it, and that, perhaps, was enough for Lurch to sense his doom.

He turned, the rusted sword in his hand falling in a clatter, as the hearth-fire, a fiery wave, perfectly symmetrical, drawn with a steady, even hand, collapsed onto him with the sound of a great inhalation, as though it was sucking up all the air, all the wind below the Sea.

Kindred let the song die on her lips. The fire would burn itself out, and Sarah needed her.

"Help me!" she shouted over her shoulder as she kneeled down beside Sarah, whose breath had gone raspy. Fourth-Folly was there in an instant, and together they brought Sarah over to the shelter of a half-wall that had fallen on some loose rubble. It would give them some protection from the fall, which seemed to be slowing but was still dropping corpses in intermittent waves.

"Kindred," Sarah said, her voice quiet, weak. "That bastard stabbed me." She gestured down to one side, where the wound continued to bleed.

"It's going to be okay," Kindred said, ripping off a sleeve from her robe and balling it up into a mass she could press against Sarah's side. "You're going to be okay."

"I'm not," Sarah said, shaking her head and giving her a thin smile. "They don't have anything down here that could heal a wound like this."

"We have a few things in the ship," Fourth-Folly said, hissing with pain at their own wounds. One arm still hung limply at their side.

"I'm done," Sarah said, her voice hardening. She looked at Kindred, eyes going wide for a moment. "Don't bury me among the Once-City ruins. I hated this place."

"I'm not burying you anywhere," Kindred said. "You're not—"

The wooden half-wall under which they crouched slammed down on Kindred and Folly's shoulders in a roar of sound as a chunk of viscera fell onto it. Fourth-Folly's scream of pain cut the air for a moment before they fainted away, leaving Kindred holding up the battered wall on her own, the rubble that had supported it pushed away or fallen apart.

"It's okay," Sarah whispered. Her voice was so weak, so quiet. "Go stop your grandmother."

"*No*," Kindred said, gritting her teeth against the weight of the wall. "Not without you."

Kindred looked around for something, anything to help, and found a pair of eyes staring out at her from under a portion of the Once-City's central staircase, the wood busy with the carvings ranging all around it.

"Madrigal!" she shouted, gesturing with one hand. "Come here! Quick!"

The young girl's eyes were all fear, and she looked as though she wanted no part in anything outside of her shelter, but still she pushed herself up into a crouch and, after a quick glance around, ran.

She moved in quick bursts, racing between bits of shelter in a zigzag rush, until finally she slid under the wall.

"What do you . . ." she began, but stopped as she saw Fourth-Folly and Sarah, their wounds ghastly and garish.

"Madrigal," Kindred said, trying and failing to keep her voice even as the half-wall pushed down on her. "I need you to drag them out of here so I can let the wall down. Hurry. I can't hold it much longer."

Madrigal stared, her young, wide eyes empty of thought or understanding. She stared at Fourth-Folly, whose breath was shallow enough to be almost impossible to see.

Kindred took a breath, letting the prairie wind fill her lungs, and when she spoke, it was calmer than before. Not totally calm, but calmer.

"Madrigal, I need you right now. They're going to be okay, but we need to get them out of here. Can you help me?"

Madrigal pulled her eyes up from Fourth-Folly with an effort, gulping once as she gave a nervous nod of her head.

"Thank you," Kindred said, grunting with effort. Sharp pain had begun to lance down her back, radiating out from the point of contact with the wall. "Fourth-Folly is unconscious, but they're going to be okay. I need you to grab them under the arms and pull them out from here. It will be hard, but you don't need to go far. Can you do it?"

Madrigal nodded again, and this time she moved, sliding tentative hands under Folly's arms and setting the whole of her body at a backward angle, struggling through each step but managing to get Fourth-Folly out. Kindred's back seized and her legs shook.

"Me next," Sarah said, her eyes bare slits. She hissed with poorly concealed pain as Madrigal dragged her backward, step by agonizing step. The young girl whispered a quick-syllable litany of "sorry, sorry, sorry, sorry" as she pulled.

Kindred let out a gasp of relief and fell to her knees beside Sarah as she slithered out from under the wall, slivers embedding themselves in her shoulders and neck as she did. The wall crashed down and settled with a clatter.

"What now?" Madrigal asked, crouching down, tears etching paths through the dirt and grime on her face.

Taking a pained breath, Kindred looked around until she found a length of cloth big enough to fit both Folly and Sarah on. She retrieved it, gasping at the effort it took to move and wanting so badly to drop to the ground and rest her aching body.

"Help me get them on," she said, flattening out the swath of cloth she'd found, something closer to the fabric of a sail but unfinished, its edges ragged and loose. Together, while the ground still occasionally erupted around them, Kindred and Madrigal moved Fourth-Folly and Sarah, who had lost her grip on consciousness, onto the cloth.

"Pull," Kindred muttered, wrapping the corner of the cloth around her hand and yanking it forward. Madrigal joined her, pulling with the whole of her body, and slowly, so slowly, they pulled the two members of their crew, of their family, around the shell and back to that quiet place behind it where it had been almost no time since Kindred and Sarah had walked out of the trees, hand in hand, tuned together.

Now Kindred could barely stagger, and Sarah's breath had gone deathly quiet, her face set at an unnatural angle, as if she were looking up at Kindred, plaintive and curious. *Where are we going, love? Will you lay me to rest away from this place as I asked? A nice, empty field, surrounded by the sentinels of the Sea, my cold body kept company by those many-beings of the dark? Well, Kindred? Well, keeper?*

"There," Kindred grunted, raising her free hand to gesture at one of the small plants—barely chest-high—seeded by the Once-City's crash, a plant Kindred knew well. It had healed her hand, had healed Sarah after their violent arrival into the Once-City.

Buried deep in the Forest, the Healing Glade had been home to just one plant—the great shepherd scrub, grown impossibly large. Here, though, as if spread and scattered by the fall and crash, the plant had multiplied, springing up small, spherical bushes throughout the area, ten or twenty of them at least, each branch and shoot glittering brightly with thorns and small buds that would soon flower into delicate white blooms.

"Are we burying them?" Madrigal asked, horror running through her voice.

"No," Kindred said, turning to look at the younger girl before flicking her eyes to Sarah. "You need to stop talking about that. I'm not burying anyone."

Kindred continued to pull, stopping only when they reached the tallest of the shepherd scrubs. She slumped down beside it and hooked her hands under Sarah's armpits, dragging her forward until her body lay still and silent beneath the plant.

"What—" Madrigal began after a moment, but Kindred put up a hand, quieting her.

She leaned forward, staring hard at the plant, willing it to move, to loose those healing vines.

"Please," she whispered. "Please, please, please, *please.*"

Sarah had not moved in a long time, and Kindred placed a hand on her chest, feeling for the rise and fall of breath and finding . . . nothing.

Nothing stirred in her lungs.

Nothing.

Kindred didn't move, didn't breathe, waiting for something to happen, anything to happen, for Sarah to move or cough, for the plant to reach out its healing vines and do its work.

Nothing.

Anguish like a wave crashed over her, and Kindred was screaming, her mouth wide enough to hurt, her voice ragged. Tears puckered her eyes and coursed down her face, and she had balled both hands into fists in Sarah's blood-soaked shirt, squeezing hard enough to send rivulets of red running down her knuckles.

A melody sounded in her mind, one as familiar as her own voice and welling with such sadness that Kindred was rocked back by the force of it. It was the song she'd heard upon landing down there, the song she'd heard on the wind while staring up at the Silent Gods and their strange, purposeless work, the song she'd been hearing her whole life on the Sea.

Emanating from no single point Kindred could see, the melody grew in cycles, voices joining together in counterpoint, harmony leading to discord and then back to harmony, singing of life and loss, of a sunrise like grace itself. It was a song Kindred had heard her first day on *Revenger* and every day since, a song that twinned with the hearthfire's melody and waited beneath the wind's moaning, patient and eternal.

It was the song of the Forever Sea itself, a lyric sung by bluestem and blazing star, by catchweed and compass plant, by sky above and soil below, by prairie rose and ragwort and windflower and prairie smoke.

A lyric of green and gold, tasting of thick honeyed sunshine and buzzing like a bee on the tongue.

Like an old friend, the song of the prairie returned to Kindred, sounding out from the great glowing plants standing their slow guard out in the darkness, and with it came their light, moving in rivers rhizomatic below the surface of the ground and floating in motes through the air itself, waves of the Sea's magic surrounding Kindred.

Along her hand, the shoots of golden grass rose with a gentle wave, stretching into the light-suffused air and spreading suddenly up Kindred's arm, no longer a tiny patch clustered along her wrist but a row, a field, a Sea of grasses erupting from the skin all along her arm, a few strands bursting excitedly into bloom.

Sing, the Sea said.

And Kindred did, letting the wordless melody of the Forever Sea lift from her, voice ragged and rough and perfect.

As if she were keeping the hearthfire, Kindred reached out into those rivers of light, feeling the Sea's magic against her fingers and palms, running through the grasses growing from her arm. It was like holding the wind, and Kindred wept anew at it.

Carefully, tentatively, Kindred directed the light down into Sarah, her hands becoming the vines that the shepherd scrub could not release, her body becoming the conduit. She placed glowing hands on Sarah's body, spreading her fingers and feeling the stillness of Sarah's body again, no longer a cold, empty vessel but a garden, holding tight to its bounty until given permission by the sun's rays.

Kindred sang love and Sarah returned, eyes blinking open, mouth dragging in a ragged breath—another note in the melody of the Sea. The wound at her side burst with new growth, tiny plants of all kinds and colors filling in the absence there, sliding roots below skin and wrapping them around bone, another webwork of life spreading delicate throughout Sarah's body.

"Kindred," Sarah said, not a question or a statement. Simply an utterance, like a breath huffed out at the rapture of a sunset or a chill wind tracing across an exposed neck.

Kindred slid her hands up around Sarah's face, cupping her jaw, and bent to give her a kiss, soft and long.

"You're okay," Kindred whispered. "You're going to be okay."

"Did you—" Sarah began, but Kindred was already moving.

"I'll tell you—I will. But I have to help Fourth-Folly."

The song in the air was fading, the Sea's gift and aid waning, and it took Kindred's focus and care to capture the rest of it for Folly, working the light deep into their body, sending the luminous lyric on a fanfare to stitch muscle and bridge bone.

Madrigal crouched beside Kindred while she worked, and when Fourth-Folly gasped awake, the young girl threw herself onto them, crying and shouting her joy into Fourth-Folly's shoulder.

Another note in the song of the Sea.

"What happened?" Sarah asked, pushing herself up carefully. "I thought..."

"The Sea," Kindred said, gesturing to the plants around them and unsure of what else she could say. It wanted life; that much she understood. It yearned for it and, for the listening ear, it sang of how to find it.

A shout behind them drew all of their attention to the edge of the shell, where Tesser Cobb appeared, fleeing and chased by Jest, Wylf, and Awn, all of whom had found ragtag weapons—wooden beams and metal poles—and were holding them out in threatening, if inexperienced, ways.

Tesser had lost his spear somewhere and had acquired a bloodied face in its place, one eye swollen shut and a thick crust of blood mixing with the dirt around his nose.

"I'm sorry, I'm sorry, I'm sorry!" he was shouting, voice pitched high.

Jest had lost her genteel composure. The hair of one braid had begun to unravel, and long, ropy strands whipped against her back and shoulders. A cut on her neck gleamed in the light, and she ran with a slight limp in one leg.

Awn and Wylf seemed mostly unhurt outside of a few scratches and bruises.

Tesser Cobb reached the trees and kept running, still screaming his apologies to the air, but his pursuers stopped as they saw Kindred and the others.

"Where's Lurch?" Jest asked, cutting a glance to Tesser Cobb's retreating form disappearing through the trees.

"Gone," Fourth-Folly said, shaking their head and sitting up. They flexed and stretched their arm, staring at the layer of dark wood spanning the space between their shoulder and elbow, the grains sparkling with soft white light.

"And what happened here?" Awn asked, looking around at the four of them before he saw the shepherd scrub under which Sarah still lay. Understanding gleamed in his eyes as he looked between the plant and Sarah and Fourth-Folly. "Oh," he said, nodding.

Kindred let him think that it had been just another healing from the plant. There would be time later to clarify. Or there wouldn't, but either way, she needed to move.

"I need to get back to the Fell camp," she said, pushing herself up. "The Marchess is still summoning those creatures. We . . ."

She trailed off, her eyes unfocusing for a moment as she looked beyond where Jest, Awn, and Wylf stood, each of them watching her with uncertainty.

Wylf's lips did not move in their normal frantic whisper, and Kindred wondered how long he had left off his focus on the Windrake. The whole fight? Intermittently?

Behind him, moving with steady, deliberate steps, as though each one were a thing to be considered, wondered at, and executed, was the Windrake.

It looked like a person—a child, barely taller than Madrigal, with thin, willowy arms and legs. It wore no clothing, and its body was covered in glittering scales and patches of silver-blue fur, the hair just long enough to curl and wave into a soft cloud that shifted and moved around its limbs.

The Windrake did not walk around the chunks and detritus of the Once-City. It did not leap light over rubble and walls or step around jagged rocks. It walked *through* the crashed remains—thick wooden poles and piles of rocks and heaps of indeterminate ruins whisping away to smoke and shadow at its touch.

Kindred watched in horror as it stepped through a length of wood that had been a mast at one point, the thick pole tensing and then, as if solidity had been a farce it had maintained until this moment, dispersing in a languorous weave of smoky tendrils.

Worst of all, worse than anything imaginable, were its eyes, set deep into its too-small skull in a face that had no nose, no ears, nothing but cold coal-red eyes fixed on Wylf and a mouth that looked torn into its skin, the lips asymmetrical and hanging slightly open, the skin along them ragged and bloody.

Wordless, Kindred pushed herself up and forward, grabbing Wylf by the shoulder and turning him around to see the diminutive figure's approach.

A gasp of terror coughed up from his lungs before the Windrake stopped, going totally still. It was not like a statue, which might move in the imagination or through force from the outside world. A statue might have been moved once and would move again, would give way to time's slow, certain dissolution.

The Windrake simply stopped, and Kindred could not imagine it moving ever again. More likely that the great grass boles standing in the darkness shift and move. Even her memory of its steps grew murky, and a growing part of her wondered if it had ever moved at all.

Only its eyes gave truth to her memories. Its eyes, which continued to follow Wylf as he moved, staring with an intensity like nothing Kindred had ever witnessed. It was not rage or anger in its eyes. If she had to say, Kindred might have thought it was something closer to love, and it scared her.

"Yes, we're coming, yes," Jest said, her gaze locked on the Windrake, her hands seeking and finding Wylf, whom she began to push away. "But we will need to commandeer the Fell vessel. Tesser Cobb, villain and coward that he is, destroyed the hearthfire basin on ours. It will take some time to repair."

"That's not going to work," Fourth-Folly said, keeping their eye on the Windrake as well. The whole group had begun to shuffle away, each of them staring at the uncanny, still being as if the force of their collective gazes could hold it in place.

"Why?"

"Kindred set their ship on fire."

"Oh."

"We could run back."

"It's a long way to run."

The frantic planning might have continued, but Wylf separated from the group, all of whom had clutched hands or reached out to grab on to arms or shoulders.

He stepped away from them, facing his pursuer, whispering its name to himself, and he began to walk toward it.

"Wylf! *Wylf!*" hissed Jest, and Fourth-Folly made a grab for his shoulder, but he shrugged them off, shaking his head.

Like an eerie imitation of the Windrake, Wylf took slow steps forward, ignoring the calls and hissed entreaties from the rest of the Court. His feet dragged as if he moved against their will, spreading dirt with each step.

Only when he was close enough to touch the Windrake did he stop, staring at it up close for a long time before moving around it, inspecting it up and down. How many years had it been since he'd seen the creature and been seen by it? How long had it lived in his mind, a constant companion to his every thought?

Kindred had imagined that he would have dreaded this moment, would have run screaming the Windrake's name from this place, but Wylf was fascinated by his pursuer, and as he crossed around behind it, putting the Windrake between him and the rest of the Court, his smile shone in the light of the Seafloor.

He reached out a few times, almost touching the Windrake, but he couldn't bring himself to.

The rest watched until he finished, stepping back around the inert form and leading the Traveling Court back around the shell, where one vessel was mostly burned away and the other would not sail.

"Are you okay?" Fourth-Folly asked Wylf.

"Windrake," he said, nodding, the word whispering out through his grin.

"What are we going to do?" Madrigal asked.

"I can take a look at the basin," Kindred said, but Jest was already shaking her head.

"It needs to be replaced," she said.

A moment of silence, filled only by Wylf's continued whispering, followed.

"We don't have time for that," Sarah said. She was holding out her book, which she'd managed to keep during the fight. A new message from Flitch glittered on the page. It said only: *Where are you? We're going to begin the attack. We need your help. Some distraction. Something. Anything.*

"It's too far," Kindred said, shaking her head. She'd walked for what? A day? Longer than a day? Time was a thick, sludgy thing down there, hard to differentiate and break apart into easy increments. She had walked. She had slept. She had eaten. She had walked more. How many times had she repeated that cycle? She couldn't remember. There were no barriers down here, no walls that stood, no here and there.

Only now. Only the Sea.

"I'll start work on the basin," Fourth-Folly said, walking forward. "Kindred, help me. We'll do it as fast as we can. It's the best we have."

"No." This was from Sarah, and Kindred grinned to hear her voice, so alive, so full of her again. "I have an idea."

"It is . . . unconventional," Jest said, holding the braided rein in her hands and staring down at the straps on the inside of her shield into which her feet had slid. A repurposed shield repurposed again, given new life with each need.

"*Very* unconventional," said Fourth-Folly, who smiled as they said it.

"It will work," Sarah said. She moved and spoke with renewed vigor now. When she had been healed by the plant in the Once-City, Sarah had been given small flowers, like gems, along the length of one leg.

Now, though, the healing had suffused the whole of her body, and the gifts from the Sea were everywhere on her: thin tufts of burnt red grasses tracing her jaw and disappearing down her neck, tiny seedpods beading the lines of both ears, vines flowering with tiny green and grey blooms swaying in her hair. There were more growths along the rest of her body, Kindred guessed.

She hoped there would be time to find and examine them later.

Kindred looked down at her own feet, tied tightly into two thin wooden slats, like long shoes angling out and up from her feet. *They're like little ships*, Sarah had said, excited, as she tied the knots to secure Kindred's feet.

"Like little ships," Kindred muttered to herself. "Just little ships."

"Yeah," Sarah said, nodding and grinning. She had only been able to scavenge a single piece of wood for herself, wider and thicker than the others. Jest, Wylf, Fourth-Folly, Madrigal, and Awn all had shields from the Traveling Court's ship. Awn and Madrigal sat in theirs, holding tightly to the reins. The others stood.

Jest looked around, her eyes wide with a mixture of excitement and fear, before muttering, "Oh, I think I'll sit, too." She settled herself into the dip of her shield, working one leg through the straps there, and nodded at Sarah. "I'm as ready as I'm likely to get."

After Sarah had proposed her idea, and after the debate in which they all quickly realized it was their best and only hope to reach the Marchess quickly, Fourth-Folly had explained the commands and movements needed to steer the pluralities.

"Although they seem to have a good idea of where you want to go," they'd said at the end with a shake of their head and a shrug. "I wonder sometimes if all the phrases and gestures we do to control them aren't more for us."

And that seemed true, because as soon as Jest said she was ready—the rest had been set and ready for some time—the pluralities moved, straining at their reins for a moment as if to ease their passengers into the movement, before taking off, running or leaping or flying or swimming below the ground at great speeds. Sensing, perhaps, the urgency of the Traveling Court, the pluralities pulled each person and their tiny ship or ships faster than Kindred had ever sailed on or in the Sea.

Once she found her balance, and after a few near-falls, Kindred found it exhilarating to cut through the Sea on her own feet, every bump and dip in the ground sending echoes up through her legs.

Once they navigated out of the Once-City fall area, the Sea opened up, and so, too, did the pluralities, weaving a frantic dance forward, rising near enough to the surface to send sprays of dirt up in arcing ridges, showering their riders.

Kindred laughed aloud, letting the joy of this moment lift her on its shoulders, knowing what lay ahead would be difficult regardless of the outcome.

Sarah's laughter joined Kindred's, and soon Awn was laughing too, and Madrigal, and all of them, even Wylf, who crowed the name of his pursuer to the sky, his voice buoyed up by his rolling, rich laughter.

They crossed the Seafloor in an ecstasy of movement and sound, their joy a bright splash against the grand stateliness of the grass towers holding up the world above.

Kindred thought of the wind, and of Sarah, and of the melody behind all things.

CHAPTER NINETEEN

The combined forces of Borders and Paths took the day and night to prepare, and though Gwyn and Flitch's father both claimed they needed the time to prepare their people and gather supplies, it was clear that both were waiting and hoping for a different message from Ragged Sarah.

They would attack at dawn regardless of whether Ragged Sarah wrote back with better news.

In the bustle of activity that afternoon and evening, Flitch found himself unoccupied, his only job to wait for a more hopeful message. He'd written back immediately, urged on by those at the planning table—a few lines begging her for some help, anything. *Don't worry about the creatures,* he wrote, *we just need a distraction.*

The empty page was his only answer.

Idyll and Ravel planned with the few guards who would join them in their mission to set the Rose on fire, tracing fingers over city maps as they considered best routes to and from or argued over numbers of guards to wait outside or go in as faux-librarians. Despite the promise of violence and possibly death should any single part of their plans fail, Idyll looked excited as Flitch peered into the room at them.

Aster had disappeared into Gwyn Gaunt's garden with the other casters, her eyes going wide as the man beside her talked through the various species they were about to harvest in preparation for their attack.

Even Zim was spirited away almost immediately after the meeting on the Sea Deck, already heatedly discussing timetable arrangements for the collected houses with the other bookkeepers from Paths.

Flitch stayed out on the Sea Deck for most of the morning, watching the vessels moving about the wide harbor, surprising himself by remembering the names of their crews along with the captains and ship names. Through the longsight he watched vessels crest green waves, sails billowing out—most bearing the royal sigil and King Faineant's colors, though a few boasted Rivers colors, too.

Some harvested the small patches of plants available so close to the coast, but most were either setting off for or returning from longer haul harvest runs. *The Arcana* floated further out, surrounded by two protective vessels. It was too far out to be much more than a vague shape in the longsight's glass, but it would be bristling with casters and keepers, all of whom were entrusted with the Mainland's most precious task.

Aster had once described to Flitch how the spellwork on *The Arcana* functioned. Unlike the now-burned island of Arcadia, which had a much smaller stretch of grasses to keep flat and could do so from a stable, central point on the island itself, the Mainland maintained huge swaths of flattened, controlled grasses. The upkeep of the spellwork needed to keep such a massive portion of the Sea in check required a mobile source, and the result was *The Arcana*—a double-hulled vessel with a massive hearthfire in its belly, fed constantly with a complex mixture of plants and bone and tended by a rotating crew of hearthfire keepers who tinkered with the spellwork like a captain fiddling with her sails, watching for any sign of inefficiency or imperfection.

More than the facts about *The Arcana*, though, Flitch remembered Aster's awestruck expression as she'd described it to him, the way her eyes widened and lifted from his face, as if seeing it there behind him. The way her hands had moved as if she were one of the keepers, reaching into the vast fire to tend the ever-burning structure there. He heard her voice in his head with such clarity that he looked around for a moment, sure that she was standing nearby, but no, she had left already.

Strange, he thought.

He reached back in his memory—an act unfamiliar to him until then, living as he so often did in heroic imaginings and wonder-filled futures—and found the moments of his life waiting for him there, clear and rich, each interaction or experience perfectly captured. He let them slide before his eyes, leaving behind the wide view of the Sea for a memory of his father lifting Flitch up onto his shoulders. It was Flitch's fifth birthday, and though he saw the cracked plates holding up the food, the dust and dirt collecting in the corners of the room, the memory shone with such bright happiness that none of that mattered.

Flitch watched himself screaming with joy, saw the faces of his siblings, their eyes crinkled in laughter, heard the low, rumbling chuckle of his father. Wind from the prairie encircled him with soft arms as he fell deeper and deeper into the memory, examining every part of it, every stretch of skin and smile, every stray movement of a hand lifting a cup, every word spoken.

Happiness lurked in every line and glow and smile and phrase, and yet it all felt somehow soft to Flitch, hard to grasp and harder to hold on to. Like food that has begun to lose its taste or the sun's light feathered and dimmed by slow-moving clouds, the memory carried an echo of its jubilance, so close to the truth that Flitch might have missed it, had he been paying less attention. But it was there, a sadness braided subtly into the joy.

The memories were like favorite clothes that no longer fit him, their every seam and stretch a reminder of who he was and could never be again.

It should have been sad, and on some distant level, Flitch understood that and even felt a vague swelling of it. But the joy of the memory and the melancholy in knowing it would never return were in a locked room, and he no longer had the key. Or perhaps he was the one in the room, the lock turned by a leaf-laid hand.

Not knowing what else to do, Flitch spent the afternoon and evening writing to Sarah. It began with him rereading Sarah's entries and his own, running a finger across the phrases and letting them live on his breath in quiet whispers.

He waited for her reply, thinking his way into her world, using every line from her short responses like a ladder, lowering himself down one word at a time until he could picture Ragged Sarah and Kindred, could imagine them moving through the darkness below, a secret held underneath the world.

And soon he was writing to them, telling them of his siblings, his father, the barony and the King and their attack, but always it came back to his family. The memories that glowed like burnished statues in his mind, untouchable and beautiful, came to life on the page, and Flitch lost himself in it, barely aware of the light changing from golden glow to evening dim to dusk pale as he wrote.

"Flitch!"

Idyll's surprised gasp broke Flitch's reverie, and he looked up from the page packed with his tall, scrunched handwriting to find Idyll staring down at him, the sun's light from the nearby window completely gone and replaced with cold starlight, itself not enough to light the pages of the book.

"You're glowing . . ."

Flitch's skin illuminated the page, the strange light picking him out of the darkness like a candle. Idyll stared down, confused and concerned, at a patch of Flitch's arm that was bleeding the faintest wispy curls of light. Idyll had seen the change in his skin after he'd come out of the labyrinth, but he had not been glowing like this then.

Was it the memories that turned him into a torch? Or was it the remembering? The thing or the act?

He wasn't sure, and either way, he was fading now, and soon they looked at one another in the darkness.

"What are you doing out here?" Idyll asked, looking down with some suspicion at the book in his hands.

"Just writing," Flitch said, tucking the now-closed book under one arm.

"Dinner is almost over," Idyll said finally, their voice emerging with a slow, uncertain cadence, as though they were feeling their way into the conversation. "I guess we forgot to come and get you. I just realized you weren't there at the end when they brought out dessert. It's one of your favorites."

Idyll frowned, thought, and then said, "Honeyed apples. That's what it was. I looked around and thought, 'I bet Flitch is enjoying these.' But you weren't there."

They shook their head and looked back at him.

"What are you doing out here?"

"Writing," Flitch said, taking his turn at being confused now. He held up the book. "You asked me that already."

"Of course." Idyll blinked at him. "Sorry. There's just so much happening right now. Are you coming to eat or not?"

Flitch nodded and stood, following his sibling back down the hallway and into a room rich with excitement and nerves, the ballroom transformed into a great mess hall bubbling with anxious chatter and too-loud laughter. The attack and the flight of the morning weighed heavy on the shoulders of everyone present.

Idyll moved into the mess of that room with ease, nodding at friends new and old, calling out across the tables and grinning in response. Ravel waved them over to his table, where Gwyn Gaunt was in the middle of telling a story of a day she spent on Arcadia evading the authorities there. A susurrus of constant laughter accompanied the tale, and Flitch smiled instinctually to hear it, drawing a curious look from Gwyn as he and Idyll walked by.

Flitch followed in Idyll's wake, sliding by mostly unseen and forgotten, thinking of Idyll in the hallway asking him twice what he was doing, the sleepy confusion underlying their voice. They were always so certain in their speech and thought, measured and careful. It was odd to see them so befuddled.

"Flitch!" Aster reached across the table to put a hand on his arm as he sat down. "Where have you been?"

She sat beside Zim, whose food lay forgotten on the plate, pushed aside to make room for the detailed tables he was working at, bottom lip caught between his teeth as he concentrated.

Farther down the table, the Borders Baron was in conversation with a few of the Paths and Borders advisors, ignoring Gwyn's increasingly dramatic retelling a few seats away.

"I got you some dinner, Flitch," Ravel said, pushing the loaded plate across the table toward him. "I'm sorry to not have gotten you before we started."

"Ravel apologizes for everything," Idyll explained, putting a hand on Ravel's arm and smiling around. "Even things that aren't his fault. It's adorable."

"*So* adorable," Aster said around a mouthful of the apples, sarcasm dripping from her lips like the honey from the dessert. Idyll gave her an arch look but said nothing.

The conversation grew animated and joyful, and even the barbs from Aster were delivered with tenderness. They sheltered against the change dawn would bring, drawing close inside the protection of good food, good friends, good stories, and hope for better.

Aster described how she and a few friends had swapped out one of the casting masters' stores of bluestem with switchgrass, knowing that this particular master had grown careless in his advancing years. Speaking in the stutter of one barely holding back her own laughter, Aster told of this master's attempts to demonstrate a double-fire casting in which the caster draws the energies from two hearthfires. Unfortunately, the spell went terribly wrong and he lit one wall of the classroom on fire. By the end of the tale, Aster had reduced herself to joyful tears, and the rest of them were laughing sympathetically at her laughter.

Idyll and Ravel told the story of their meeting, this time in more detail, each sharing their perspective on that morning when they'd first seen one another. It was a quiet, sweet thing, listening to them go back and forth, telling the story to each other as much as if not more than to the others at the table.

Every tale felt like an invitation to come in from the cold, and Flitch watched the others eagerly accepting it, stoking the fire of that little community against the chill of the night. They would think on this night tomorrow as they anxiously prepared for whatever their tasks were, and if they lived, they would think on it afterward.

Flitch pushed the food on his plate around, waiting for any of it to seem appetizing. Outside of tea on the Sea Deck, had he eaten or drunk anything? He didn't think so, but he couldn't bring himself to eat any of the food on the plate in front of him, even the generous helping of honeyed apples there. Perhaps it was the imminent promise of tomorrow, but he wasn't so sure.

The stories at the table and the warmth they created had that same distant feeling he'd been experiencing before. He felt like an outsider staring in through a window, watching the fire flicker in the hearth and unable to feel its heat. Seeing words spoken but unable to hear them.

This is my gift, Flitch thought, looking down at the book from Quietus. *And it has come with a price.*

The night was rich, and it lost its revelers and rememberers one by one, two by two to rest's promise.

"Don't stay up too late," the Borders Baron said, putting a heavy hand on Flitch's shoulder as he excused himself.

"I won't," Flitch lied, nodding and watching his father walk off, still in conversation with guards and advisors. He wouldn't sleep more than a few hours that night, Flitch was sure. He would worry. He would pace. He would look in on his children to make sure they were sleeping soundly.

Would he remember to look in on Flitch?

The world was bursting into violent, adventurous, exciting bloom around Flitch, and he was curling up into something small, empty, and enduring.

Gwyn was the last to leave, and she sat down across from him, giving him a long, critical look but saying nothing.

"How did you know about Faineant's fake prophecy?" Flitch asked. He'd been thinking about it that morning while they were out on the Sea Deck. She knew more than she should and acted like the events of the day were nothing more than rain—inconvenient and best enjoyed.

Gwyn let out a low chuckle and nodded.

"The best poor old Faineant could come up with to scare everyone was the Supplicant Few." She let out another laugh and looked up at the ceiling above for a moment. "Specters from the past that no one really remembers. He's so *obvious*."

Gwyn brought her eyes back to Flitch's.

"Do you know how long ago the Supplicant Few set sail?"

Flitch shook his head.

"One hundred and seventy-two years!" Gwyn said, voice bright. "Four sailors filled with dreams, fed up with this place and set on answering the only question anyone had ever asked: what is out there?"

She let one hand rise through the air, gesturing off toward the Sea to the east.

"Four fools, of course. Unable to see what was around them, unwilling to fix the problems in their own house, they set off to find another one."

"You talk about them as if they were real people," Flitch said, thinking of the stories he'd heard of the Supplicant Few, each one more impossible and more exciting.

Gwyn gave a noncommittal *hmm* but otherwise ignored the implication.

"The stories have it right. They sailed their vessel—*Rau's Glory*, named after a woman who sailed to the stars to bring her love home—and pushed out past Arcadian grasses, out into the Roughs. Did you know the grasses grow smoother the further out you get? Everyone thinks the Roughs continue on to Forever, but they don't. It's almost like the Sea grew a barrier to dissuade all but those with the strongest desire to sail east.

"Those four had the conviction, no matter all the other things they didn't have—*sense* highest among them. They made it out into the unmapped grasses, well beyond where even the oldest and most imaginative maps dared depict, and they found their forever."

"They made it to the end of the Sea?" Flitch asked, realizing he was leaning forward in his chair, barely breathing.

"Oh, no," Gwyn said, shaking her head. She had begun to fold a cloth napkin on the table into a tight-fitting, complicated shape, compressing and tucking the material without thought. "There's no end to the Sea. It goes on and on and on. Of that, I'm sure. But the Supplicant Few did reach their own forever. They saw many wondrous things, magics and oddities and terrors that make our Sea—even with the Marchess's monsters rising up from below—seem banal by comparison. But they didn't stop until the island."

She paused for a moment, setting the folded napkin onto the table. It was a ship, elegantly made, no bit of cloth wasted. Gwyn pushed a spoon into it to make the mast.

"Anchors aweigh," she said in a small voice, pushing the ship forward on the table until it fell apart, even her expert folding unable to hold up for long.

"What was the island?" Flitch prompted.

"Small, stone, no bigger than this room," she said, gesturing around at the ballroom, which was quite large for a room and quite small for an island. "They weren't going to stop, but the island, despite being bare of any house or home, was occupied. Dangling his legs off the edge was a man. Or, at least, what looked like a man.

"It was the first person they had seen since leaving Arcadia behind. They stopped by the island, checking with long poles for a stone reef hiding in the grasses around it, but there was nothing, so they sailed as close as they could, shouting out their hellos.

"He did not speak at first, and as they turned to each other in confusion, the man leapt onto their boat, crossing the distance as if it were a simple step. Too stunned to move, the Supplicant Few watched as he sank his hands into the wood of the deck and the mast, his fingers touching and then pushing in past the surface. He was like a gardener sinking his hands into fresh dirt, not because he is working but because he wants to feel the earth against his palm.

"One of the Few attacked him, thinking he was trying to destroy the ship, and he tossed her overboard without a thought, his face perfectly

serene the whole time. The others waited, terrified, and when he was finished examining the vessel, bones and all, he sat down on the deck and
said only 'One wish each.' He wouldn't respond to any of their questions,
and showed no reaction to their rage and sorrow at losing their friend. He
just waited, until the youngest of them, a tiny nothing of a girl who looked
like her mother and talked like her father, said, 'We came out here for forever. I want forever.'

"The man nodded and said, 'It is so.' The girl felt nothing, no change at
all, and the others thought it was a nonsense game. One asked for her
friend to return at almost the same moment the other asked to become a
bird. Again, the man said, 'It is so.' But this time, the change was immediate. The first of the Few, the one who had been flung from the ship, was
suddenly back, broken and bruised from the fall she'd still been experiencing, but alive. One moment she was not there, the next she was on the
deck, gasping for air and screaming in pain.

"The one who had wished to be a bird gave a squawk of surprise, changed
as he was into a small red bird, wings glittering a dark crimson and breast
shining like a sunset. He was beautiful. I cried when he flew off."

Flitch blinked and said nothing.

"We sailed back, the three of us remaining on the ship. Nan, that's the
woman who'd wished for the return of her friend—a woman named Rilla
who I never really liked—Nan died on the return voyage. We were running so low on food and water, and we'd been unable to harvest much of
anything with only three of us. She was too hungry and thirsty to know
what she was doing, and she slipped while tying off a sail. She fell into the
Sea, and do you know what she did as she was falling?"

Gwyn stared at Flitch, head cocked just slightly to the side.

"She laughed. Maybe she didn't understand what was going on. Or maybe
she did. But she let out a laugh that disappeared into the Sea with her. After
that, it was just me and Rilla. We made it back to Arcadia, and no one
there recognized us. We listened to the stories of the famous Supplicant
Few, which had spread from the Mainland, and it was fun for a little while.
Rilla left after a few days, saying she never wanted to see me or talk about
our voyage again. I never knew what happened to her. Sometimes, I wonder if it wasn't actually a mercy to save her when we did. Who can say?"

Gwyn stopped, looking down at the mess of cloth her ship had become.

"You were one of the Supplicant Few," Flitch said, speaking quietly.

Gwyn spread her hands and said nothing.

"You were the little girl who asked for forever almost two hundred years ago."

"No, I *am* that little girl. I asked for forever and I got it."

Flitch stared at her, thinking back to the artwork he'd seen on the walls. *Gwyn, Age 195.* He'd assumed it was a joke, the old lady painting with all the kids and pretending to be even older than she was.

"Does everyone around here know?"

"No," Gwyn said, shaking her head. "Although most of the people around here know that I'm a bit odd. It's why I make so few appearances at court. Even Faineant isn't thick enough to miss such a fact. His father was the same way, and his before him. I've pretended to be my mother, one of my aunts, my grandmother. It's amazing what they will believe when they already think you're strange."

Flitch could only watch her in astonishment, every story he'd ever heard about the strange and mysterious Paths Baron now coming unraveled in his head, each one threaded through with this simple truth: Gwyn had lived a long, long time.

"Will you live forever?" he asked finally.

"I'm not sure," Gwyn said, shrugging. She reached over to the plate that had been Flitch's father's and ran her finger around it, collecting the crumbs and bits of honey still sticking there and popping it all into her mouth with a satisfied moan. "I can be hurt, and I can be badly hurt, which leads me to believe that I can be killed. I've never tried it, though. Perhaps tomorrow will give me my first and possibly only chance at it. But yes, without outside intercession, I suspect I would live forever."

"Why haven't you . . ." Flitch said, tracing off and gesturing around.

Gwyn watched him, curious.

"You can live forever and you're a hero from actual stories. But you spend your days doing finger-painting with kids?" It was a blunt, rude way to say it, but the social muscles that might have kept him from speaking so had gone slack.

"Have you ever tried finger-painting with kids?" she asked, frowning at him. "It's *very* difficult to get the right spread and coloring. You could spend several lifetimes working at it before finding mastery. I certainly have."

When it was clear that such a flippant answer wouldn't satisfy Flitch,

Gwyn put her hands in her lap, sat up straight, and looked him in the eye, a wistful expression on her face.

"I tried doing the big things right away when I realized what I had received from that thing on the island. Fame could never be mine, but riches? Power? Authority and control? Oh, yes, I sipped from all those cups, and each one left me feeling thirstier than when I'd started. The only thing that's ever left me feeling full—*really full*—is the simple stuff. That's where real joy is. That's where the good bits are, waiting in plain sight for anyone to find them."

Flitch nodded, seeing the truth in what she said.

"I think all of that might be out of reach for me now," he said. The words tumbled out without any planning or forethought, a sad cry from somewhere deep down inside him, somewhere distant and getting further away with each moment.

"Maybe," Gwyn said, untroubled and thoughtful. "But isn't it better to think on what you have before you than to stare longingly at what's behind?"

She stood and stretched, lifting her arms to the ceiling and going up on her toes. The smile as she settled back was one of pure contentment. She carried none of the danger tomorrow would bring on her, no worry lines creasing her face, no anxious fidgeting moving her hands.

"Have a good night," Gwyn said, turning and walking toward the door. "The library is on the third floor—if you want somewhere nice to sit while everyone else sleeps. Lots of good stories in that room."

Flitch watched her go and, after some time, took her advice. The library was a tall, beautiful room, every wall lined with books of every size and quality, the floor littered with comfortable couches and chairs, sturdy desks and tables. He walked around the space, running a hand across the spines of the books, recognizing stories he had read as a younger boy, each one a set of clothes he had worn.

There was the tale of Resik of the Clouds, there the Queen Who Laughed, there a chronicling of the Six Spirits War, all of them stories Flitch had loved and lived in, pretending to be the heroes, the villains, anyone of consequence. As his siblings had grown up and gone off, he had leaned more and more on those stories and the promises they held for him, a boy with his whole life ahead, last of the Borders siblings, always in danger of being forgotten.

Alone in a sleeping house, Flitch sat surrounded by stories and thought on what lay ahead of him. His breath came slower and slower, and before dawn broke, he had lost the need to breathe at all.

When they arrived, the summoning was already well underway, a monstrous menagerie emerging from the Greys, pulled by the Marchess's magic and sent above by her command. She looked so small kneeling there in front of her fire, dwarfed by the flames and the Greys, by the monsters and the space above into which they disappeared.

Just a person, Kindred thought. *Just.*

She pulled on the braid of grass, slowing and stopping her steed. She tried to step from the slats of wood and found that her legs had turned to weak, quivering masses, barely able to hold her up, and she staggered for a moment before kneeling. The other members of the Court who had stood for the trip looked to be in a similar state.

Only Madrigal, Awn, and Jest were able to walk, and they ran toward the Marchess, screaming for her to stop. Kindred followed but at a distance, slowed by her legs, which would not cooperate and felt like rocks had replaced her flesh and bone.

"Tell Flitch that a distraction is coming. Tell him to look to the Greys," Kindred said to Sarah before turning back and focusing on her grandmother.

The Marchess did not stop her song or her summoning, and yet she managed to turn, mouth still working, hands still busy in the fire, to see the Court's approach. Her eyes flicked around, hoping perhaps to see her own friends coming to her aid, and when they found only Kindred approaching, a grim look came over the Marchess's face.

With an effort of will that felt like someone screaming inside Kindred's head, the Marchess yanked through another creature, its huge mass obscured by violet flames roaring across its body. As she had done before, the Marchess flicked a spray of flame at it, driving it up and away, and the creature vanished into the black.

Blood and feeling had begun to return to Kindred's legs, and she caught up to the others, stepping forward to shout at her grandmother.

"Enough!" she cried, pitching her voice to climb over the tumult of the mephitic hearthfire song in her mind. "Stop this, Grandmother!"

Still singing, the Marchess shook her head and stooped closer to the flames. Her song, the broken almost-melody of it, shifted slightly, and Kindred couldn't help but marvel at her grandmother's range and control, the delicate slide of her voice from one minor key to another, her ability to hold off harmony's pull and maintain a tension that kept the fire going.

The blaze, soot-colored and sludging up through the tower of bones, reacted to the shift immediately. Black and brown and grey flames fountained overhead, stretching wide up and out like a pestilent tree stretching limbs for the first time. The fire curtained all the way down around the Marchess, creating a space inside for her to work and a barrier through which it would almost certainly be lethal to walk.

Through the shifting thickness of the flames, Kindred saw her grandmother, resolute and sad, resume her work.

A blur of movement beside her caught Kindred's attention, and she turned to see Sarah completing her throw, the knife already slicing dangerously through the air. Kindred had time to think, clearly and with a deep sadness, that this attack would kill her grandmother, when the wall of fire around the Marchess contorted and reached out one oily tentacle to slap away the knife, sending it skittering off into the dirt.

Jest and the others had backed up, looking around with fearful, uncertain gazes. It had been an almost-impossible task for them to fight with Lurch and Tesser Cobb despite outnumbering them.

This was different. The Marchess had been the most capable keeper above, her ability with the fire unmatched by anyone Kindred had ever met. The tales about her bravery or grand sailing deeds might have been stretched or romanticized, but those about her skill with the fire were not.

She was an artist who worked in bone and flame and song, and she would kill the Traveling Court without hesitation.

She'll kill me, too, Kindred thought, certain of that fact.

That tendril of flame snapped once at Sarah, driving her back, before receding into the curtain of fire surrounding the Marchess. Through the Greys, another monster had begun to emerge, a toothy snout sprouting long, thin, waving arms.

"We can't get in there!" Fourth-Folly shouted at Kindred, backing off like the rest. They picked up a stone and hurled it at the fiery wall as if to prove the point, and one of those thick tendrils flicked out again, moving fast enough to blur.

"What do we do, Kindred Captain?" Jest asked, having to yell over the high-pitched keening emanating from the summoned beast.

But Kindred had turned her ear inward, hearing the slight shift in her grandmother's song, the tiny leap in intensity that occasioned the defense of the fire, the somber dirge sung to bring down the wall of flame around her. The songs of the Greys, of the hearthfire, and of her grandmother all twined together in Kindred's head, and she pushed through them, just as the Marchess had taught her, to find the central strand.

She listened as she had done on the deck of *Revenger* so many days and nights, straining to hear what her grandmother found so simple, so easy, until it became easy and simple for Kindred, too.

Slowly, Kindred mimicked the Marchess's song, stealing her technique one melodic slide at a time.

The fire was a rambunctious, wild thing, wrong in its creation and wrong in its continued existence. The hearthfires that burned above were like gentle creatures, capable of great power and violence but, at their core, slow and easy. They were beautiful in their way, elegant and wondrous, singing in a language shaped by the wind.

This fire was nothing like those, and yet it was not an evil thing. Turned to an evil purpose, perhaps, but strange and wondrous in its own terrible way, the edges of its song clipped, a rhythm never finding itself and a melody never reaching home.

Singing to it made Kindred feel dirty, her hands suddenly oily and sticky, her skin itching and hot. She resisted the urge to stop, to spit out the rotten taste flooding through her mouth with each syllable.

She sang to the fire, feeling the Marchess's control over it, the echoes of her voice, and the fire sang back. It reached for her with grubby, grabby fingers, knowing nothing else, and it took every bit of control and power Kindred had gained as a keeper to stop it from shattering her consciousness.

Inside of that song, distant from where she stood, was the power to pull forth the monsters from the Greys, and it was this that the Marchess was tapping into, this that Kindred had to stop if she was going to stop anything.

A broken melody in her mouth, Kindred took a step forward, eyes following the swirls and patterns moving through the fire, straining to hear for any change in its song. She could beg the fire to burn down or halt its grave work, but only the woman kneeling before it, hands working inside its body, could truly control the flames.

Kindred took another step, and now the Marchess felt her, looking up from the bones to see Kindred approaching, a look of surprise and—was that pride again? She locked eyes with Kindred, singing louder, more insistent, and Kindred felt the fire push back at her, tripping along ahead of her, climbing higher and diving lower without warning—a creature trying not to be caught.

She felt the change in its song and threw herself to the ground a moment before a lash of flame whipped out, singeing the air where her head had been. Voice cracking from effort, Kindred redoubled her melodic assault, listening for her grandmother's voice and pulling out the strands of control, harmonizing her and pushing the melody faster there, agile and quick.

The next lash came more slowly, a sluggish swing of flame that Kindred easily avoided, and now she stood before the wall of fire, close enough to touch it. But she couldn't keep up her defense against the Marchess and form a doorway at the same time, a fact the Marchess seemed keenly aware of. Inside her fiery bunker, she smiled at Kindred and continued her work, unworried. Once again, as ever, her granddaughter had come up short.

It was dangerous—impossibly so—but Kindred would have to part the Marchess's wall fast enough to slip inside before she could be struck by one of the lashes of flame. Maybe the Marchess would not be able to maintain the musical spellwork of the wall and attack her. She had to hope. There was nothing left.

Kindred sang in a high, clear voice, pushing past the strain in her throat, finding the melodic spellwork holding the wall together and begging it to part, offering harmony to its shattered tones, following the vocal maneuverings of her grandmother as best she could. It was a tangled mess, chaos and revelry worked through every line of song and spread of fire, and Kindred was just beginning to find her way through when the Marchess sent a lash of coal-black flame whipping toward her.

The shift in her grandmother's voice was her only warning, and Kindred hurled herself back from the wall, crashing to the ground as the long fiery limb splashed against one shoulder, burning her clothing and skin. She let out a gasp of pain and rolled away, driving her wound into the ground to put out the flames and feeling the touch of unconsciousness as the pain moved through her body.

"No," Kindred groaned, shoving away the promise of rest in that unknowing sleep. She pushed herself up in time to see two more lengths of fire extending from the wall, arcing back to swing at her, moved by the Marchess's melody. Kindred could almost hear her grandmother's cawing laugh inside that melody, her victory assured, her power affirmed. She would triumph. As she always did. As, it seemed, she always would.

The lashes flexed before whipping forward, and Kindred threw up her hands, as if they might do anything against such an attack, no time to sing, no time for entreaty, for her own songwork.

Kindred waited for the fire.

Instead, voices behind her raised their own defenses, one light and quick, the other deep and driving. Their song, a complicated thing made of simple melodies, each of which mimicked Kindred's own song, worked on the Marchess's fire, besieging it with plaintive entreaties and commands, a cavalcade of choruses driving the lashes back into their source, confusing and confounding the blaze.

It was a cacophony of music, and Kindred whirled around to find Awn and Madrigal, hands joined, standing behind her, staring hard at the fire, mouths open in song. Madrigal's melodies were quick, symmetrical works, and Awn's were the wild, whirligig wanderings of a pirate keeper. Together, they followed in Kindred's musical footsteps, offering their own approaches and tonal shifts, stealing what they could from her and making it their own.

Awn, looking down at her, nodded and gestured with his one free hand. *Go on*, he said.

They were giving her a chance, an opening, and Kindred would not let it go.

The song burst from her mouth, insistent and dynamic, the mirror of her grandmother's but taken an octave higher, two octaves. She ran an ariose riot through the tangled web of melodies sung by her grandmother, the fire, Awn, and Madrigal.

Forward.

One step and then Kindred was running, racing for the wall, her shoulder singing its own song of pain, and when she reached it, the oily flames cascading down before her parted into an archway, the edges flickering and shuddering with the contested wills of the Marchess and her grand-daughter, two captains, one old and one new.

Kindred walked through the archway and the fire closed behind her with a *whoosh* of heat and air.

She was inside, the light murky and strange, the fire a kaleidoscopic dome all around her, black and grey and brown run through with dizzying scintillas of arcane power, all radiating up and out from the hearthfire at its center.

And before the fire, attendant to its needs, a careful shepherd watching over it, was the Marchess.

She broke her song for a moment, somehow able to draw steady, even breaths despite the work of maintaining the fire, building and holding its defenses, and pulling through the monstrosities above. Even now, even after everything, Kindred could see she was a wonder.

"Do not do this, child," the Marchess said, glaring at her, eyes moving across the shoulder wound. "You're already injured, and I will not be so kind the next time."

Kindred stepped around the fire until it burned between her and the Marchess, distorting her grandmother's features in its heat and dark flames.

"No," she said, shaking her head. "You can't keep doing this, Grand-mother. Those people above matter. There has to be another way. This cannot be it."

As she spoke, Kindred reached out with her senses, feeling the fire anew now that she stood before it, listening for its rhythms and rises, the too-long gaps between its notes and the staccato-skip of its melodies. She listened as her grandmother had taught her, turning her mind into a stalk of grass to be blown about by the song of the fire, a sail to be filled by its wind.

Let it *show* you, she had taught Kindred on *Revenger*, and so she did now, becoming a blank page on which it might write itself.

"They've lost the ear to hear," the Marchess said, speaking with quiet sincerity, as though all of this was a deep pain to her, like watching a loved home abandoned during a storm. "The Sea has been sending its messages every day—every new run of the Greys was like a shout from the Sea, and not one of those fucking people knows how to listen anymore. Sunrises and blooms of coneflowers and sprays of bluestem seeds caught like lanterns in the sunlight, all of it, every day, every moment, and no one is listening, Kindred! No one is listening."

"This isn't the way," Kindred said, shaking her head. The song of the Sea could be heard out on the periphery now, almost blocked out completely by the chaotic sounds of the hearthfire, and Kindred pitched her ear to find its wisdom again, that same knowing that had moved through her when she'd healed Sarah, that same knowing that whirled and rushed in light and wind, waiting to be found, waiting.

When she spoke next, Kindred let the words of the Sea move through her.

"We look at the Sea and see ourselves. We look and offer our own hurts and healing, our own good and bad. We look and ask what the Sea wants, as if wanting is anything more than a broken human creation. Wanting and having, and in the having, wanting more.

"But the natural world isn't our reflection, not mine and not yours. It's not here to teach us lessons about ourselves. It's not our god, to be prayed to above all else. You talk about seeing messages in nature, Grandmother, of reading in the Sea its thoughts and desires, but you have it wrong."

Kindred stepped closer to the fire, letting one hand drift toward the huge blaze, captains' bones stacked high.

"We are not the audience, Grandmother. We are the message, too. Just as wind and Sea and sky are nature's words, just as every strand of bluestem is letter and language both—so, too, are our lives medium and message. You've grown haughty in your care for the world, so sure that it speaks in secret whispers only for you.

"The world is speaker and audience both. We are its words, Grandmother. *We* are the message."

When she sang this time, it was a challenge, voice raised and powerful, syllables cracking like thunder, and Kindred plunged her hands into the flames, reaching for the tangled structure of bone at its center. If she could break the tower of bone and steal its fuel, everything else would fall.

Her song was a high, glittering bridge racing over the tangled melodies below, but the Marchess would not be outdone so easily. She sang again in that broken language, so near to that of the hearthfire, *almost* sensical, *almost* meaningful, and her power surged through the hearthfire.

But the blaze thickened around her wrists, urged by the Marchess's song, trapping Kindred where she was.

"I taught you everything you know, child," the Marchess said, shaking her head. "I am the outside bound of your knowledge."

Kindred redoubled her efforts, sweat bursting from the back of her neck and temples, stringing together musical entreaties and plaintive lyrics with every breath, long passages of soaring notes, gliding between registers and letting her voice thrum with all the power she could manage.

The Marchess's answer was a doomed rhythm, brutal and unyielding, a stone wall against which Kindred's efforts came to nothing. She was simple lines and smooth utterances, short words and direct meanings. It had always been her way, and Kindred's frenetic songwork seemed nonsensical in comparison.

Memories like motes of light glittered along the paths of Kindred's mind, and even as her hands and wrists and forearms began to grow hot, she let the past work in her, digging up the old, dry dirt there and seeing what might grow.

She was sitting on the deck of *Revenger*, surrounded by her grandmother's crew and yet still alone. The music of the ship—the old-woman groans of the timbers and the familiar, smooth-leather patter of the sailors' voices, the strain of the sails catching the wind and the constant sound, like a parent telling their child to *hush*, as the ship cut through the Sea.

She was nursing burns on her hands after another day of failure at the hearthfire, sitting on her hammock belowdecks and listening to the raucous laughter of the crew, her grandmother included, above. With every dip of salve and every bit of skin that would not come back, she promised herself that she would be stronger, better, so that she, too, could sit up under the night sky and send her carefree laughter to the stars.

She was walking through Arcadia with her grandmother, sharing a cup of precious water, and glowing as the Marchess laughed at one of her jokes.

She was watching *Revenger* sail away without her on it, the final spat with her grandmother still a bitter herb on her tongue. For a moment, just a moment, she hoped the Sea would rise up and swallow her whole.

Laughter and stories, hard moments and easy ones, days in the sun and nights screaming their thanks to the sky for the spare bit of rain filling their water buckets—all of them and every one in between came back to Kindred as she set her will against her grandmother's, knowing that what she said was not true.

She had taught Kindred so much of the world and its ways, but Sarah was right—the best of Kindred, the parts she was proudest of, she had found like gems in the mines of her grandmother's teaching. She had worked for them, and she would not give up now.

"It's over, child," her grandmother said, voice a low growl now. The strain of her defense was beginning to take its toll on her, and she breathed heavily now, leaning over the fire with a hungry look on her face. "Do not make me burn your hands to nothing. It would be a waste, and I do not want to do it. But I will if you don't stop."

It would be a waste, Kindred thought, and what she needed to do clarified in her mind like a terrible truth.

Hearthfires burned captains' bones, drawing out the magic worked into them by the rites and vows every would-be captain took and intensified by every journey on the Sea, the wind and sky and Sea all sinking deep into a captain's bones, pulled in by their magic and held there.

To burn such a bone in the hearthfire was to release that magic and shape it back into the world, to take sunlight of old, wind across a face long left of the world, and turn it into lift and speed, into stability through flame.

The Marchess, most storied captain of Arcadia, oldest among the fleet at the time of her disappearance, and oldest still, glared at Kindred across the fire, a challenge girded by the certainty of her superiority.

When Kindred sang this time, it was a tapestry threading together every melody she could remember singing to the fire, a weaving together of her past and present, harmonies and phrasings and tones all gilded by memory's slow work.

She sang, letting her voice trill and trail, echo and bellow, the words simple ones she had used many times for many hearthfires, each line less important than the emotion and music she layered on top of them.

"Burn bone, ay lay, burn bone to black," she began, feeling the hearthfire respond immediately to her litany, the flames slackening around her wrists and hands. She did not fight the blaze or its urge to burn.

The Marchess's power rushed past her, burning for a moment before releasing, lost without resistance, as though she had been leaning forward, hands on Kindred's shoulders, the two of them gaining and losing ground. And suddenly, instead of pushing back, struggling for control, Kindred had simply released, let go, given in and turned aside. She could not change who her grandmother was or what her grandmother would do.

When the fire surged, Kindred gave in to it, turning herself into a long, slender length of bluestem arcing in a wind.

"It will be and it will be and it will be," she sang, and the fire glowed with sudden vibrancy, greens and blues, reds and oranges—all the colors of a prairie in bloom—cutting briefly through the swamp of oily greys and blacks. The Marchess's eyes grew wide as she realized what Kindred was doing, but it was too late. She had pushed, and Kindred had let her. She had spoken, and Kindred had listened.

The fire rippled and rolled, shuddering underneath this new direction from Kindred, who had resumed her chant. Flames jumped out erratically, like a child feeling its limbs for the first time, snapping out an arm or flicking fingers in wild waves. Greys burned up into vivid blues and midnight black gave way to sunrise oranges as Kindred sang and let the fire do what hearthfires were meant to do: burn captains' bones.

> *"For ship and Sea and crew, ay lay,*
> *For past, come blaze, to light the way,*
> *This prairie wind return, return,*
> *Take bone and past and . . ."*

The pressure of the hearthfire, its song and heat and power, built in Kindred's mind and around her hands, which moved gently among the flames, no longer reaching for the tower of bone but fluttering open, inviting and warm. She held the final word of her song, letting the fire long for it, meeting her grandmother's eyes and hearing her song one last time, finding in it all the strands of her grandmother, a woman capable of so much kindness and so much anger, so much goodness and so much evil, all of it her, all of it.

Was it defeat welling in the Marchess's eyes? Resignation? Contentment?

It was impossible to say, but Kindred did not let go of her grandmother's gaze. She wanted it to sink deep inside her, a weight and a gift and promise and warning to carry forward into whatever was next. It was a moment she would not let herself forget. If a captain's body became the product of every morning wind and seedy spray and success and failure, all of it sinking down into her bones, then this would be Kindred's rite and curse, the burr in her bones, the crack she would carry.

"*Burn*," Kindred sang, the word a whisper in her mouth, a flicker of flame in her throat, and a roar in the hearthfire, which woke around her, leaping from the fell tower to the Marchess, one set of captains' bones to another, racing along her body and making of her a lantern to light the dark, rapturous and riotous, a panoply of color and heat and song and sadness and joy that burst up from Arcadia's oldest captain, urged on by Kindred's song, leaping for the Greys above and *exploding*.

The fire devoured the Greys, blazing up along it and shining a sudden and strange light in the sky of the Seafloor, illuminating creatures and plants above previously hidden by the dark, sounding out a depth that Kindred had already taken to be as endless and fathomless as the night sky.

The burst of light and heat was enough to throw Kindred onto the dirt, shoving her back with a heavy hand and blinding her for a long moment. Voices echoed from far away, and they might have been from the hearthfire or the Traveling Court or memories from her past; Kindred couldn't tell.

Her throat burned from her song and the heat of a fire built for a wrong purpose wrenched around to be used for something better. She swallowed against the pain.

In her mind, the sounds of the world distant curiosities, she held only her grandmother's face at the end.

The set of her mouth as she sang one last song.

The flush along her cheeks at the sudden heat.

The shine of her eyes, which said so much.

CHAPTER TWENTY

The combined forces of Borders and Paths moved in dawn's grey light, nothing more than shadowed shapes rushing toward the stables where the wagons and horses were already packed and ready for their flight west. A friend of Gwyn's who lived in the Gloaming Woods had sent a message back with a silver-winged raven promising to shelter any who came. Any who wanted it would meet there.

Zim moved among the packs of people, directing and organizing the work, completely comfortable and in control. It made Flitch smile to see his brother so confident and valued. How far he had come from that little boy crying in frustration at Aster's jokes and trickery. He moved with a cluster of other bookkeepers, talking in quick, descriptive bursts about the logistics of moving this or that, the number of people who should be on this cart or that one, timetables for leaving and meeting up.

Nearer the house, Aster was moving through a series of warmup stretches with several of Gwyn's casters, talking in the overly jocular way she did whenever she was nervous. To anyone who didn't know her, it might have seemed like excitement or confidence, but Flitch knew better. Laughter that went on a little too long, hands that never stopped moving, a brittle smile that showed too many teeth. Behind all of her bravado and bravery, a little girl seeing her barony in ruins still reached, anxious and unsure, for greatness.

"Are you sure you want to be on the boat?" Idyll asked, checking and rechecking their supplies and the saddle on their horse, which stood still and easy under Idyll's calming touch. "You could still come with us. It won't be nearly as dangerous. And . . . we won't . . ."

They frowned down at their pack, muttering something about candles

and flame, and when they looked back up at Flitch, it was with some fog-
giness.

"I'll be okay," Flitch said, putting a hand on Idyll's arm and nodding.
"It's where I should be, I think."

"You sound old and mature all of a sudden," Idyll said, recovering themself and smiling at him. "You're supposed to be my little brother, scared of
the thunder and needing a story to settle him down."

They stepped forward and wrapped him a hug so tight, it might have
squeezed the air from his lungs if any yet remained. Flitch closed his eyes
and committed the moment to memory, knowing it might very well be
the last he had with his oldest sibling and oldest friend. This, still, stirred
the slow trudge of his heart.

"Okay," Idyll said, stepping back and putting their hands on his shoulders. "We're off to set fire to a library."

"No books," Ravel said from where he was saddling his horse nearby.

"No books," Idyll agreed, nodding at him before returning their gaze to
Flitch. "We will burn no books. Stay safe on the ship, all right? Stay back
when they attack. I want to see you stepping off that ship afterward, okay?"

Flitch nodded, smiling up at Idyll and feeling like he was moving through
a memory, unable to feel the rough edges of the moment, the sweet stench
of now.

"I'll be safe," Flitch said. Idyll needed to go if they were going to play
their part in the theater of the day.

"Good," Idyll said, smiling at him. "I'll see you after."

With that, they climbed up onto their horse and set off toward the
capital, surrounded by the few guards going with them and Ravel, all of
them merging into a cluster of shadows in the early morning and disappearing quickly.

"Goodbye," Flitch said, his voice merging with the wind.

⬤▬◆▬⬤

"Boat group!" Gwyn said, clapping her hands as Flitch joined them. In
addition to the crew, the Borders Baron, Aster, Flitch, Gwyn, and six of
Gwyn's best casters would be going. The other casters and guards from

both baronies would escort those fleeing west. *We need to be small, agile, and deadly,* Gwyn had told them when deciding how many would sail on the ship. The rest of them clutched swords or axes, throwing knives or maces, but Flitch had elected to carry only a small blade that he'd tucked into a slim leather sheath at his belt. He wouldn't need any weapons, wouldn't know what to do with them even if he did, but the woman passing out weapons that morning had looked alarmed at his initial refusal.

The group wore the drab, brown clothing of sailors, except for Gwyn, who had found and donned robes in the color of Rivers.

"Maybe Cantria will never hear about this," Gwyn said, running a hand across the white and red checkers of Rivers, "but if she does, I hope she chokes on her rage."

That elicited a grim chuckle from everyone present, including Aster, who looked to Flitch for a moment, smiling at him.

"Now, casters, let us prepare before we go down to the ship and kick this shitpile of a day over," Gwyn said, turning to a low fire burning in a movable metal basin she'd brought out from the house. The casters around her nodded, a few running their hands over the bandoliers crisscrossing their chests, the pouches sewn into the fabric each carrying a pinch of powerful casting plants.

Flitch understood little of casting—it had always been Aster's passion, but for him it had been another necessity of planning for the voyages he'd imagined himself taking. You had to hire the crew, but you had to hire casters, too; they were workers whose labor led to magical protection instead of simply stowing cargo or reefing sails. How they did their work, he didn't really know or particularly care to know—they did, and that was enough.

But he *did* understand that casters needed a fire to burn their plants, and he had been surprised that morning to see no one wearing rush pits—the mobile hearthfire carriers shaped like great metal shells slung over the backs of their wearers. If they intended to board *The Arcana* or either of its protective vessels, wouldn't they need their own hearthfires?

Gwyn gestured down at the chuckling blaze burning in the metal basin, and one of her casters dropped a complicated weave of plants—big as her hand and impossibly intricate—into it, her voice a husky, dry thing as she sang. The fire belched a thick, strangely concentrated stream of dark-orange smoke that twisted and writhed through the air, tipped by a point of fiery red that moved like a newborn animal's nose sniffing at the wind, finding and following a scent.

A second voice had joined the first woman's, and it took Flitch a moment to realize it was Gwyn's. Her singing voice was different from the one she spoke with—she sang in a high, controlled waver, every syllable like a paean to something lost, every melodic run tinged by a deep, weary sadness. The Gwyn of conversation was light, airy, funny, weird; the Gwyn of song breathed sorrow into every note.

The stream of smoke cut a line toward her, and as it neared, Gwyn reached out a hand to cup the fiery red heart of it, her song climbing high as she did.

In her hand, the smoke stilled for just a moment as she sang a single note, high and pure and melancholy.

Like lightning, the burning thing in Gwyn's hand struck, forking out, splitting and splitting and splitting in fractured lines of tightly curled orange smoke that lashed out and into the mouths of the casters standing around, including Aster's and Gwyn's. A few jerked their heads back, surprised or not prepared for whatever Gwyn had just done, but most did not move except to close their mouths after the smoke had already disappeared down their throats.

Gwyn's song cut off and she raised her now-empty hand.

"A fire in hearth and a fire in gut," she said, nodding around at them. "As long as this fire burns, so, too, will the fire inside you. Feed it with plants and draw your power out."

Gwyn reached into a pouch on her own bandolier, pulling out a pinch of plant and popping it into her mouth. She chewed for a moment before swallowing the whole mass of it, sending it down to where the fire burned in her belly.

"Farewell, house," she said, looking up at her architectural wonder. "Thank you for everything."

Her casting was a simple thing, the violet magic glowing suddenly on her hands as she sang in a clear voice. The metal fire pit in front of her shook and lifted into the air, the flames inside it roiling and swelling beyond the bounds of the structure. Gwyn's song crested and she flicked her hands forward, a gesture that might have been one of finality, a gesture that said *I'm finished with this.*

The fire pit hurtled in through the open door of the now-empty house and erupted in gouts and rivers of flame, the blaze moving as if possessed, spreading out and expanding into every room, climbing walls, running along stone and wood alike in its urgent need to devour everything.

Flitch watched as the inlaid floor, its depiction of the Sea so idyllic, was consumed in the biggest casting fire he'd ever seen.

"Let's go," Gwyn said, not meeting any of their eyes as she gave her house one last look. She jogged toward the path that would lead them down to the secret cove where one ship, outfitted to bear the King's colors, waited for them.

Two ancestral homes gone in the span of a few days, one burned and one burning. Flitch wondered what other foundations of the Mainland would be gone by day's end.

Flitch checked the book as they walked down the winding, thin path, crowded in by the tall stands of prairie grasses growing on either side, following close behind Aster and hearing his father's breath at his back.

Nothing from Sarah, his pages and pages of writing unanswered. The possibilities of why she hadn't written back yet moved through Flitch, each scarier than the last, shaking him as so little over the last few days had.

"There it is," Gwyn said from ahead, pushing through a stand of bluestem and revealing the small cove beyond, well hidden by rocky outgrowths. She paused for a moment at the end of the path and said, quietly, "Oh, dear."

Flitch looked around the tangle of bodies ahead of him and saw two ships anchored in the cove, both bearing the King's colors, Faineant's sigil sewn into the mainsail.

On the small crescent of rocky ground leading toward the dock stood Cantria and a handful of her warriors.

"Paths Baron," Cantria said, hefting a pair of huge axes effortlessly. "I have been charged by King Faineant Lark to relieve you of your lands, home, and authority. The King's soldiers, aided by my own, are already moving on your house. You and the disgraced Borders Baron are to accompany me to the castle to await His Majesty's judgment. If you resist, I will bring your bodies."

"I don't know if you're going to want the home," said Gwyn, her voice light and easy. "I accidentally set it on fire. Oops."

"Joke all you want, Baron," Cantria said, "Faineant's patience with you has eroded, and you would do well to surrender to me now if you hope for anything resembling kindness from our King."

Cantria smiled at them, smug and confident, until she really looked at Gwyn's clothing. She stared for a moment, sucking in a slow breath.

"Oh, no," she said, voice quiet, murderous. She turned slightly to the guards around her. "They're resisting."

"I'm glad I got to see your face when you found out," Gwyn said, bringing a hand to her face to hide her chuckle. "I'll hold the memory close all of my days."

Cantria turned to her collected warriors, a group of people who looked every bit as dangerous as she did, and nodded, as if giving permission for the fight to start. What she didn't realize was the fight had already started, because Gwyn was not hiding a laugh when she brought a hand to her face. Flitch had seen the small weave of green plants in Gwyn's palm, and he watched her now as she chewed, swallowed, and *moved*.

Flitch had seen his father's guards training in the yard, the best among them leaping and striking with deadly precision and impossible speed. He had watched the fastest people on the Mainland racing on festival days, sprinting from one end of the Long Road to the other. He had seen birds and beasts cutting through air and churning earth at blurring speeds.

None of them came close to Gwyn Gaunt.

In the space between Cantria's nod to her warriors and swiveling her head to look forward again, Gwyn crossed the space between the two parties, a span of rocky shore easily the length of a ship if not more. And though she moved with unnatural speed, Flitch saw every movement, his vision tunneling briefly on just her, the flick of her legs and feet, the push of her arms, the wide, wild grin on her face. He saw it all and understood that if he were to have a place in this fight, in this day, it would be seeing the events enacted by those around him. Seeing and remembering.

Gwyn passed by Cantria, lashing out with a fist that struck the powerful Rivers Baron in the side of her throat. Her momentum carried Gwyn into a roll that brought her up in front of a Rivers warrior with thick metal armor and a quicksilver sword, which flashed out in the sunlight, shearing the space beside Gwyn's head and sending the Paths Baron rolling away. Cantria let out a gurgle of rage before leaping after Gwyn.

More Rivers warriors collapsed on Gwyn, whose agility kept her just out of their reach, propelling her through the increasingly thin spaces between sword cut and shield push. Even going as fast she was, there were too many Rivers bodies pressing too close, and Gwyn's blurring movement became a bound, agitated thing, edged in closer and closer with each slash.

Aster's voice, rising in parallel with the other Paths casters, signaled the real threat of Gwyn's attack. She was the bait, and they were the jaws of the trap.

As one, they chewed through the plants pulled from their bandoliers and loosed an arsenal of magical attacks, lashes of purple, crackling power, rolling wheels of black arcane fire, and hails of sharp blue shards, all flung forth by the casters. Gwyn leapt clear of the fray just before the magical onslaught hit, vaulting high and back toward her own lines.

But Rivers had come prepared, and while the warriors at the front carried metal weapons and thick armor, those at the back wore rush pits and had already begun pulling out the magical energies to form a barrier of glowing blue in front of their soldiers. It stopped some of the attack, cobalt and azure waves of force rippling along the still-manifesting barrier.

Others, though, it could not stop, and Flitch watched a great wheel of black flame crash into two soldiers, throwing them to the ground and leaving them still and lifeless. Aster's attack—a bright red comet that screamed through the air—smashed through the barrier too and slammed into Cantria, who took the blow on her shoulder and dropped to the ground, still alive but bellowing with the pain.

Rivers warriors scattered and raced forward, diving and dodging what magical attacks they could and closing the distance to their enemies. Miraculously, Cantria was at their head, one arm hanging limp from the damaged shoulder, but still she carried an axe with the other, and still she raced forward, Faineant's best and most reliable instrument.

She had her eyes on Aster, dodging the next attack with surprising agility and raising her axe high for the felling blow, but the Baron o' the Borders, Flitch's father, interceded, stepping in front of Aster and flinging up a sword to catch and deflect Cantria's attack. Her axe glanced to the side but she bulled on ahead, throwing her good shoulder into the baron's chest and driving him down to the ground, his shout of surprise turning quickly to a moan of pain.

Aster spun around, grabbing for the pouches on her bandolier as Cantria rose up, axe forgotten, one balled fist swinging to meet the baron's jaw once, eliciting a *crack*. She swung again, and the baron brought up his arms to shield his face, but still Cantria pummeled at him, swinging over and over as Aster searched for the right plants, dropping them to the ground even as she found them, shouting in frustration. Rivers warriors were closing on the Paths casters all around her, and she had lost her control.

The sounds and stresses of the battle crashed against Flitch's ears, as they did everyone else's, but they could not reach inside him as they had for Aster, and so it was with a strange calm—something like serenity— that Flitch dropped the book he'd been carrying, stepped forward, and stabbed Cantria through the neck with his small blade, the one he had been so sure he would not use. He felt the skin part with almost no resistance, the blade sliding in cold and impersonal, just another length of metal and another neck. It cared nothing for Cantria's authority or lands, her reputation or power. It brought about the end of her life as if she were no one.

Flitch stepped back, horror and revulsion rising in him as Cantria fell over, clutching at her neck and straining to look around for him until her muscles relaxed and her face went slack. Her blood was on Flitch's hands, staining them, and he wiped at his clothes, trying unsuccessfully to clean it away.

"Are you okay?" the baron asked, pushing himself up, his face bloody, jaw not working right. He tried to stand but couldn't, wavering with dizziness, and so he settled for kneeling. He took up Cantria's axe, which lay on the ground beside him, and looked around, holding it up as if he might protect his children from the ground.

The battle had turned into a chaotic skirmish, packs of two or three fighters tangling together, and among these clutches of violence, Gwyn moved lithe and quick, the short blade she'd found during the fight flashing out, severing tendons and parting muscles, never delivering a killing blow but incapacitating wherever she went.

With her aid and the loss of Cantria, Paths and Borders managed to overcome the remaining Rivers warriors, ripping rush pits from the backs of the casters and disarming the rest.

Gwyn was walking between her people, checking on injuries and giving what aid she could, when she saw Cantria on the ground, and a look of unbearable sadness swept over her face. She kneeled down and checked her for life, but it was clear that she was gone.

"Goodbye, daughter of the river," she said, laying a hand on Cantria's armored chest and bowing her head for a moment. When she looked up, tears were beginning to course down her cheeks. Flitch caught her eye, and she said only "I knew her mother very well."

Some of the injured were well enough to continue, but a few casters were in no fit state to sail or assault *The Arcana*, and with the crew who had been injured in the fight, they elected to remain behind with the Rivers warriors who had been tied up or left free, depending on their injuries.

"That leaves us with a skeleton crew," Gwyn said, looking around. Four casters, including her and Aster, three crew, the Borders Baron, and Flitch. "A little lighter and more mobile than I had imagined. We'll just have to make up for it by being extra deadly."

"Perhaps we should rethink our plan," Flitch's father said, his voice coming out strained and awkward from the jaw injury Cantria had given him. "If they knew about this, they may know about the rest."

"They don't," Flitch said, shaking his head. "Cantria said the King's people were moving on the Paths house. If they knew the other parts of the plan, they wouldn't bother going there."

"Your strange boy is right," Gwyn said with a nod. "Cantria must have thought we were using this ship to escape. I say we continue with the plan."

Gwyn turned to Flitch.

"Has there been anything from Sarah or Kindred?"

Flitch looked around for the book, suddenly aware that he didn't have it, his hands moving, empty and dry, against his clothing, still trying to clean off the blood now staining his skin.

He scooped the book up from the ground and flipped to the last filled-in page, the white of it blocked out by his own handwriting—a long, wandering description of what it was like to wander the Borders lands with his siblings as kids.

"Nothing," he said, shaking his head.

"We have to hope she is working at her goal just as we are toward ours," Gwyn said, looking around at the faces of the skeleton crew. "Yes?"

One by one, they all reaffirmed their commitment to the fated plan, and then they were moving across the dock and onto their vessel, a two-masted ketch, smaller and sleeker than most of the large harvesting and patrolling vessels in the Borders fleet.

The crew got to work immediately, pulling at the sails and checking over the hull and masts to make sure no one from Rivers had sabotaged them. One man kneeled before the hearthfire and began building a simple structure in the basin, singing a flame into life which lifted the ship up from the metal cradle that had been holding it.

Gwyn settled at the wheel only after moving quickly through the ship with her people, nodding when everything seemed to be in place and untouched by Rivers.

High above them, at the top of the cliffs, the Paths house was a torch burning in the wind, a tiny conflagration waving them onward.

"Give us steady speed, keeper," Gwyn said from behind the great wooden wheel as the ship slid from the dock and out through the cove, sails hanging limp until they reached the open harbor and caught the wind, which bellied them out with a satisfying snap and pull.

Crew and casters alike moved around the deck with busy efficiency, calling out when they needed help and readying the materials for the assault. Aster kneeled on the deck, the bandoliers of the casters laid out before her, and larger packs of casting plants in her lap, portioning out refills to supplement what had been used up in the first fight.

"There's not enough," she said, shaking her head. "We didn't plan for two fights."

"Do what you can," Gwyn called down from the helm, her mouth a grim line. "We'll make do."

Flitch's father was working with a few others to hoist one of the sails and the King's flag with it, their chatter filled with the kind of seafaring argot Flitch had loved and longed for as a boy. Sheets and lines and halyards, tacking and headsails, luffing and heeling, keels and jibs and all the rest. Flitch had chewed on those words for days and days, letting them roll around in his mouth, whispering them fiercely to himself as he stood at his window, pretending he was a famous captain shouting out orders to his crew, pirates beyond and glory ahead.

They're coming abeam! he would say, gesturing at the phantom boat bristling with pirates and danger. *Swing away! Helms alee!*

That young boy would leap onto his bed, whisper-shouting his orders as he clutched at the wheel—some repurposed book from his desk—turning hard into the wind and crying out for his hearthfire keeper to *Sing speed! I need more speed!*

Now, aboard this vessel and sailing out into the harbor to save the world or die trying, Flitch settled for simply helping where he could, quietly hauling on a rope or passing supplies up from belowdecks, a crew member in someone else's fantasy.

And when Gwyn called out to say *The Arcana* was in sight and that those aboard should prepare themselves, Flitch felt sad that this pocket of quiet work was over. Aster was passing out partially refilled bandoliers and putting her own on, and his father was strapping on a sword and knife, and even Gwyn had given over the wheel to one of the crew to prepare herself for the attack, but Flitch could not part with this moment yet, and he stood at the bow, knowing that the wind was rushing by his face and trying desperately to feel it.

The Sea was a green, blurring mass rushing by the ship, no single plant identifiable, and yet Flitch could hear and feel them all, could sense their quiet yearning for growth and the noxious power of the spellwork holding them back. Creatures, furry and scaly and chitinous and slithering, moved beneath those sunlit waves, and he could sense them, too, could feel them pulling back from his approach, giving whatever he was and was becoming a wide berth.

All of this Flitch knew and accepted without concern. *Better to think on what you have before you than to stare longingly at what's behind,* Gwyn had said, and Flitch raised his eyes to *The Arcana.*

It was a many-masted vessel—four or five, maybe more. Impossible to count them with so many sails crowding the sky above its two-hulled deck, outsized aftcastle flashing with windows and gilded decorations. It was a huge, beautiful ship, hulls reinforced and strengthened, sails replaced several times a year, masts checked every span or so for degradation or damage.

It was perfection on the Sea, and they were sailing straight toward it.

Floating starboard and port were two protective vessels, each bigger than the one on which Flitch sailed, busy with warriors looking to defend *The Arcana.* These were the King's vessels, maintained just as *The Arcana* was. This they had planned for.

But the swarm of pirate vessels crowding the Sea around *The Arcana* were a surprise. Six ships of ramshackle upkeep and design sailed in a rough constellation around the two defenders, each one now flying the King's colors, an extra line of defense, easily expended and easily refilled.

"Oh," Gwyn said, as though spotting a leak in a water bucket. "Shit."

"They're not outfitted to be defensive vessels," Aster said, peering at them through a longsight. "Two or three casting fires. Slim crews. The ships look rough, too."

"Look at that one, the three-master," the baron said, standing beside Aster and pointing, one thick arm around her shoulders. Flitch was near enough that he could have placed a hand on his father's arm, could have leaned in close to look along Aster's eyeline along with his father. He could have made himself part of that moment.

Instead, he stayed still and took one unnecessary breath, pulling the prairie wind in through his nose and holding the myriad scents in his lungs until the bright fizz and glow of them slowed to nothing.

"It looks like the bowsprit has been modified somehow," Aster said, and the other sailors nearby began gazing through their own longsights.

"They've reinforced it," one sailor said.

"It's coated in metal, too," came another voice.

"Sometimes, it's nice to just watch them watch the world," said a voice from just beside Flitch, and he turned to find Gwyn Gaunt there, too close for comfort.

Flitch opened his mouth to respond, but an eruption from the grasses off to the north drew his attention. One of the Marchess's monsters was surfacing, a creature shrouded by violet flames and keening at an earsplitting volume. Arms emerged, armored in dark blue scales, and began searching around in the air, claws snapping shut and flying open with bright *clicks*.

"I believe we've found the Marchess's Greys," Gwyn said, voice loud enough to direct her crew as she gestured toward the monster, which shuddered and moved in small jolts atop the slick, oily mass of sickened plants.

If Gwyn was right, that thick, tangled body of decaying prairie plants reached down and down through the darkness to a Seafloor where, even now, a woman was summoning monstrosities to cause horror and death above.

And yet, despite the danger of it, despite the wrongness of its existence,

Flitch felt bad for the creature. Confused and driven to violence, it had become the maddened product of a madder mind. Nearby boats had begun to converge on it, the brilliant shine of violent castings already lighting their decks.

Four of the pirate vessels turned toward the creature, their meager casting fires burning bright.

"They won't be able to stop it," Aster said, shaking her head. "Not with so few casters."

"They're just the distraction," Flitch said. "Faineant isn't using them for their casting."

Aster turned and looked at Flitch with surprise, as though she had forgotten he was there. The baron, too, sucked in a quick breath as he considered Flitch, the memories rushing back in to fill the gap, like sand caving in on a sinkhole.

"Look," Flitch said, gesturing with one hand.

Two of the pirate ships neared the creature and bright red flashes of magic crackled out from their decks, crashing into the creature and pushing it back for a moment, stunning it with their power.

It was frightful magic but far too little to kill or even frighten away the monster.

The casters sent another volley and then another at their target, each time arresting it and carving chunks of its flesh away. If they meant to destroy it that way, they would be at it for several days and nights before they succeeded.

But as Flitch said, they were merely there to draw the monster's attention while the other two vessels circled and cut in from behind, their bowsprits gleaming in the sun, looking like lances from so far away.

When they slammed into the creature from behind, it let out a great, strangled cry, lashing around in vain to respond, but the great bowsprits held it in place, pricking out through its front now like spits ready for the cooking fire.

It screamed and reached, but it could do nothing, and soon the other pirate vessels were nearing, lashing it with magical attacks.

The creature might have fallen then or fled with the dregs of its life, but it couldn't escape, the two bowsprits holding it firmly in place, and the crew on Flitch's ship watched as the pirates drove the life from the creature before approaching.

"Of course Faineant would want the creatures," Gwyn said, looking away with disgust as the crews of the vessels sailed up close and began their work of stripping away the skin and muscle and membranes of the creature. Flitch had heard of wyrmers doing such things, the endeavor almost impossibly dangerous but equally profitable if it could be done.

"He's probably going to decorate his throne room with its skeleton," Flitch said, imagining the Fickle King sitting on his milky-white throne, the vast space around him garlanded with the spiny, illogical skeleton of that creature.

"No, he's not," Gwyn said, returning her focus to their task. "Not after we end this. Eyes up, everyone!"

The chaos of the monster's attack subsiding, one of the King's protective vessels had noticed them and was coming around to show off a portside dotted with casting fires to meet their approach. How long they had until another creature emerged was hard to say, but Flitch would have guessed they didn't have much time.

Gwyn nodded at the crew, who ran up a flag that was supposed to mean *supply refill*. The protective vessel gave no sign that the message had been received.

"What should I do? Ramming speed?" asked the hearthfire keeper, but Gwyn shook her head, frowning at the nearing ship.

"Slow us down and bring us close," she said to both the keeper and the crew member at the helm. "We didn't get dressed up in these costumes to just resort to violence right away."

A nervous chuckle sounded around the deck, but as Gwyn turned away from the crew, she eyed the casters and mouthed *Be ready*.

Their ship slowed and angled so they ran parallel to the other, and Gwyn walked up to the gunwale, calling out a hello to the other ship. The casting fires were lit and ready, casters standing nearby. A man walked over to the edge of the deck and peered down at them.

"What's this?" he shouted down. "We're not due for supplies for another three days."

"They thought it better to send supplies sooner, what with the beasts coming up and everyone working longer shifts," Gwyn said, and Flitch looked up at the man, wondering if Gwyn's guess at the strain on the crews would pay off.

The man peered at her for a long moment before squinting off toward the Greys and spitting down into the Sea.

"That's the truth, ain't it," he said, nodding. "Come on around and link up portside with her." He jerked his head back at *The Arcana*.

"Aye," Gwyn said, stepping back and turning to the crew. "Bring us around. Ramming speed once we clear this one."

"But he said—" began the man at the hearthfire, but Gwyn cut him off.

"He knows. He's just trying to bring us between the two vessels so they can attack from both sides. Apparently, he and I are both shit at lying."

Their ship began to move slowly across the front of the defensive ship, and Flitch hazarded a glance over at it. The deck was a mess of activity, and though none of it was obviously the preparation for an attack, it was clear that something was amiss.

Meanwhile, Gwyn was giving her directions in a terse, low voice.

"I'll give us protection against the attack from behind. Aster, Woods, you both are in charge of defenses ahead. The rest of you, send whatever attacks you can manage. We want area, not precision, do you understand? I want that ship swarmed with magics. Once we're rammed and on board, I'll join you. Those casters from the other ship won't send attacks onto *The Arcana*."

Their vessel had begun to pick up speed on its turn into the space between *The Arcana* and the protective ship, the Sea sliding by quicker and quicker, the hush of grasses against the hull growing steadier, like sand sliding through an hourglass.

Shouts from the protective vessel came a moment before their attacks did, but Gwyn was prepared, her mouth already working at the casting plants, and when the spells came from that other deck, the Paths Baron threw up a wall of such brilliant blue that it put the sky above them all to shame, the great span of it shifting and rippling in response to the attacks it was holding back. Gwyn had begun to laugh through the words of her spell-song, a great grin stretching across her face.

The woman at the helm swung them hard toward *The Arcana*, which loomed ahead now, the decks aswarm with casters hurling plants into their fires to attack. Aster and Woods joined voices as they brought up a dome of arcane power ahead, weaker somehow than Gwyn's but enough to hold off the early rain of magics thrown by those on *The Arcana*.

A pulse in the book Flitch held in his hand dragged his attention away from the imminent crash and down to Sarah's message. It had to be her; it had to be. He opened it, mouth gone suddenly dry as he reached the last written page, no longer his own handwriting but Sarah's.

Look to the Greys; a distraction is coming.

Flitch slammed the book shut and cursed. He found Gwyn's gaze and relayed the message to her, eliciting a string of curses from her. Was this just more of the Marchess's creatures? Was the distraction the one the pirates were even now butchering? And even if it were more creatures, what good was such a distraction now? It was too late for that.

"Hold on!" the woman at the wheel shouted, and Flitch did, reaching for the mast his father also grabbed for, feeling the baron's arm tighten around his back. The casters had prepared for this, weaving braids of seagrass through exposed eyehole screws and holding tight to them.

The ship angled into *The Arcana*, crushing into its hull with a sound like the earth grinding itself apart, wooden hulls scraping against one another, ripping holes and tears in both vessels, until the force and tension brought the Paths ship to a halt, pointing drunkenly into the larger vessel, bow buried in the hull of *The Arcana*.

"Off!" Gwyn shouted, threading the word into her song but already taking steps toward *The Arcana*. Aster and Woods continued to hold up their defense, but it was clear that they would not be able to maintain it for long. Luckily, the other Paths casters had begun flinging their own magical attacks in return, following Gwyn's advice and blanketing the deck with bright, loud, wide spellwork, wavering clouds flicking with indigo lightning and gouts of cerulean flames that splashed across the deck in fountains.

It was enough to give them entry, Flitch and the others climbing across the shattered edge of their own ship and onto *The Arcana*. The Borders Baron lashed out immediately with his sword and blade, cutting down the nearest casters, who, even as they prepared their attacks, looked shocked.

Who would attack *The Arcana*? Who would profit from such a thing?

Flitch sheltered behind Aster's defenses, peering through the blue spellwork at the huge deck spread all around them, packed with warriors appearing, all of them with that same confused look.

"Hold them off for a little while," Gwyn said, leaping onto the deck behind them and finally dropping her spell. Sweat dripped down her face, and the signs of fighting were finally making an appearance on the seemingly unbreakable Paths Baron. She breathed heavily, mouth open, and one hand had begun to tremble slightly.

"What do we do?" Flitch's father cried, darting out for a moment from the protective dome to cut down a nearby enemy advancing with a drawn blade. "There are too many of them!"

"Not for me," Gwyn said, winking at Flitch and taking a healthy pinch of several casting plants from her bandolier's pockets, more and more until she had stuffed her mouth full.

Amid their ramshackle defenses, from the tiny foothold they held on *The Arcana*'s deck, the Paths Baron sidled forward, as if stepping through the delicate movements of a dance only she knew, one set to music only she could hear. The muscles of her jaw moved in quick flexes to chew and swallow the mouthful of casting plants, and as they disappeared, she sang a quick-syllabled song, the words percussive and hard.

A hazy afternoon light coalesced around her hands and arms, her head and neck, her feet and legs.

It was a patchwork thing, some sections of armoring thicker or thinner, some glowing brightly and others emitting only a dim throb of magical energies, but even so, it was a miracle of control and power. Worked with Gwyn's ability, the spell condensed into a sheen of solid protection that covered her whole body, and as she lunged forward out of the protective confines of Aster and Woods's spellwork, she bit into another pinch of plants, this one smaller.

Warriors crowding the deck leapt for her, and she sang a twinned note, two rough sounds emerging from her mouth that called into being twin blades blooming brilliant and sky-blue from her fists. But unlike swords, these blades wrapped around Gwyn's fists and extended back along the outside of her arms, running the length between wrist and elbow with a wickedly sharp edge.

Gwyn continued her dance, stepping and twisting and sliding and leaping, her movements graceful and quick. She did not meet her enemies so much as move through them, her shoulders rolling away from their thrown punches and swinging swords, her body arching back and forward to duck under their outstretched arms.

She pivoted from casting fire to casting fire, leaping across stretches of the deck, up to the aftcastle and back, always graceful, always purposeful.

And as she danced forward through them, the defenders of *The Arcana* fell like grass beneath the blade, and Flitch was reminded of something she had said to him. *If we fight, I will kill Faineant and all who stand between he and I. But many, many, many people will die in the doing of it, and that's not something anyone should want.*

She had seemed so confident, so sure that she could do if she needed to, and now he saw why. These other casters had trained for forty years, perhaps. Fifty, even. Gwyn had been training for almost two hundred, and she moved around them with a grace and precision they could never hope for, leaving bodies falling to the ground in her wake.

It was an awful, terrible sight.

Gwyn did not make it unscathed, though. When they realized what they were up against, the King's casters began hurling their magical strikes at the Paths Baron regardless of who or what else they might hit, and focused as she was on the lithe, quick movement of her deadly dance, Gwyn could not protect herself.

A lash of red power, burning in juddering, sharp flickers, struck her across the back, slamming her forward and sending a shiverwork of cracks running along her spectral armor. Another, a wave of silver fire, roared across her and the three casters she was tangling with, burning them all. Only Gwyn emerged afterward, still moving but sluggishly now.

"Push!" Aster shouted, looking around at the forces still huddling behind her dwindling defenses. "She's dying!"

The last of the skeleton crew rushed forward, shouting their cries of war or loyalty or battle or fear. Aster and Woods dropped their spell and launched themselves forward, too, Aster flicking through the steps of a complicated movement that left two huge, broad-tipped spears in her hands, dark blue and tipped with a white light that Flitch couldn't bear to look directly at. Paths and Borders surged forward to protect Gwyn Gaunt, and soon the deck was overrun with their force.

Flitch might have joined them. He had left the knife behind, on the shore next to Cantria's body, but weapons lay forgotten all around the deck, and it would have been easy enough to pick one up. But he was distracted by something, some pattern in the movement he saw but could not yet work out.

He looked up and saw his father battling with a barrel-chested man swinging a mace to keep the baron back but never stepping forward. He saw Aster driving one of her spellwork spears at an enemy caster who had surrounded himself with a blue wall of force.

He watched Gwyn Gaunt stumble through the steps of her dance and fall to one knee, the armor covering her body reduced to jagged shards clinging to bloody skin, and though one of the King's men stood near enough to strike at her, he instead ducked back, down to the stairs leading belowdecks.

They weren't fighting anymore. They were stalling.

Flitch cast a quick look behind him, the sinking feeling in his stomach confirmed by the sight of that first defensive ship drawing close, its swarm of fighters ready to leap across the Paths boat and climb aboard *The Arcana*. And on the other side, the second defensive vessel was doing the same.

"We need to . . ." Flitch began, but stopped. They needed to what? What could they do?

The spellwork holding the Sea hostage was in the belly of *The Arcana*. This was all distraction; the hearthfire below was the real goal.

Flitch rushed forward, the book clutched in one hand, raised as if he might use it as a weapon, but those on the deck had concerns other than him, and he reached the stairs leading below without trouble.

At the base of the stairs was a door, and when Flitch threw himself against it, he met solid resistance. Unlike the rest of the ship, the door was metal, reinforced at the hinges and locked.

Flitch screamed in frustration and slammed a fist against the door, but it was unyielding, and whoever was behind it had no reason to undo the lock. Let those above claim they owned the deck. The true prize of *The Arcana* would remain safe until reinforcements arrived.

With nothing to be done, Flitch raced back up the stairs and found those on deck preparing as best they could for the next wave, though not one of them looked ready. One of the Paths casters lay dying, his head supported by Aster, who was herself badly injured, a burn ranging down from the back of her neck and across one shoulder, cuts tracing along much of her body. The Borders Baron was the same, and he sat slumped against one mast, his head turning slowly from one side to the other, staring at the nearing vessels with their fresh fighters.

Sitting next to him was Gwyn, her breath coming in painful lurches, mouth and chin wet with blood.

"The fire below," she began as Flitch neared, but he shook his head.

"Locked behind a door like a vault," he said, and Gwyn dropped her eyes in defeat.

"We did what we could," the Borders Baron rumbled. "At least the others will have gotten away by now."

Gwyn nodded, and Flitch was opening his mouth to say that he hoped Idyll and Ravel would leave without them when a sharp cry from the Sea cut into his mind, nothing human or animal, a cry deeper and harsher than anything a living creature might make.

He turned toward the Greys, which now boasted a group of monsters, each one doing battle with a ship or two nearby, though all of them shuddered at the cry, recoiling and shrinking back.

The slick mass of oily plant, sick and sickening, burst into flame, a gout of fire leaping up from the Sea, hundreds of lengths into the sky, a blaze burning in a swirling range of colors. The nearby monsters were either caught in the inferno or flung themselves into it, moths pulled toward the destructive flame, and still the fire raged, never spreading to the healthy plants but roiling and boiling up from the Greys alone.

A distraction. Look to the Greys.

"It's Sarah and Kindred!" Flitch shouted, looking back at those on the deck and realizing all of them were staring slack-jawed at the fire still searing the sky. And if they were staring?

Flitch looked to the advancing enemies and saw the same. Maybe a distraction *was* what they needed.

A plan, rushed and simple and brutal, came together in Flitch's mind, and he swung back around. It was finally his moment. He finally understood why he was there.

"Someone get to the hearthfire!" he shouted, racing for the wheel, which was located up on the aftcastle. He slung himself up the stairs, taking them three at a time, until he reached the wheel. "Get to the hearthfire!" he screamed again, shocking at least one of the crew members to race for the huge blaze set in the middle of the deck.

"Get us moving," Flitch shouted. "Speed! As much as you can give!"

The Borders Baron and the Paths Baron, both laboring with the movement, crested the steps and came close.

"What are you doing, Flitch?" his father said, looking around.

"Get everyone you can onto the other ship," Flitch said, not bothering with his father's question. The wheel felt smooth and right in his hands as he swung it around, pointing the bowsprit at the tower of raging flames. "Quickly!"

His father frowned at him but nodded, lumbering over to the edge of the aftcastle and shouting the order down. Even as *The Arcana* swept forward, leaving the approaching defensive vessels wheeling hard to follow, the Paths vessel remained stuck in the larger ship. How long it would hold, Flitch didn't know. He just hoped everyone could get aboard before it broke away.

"Speed!" he called out, staring out his window at the Sea no longer. "Speed, keeper!"

The Arcana raced ahead, its massive hulls churning Sea grasses into seedy spray and scattering of pollen. Below, on the deck, the ragged remains of the skeleton crew limped and struggled across to their vessel, making the leap from one to the other carefully, painfully, knowing that the two vessels might detach at any moment.

Soon, it was just Flitch and the hearthfire keeper, who set the blaze as best he could before standing and nodding, racing across the deck as best he could.

"Speed," Flitch said to himself, eyes ahead, full of the fire. He could picture *The Arcana* racing ahead into that blaze, the flames consuming the ship, burning through that metal door and destroying the spellwork inside. Kindred and Sarah had offered a distraction, but it turned out to be so much more. How perfect that the fire from the Greys would be the very thing to undo their cause. He smiled at the neatness of it all.

"Your turn now, strange boy," came a voice beside him, and Flitch looked with surprise to find Gwyn standing there, the jagged remains of her armor gone now, leaving only her small, broken body. "I'll take over from here."

"No," Flitch said, shaking his head and gripping the wheel. "This is why I'm here. This is what I'm supposed to do. It's my fate."

"There's no such thing as fate," Gwyn said, her voice tired. "But if there were, yours wouldn't be piloting a ship into a magical fire. I don't know what's in store for you, but it's more than that. Now move before I move you. That ship won't stay caught in this one forever."

"But . . . this . . ." There would be no returning from what lay ahead, Flitch knew. Gwyn had lived two hundred years, and she was going to die here and now, running the King's favored ship into that fire?

"What do I do if not this?" he asked, dropping one hand from the wheel and staring hard at Gwyn. "I can't go back with them. I'm not . . . me. I'm not Flitch anymore. This was my story."

Gwyn stepped forward, her every movement pulling a spasm of pain across her face. She took the wheel, pushing Flitch gently toward the stairs. Ahead, the fire loomed.

"No one has just one story," she said, setting her feet and looking ahead, the blaze setting her face aglow, filling the wrinkles and creases with rivers of riotous colors. "If you can't go back, then go forward, one step at a time. Sing the songs you know."

⸻◆⸻

Flitch watched *The Arcana* race headlong into Kindred's blaze, sitting between his father and sister, their vessel wrenched free with the help of the crew.

Those on board said what goodbyes they could to the Paths Baron, who disappeared into flame and never came out.

It took almost no time for the destruction of *The Arcana* to reverberate across the Sea. Grasses grew unruly and wild immediately, shoots rising in uneven leaps, clumps of plants breaking the surface in chaotic swirls and patches.

Their vessel held, though the cove they planned to return to was gone as they neared the Mainland coast, the rising Sea level having consumed it. Instead, the crew member at the helm and the man at the hearthfire contrived to bring their vessel up along the edge of the cliffs, which had ceased to be cliffs and were now simply ledges growing nearer with every moment. Flitch and the others leapt from the ship and then helped the remaining crew onto land, watching with surprise as their ship listed off starboard-way for a time before sinking, the hearthfire no longer able to keep it up without someone maintaining it.

The group walked inland, crossing the road that connected what had been the Borders house with what had been the Paths house. Behind them, the Sea crested the edge of the cliffs and began to grow up onto the land, creeping forward with a steady, unrelenting pace.

Horses on the hillside above them brought initial cries of dismay, but as they neared, Flitch saw it was Idyll and Ravel, their faces going slack with relief as they saw the party.

"Idyll!" Flitch's father called out, waving. "We're here!"

Idyll leapt from their horse and ran the remaining few steps, wrapping their father in a huge hug before turning to Aster, tears in their eyes, and embracing her, too. Ravel moved among his people, one or two of whom gave him the story of what had happened, and Flitch watched the shock of realization form on his face as he saw Gwyn's absence and learned the reason for it.

Flitch stood on the outside of all of this, hearing the Sea's slow approach from behind him. He noticed that his skin had begun to glow again, and when Idyll looked up from their hug with the baron and Aster, their eyes briefly met his. Idyll, who had ridden back on horseback to bring salvation; Idyll, who had spent all of their time reading and writing stories, now living one.

Idyll looked at him for a moment, and in that space, anything whole left in Flitch broke. Thin strings that had been holding him together snapped with a finality that Flitch felt in his bones.

Confusion wrinkled Idyll's face for a moment, searching through their memory for him and finding something fuzzy and strange, something faded and fading, partially lost.

This was Quietus's gift, to sing what might be forgotten and must be remembered, but to be forgotten himself. A young boy who dreamed of living grand stories, given the gift of telling them forever, lost and found and lost again.

Flitch's oldest sibling, nearest to his heart, looked at him without recognition. Eyes he had longed to see again passed over him with a confused glance, absent of memory, of the stories they had lived and told together. Idyll remained, but Flitch had gone, disappeared in those tunnels beneath the crumbled ruins of the Borders home.

He was not even something lost for Idyll, not even something forgotten. To be lost is to leave a space behind, and as Idyll turned back to their father and Aster, Flitch heard them speaking in quiet, comforting tones, mourning the loss of Gwyn Gaunt, who gave her everything to save what she could.

"Goodbye," Flitch whispered to Idyll, quiet enough that it might have been just the wind. Already he had begun to step back, away from the circle of grief and reunion, his skin glowing with a faint light. "I'll see you after."

As the party set off, some on horseback, some walking with the aid of others, Flitch turned and walked toward the coastline that had disappeared in the Sea's new growth. Step by step, he left everything behind, and when he reached the grasses, the storyteller, carrying only a book, walked into the Sea's wild embrace, forgotten and forgetting.

CHAPTER TWENTY-ONE

I t took many days for Kindred's voice to return after the burning of the Marchess.

It did not matter. There was so little to say in the aftermath that she didn't mind.

Sarah was safe. The rest of the Traveling Court were safe. Madrigal sang again, Awn gripped Kindred in a tight hug, and Fourth-Folly grouched around as they caught new pluralities with Sarah. Jest wondered and wrote about the importance of these events for the Lost Monarch, and Wylf whispered *Windrake* and cast his eyes often and longingly back in the direction of the Once-City's fall, where the Windrake still stood, they all hoped, fossilized there by Wylf's dogged attentions.

Once Kindred's fire had consumed them, the Greys were nothing but a burnt skeleton, brittle and lifeless, at odds with the rest of the Sea, which had begun to glow with fresh light and hum with the voices of creatures above. The growth, they all assumed at first and knew after reading Flitch's messages, was happening above, but life was returning to the Seafloor as well. Huge shadows flew and skittered and raced and swam above them as creatures of all kinds moved through a Sea cured of its disease.

Awn began a journal of all the creatures and new growths he found, sketching them and cataloguing their movements and characteristics, their coloring and glow.

They recovered the Traveling Court vessel after a few days, deciding to walk back instead of being pulled by their pluralities. Those who had stood for the trip back to confront the Marchess still had aching legs.

While Kindred, Awn, and Madrigal worked at the hearthfire basin,

slowly repairing and rebuilding the physical and magical connections holding it to the ship, the rest of the Court scavenged what they could.

Wylf simply stared at the place where the Windrake had been but was
no longer.

When they weren't working and when Kindred was not otherwise encircled in Sarah's attentions, she wrote to Flitch.

It had been Sarah's suggestion. A practical value to know what was happening above, but a chance for her to communicate without speaking, to
tell the story—the myth—of Kindred and Ragged Sarah, of Captain Caraway and Little Wing and the crew of *The Errant*, of the Traveling Court,
and the world below.

Of the Marchess and her granddaughter.

Flitch seemed hungry to know more even as he sent shorter and shorter
messages in return, saying only that the Sea had returned, that those above
had either retreated much farther back along the Mainland coast or been
stranded inside the Sea itself, their sky replaced by a prairie lattice. He would
visit them, he promised. They would not be forgotten. No one would.

So Kindred wrote, and the soft space of remembering began to fill in
her waking hours. Memory became her sea, every written word a new
craft. What treasures she found.

Amid adventure and life, time passed.

Madrigal grew into adulthood and found her myth, which involved a
woman living in the vast husk of a long-dead plant. She spoke a strange
language and embraced Madrigal as family when she saw her.

The Traveling Court woke one day to find Wylf gone, all his belongings
taken, every bit of him scrubbed from the ship, lingering only in their memories. Outside, they found a pair of footsteps leading to the ship. Nearby, a
small blue flower, wilted and used up, lay on the ground.

Jest never gave up her search for the Lost Monarch, and she took the
Traveling Court to distant lands and through strange places on her quest.
Ever curious, ever energetic, she led them through many adventures, sow-
ing kindness and love everywhere she went.

While crossing a stretch of Seafloor populated by strange creatures, half-plant and half-animal, each one tracing curious diagrams in the dirt and paying the Court no attention, Fourth-Folly told the whole of their story, tracing meaning between the tragedies of their life like a constellation between stars. Kindred never told it to Flitch, though he asked many times. It was not her story to tell, and she kept it like the gift it was.

Awn grew old and died, every day a small and wondrous joy, smiling until sleep carried him away with soft hands. Kindred and Sarah buried him, sharing stories of the man they had known and loved.

Kindred wrote less and less as those around her disappeared, until finally she stopped writing altogether, her life a mystery to Flitch.

Time passed and the world grew older and stranger, but Kindred and Sarah continued on. Whatever magic had hidden in the Sea's song when Kindred had healed Sarah lingered now in both of them, fending off time's steady advance.

More growths of plants appeared through their skin, and when they at last bid farewell to Madrigal—an old woman herself by that time—the former hearthfire keeper and the crow-caller had both begun to look like the Sea, grasses and vines interleaved in their hair, flowers growing in ranges across their arms and legs, plants bursting from the soft skin behind ears and along collarbones.

They disappeared into the Sea, moving among the grasses as one moves among family.

In the darkness outside of Twist, moving ever onward to his next audience, the storyteller-that-was-Flitch feels the slow swell of memory overcome him.

At first, in those years after the Sea grew up over Arcadia and huge stretches of the Mainland coast, he had wandered, seeing all that the Sea offered above and below. Wonders that even the most fantastical stories could never touch. Sunrises that sang rapture. Darkness that wrapped around a body like a blanket.

He read the missives in his book and wrote in return, finding in the correspondence a new life.

But soon his steps returned the storyteller to the Mainland, and he walked until he found homes rising from the land, paths packed into tributaries feeding ever inward. These the storyteller followed, seen and forgotten by everyone he passed.

He found Aster first. She was living in a community of people from Paths and Borders who were building a new fleet to sail the new Sea—ships imagined and built to handle wild and unpredictable grasses. He had watched her teaching a new crop of casters, had smiled as she demonstrated with strange tenderness how to sense and shape the power of plant and flame.

For just a moment, she had looked up from her instruction and seen him, but aside from a slightly furrowed brow, Aster had paid little attention to the thing that had once been Flitch, and after that, he was more careful.

Zim he found working as the head of that same community, the comings and goings of every tradable good and bit of currency carefully noted in his books, traced and categorized and recorded. People had never been Zim's strength, but this—the intricate webwork of how people moved through the world—*this* he excelled at, and the boy that was Flitch left Zim to his work.

It took some time to locate the baron, and night had fallen by the time the storyteller sank to the ground before his father, putting a single unfeeling hand on the gravestone.

Uthe o' the Borders That Were, the stone read, and then below. *Father to three, baron to many.*

The storyteller, Flitch, spent that whole night beside his father, remembering those happy times in their home, the joy of riding on his father's shoulders, of being swallowed in his embrace, of seeing a smile move beneath his father's great beard. He had not yet begun to bury those painful memories, and so he relived each and every one, smiling and imagining his father there beside him, the man's deep laughter joining his own.

When the sky blushed with dawn's light, he said goodbye to his father and moved on.

After days and days of searching, stretches of time walking through rain and cold and harsh winds, he found Idyll.

They were living in a small house outside a city far inland, tending a small garden and writing throughout the day at a thick wooden desk. In the evening, when Ravel returned from working in the city, the two would make dinner and take walks around their property, sharing secret smiles and quiet joys.

The boy that had been Flitch watched his sibling grow, watched as the world changed and moved around them, unchanged and unmoved himself.

He watched as Idyll and Ravel made their community better, tiny changes like seeds that might grow into something strong and mighty.

He watched as Idyll wrote book after book, story after story, brightening the world with each one even as they lived the only story that ever mattered.

He watched Idyll mourn Ravel's death, searching for and not finding his own tears as one by one, the other mourners departed and left only Idyll, their long fingers buried in the dirt where their beloved lay.

He watched as Idyll's back curved and their shoulders hunched over, as their hair silvered and thinned and their hands gnarled and wrinkled. And when they were struggling for breath on their final night, shivering and cold in bed, dreaming troubled dreams, it was the boy that had been Flitch, the boy who had listened to their stories and loved them beyond all else, who stood close and covered them in a blanket, whispering a story into the night to comfort them.

"Sing, memory," the storyteller says now, looking back over his shoulder at Twist, where the inhabitants will soon wake with a hollow memory of the storyteller. A figure from dream and myth who, if they are lucky, might one day enter their community with his strange, singsong cry.

As the storyteller turns back to the path, he opens the book and looks down at the pages filled with his messages to Kindred. His final plea—*Kindred, are you there?*—remains unanswered, as it has for so long.

He flips back a few pages, finding her final entry, and as he steps forward, Twist behind him, darkness ahead, the storyteller reads.

———◆———

Flitch,

It has been long since I last wrote. Or maybe it hasn't. Time has grown thick down here, and without sleep for either of us, neither Sarah nor I have much luck keeping track of it. I think often of that old scribe writing of the prairie as a daydream. I dream without sleep now, every moment, every breath.

We walk less and less. Why move when so much waits to be seen around you?

Sarah and I have stopped to consider a length of bluestem connecting ground to sky. We sit near and watch the slow turning of the world around it. We have been here a long time, I believe, and will be here much more.

I have picked a small blade of grass, barely grown, for my love, and still I find joy in anticipation of giving it to her.

In the end, I have known only this—my hand in hers, my eyes on the world around me, an unassuming strand of green ahead. I have known only this, and it has been enough. It has been more than enough.

Remember, the prairie holds worlds. If you're looking for yourself, start there.

In a moment I will put down this book and take Sarah's hand. I will say what has always been true: Let them forget us. Only this matters. Only this.

Kindred Greyreach, Captain of the Lost

ACKNOWLEDGMENTS

With my whole heart, thank you:

To Alex Cochran, Craig Leyenaar, Sophie Robinson, and the teams at Titan and DAW. I've loved working with all of you, and I'm so proud of these books we made together.

To anyone who has taken the time to read my stories. Thank you for the gift of your attention.

To Marc Simonetti, whose work any author would be lucky to have on their cover.

To Ben Wheeler-Floyd, who read a draft of this book and promised it did not totally suck.

To the Saint John's Abbey Guesthouse, which provided the space, the solitude, and the silence to make a rough draft less rough.

To the students of my Advanced Fiction class, Spring 2022 edition. You all taught me more about writing than I could ever have hoped to teach you. Thanks for all the reminders of what fiction can and should do.

To Megan Steblay, who long ago helped me research what I thought book 2 was going to be. I was very wrong, but I'm grateful for your help nonetheless.

To Farah Naz and RK, who give the best pep talks.

To Shecky, the most sedulous copyeditor I know.

To Leah Spann. Thank you for supporting me and these stories with your kindness, your wisdom, and your ideas. I've grown as a writer under your editorial guidance, and I'm endlessly grateful to you.

To Agnes, the joy monster, who sees the world as the wonderful place it is.

To Rachel. Without you and your support, I couldn't and wouldn't have written these books. Thank you for believing I could do it even when I didn't. I love you.